DOUBLE CROSS TRAIL DRIVE

The journey begins as an ordinary trail drive from Texas to the railroad in Kansas — but soon turns deadly as bullets fly and rustlers try to steal the whole herd of steer . . . Back at the ranch in Texas, the violence continues, as the ranch owner seems to have become a sitting target. Whoever is out to ruin the ranch and kill the owner must be discovered, especially as the final deadly cattle stampede threatens to settle the matter once and for all . . .

CHET CUNNINGHAM

DOUBLE CROSS TRAIL DRIVE

Complete and Unabridged

LINFORD
Leicester

First published in Great Britain in 2012 by
Robert Hale Limited
London

First Linford Edition
published 2014
by arrangement with
Robert Hale Limited
London

A catalogue record for this book is available
from the British Library.

ISBN 978–1–4448–2065–2

Published by
F. A. Thorpe (Publishing)
Anstey, Leicestershire

Set by Words & Graphics Ltd.
Anstey, Leicestershire
Printed and bound in Great Britain by
T. J. International Ltd., Padstow, Cornwall

1

Near Jackson, Texas
June 12, 1869

Matt Hardy swore and kicked his bay into a gallop across the Texas graze land. Three steers moved slowly across the thin grass away from the large herd heading into the pasture just west of the ranch buildings of the Bar-H spread. Matt came up to another cowboy who sat on his sorrel watching the three steers.

'Hal, don't just sit there like a zombie,' Matt bellowed at the rider. 'Go get those three steers turned back to the bunch. Don't you know anything about herding cattle?'

Hal Westover, the sorrel rider, sent a withering glare at Matt, spurred his mount and galloped after the strays.

Westover did not ride with confidence, Matt could see. He was a tenderfoot in the saddle but he was family.

Westover was slight, twenty-five years old, married to Matt's sister Ginny, and had been working to be a passable cowboy for the past two years. Matt figured the guy could learn enough to pull his weight.

Matt, twenty-eight and son of the ranch owner, Gregory Hardy, was five feet ten and 160 pounds. He had short black hair, a round face with a thin smile, high cheekbones, heavy brows over light-brown eyes, and strong, rope-scarred hands.

The two riders pushed the steers into the main herd which was soon funneled into the holding pasture at the edge of the ranch buildings.

Matt shook his head as he rode back to the big corral. Tomorrow morning, bright and early, they would start the drive of 2,500 head of steers up the Chisholm Trail heading for the railroad pens in Kansas. Matt had pleaded with his father to leave Hal Westover at home. His father had been firm.

'The boy has to learn to be a cowboy. One day he and Ginny will be half owners of the Bar-H along with you.'

Matt had been surprised when two years ago Ginny had married Westover after a three month courtship.

Westover had a reputation in their small town of Jackson as being a wastrel with no job and no direction, and a kid who gambled and drank too much. He was the son of the town's banker. His father had tried to get him to work in the bank but he had shown no talent in that direction.

Matt rode up alongside Westover as they unsaddled their horses and put them in the corral.

'On the trail drive you're going to have to do better than you did today.' Matt said.

Westover glared at his brother-in-law. 'Shut your big mouth. You ain't my boss.' He snorted, threw his saddle on the rail, and headed for the big ranch house.

Matt watched him go. He walked with a slight limp due to a poorly set broken leg when he was ten.

By the time Matt had washed up and come into the dining room, he found Ginny standing toe to toe with her husband. Her fists set akimbo on her hips and her face red with fury.

'I won't do it, Hal, and that's the end of it.'

'Woman, you're my wife and you do what I tell you to.'

'No, never!' Ginny shouted.

Hal slapped her across the face, pivoting her away from him. Matt surged across the room and grabbed Hal by the shoulders spinning him around. His right fist shot out, hit Hal on the jaw, and dumped him to the varnished wooden floor. Hal jumped to his feet but before he could charge Matt, Ginny ran between them.

'No, now stop it, both of you. I won't stand for you two fighting. Now act like grown-ups and not angry little boys.'

Matt backed off and lowered his fists.

He saw the red mark on Ginny's face but it didn't look serious. His sudden flare of anger drained away. 'Hal, you ever hit my sister again, I'll track you down and take you apart.'

'Anytime. That was a sneak punch. You won't be so lucky next time.'

Matt snorted and looked at his sister. 'Ginny, you are a feisty one. Why did he hit you?'

'My business, big brother. Now I think it's time for supper.'

'I won't sit down to eat with a wife who won't do what I tell her to do,' Hal snarled with fury flaming his face, 'I'm getting out of here.' He turned, stormed out of the dining room, through the living room, and out the front door.

'What was that all about?' Matt asked Ginny.

'Not your affair, Matt. Stay out of it. My problem and I'll deal with it. Now, it's supper time.'

Matt grinned and nodded. She was something. A small bundle of energy and with an independent mind. She

5

was twenty-three and five feet two inches tall. She wore her brown hair long, framing a slightly pinched face with soft brown eyes and she smiled more than frowned. Now she was three months pregnant.

Gregory Hardy had come into the room just after Hal had rushed out.

'Trouble?' he asked. The owner of the Hardy Bar-H ranch was two inches under average for men of the day at five feet six. He had husky shoulders and arms and a strong upper body from long days roping and bull-dogging cattle. The top half of his face was almost white but the lower half was burned brown by the Texas sun where it was not protected by his well worn low crown hat. He had brown eyes, a round bald spot on the top of his head, and kept his hair cut short by the cook.

'No trouble, Pa. Just a little argument with my husband. Now, are we ready for supper? I'm starved.'

'Should we wait for Hal?' Gregory asked.

Ginny shook her head. 'No, I think we better start. He won't be back to eat.'

Gregory Hardy lifted his brows. 'Fine, just so he's ready for an early breakfast at five. We start the herd moving at six.'

★   ★   ★

The next morning, after a huge breakfast, the twelve men saddled up for the trail drive. They would be moving market-ready steers to the northwest toward the Chisholm trail with their sights set on Ellsworth, Kansas, some 450 miles east and mostly north.

Gregory Hardy sat on his pinto at the head of the quarter-mile chute leading from the holding pasture. It was designed to funnel the steers into a stream four to five wide in a long line ready for the trail north.

He had assigned the ten cowboys to their jobs. Three would ride as drag at

7

the very end of the line of animals. They were responsible for finding any strays and driving then back into the herd. It was the worst job in the drive since there were ten thousand hoofs ahead of them kicking up dust that boiled back at them like a hostile dust storm. Kerchiefs over mouths and noses helped. That's why the men were rotated every day to balance out the easier jobs with the harder ones.

Gregory watched the rest of the men moving the herd along. He had one man on each side a quarter-mile from the end. These were the flank riders who were responsible for keeping the animals in line and moving north. Ahead of them a mile or so was a cowboy on each side of the herd called a swing rider. They also kept the cattle in line.

At the head of the line were two more men called the point riders who kept the herd aimed in the right direction that the trail boss had laid out for them. The trail boss, on this drive Gregory

Hardy, usually rode out in front marking the trail and watching for water, Indians or any trouble spots such as a swollen river that had to be crossed, deep canyons, or heavily wooded areas.

Off to the left side of the drive rode the wrangler. He was often a boy or a young rider, who had the job of driving the remuda of spare horses, remounts for the cowboys. They changed horses every day to give their mounts time to rest. With sixty spare horses in the remuda, the mounts would get five days' rest.

The twelfth man on the drive was named by the cowboys as the most important — Ponchy, the cook. He drove the chuck wagon that served as supply rig and as a rolling complete trail kitchen. The cook sat on a high seat to drive the two horse hitch and usually ranged well ahead of the herd to pick out a spot where he could stop and start cooking the next meal.

Ponchy was a half-Mexican in his late

forties who did the cooking both at the ranch house and on the trail drives. He was short with a fat belly he blamed on his good cooking. He wore a full beard and moustache, had black eyes under heavy brows, and a thick thatch of black hair. He had been with the Bar-H for eight years.

Some trail bosses liked to make four or five miles in the morning, then let the steers rest for an hour or so. This also allowed the men to get their dinner. The chuck wagon was a marvel of efficiency holding all the food for the drive, all the kitchenwares needed, flour, spices and lots of dried fruit. They picked up meat by hunting along the way. Ponchy drove the chuck wagon ahead of the herd for what he figured was four miles and stopped beside a small creek.

With the herd, Gregory Hardy had positioned Hal and Matt as far apart as he could. He knew about the rancor between the two.

The landscape here was typical of

central Texas — a lot of open plains and grasslands with a few small hills here and there, hardly any trees or brush except along the few wet weather creeks that provided some moisture for them. It was open plain and made for easy traveling.

The drive went well that first morning as the herd, led by an old broken horn steer, moved them across the west Texas grassland. They were heading north-east where they would pick up the Chisholm Trail about thirty miles north of Fort Worth at the Red River crossing.

When they stopped at noon the first day, Ponchy had built a fire, balanced an iron grill over it on rocks and fried steaks. He heated up beans he had cooked at the ranch and was ready for the hungry crew. It was the last of the fresh meat from the ranch. From now on any fresh meat they could get would be from a steer that got killed on the drive or some rabbits or maybe a deer one of the outriders had shot.

The drive continued and by six o'clock on Matt's pocket watch they had the herd bunched and bedded down in some fair graze. He figured they had made about eleven miles the first day.

Gregory Hardy shook his head as he worked on the supper of beans, boiled potatoes and slabs of bread from six loaves that Ponchy had brought from the ranch house kitchen.

'More like nine miles,' Gregory said. 'It's always hard to figure the distance the first few days.'

The two men riding guard around the herd were replaced and they dug into their supper. All night there would be two riders circling the herd in opposite directions on four-hour shifts.

Hal had been the third man riding drag and it took him a half hour to wash the grime and dust off. Two or three times he had wanted to turn around and ride back to the ranch. The dust was unbelievable. The coughing

12

and racking had made him throw up once and the other two drag riders laughed at him. But he stuck it out. He had to. At least tomorrow he would rotate to the left side of the herd as a flag rider. He would make this drive and do it right.

After a few wild tales around the camp-fire, the men took their blanket rolls out of the chuck wagon and spread them out for the night's sleep. A brisk wind had sprung up and Matt thought he saw some clouds, building in the west, heading their way. Two of the older hands saw the clouds as well and rolled their blankets out under the chuck wagon.

Hal watched them a minute. He knew that Gregory figured he'd see what the old hands did and learn from them. But he couldn't figure out this sleeping under the chuck wagon. So he asked them.

'Playing the odds, kid,' the older range hand said. 'Never can tell when it might rain.'

13

'Don't look like rain to me,' Hal said and found a spot away from most of the others to put down his blankets. He had brought an extra blanket for a ground pad.

Matt and his father talked over the day's drive as they always did. The camp-fire burned down to red coals.

'Not bad for the first day,' Gregory said. 'We should make the Red in five days.'

'Unless we run into some trouble,' Matt said.

'Not much to stop us out here,' Gregory said. 'No Indians, no rivers to cross, no rustlers trying to run off a hundred herd.'

'You heard about that outfit up near the Kansas border?'

'Yep. A bunch tried to take over a small trail drive herd but they didn't count on all of the cowboys riding with repeating rifles in their saddle boots.'

'A dumb thing to try,' Matt said. 'I talked to Bill Fowler. He said Hal did OK on his first day at drag. He brought in six or eight steers.'

They said goodnight and spread out their blankets. Matt took one more look at the clouds building to the west. Please no rain, he thought.

The next thing Matt knew was when a crack of lightning brought him up to a sitting position. He heard the rumble of thunder to the west. Then a bolt of lightning hit so close he could smell the sulfur. He grabbed his boots, sure of what he would hear next. A hundred steers stared bawling then he heard the pounding of hoofs on the dry Texas range.

'Stampede! Stampede! Stampede!' the cry came from the two night riders working around the herd.

2

Matt jammed on his boots, grabbed a jacket, and ran for his horse. He had picked out his mount for the next day before supper. Now he slammed the saddle on her and cinched it up quicker than he ever had before. The steers kept bawling and running. Now the rain came, huge cup-sized splashes that wet him through before he could mount up.

Once astride, he could see the shadows of the rampaging steers moving north. He raced the brindle after them, hoping he could catch up with the lead steers and turn them.

He rode hard, gaining on the steers. They kept breaking off to the right and left, scattering with no one to contain them. Still a stream of animals kept running almost due north. He was nearing the lead animals when he heard two pistol shots, then two more.

Someone was there ahead of him. The night riders must have reacted quickly. He saw the lead animals hesitate, then veer to the left, then to the left again until they were heading back the way they had come. They slowed and after another quarter of a mile the main stream of steers heading south now came to a stop. He saw Vince and Wally, the two night riders moving along the animals, trying to calm them, slapping one now and then with a rope to stop it moving and to urge it to lay down. Bit by bit the steers lost their fright and milled around, then with nothing better to do, they dropped to the ground.

Vince saw Matt in the gloom and rode over.

'At least we got most of them stopped,' Vince said.

'Good job. Consarned lightning. How far are we from the chuck wagon?'

'My guess is about a mile. We'll burn up most of tomorrow rounding up the rest of them. We might have half of them in this bunch.'

'We had such a good start,' Matt said. 'See if you can bunch some more of these on this end together. I'll get some hands to gather some more back toward the chuck wagon.'

They waved and Matt rode back along the still milling cattle toward the chuck wagon and the rest of the hands. Five or six of them had got up, put on their boots and had horses saddled.

'Good, guys,' Matt said. 'Let's do an easy gather here and see what we can find in the dark. What we find we'll pull back here by the first bedding-down spot and get them settled down again. We'll do what we can before sunup. Then our real work begins.'

Matt saw only half a dozen steers still in the night's bedding place. The men worked in pairs moving north slowly and spread out over a hundred yards. They found few steers and what they did they drove back to a line in the center of their sweep. Matt lit a match and checked his pocket watch. It was just after five o'clock. The heavy downpour had slacked off to a steady drizzle.

When they found all they could on the sweep, Matt called the men in and then drove maybe fifty steers north into the end of the larger bunch.

'Let's break it off until daylight,' Matt told the riders. 'Get some sleep if you can. George and Bob, go up front and relieve Vince and Wally. I'll send up riders to replace you in two hours.'

Back at the chuck wagon, Matt met his dad coming in. He shook his head.

'Blasted ornery luck. A lightning storm. Ruins tomorrow. Just hope we don't lose too many steers.'

'We'll find almost all of them,' Matt said. 'They won't run far now that the lightning has moved off.'

Matt saw movement under the chuck wagon and when he went over found Hal huddled in his dry blankets under the shelter.

'Thanks for the help,' Matt said and snorted. Hal pulled the blankets around him and looked away.

By six o'clock the sun was up and already Matt had taken two riders and moved to the west three miles. They came back in a wide sweep that netted more than three hundred steers nibbling on the sparse graze. The animals moved slowly but steadily toward the chuck wagon. They seemed to recognize where they had bedded down before and sank down there.

Gregory was up and in the saddle. He sent three riders west to do the same sweep. Hal rode with the trio to the west. Matt took the same three riders and rode north a quarter of a mile, then rode to the west again and made another sweep. This time they found more than four hundred steers.

By noon they had driven the chuck wagon north a mile and a half to the rest of the steers. Gregory looked over the resting animals and figured. He was good at estimating the number of animals in a herd. He came over to

Matt with a worried look.

'We're missing at least two hundred,' he said. 'Let's send some long-range riders out each side. Have them go out five miles, then swing back in a wide sweep pattern.'

Ponchy stood behind the chuck wagon with all of his plans for breakfast on hold. He'd been in situations like this before. It was find the missing steers first and breakfast would come later.

They made two more deep sweeps out five miles and netted almost two hundred and fifty head. Matt figured they had most of them. When Gregory got back he was smiling.

'Figure we got almost all of them. Maybe ten steers down there somewhere hiding in the brush. Ten steers, that's four hundred dollars. I'm taking that out of your pay, Matt.'

'That's if we get forty a head. Now have some breakfast. It's after ten o'clock. We should be all fed and the crew ready to go by noon.'

'Oh no,' Gregory said. 'What about the remuda? I never thought about them.'

'Wilbur said he has all of the mounts,' Matt reported. 'He had a double-rope corral rigged up and none of the horses spooked, so they are all safe and sound.'

Ponchy fed the men a double breakfast since it was after ten and there was no time to get a noon meal. They would be moving by eleven so he pushed hot cakes and syrup and biscuits and gravy on them and lots of coffee.

Getting the steers back into a line to drive north was their next task and one they had to take on each time after a stop and every morning.

The cowboys began by heading a few steers up the trail, then squeezing the herd into a line four or five wide. They worked from both sides and forced the steers to quit the resting spot and move up the trail in a thin line that could be handled. The riders on the rear of the herd and sides held firm forcing the animals into the line.

When the whole herd was in the long ragged line about one o'clock it stretched back almost two miles. Ponchy had shut down the noon feast, packed up, and headed out looking for a good camp spot five or six miles ahead. Matt had rotated to the right-side point rider and kept the herd moving toward a sharp rock cliff that Gregory had told him was the next landmark to head for.

It took the Hardy trail herd four more days to reach the Red River crossing. Matt figured they had covered about fifty-five miles from the ranch. The Red River crossing was just that, a shallow and wide stretch of the river that could be crossed with few problems — if there was no sudden flash flood or high water runoff. The Hardy trail drive had experienced no problems with the Red River crossing the last two years.

One herd was in the process of

crossing when Gregory came up to the spot about four o'clock that seventh day. He rode back three miles and had the herd bed down there.

★   ★   ★

The next morning Gregory rode ahead and saw that the herd that had been crossing had finished and was out of sight to the north. He brought up the steers. The Red was a little on the low side this year and none of the steers would have to swim.

Gregory posted three riders in the water downstream twenty yards from the string of cattle as they crossed. The riders would turn back any steer that decided he wanted to take a down-river walk.

They hit the water a little after nine-thirty and had all of the steers across the Red River by noon. It was a slow process.

Ponchy had dinner ready for them two miles beyond the river at a small stream where he had filled the water barrel.

This time they kept the herd moving and the riders ate in shifts, two at a time. They let the lead steers slow a little as the herd paced up the real-life Chisholm Trail. It was named after a Scotch-Cherokee by the name of Jesse Chisholm. He was a trader working out of his post on the Canadian River in Texas and wanted an easy drive for his wagons up to the rail line in Kansas. It was first used as a cattle trail in 1867 and in five years would see more than a million head trample a path four hundred yards wide through the plains.

★   ★   ★

It turned half past six before the riders had the herd bunched in a small meadow near the chuck wagon. Ponchy had estimated the afternoon's drive a bit long, but nobody complained. This time Ponchy had fire time enough to cook up a big pot of beans, flavored with some cut-up rabbit. He cooked them in a big iron pot that took well over four hours of constant fire.

Hal had been keeping away from Matt. He knew that the big guy was checking up on how he did each day. The only defense he had was to be the best cowboy on the drive.

That night Matt took his turn riding night herd on the bunched mass of steers. He went on for the third shift, from ten to midnight. When replacements came for the two circling riders, Matt headed for his blankets. He had rolled them out and rested on them before he went on duty.

Before he went to sleep he started thinking about the dangers of the trail. If he somehow turned up dead on the trail drive, then Hal and Ginny would own all of the Bar-H when their father died. Yes, from now on he would be extremely careful in any dangerous situation and he would be ever watchful around Hal Westover.

*   *   *

The next morning Matt was reminded
that the Chisholm trail wasn't only for
cattle. He saw two freight wagons
rolling past the herd. They were
hauling something north to the rail
line. Then they would load with goods
for the mid-Texas area that had not yet
heard the whistle of a steam railroad
engine.

3

The next morning Matt settled down to his job of keeping the steers aimed at the right spot. They were making good time. By noon they should have almost six miles under their hoofs. Matt did not worry about Hal but he was concerned with his mood. The man had never seemed dangerous before. Now he was more calculating and devious. Hal was three men behind him on the rotation around the herd so they had little contact.

*   *   *

Three days later they entered the heart of the Indian Territory — that area between Texas and Kansas that had to be crossed. The progress had slowed. Sometimes the steers developed a reluctance to move ahead at a reasonable speed. After a breakout of a couple of dozen steers, the whole herd almost stopped as the cowboys rounded up the malcontents and pushed them back into the ragged line of animals.

They had seen Indians in the distance but none had approached the drive. Gregory kept well ahead of the herd and watched out for any more. He knew that there were five or six tribes in the area. The toughest were the Comanches. Matt knew that they were well into the 300 miles of Indian Territory where the only law was that of the Indians.

The drive was nearly halfway across Indian Territory. So far they had not seen a hostile redskin. Each man had a repeating rifle in his saddle boot and his six-gun in his gun belt. Today they had just forded the South Canadian River when Matt spotted twenty mounted Indians on a slight rise watching them. Matt was in his swing position and called to the two point-men about the savages.

They waited.

A few minutes later the Indians came charging at the head of the drive, screaming and brandishing rifles and bows and arrows. They slashed forward in a long front and raced up to within thirty yards of the nearest point-rider. The men had been carefully coached about the Indian threat. They were warned never to fire the first shot. Gregory said the Comanches particularly were good at bluffing a charge then stopping. Matt rode slowly toward the head of the drive until he was near the right point-man.

'Hold steady,' Matt called to the point-man who had his rifle in both hands but not aimed. Thirty yards from the two men the Indians came to a skidding stop. The screaming and yelling ceased and one Indian rode forward at a walk to meet the two cowboys. Matt's father had ranged far ahead of the herd this afternoon and missed the Comanches. Matt watched the Indian leader ride up. Something about him triggered a memory. The single black feather he wore in a knot of hair. Black Feather. The same one who had met them the past two years. Matt held up his hand in a greeting gesture.

'Black Feather. Good to see you again.'

The Indian scowled and shook his head. 'Not know you. You on sacred Comanche land. Must pay to pass. We take twenty white man buffalo.'

'Twenty?' Matt kept his face flat and showing no emotion. 'Too many, Chief Black Feather. My name is Hardy. Last year we gave you seven steers.'

'No, not seven, must have twenty.' He turned and waved a long lance in the air. The twenty warriors surged forward shouting and bellowing screams of fury until they were ten yards from the cattle in the long line, then split both ways. Matt never moved as the Indians raced past him. He sat on his mount with hands folded on the saddle-horn.

'We can give Black Feather eight steers.'

The Indian who wore no war paint or other facial decorations shrugged. 'We take eighteen.'

They talked for fifteen minutes, each changing his offer as the bargaining went on. Once Matt dropped his offer by one instead of raising it one steer. The Indian shook his head and increased his demand by one.

At the end of half an hour of bargaining, the two agreed on eleven steers that the cowboys would cut out and herd toward the Indians. Hal rode up and shook his head at Matt.

'You gonna get your ass chewed when your old man gets back,' he said. 'You just cost the Bar-H over four hundred dollars.'

'True, but at least I saved your scalp from hanging on a Comanche lodge pole tonight. We'll be lucky if that's the only Indians we have to bargain with. Now get back to your post, swing right as I remember.'

Hal scowled and was about to say something when a shot went up by the flanker right and twenty steers turned away from the main line and ran toward some trees and the smell of water.

'Get them,' Matt shouted and headed that way.

* * *

It took them nearly a half hour to outrun the steers, then turn them, and drive them back to catch the tail end of the line of cattle. When the steers were back in line, Matt rode around to Hal and growled at him.

'Don't you ever leave your post again unless you're almost dead. Got a notion to send you packing back to the ranch right now.'

'You can't do that, Matt. I work for Pa Hardy, not you.'

'You sure better. When Pa ain't here, I'm the next in command. Next time you mess up, your puny little ass is heading down the back trail.' Matt pulled his mount around and rushed back to the head of the line.

They were almost to the chuck wagon that evening when Matt heard rifle and pistol shots ahead of them. They were in a little hilly country and he could see less than a quarter of a mile north. He called on three riders and they rode hard up the slope so they could see what the trouble was.

At once Matt saw that a small band of Indians had stopped a pair of covered wagons and were shooting at them with two or three rifles and bows and arrows.

'Let's give them a hand,' Matt bellowed and the four men galloped down the slope a quarter of a mile toward the fight. Matt fired his rifle twice to get the Indian's attention but it didn't stop their attack.

'Get in rifle range and we'll try to pick off the attackers,' Matt yelled to his three men. At two hundred yards they stopped, dismounted, lay in the grass, and began sharp-shooting at the savages. Two of the Indians went down, then a horse screamed and fell. Matt could hear rifle and pistol fire from the two wagons.

Suddenly two of the Indians turned toward the rifles up the slope and rode straight at them. Matt waited until the lead rider was a hundred yards away, then he sighted in carefully on the bouncing Indian rider and fired. The round hit the Indian in the left shoulder and pivoted him off the horse, which turned and galloped to the east. The other attackers broke off their charge, picked up the fallen warriors and rode away fifty yards and stopped.

After another volley of rifle rounds from the nearly concealed cowboys, the Indians yelped and rode off to the east and were soon out of sight.

Matt sent his three men back to the herd then rode down to the two wagons. As he neared the white canvas-covered rigs, a man stepped out holding a rifle. He had no hat and was grinning.

'Got yourself in a little trouble,' Matt said.

The young man waved. 'Yeah, you might say that. I heard these Indians were friendly around here and could be bought off for a few beef. They came up peaceful enough but demanded all of our horses and cattle. I told them not a chance. They got furious, rode away, then came back shooting.'

Matt stepped down from his horse just as a woman screamed from the first wagon. Both men ran to the wagon and found a woman tearing at her hair and screaming in agony.

Another woman came and shook her head when she talked to the wagoner.

'It's Waldo,' she said. 'Must have been one of the last shots. He took a bullet right through his forehead.'

The man left and came back quickly. 'It's Waldo alright.' He wiped his eyes. Not a day over thirty and stone cold dead. Don't know what we're going to do now. Waldo was a crack shot and our best defense.'

Matt nodded and held out his hand. 'I'm Matt Hardy. We have a trail herd just over the hill. Looks like you need some protection. Why don't you turn around and come back half a mile to our night camp. We have two guards out all night. That was probably a bunch of renegades. They don't like a fair fight. We can give you some protection and maybe in a few days you can join a larger wagon train heading up the trail.'

The man held out his hand. 'I'm Sam Simpson. Good to meet you and thanks for the rescue.' He made up his mind at once. 'Sounds good. We'll try not to be a burden on you. It will slow us down a little, but that will be better than another Indian raid. Come and I'll introduce you to our group.'

* * *

Ten minutes later, Matt had met the wagon folks and headed back to the herd. He told them how to find it. Matt rode up to the head of the herd. His father had come back from his scouting and knew about the Indian raid.

'Had to be some renegade Comanches,' Gregory Hardy said. 'Some of the young bucks don't like the big bellies telling them what to do. You say you killed two of them?'

'Near as I could tell. They picked them up and rode away fast. Hope it's all right that I asked the wagons to go with us. That way they'll have some protection until they can hook up with a bigger bunch of wagons.'

'Fine with me,' Gregory said. 'Wonder if they have any milk cows. Bunch that big can't use up four to six gallons of milk a day.'

Twenty minutes later they met the covered wagons which swung onto the trail ahead of the point men. Sam waved at the cowboys and kept the wagons fifty yards ahead of them.

They met the chuck wagon about five and the two covered wagons turned off to the left as the cowboys bunched the cattle in a little draw for the night's bed-down.

Before Ponchy could get supper

ready, one of the women came over with a bucket and handed it to him.

'We got more milk than we can use,' she said. 'Figured you might be able to use it.'

'Hey, lady, thank you. I'm Ponchy. Yeah, oh yeah I can use some fresh milk, might bake some small loaves of bread, even.'

'You're welcome. I'm Martha. We'll have milk for you morning and night. Now I better get back and get my supper going.'

Ponchy couldn't stop grinning. He poured out a cup of milk and drank it, then hurried to bake some extra-large biscuits with the milk. They were down to beans and a few dried apples. He hoped he could spot a deer or an antelope or some kind of game soon. Now with the wagons, they could eat up most of a full-grown buck.

Ponchy used half the milk for supper and with the men for drinking, then kept the rest and skimmed off the cream that rose to the top. He would put it in a jug and let it bounce along under the chuck wagon for two hours in the morning and have butter.

That evening, just at sunset, they buried the emigrant and marked his grave with a wooden cross. It was a sight on the trails that happened too often. Matt helped with the grave and hoped that none of their men wound up under wooden markers.

$\star \quad \star \quad \star$

In the morning they strung out the steers in the usual long line and got them moving north. They had been all day yesterday without hitting any good-sized streams where the herd could drink. Gregory worried about it. He talked to Matt as the two covered wagons led out the long parade.

'Critters are going to get thirsty by noon,' he said. 'Ain't no good-sized streams up this way for another full day. We could have some trouble keeping them in line. Let's string them eight wide instead of four and bunched up that way, we'll have more control.'

Breakfast that morning had been flapjacks with real milk instead of water. All of the crew had milk to drink as well as coffee and they got into the saddle feeling good.

★   ★   ★

By noon the animals were bawling and getting harder to control. By four o'clock Gregory came riding back fast from the front to find Matt.

'We've got a good-sized stream ahead about three miles. We'll get them to it. But we won't have much control. In another two miles they are going to smell the water and we'll have a minor stampede on our hands. All we can do is stay with them. I warned the two covered wagons to pull off a couple of hundred yards. These steers are going to go charging.'

★   ★   ★

Ah hour later the lead steers sniffed the air, bellowed in delight, and took off at a steady trot toward the wetness. Those behind followed and soon smelled the water as well.

It wasn't a stampede, Matt decided. But it certainly wasn't an orderly cattle drive. The steers were soon in a swath a hundred yards wide charging the last mile to the water.

Matt rode along, keeping up with the leaders. He didn't remember the stream. It wasn't huge, maybe twenty feet wide and three or four feet deep. The first steers there plunged into the middle of the water and began drinking. Some wallowed in the cool water and just stood there.

A hundred yards downstream two steers jumped over a four foot bank and into the water. Matt winced as one of the animals bellowed in protest. Matt took out his six-gun and rode through the cattle to the bank. One of the two anxious steers was down, half in the water. Her right front leg lay broken

42

with the white bones sticking out through her skin. Matt rode close and dispatched the steer with two well-placed shots. Then he got down, tied his lariat around the horns and dragged the animal downstream until he could get it out of the water.

Ponchy would find it soon enough. Matt went to work moving some of the cattle out of the water and letting others in. Some would drink too much and cost them a day while they recovered.

★　★　★

It took the ten cowboys two more hours to get the cattle into the water, let them drink, then slap their ropes on the steers to move them out the other side and into a bed-down location.

Ponchy had heard the shots, guessed what had happened, found the steer, and butchered it on the spot, cutting it up into quarters. Supper was late that night but nobody complained. They had all the steaks they could eat.

Ponchy had taken a quarter of the steer over to the covered wagons. Martha had thanked him so much that it embarrassed Ponchy.

Ponchy hummed as he cut up the third quarter. They would have thin breakfast steaks in the morning. Tonight he would keep his fire going. He'd grill as much of the beef as he could. It would last a little longer that way. Even with all of his planning, at least one quarter of the beef would spoil before they or the wagon train people could eat it. He shrugged. He would enjoy it while he could.

4

The next morning found the cowboys hard at work getting the steers ready to trail. About two dozen had drunk too much too fast and were still recovering. The men had breakfast steaks and again at noon they had more of the leg-broken steer. Ponchy figured the men were fed full of beef for a few days and discarded the rest of the third quarter.

Just after breakfast, Matt had saddled his new mount and then moved away from the horse and had a long talk with his dad about the drive and how it was going. They tried to figure out any problems that could come up the trail.

Matt went back to his mount, put his foot in the stirrup, and started to swing into the leather. Instead the whole saddle came crashing down on him sprawling him in the grass and dirt. It was an old trick cowboys sometimes played on each other.

Matt sat up, pushed the saddle off him, and looked around. He heard no one laugh. Not one of the men in the area was watching him. Matt snorted and shook his head. None of the cowboys would play that trick on him. He was sure that only one man in the crew would do it and that was Hal Westover. The man had been quiet lately. Matt understood the frustration Hal felt as if he was the tenderfoot on the trail. But there must be more than that. Matt stood, put his saddle back in place and cinched it up.

$\star$ $\star$ $\star$

The drive got underway about one o'clock that afternoon and moved northward. Gregory and Matt did not know what to expect. They were still in Indian Territory.

About three that afternoon two covered wagons loaded with migrants overtook them. Matt saw two men from the new wagons ride over and talk with Sam at the other two wagons. They talked as they drove ahead. Ten minutes later the new pair of wagons moved out and soon vanished up the trail. Sam rode back and talked to Matt.

'They asked if we wanted to team up with them,' Sam said. 'But they had only two men and a mess of kids. I decided that I wanted a little more protection than that.'

'Be Indian Territory for another hundred mile. I think you made the right decision.'

They had come to a section of the country that had some low hills and a few patches of trees. Hal talked to Gregory when the herd was bedded down and soon Hal rode off toward a section of hardwood trees. Matt frowned and asked his dad what it was about.

'He said he thought he saw some deer over in that bunch of trees. Asked if he could go over there on a quick hunting ride. Told him he could.'

Matt shrugged and headed for the chuck wagon where the beans and biscuits were ready. He wondered why the man was feeling so helpful all of a sudden. He shrugged again and dug into the beans. They tasted different tonight.

Just before dark Matt saw Hal ride back from his hunting trip. He had one rabbit which he gave to Ponchy.

'Yeah, spice up the beans a little,' Ponchy said. 'Never can get enough rabbits.'

That night on his herding ride, Matt thought he heard some horses somewhere behind them. He rode out a ways and stopped, listening. He was sure of it then. There were three, maybe four horses and they were moving away from the herd at a gallop. What in the world would four horsemen be doing out there? Maybe they were Indians scouting out the camp. But then why not just make a raid? No, he'd heard that Indians never fought or raided at night.

Matt shook his head and continued his ride around the bedded-down herd. When he met the other night herder coming the other way he asked him about the horsemen.

'Yeah, thought I heard some horses out there last time around, but decided it was just my imagination. Could be some wild Comanches out there, but don't think a renegade bunch would make a try at us. Not when we have ten rifles.'

'Never can tell,' Matt said. 'Keep your ears on and we might hear them again.'

But neither of them heard the riders during the rest of their two hour shift. They told the new riders about the sounds and to listen for them. Then Matt hit his blankets.

★   ★   ★

The next two days went by with no problems and Matt figured they had made twelve miles each day. At this rate they should be out of Indian Territory in four or five more days.

Late in the afternoon on the third day from the river a train of six emigrant covered wagons and a dozen or so cows and horses came up the trail. Matt saw Sam ride over and talk with the mounted men. Five minutes later he rode up to Matt where he was on drag, fighting the dust.

'Matt, this looks like a good bunch. Six families of Baptists looking for some new country in Kansas or Nebraska. I like the men. They asked us to join up with them for a little more protection through the rest of Indian country. We're going to do it. I thank you for your help in the past, and the beef.'

Matt held out his hand. 'Our pleasure, Sam. You take it steady and get to where you're heading.'

The men waved and Sam rode back to his two wagons. Within ten minutes Sam and his wagons had joined the end of the new emigrant train and moved up the trail.

* * *

The good streams were getting farther apart. Somebody told Matt that a steer needed twenty gallons of water a day to stay healthy. Ponchy had found a good stream in a small valley and had pulled the chuck wagon in an hour early. Gregory approved the stop and they got the herd gathered, watered, and bedded down.

* * *

Just after a supper of beans and rabbit gravy over big biscuits, Hal asked Gregory if he could go hunting. Gregory said only if he guaranteed a two-point buck.

'Can't guarantee a buck but I'll be sure to get a pair of rabbits.'

Matt frowned. He had heard the exchange. It didn't look like good country for deer but you never could tell. He put another few sticks on the fire. Be two hours yet to dark. The days were getting longer. He got a penny ante poker game going, with a nickel limit bet.

Matt had told his dad about the four horsemen he had heard that night but he wasn't too concerned.

'Probably some renegade Comanches checking us out. They probably were within fifty yards of us and you couldn't see them in the dark. Course they never attack at night.'

'If they left their tribe, they just might be desperate enough to attack at night,' Matt said.

Gregory nodded. 'Never put anything past a Comanche.'

* * *

At seven o'clock that night Matt checked the riders coming in off watching the herd.

'Quiet as the inside of a church at midnight,' Bob said. 'Nothing stirring out there.'

Matt thanked him. He was due to go

riding herd on the steers at nine. It wasn't dark yet at seven o'clock. He settled down to feeding sticks to the small fire to help chase the chill night air.

Matt jerked up his head and looked toward the herd. Something wasn't right. Then he heard the beat of hoofs on the hard Indian Territory ground.

Three pistol shots shattered the stillness. It was the universal signal that there was trouble. Matt heard somebody yell from the direction of the herd but he couldn't make out the words.

'Trouble,' Matt bellowed, his voice blasting out like a steam locomotive's whistle. Before he could stand, two rifle shots jolted through the air. One hit the fire in front of Matt and sent up a shower of sparks. The second brought a scream of pain from a cowboy on the other side of the fire.

'Take cover,' Matt screamed. 'Rifles to the north of us. Stay low.'

Three more rifle shots slammed into the little camp, one slashing through the chuck wagon's top. Matt dove for the ground away from the fire. He was too good a target even in this half-light. What was going on? His first thought was Comanches. Steers moving. Somebody trying to rustle the whole herd? He crawled away until he came to a good-sized maple tree and stooped behind it. He looked to the north but couldn't see any men with rifles or any gunfire flashes. A dozen more rounds slammed into the camp.

5

'Anybody hit?' Gregory Hardy yelled over the gunfire.

'Yeah, got a shoulder could be better,' one of the hands called.

'Get to you in a minute,' Matt shouted. 'Meantime everyone stay low and fire back to the north. Shots came from there.'

Three or four rifles and some pistols fired to the north and the firing from up there cut off.

Matt waited a minute or two and when no more shots came into the camp he called out.

'Who got hit and where are you?'

'Paulie . . . other side of the fire. Just a scratch.'

Ponchy beat Matt to the cowboy. He had the man's shirt off and was stopping the bleeding.

'Don't look too bad,' Ponchy said.

'Slug went on through and missed the bone. Be in a sling for a while.'

'No sling,' Paulie growled.

Matt ran toward the herd. Even in the pale moonlight he could see most of the herd moving. He ran back to his horse near the fire.

'Everybody up. We've got a stampede going on. Somebody spooked the herd. We've got to cut them off as soon as we can.'

Even as he talked, Matt threw on his saddle and cinched it up. He was the first one moving and rode hard to the north where the cattle had been spooked. Not all of them were running. He rode harder and five minutes later was at the head of the herd. He fired some shots and tried to bend the running steers back the way they had come. They didn't alter their course.

He'd heard it done before but never tried it himself. Now he rode hard to the lead steer in the stampede, came in close and shot the animal in the head. It went down in a flurry of flailing hoofs and legs, tripped several steers behind it and slowed the whole mass. Then the rush forward broke up little by little as if the steers had no leader. Five minutes later the stream of steers had stopped.

By then there were eight horsemen on hand and they herded and bunched the animals in a long line about fifty deep.

Jordan, one of the younger cowboys, found Matt and shook his head.

'Matt, you better come with me. I was one of the guys riding herd tonight when it happened. I didn't hear a thing until the first gunshots spooked the herd. I wondered what happened to Billy. After things settled down I hunted for him. You better come take a look.'

They rode back to the chuck wagon and then out to where the herd had been bedded down. A horse stood ground-tied and a dozen feet away lay a body. Matt came off his mount quickly and ran to the cowboy. It was Billy and he lay on his back in the grass with a six inch hunting knife sticking out of his stomach. He was dead.

'Figure I must have been on the far side of the herd when they hit Billy. Nothing I could have done. They killed him, got in close to the herd and hurrahed it up to its feet and then blasted some shots to get them moving.'

Matt stared down at Billy's face. It was in repose. His open eyes stared at the heavens.

'Let's get him on his horse and take him back to camp. Looks like somebody was trying to take over the whole herd and didn't mind killing a few of us to do it.'

They got Billy back to the camp then Matt and Jordan rode out to the herd with eight other cowboys. Matt stationed them around the herd in its elongated position.

'Ride around the herd and keep your rifle across your saddle. They tried once, they may try again.' He told each of the men the same thing and soon the eight were riding herd on the animals. Matt wondered how many they had lost. They would lose a whole day tomorrow. By morning Gregory would have estimated how many they were missing. First they would have a burial for Billy. Matt would write a letter to his parents back in Ohio.

★   ★   ★

They laid Billy to rest just as the sun came up. One of the men had carved his name in a tree limb and they nailed it to a three foot high cross. Nobody said any words over his grave.

Flapjacks with syrup and lots of coffee got the men out on the hunt. Gregory came back a half hour after sunrise.

'Looks like we're more than five hundred short,' the rancher said. 'We can't take a loss like that. We'll stick right here until we get them back. Chances are most of them could be in a herd the rawhiders got away with. If so, it should be easy to follow them. We'll move out in ten minutes. Be sure each man has his rifle and thirty rounds of ammunition.'

* * *

It took them a half hour to find where the heavy trail of the herd split about a mile north.

'Could be five hundred by the looks of the tracks,' Gregory said. 'We ride hard. Put one man out a quarter of a mile ahead so we don't get surprised.'

Bob Womack took the job. He'd been good friends with Billy and was anxious for some revenge.

Two miles down the easy to follow trail they found six steers to one side munching on grass. They all carried the Bar-H brand.

'We'll pick them up when we drive back the rest of the herd,' Gregory said. They rode on. At even five miles an hour on their mounts they should overtake the slow-moving steers by midday.

* * *

It was just past eleven that morning when Bob Womack galloped up to the eight riders sporting a huge grin.

'Got them,' Bob told Gregory. 'They must have tried to push the animals too hard and had been losing quite a few. Now they are stopped and bedded down in a small valley about two miles ahead. I saw only six horses, so must not be more than six men. No chuck wagon. They have two men circling the herd.'

Gregory nodded grimly. 'All right. We move in and get some positions where we can stay hidden and yet be in good rifle range, say two hundred yards. Is that possible?'

'You bet,' Bob said. 'Quite a little bush and a few trees on this end. Some real timber to the left side. No trouble getting to within two hundred yards.'

The rest of the riders had gathered around and heard most of it.

'All right,' Gregory said. 'We move up cautiously. Bob will tell us when we should vanish into the trees and brush.

Those men are outlaws, white men, not Indians. Anyone have any problems shooting to kill?' He looked around. Nobody responded.

'Good. We take out these guys, or get them on the run. I'll settle for either one. Don't shoot their horses. Give them a chance to get away. Any question?'

'We sure those are our steers?' Jordan asked.

'Trail says so,' Matt said. 'Should be proof enough. I'll give my famous imitation of a coyote call when everyone is in position,' Matt said. 'Then we start shooting. We'll spread at least ten yards apart and find good protection to hide behind. Let's ride.'

★ ★ ★

They moved at a walking pace for a half hour then Bob motioned for a stop.

'Just over this slight rise is the valley. We can split on both sides of the trail. Lots of trees.'

They rode up to where they could see

the herd slightly below. They went back twenty yards and tied their horses to trees. Then they eased up to the brow of the small rise and forward through a thin set of trees. Gregory held up his hand when he figured they were two hundred yards away. The men had spread out on both sides of the trail and found good cover.

Matt watched the cowboys each lift one hand when ready. Then he gave a poor try at a coyote call. Eight rifles blasted rounds at the small camp below. They had a cooking fire going and two men rode around the herd.

Two men went down on the first rounds. Two others scrambled for saddles or rocks or any cover. Only one found cover before the other one took bullets. The two men riding herd hesitated, then took off fast into the heavier stand of trees and vanished.

After five or six shots per man had riddled the camp site, one rifle came up high with a white cloth on it and waved back and forth.

'Trying to kill us all, you crazy man?' a voice carried from the camp-fire.

'You murdered one of my men,' Gregory bellowed back. 'You all deserve to die.'

'You killed three of us. Ain't that enough? Let me ride out of here and you can have your steers back.'

'Leave the three horses there,' Gregory shouted. 'Cease fire, men. Let him go. Get out of there. Stay out of the trees so we can see you and leave your rifle by the fire.'

They watched as a man stood, lay down his rifle and moved toward a saddled horse. He turned.

'Hal Westover you stupid no-good slimeball. You always have been and always will be. Too bad we didn't kill you last night.' He stepped into his saddle.

They stood watching the man ride to the south. Gregory waved at Hal.

'Westover. How come he knew your name?'

Hal walked up shaking his head.

'Beats me. Sounded like he could have been Slade Watkins. Had some problems with him in town. He's been in jail half a dozen times.'

'Yeah,' Matt said. 'I've heard of Slade. But why would he know you were on this trail drive?'

'Drives are no big secret. Half the town knew when we were leaving.' Hal shrugged. 'Easy enough for him to find out, get some of his no-good buddies to form up a six-man raiding team and come after some of our steers.'

Gregory didn't look convinced. 'Might be. No matter. I'm filing a murder charge against him as soon as we get back home. Now let's get our beef back up the trail to join their cousins.'

* * *

By supper time they had the steers back in the elongated bed-down. That afternoon Ponchy had gone hunting and came back with four big rabbits. They had roast rabbit, biscuits and gravy, and beans for supper.

While gnawing meat off the rabbit bones, Matt had a worried look.

'Dad, when did Hal come back from his hunting jaunt last night? I didn't see him come in.'

Gregory frowned. 'Come to think of it, I didn't note him come back either. He was here when the shooting started. Remember him ducking behind the chuck wagon. Why?'

'Not sure. But it seems strange that Hal knew one of the raiders who stole our steers. Downright weird. Somehow it doesn't seem like a coincidence.'

'He was here when the shooting began.'

'True, but how long was he here before that?'

Gregory shook his head. 'Don't think that way, Matt. No good reason that Hal could be a part of the try for our herd. Forget about it. We've got to concentrate on getting these walking beefsteaks from here into Kansas.'

6

With daylight, Gregory was out taking a long look at their elongated bed-down. He came back to Ponchy's cooking fire not in the best mood.

'Looks like you lost your best coon hunting dog,' the cook said pouring Gregory a steaming cup of boiled coffee.

'About it,' Gregory said. He took another few swallows. 'Best coffee in town. It's hot and keeps me awake. Yeah, looks like we lost ten maybe twelve head. We can't afford to lose any more.'

Breakfast was usually at sunrise and the cowboys jawed and swore at the cook and the sun. After letting the cattle drink at the nearby stream and do a little moving around, the crew started wedging them out of their long bed-down and into the trail drive's six wide line.

Matt kept well away from Hal who had drawn the drag assignment again in the rotation. Over a mile ahead, Gregory looked over the country and found some of it familiar. They were coming into the part of Indian Territory where the Cheyenne usually pitched their camps. Gregory thought he saw some smoke well to the east. Indian fires.

Just before noon as he came to the top of a small rise, Gregory saw three Indians riding toward him walking their ponies. Gregory stopped and let them come up to him. They wore no feathers and no war paint. They didn't threaten or charge the herd the way the Comanches did. He watched them but didn't recognize any of them.

They came to within six feet of Gregory and stopped.

'Welcome to land of Cheyenne,' the one in the middle said.

That sparked a memory in Gregory. He was Running Mouth, the Cheyenne who usually did the bargaining for the tribes.

He had grown up in a preacher's home in a settlement near the army post and learned to speak English and do sums. When he was fifteen, he ran away and found his tribe again.

Running Mouth sat with his arms folded and stared at Gregory.

'The Bar-H comes again. Getting rich. Must pay the Cheyenne ten cents a head.'

'You tried that last year, Running Mouth. It still won't work. Your people need beef more than the white man's dollars. It's been a bad hunting year for you.'

'Good hunting. Plenty dried meat in baskets for summer and fall. Need money for blankets.'

'The money would never get blankets. Tell you what, Running Mouth. I'll give you one cent a steer or three animals you can butcher for your people.'

'No, no, no. Not fair. Bar-H give us

nine cents or seven steers.'

Gregory grinned and kept bargaining. He knew the Cheyenne would not attack. He also remembered that Running Mouth loved to bargain.

*　*　*

More than an hour later, Gregory held up both hands in a gesture of agreement. They had decided on five steers for the right to pass through the Cheyenne's 'sacred' hunting lands.

The four rode over to the long line of steers and Gregory cut out the five steers that the Indians pointed to. With whoops of delight they rounded up the five steers and drove them to the east.

*　*　*

Back at the herd, Matt had been keeping away from Hal as much as he could. He sensed resentment and anger from his brother-in-law. Just after supper and with the herd bedded down

Hal stalked up to Matt and confronted him.

Matt had been sharpening the hunting knife he carried on his belt. He was sitting on his blankets away from the fire and didn't look up until Hal spoke.

'Brother, I don't like the things you've been saying about me behind my back.'

Matt put the knife in the sheath and stood.

'First off, I'm not your brother. Second I haven't said anything behind your back that I haven't said to your face.'

'You told Pa it was strange that rustler knew my name the other day.'

'True, and it still is strange. Your explanation of it was impossible to believe. And remember, Gregory Hardy isn't your Pa.'

'You stinking sidewinder. You accusing me of lying?'

'You're a slow learner, Westover. I'm not accusing you of lying, I'm charging you with it. We'll know for sure once we get back home and we grill Slade for a few hours over an Indian melon head fire.'

'You've got no proof. You've got nothing. I was out hunting that evening before dark and I can prove it. I brought back three rabbits. Ask Ponchy.'

'Right. You shot some rabbits. I never did see you come back to camp that night. You could have been one of the guns out there shooting at us.'

'You idiot. You want me to draw down on you so you can kill me?'

'Never have killed a man close up but you tempt me.'

'You no-count slime. I'll take you apart with my bare hands. I'm not wearing a gun.'

Hal lunged at the surprised Matt who took a step back but not in time to avoid a stinging right fist to his jaw. He staggered back a step, got his hands up, and ready to fight.

'Didn't think you were man enough to try it with your fists,' Matt said.

Gregory Hardy had seen the first blow. He frowned, then settled in against his saddle to finish his beans. He knew this fight would be coming.

Matt feinted to the left, Hal moved away from it just in time to take a left jab on his nose. It splattered and began to bleed at once. Hal howled in fury and charged forward into two more sharp blows from Matt. He got in a right fist to Matt's stomach but took a stiff right hand from Matt on the side of his face.

Hal staggered back a step, fury building in him. Hal had never liked this rich kid but he didn't think he was this good with his fists. Hal hesitated, then did a bull rush at Matt, caught him around the chest, and wrapped both arms around his back and hung on. They slammed forward, Matt tripped over some blankets, and they went down in the dirt and rolled.

Matt came out on top and smashed two hard fists into Hal's jaw. The blows slammed Hal's head to one side and brought a long bellow of pain and frustration from the downed man.

'Enough,' Hal choked out. 'Stop it. So you can whip me. I'm giving you twenty pounds. Get off me.'

Matt stood but didn't offer to help the other stand. He scowled down at Hal.

'Look, we have some problems, you and I. Let's let them wait until we get these steers delivered and are back home. Then we can work out something so we're not at each other's throats all the time. Agreed?'

Hal stood warily, backed off a step, and slowly nodded.

'Yeah. OK, for the good of the ranch. We will settle this.'

Gregory Hardy gave a sigh of relief. He couldn't afford to lose either one of them. Then he would watch the situation closely. This would be his last trail drive. The ground was getting harder every year.

7

After the fist-fight things settled down on the drive. The men had been waiting for the blow-up and now that it was over they had only to think about their job of getting this herd into Kansas. Matt and Hal seldom spoke and then only when it was about the herd.

★   ★   ★

The next day Gregory came back from his morning scouting ride and waved at Matt.

'Damn if the country isn't looking familiar. I'd say we're about twenty miles from Kansas. Then it's a short run the rest of the way into Elmore and the cattle pens.'

'And the pay-off,' Matt said. 'Going to be good to have some cash around the old ranch for a change.'

'Should have seen the last of the Indians,' Gregory said. 'Unless we stumble over a bunch of renegade Comanches. Doubtful.'

The rest of the day went well. Matt brought the herd into a small stream where they could drink and then got them back on the trail. He figured they had made almost twelve miles that day. Ponchy had bagged four China ring-necked pheasants and they made a meal of them roasted whole over the fire.

Gregory had been assigning one of the cowboys to spell Wilbur, the remuda rider, when the horses were bunched together behind a rope and pole corral that he set up every night. Gregory didn't want some wolf or coyote to spook the mounts this close to the end of the trail.

★　★　★

The next morning the steers were ragged in getting back into a trail drive line, but the rope-slapping cowboys did their work and soon the long line of steers stretched out and moved on north through easy country then up. They finished the day when they caught up with Ponchy about five o'clock.

Ponchy was all grins and laughter.

'Damnedest luck I ever had. There he stood, sideways to me, off more than fifty yards and looking away from me. Took him down with my first shot. I hadn't been in that patch of woods over there for five minutes. You guys are gonna eat venison till it comes out your ears.'

They did.

* * *

The next two days went smoothly as they traveled more than twelve miles each day. At the end of the second day, Gregory announced that they were in Kansas. Everyone gave a big cheer.

'Not there yet, but should be no

more trouble from here on in to Ellsworth. Can't be much more than about ninety miles. Eight or ten more days.'

★ ★ ★

It rained the fourth day into Kansas then the weather cleared and it was a cakewalk the rest of the way up to Ellsworth. The stock pens were full and the Bar-H herd was pushed into a line to wait its turn at the stockyard counting pens.

Gregory went into the small town of about two thousand souls and found Jamar Winston at his office, the second table in the Cattleman's Saloon.

'Hardy, you old polecat, wondered when you would get here. You still got those half-starved Texas steers in tow?'

Gregory liked the cattle buyer. Had dealt with him for the past two years.

'Jamar, you quick-striking sidewinder. Thought you'd been caught by now for skimming twenty percent of the cash.'

The two men laughed and shook hands.

'Price went down when we weren't looking,' Jamar said. 'Home office wired me yesterday. Top dollar is now thirty nine. Just one lousy Continental off the best price, but still pretty good.'

'You just cost me twenty-five hundred dollars,' Gregory said wincing. 'But if that's the price, that's it.'

'You have twenty-five hundred head for me?'

'What we had when we started out. Figure we may have lost a dozen or so along the way. Some for the Cheyenne and the Comanches.'

'Figures. Just the way it is down there. Let me give you a ticket for the counting pens. Should be able to get you into the flow in a couple of days. You want an advance to pay off some cowboys?'

'Yeah, Jamar. The usual. I give them half their pay now and the rest when they get back to Texas. We lost one man along the way. Rustlers stampeded our herd. But we stopped them. So I'll need six hundred for my nine cowboys and the cook. And a hundred for me.'

Jamar produced the money in green-back bills and the men shook hands.

'A day to get you to the pens. You should get a hotel room and sleep on a bed for a change.'

Back at the herd, Gregory paid each of the men fifty dollars and they were yelping and yelling for glee. They set up a six-hour two-man shift to ride herd on the bedded-down steers. Then the rest of them went into the little town of Ellsworth, which was one of the roaring cattle shipping towns in Kansas.

★ ★ ★

The next day about two in the afternoon, Jamar rode out to the Bar-H herd and told Gregory to get his animals moving to the second set of pens next to the box cars. They drove the animals up in a six-wide line to the counting shoot. The buyer's man counted the steers as they went through the chute and into the box cars. The two counters used clip boards and put down a mark for each animal.

It was just starting to turn into twilight when the last steer was counted and loaded.

'Twenty-four hundred and eighty-two,' one of the counters said. The other shook his head.

'You were sleeping at the switch, Chuck. The real count was twenty-four hundred and eighty-three.'

Jamar laughed, wrote down the higher figure and took Gregory back to his office to write out the checks and deliver the cash. Gregory and Matt each took five hundred dollars in cash.

As usual Gregory and Matt split up the money. Each took half of the rest of the money in bank drafts. It all went in money belts that cinched tightly around their waists under their shirts. The total sale price came to $86,905. Matt marveled at the amount of money. It was more than he had ever seen.

'That's my biggest buy so far this season,' Jamar said. 'You have a good trip back to Texas.'

They shook hands with Jamar, and smiled as they saw a bear of a man leave the bar and walk over. Jamar nodded at him and then at Gregory.

'Monk here will see you safely to your hotel. We've had a few hard-headed drunks going after trail bosses after they talk to me. Monk discourages anyone bothering you. He will be with you until you head back for Texas.'

Gregory smiled at Monk and held out his hand. Monk ignored it and stood there waiting for Gregory to move. Gregory laughed softly. Monk was at least six feet six, must weigh over three hundred pounds. Gregory went back to the hotel and had a big supper, then a glorious night's sleep on a real bed.

★ ★ ★

The next morning Gregory met the rest of the crew where Ponchy had parked the chuck wagon. Two men were trying to buy it. Ponchy explained.

'Seems they are on a drive on up to Montana with a mixed herd of cows and calves and their chuck wagon tipped over and got washed downstream for a total loss. I don't mind riding back home.'

Five minutes later Gregory had come to a price of a hundred and fifty dollars for the set up, including what food they had left.

Matt had sold most of the remuda to an army captain from the cavalry. He had kept back mounts for himself, Ponchy, and each of the cowboys.

'You men are on your own going home,' Gregory said. 'I'll give Ponchy fifty dollars to buy a cooking outfit and grub for your return trip. Thirty miles a day, you should be home in fifteen days. Matt, buy a pack horse for the food. Tell the truth, got my fill of sleeping on the ground. Going to rest my old bones here for a couple of days, then grab a train or a stage for my ride back home. I'll be back there a few days after you arrive. So have a good ride.'

8

As soon as the men were paid, Ponchy and Matt herded Paulie into the only doctor's office in town.

'I'm fine, I'm fine,' Paulie kept saying. 'I can ride good as I ever did, even with one wing here in a sling. Don't want no sawbones poking around my hurt arm.'

They nodded and aimed him for the doctor's office where they found three other men waiting. Two had gunshots and one was coughing constantly. They had to wait almost an hour.

The doctor was a bearded older man with a quick eye; a fast talker with a gentle touch.

'Rifle slug, you say, and somebody dug it out? Good. The second day?'

'Next day,' Ponchy said.

'Good job. Give you some ointment to put on the wound. Need to take some stitches so the scar won't be a half-inch wide. Gonna hurt some, son.'

'Been hurt before. Get it done.'

He did.

Afterward the medic put salve on the wound and bandaged it up tightly. He gave Ponchy some white rolls of cloth for bandages.

'Heading back to Texas?' the doctor asked.

'In the morning,' Matt said.

'Watch it. Change the bandage every other day and keep it clean. Keep the arm in a sling. Riding?'

'Yes,' Paulie snapped. 'I can still ride, Doc.'

The old medic chuckled. 'He sounds in fine spirits, that's good.'

Matt gave the doctor three dollars which surprised him.

'Usually just charge a dollar,' he said.

'Like to pay our way,' Matt said. 'Anyway we just sold our herd. We thank you for your help.'

The men had saved their saddles and bridles, and now got their mounts tethered near town. Two men volunteered to stand watch over the mounts the rest of the day and until morning. The rest of them headed for the café and then the town's one hotel for real beds to sleep in. The town was crowded. Only three of them found rooms. The rest, including Matt, went back to where the horses were and rolled out their blankets. Monk, the huge security man, had followed Gregory for a while, now he was with Matt everywhere he went. Nobody even looked sideways at Matt.

Ponchy had bought trail cooking gear, tin plates, tin cups and spoons. He bought enough food to last for three days, figuring they would find a small town before then. Matt said they would slant to the east off the edge of the prairie where they could find more towns.

With Gregory resting for a few days, Matt took over as the trail boss for the return ride. They all understood that. The next morning they had a good breakfast at the small café and then they rode out of Ellsworth, Kansas. The sun was up when they hit the trail shortly after 7 a.m.

* * *

The ride was uneventful and eighteen days later they rode into the Bar-H and Matt paid each man his other fifty dollars. He added an extra ten dollars for each man and later gave Ponchy an extra twenty. They were delighted. Matt took his time. They had arrived about noon. Ponchy rustled up dinner for the crew and then Matt took a long hot bath in the new spaddle-legged bathtub they bought from Fort Worth. He figured he washed off three layers of dirt and grime before he finished. He shaved off his trail beard then had Ponchy give him a hair cut. By four o'clock he was ready to go to town. He had on a new pair of blue jeans, a blue-striped shirt with snaps instead of buttons, and long sleeves.

He had two tasks. The first was to deposit the big check in the Bar-H account in the bank in town. He'd take out a thousand for emergency money at the ranch. Second he wanted to find Slade Watkins and grill him about his connection with Hal Westover. There had to be some tie between the two. His one big question was why Slade had given himself away at the shootout. He didn't have to do that. It could have been a fatal mistake. How could Hal profit from such a deal? Slade had a lot of answering to do, if he could find him. Slade often took off for days at a time. He had no steady job that Matt knew about. The rumor was that he lived by rustling one or two steers at a time and selling them to the local meat market. It would be an on demand and on need by the butcher. Nobody had proved it. Most ranchers couldn't tell if one or two animals were missing.

The Bar-H lay six miles from town, so it took Matt an hour and a half to make the ride. Once there he tried the

Laughing Lady Saloon, one of Slade's favorite haunts. He wasn't there and Sylvia, the lady who ran the place, said she hadn't seen him for two or three days. Matt tried the hotel where Slade stayed sometimes when he had any money.

One-Hand J. Johnson ran the Johnson Hotel. It had twelve rooms and most of them were usually vacant. They called him One-Hand because he lost his left hand in the war. He was the most cheerful and upbeat person Matt knew.

'Nope, Matt, haven't seen him for more than a week. Don't know what's happened with him. Meat business must be slow.'

They both chuckled.

'One of these days a stout rope from the town marshal is going to take away one of your customers. You know if he was partial to any of Lucinda's ladies?'

'Now, Matt. How would I know that?'

'As mayor of our glorious little berg

you know almost everything that happens in the county.'

'Wish it were so, Matt. You might talk to Sally about Slade. Seems to me I've heard him refer to her a time or two.'

'Thanks, Johnson. I appreciate it.'

Matt remembered Sally. She was the generous-sized soiled dove at Lucinda's home for wayward girls. She had to weigh at least two hundred pounds.

When he walked in the front parlor at Lucinda's over-decorated place of business, Lucinda stood from a small desk at the near side and grinned at him.

'Lordy, look at here. I do hope this is strictly a business call.'

Lucinda was a frail little quail, just five feet tall and couldn't weigh ninety pounds with her clothes on. She was about fifty and all kinds of cosmetics hid any wrinkles or age lines that might be there.

'You're looking good, Lucinda. You must be at least thirty by now.'

'Now I know you want something. What gives?'

'Looking for Slade. He been around today?'

'Bit early for him which surprised me. Yeah, he's here. Can't tell you where.'

'I could kick in doors until I find him.'

'Could, but you won't.' She looked at a small watch on a gold chain around her neck. 'He's a one-hour man. Should be down in another ten minutes. Want some company while you wait?'

'Don't distract me, Lucinda.'

'Hey, entertainment is my job.'

'Sorry. I'll wait outside. Don't tell him I'm looking for him.' Matt went out the door and perched on a chair in front of the hardware store across the street.

Ten minutes later Slade came out Lucinda's door and started up the street. Matt cut him off just past the bank and stood in front of him.

'We need to talk, Slade.'

'What the hell for?'

'Because you rustled half of our trail drive herd and you're going to hang for it.'

Slade was tall and Texas slim. He had shaggy hair, a full beard, and moustache. His dark eyes snapped in anger.

'You don't say. When was that?'

'About a month ago when we were halfway to Ellsworth.'

'Not a chance, you wild-eye vigilante. A month ago I spent three weeks in Fort Worth with my relatives. A regular family reunion. I got me about twenty folks who will be glad to testify to that. What proof do you have?'

'A witness at the rustling site identified you by hearing your voice when you identified one of the men in the trail drive crew.'

'He's lying.'

'Why would he do that?'

'To get me in trouble. Must be somebody who has it in for me.'

'That could be half the men in the county.'

'Yeah, I am popular. Now, get out of my way.'

'You talk better than you fight. You will still hang for rustling.'

Matt watched Slade move past him and down the boardwalk. No sense going to the town marshal or to the county sheriff. Slade was right. There was no firm evidence against him and he said he had an alibi for the days of the rustling. But he would keep watching Slade. He continued down the walk to the Lenore General Store. He needed two new pairs of blue jeans and one blue work-shirt. Of course the fact that Francine Lenore probably would be helping her dad mind the store would be a bonus.

Inside the store, Francine met him with a big smile. Her father was probably in his office working on the books.

'Hi there, cowboy. Heard your trail drive was over.'

Matt grinned at her and felt giddy. She was so pretty and nice that it made him shiver. Long brown hair around her shoulders, soft green eyes, a funny little up-turned nose, and a round face that smiled and laughed a lot.

'The trail drive went well. But we had one man killed by rustlers.'

She was taller than most girls and slender. Francine was two years younger than he was and determined to make the store a success.

'Sorry about losing the hand but I'm glad it wasn't you.' She almost blushed. 'Can I get anything for you?'

She found the jeans for him then showed him three shirts.

'Can't make up my mind. Which one is best?'

'The all-blue one. It'll last for years.' She held up another one, with a wild red pattern, long sleeves, and snaps instead of buttons. 'Now this is one that you should wear to the fandangle. You probably forgot about it coming up this Saturday.'

'Fandangle? Isn't that mostly a dance?'

'True, but there will be a barbecue and cake sale and maybe a picnic basket auction. You coming?'

'Well, yeah, I guess.' He looked away then turned back. 'Francine, are you going?'

'Of course. I'm in charge of the bake sale.'

'I'll take that fancy shirt as well. How much do I owe you?' He paid and hurried out of the store. Why didn't he ask if he could squire her to the dance? Dumb. He was dumb and near tongue-tied when he was around a pretty girl. Especially Francine.

Matt headed for the bank. He'd get the check deposited and money for the ranch, and then get back to the Bar-H and see how things had fared while they were gone.

Hal Westover had seen the meeting between Matt and Slade on the street from where he watched from a second-storey room at the Johnson Hotel. It did not look like a friendly session between old friends. He had come up to this room by way of the back entrance. Room 204 was unlocked. He had arrived in town two hours ago and left a message at the Laughing Lady Saloon for Slade. He found it and wrote on the bottom of it to meet him in this room in an hour.

A few minutes later the door banged open and Slade barged in with an angry scowl.

'Westover, you ornery sidewinder. You just about got me killed.'

'Slade, you dumb horse's rump, you're such a bad shot I don't know how you stayed alive.'

Both men stared at each other for a tense moment then they burst out laughing.

'What went wrong?' Slade asked.

'Everything that could. I got back late to the camp. You started the rustling ten minutes early and I had no chance for an outside shot. The shooters from the woods must have been idiots. Didn't kill a one of the trail drive crew.'

'Total mass confusion,' Slade said. 'I

took one rifle round about a foot from my head. Man, I was spooked.'

Hal nodded then turned serious. 'Is that why you screamed out my name? I could have gut shot you right then if I'd been close to you.'

'Yeah, I was wild. Afraid I was dead. Knew the minute I yelled it that I shouldn't have.'

'I talked my way around it. They believed me. What can we do next?'

'Gonna be a next time?'

'Damn right. I'm not giving up.'

'I could use about ten head of fat steers for that little box canyon I got staked out.'

'We cleaned out of steers. But we could grab eight or so yearlings from one of the far-out ranges. That canyon of yours is north or south?'

'North up from some of your range.'

'You lost two men?'

'Yep, but both were newcomers to town. I do need at least fifty dollars to pay off the two I got back with. Both locals and if I pay them they won't talk.'

'Done, I've got the cash with me. Now, when do you want to set up a small drive of some Bar-H yearling steers?'

'Soon, this week. You set the time and I'll be there. But what about our other business?'

'Let me worry about that. We have plenty of time,' Hal said.

* * *

When Matt rode back to the ranch he was still wondering about Slade. They had to wait and see if he made another move. Then he thought about Saturday and the fandangle. He wasn't a good dancer but he had to go. The basket auction? Yes, the women made picnic baskets full of supper for two and they auctioned them off. He would have to find out which which one was Francine's and buy it. He shook his head. He didn't look forward to the whole thing but he would do it just so he could talk to Francine.

9

Matt and Ivan, one of the hands, spent most of Thursday riding a big circle around the close-in ranges of the Bar-H spread, counting brood cows and calves, looking over the yearling steers, and generally checking out the grass left on the ranges. There was no high country to go to when the summer grass ran out. All looked to be in good shape.

'What about the north ranges, Mr Matt? We've never used a line rider up there permanent. Time we sent somebody to check out back?'

'Good idea, Ivan. Going to be a long all day and half the night ride. I gave my trail guys two days off, today and tomorrow. They just rode four hundred and fifty miles twice.'

Ivan grinned. 'Hey, be a good job for Hal. He's never done it before.'

Matt chuckled. 'Oh yeah, I'd like to do that. But I can't go back on my word. One of your stay-at-home men needs to do the job.'

'I can ask them for a volunteer?'

'Might work. If it doesn't, you'll have to pick out one. Do it tonight so the man can have an early start tomorrow.'

Just after supper, Ivan knocked on the ranch house kitchen door. Ponchy went and brought Matt to talk to him.

'Mr Matt. Got a surprise for you. I talked to my men about the job, and nobody lifted his hand. Then Hal, who was in the bunkhouse paying off a loan he had taken, spoke up. He said he'd do it. I told him what he had to do, what to watch for, how to keep a record of what he found.'

'Now that is curious.'

'Oh, then he said he almost forgot. He had promised to settle up his account at the Lenore General Store tomorrow. I told him to ride in tonight and pay it, then he'd have tomorrow free. He rode out about ten minutes ago.'

'Will wonders never cease?' Matt asked.

'Surprises me too, Mr Matt.'

Matt snorted. 'Sounds almost like Hal Westover has found religion or something.'

* * *

Hal rode hard into Jackson. He made it in a little under an hour and a half. He found Slade in the first place he looked, in the Laughing Lady Saloon. He was in a nickel-limit poker game and had lost two dollars. He pushed back when he sat. Hal signaled and walked outside. Slade followed three or four minutes later. They met in the shadows.

'Yeah, Hal. So what's happening?'

'We get your eight little friends tomorrow. I'll be line riding the upper stretches of the north range. It's perfect. I can help you and no suspicion.'

'Good. Timing will be just right. Then tomorrow night after dark, I'll take one of the yearlings into the butcher shop.'

'What about the brand?'

'No problem. I always slice off the brand before a steer hits town.'

'How will I find you tomorrow?'

'You know where Jutting Rock is?' Slade asked.

'Yeah, sure. About ten miles north of the ranch house.'

'I'll meet you there. Some of those yearlings up that way?'

'Last time I knew. I should be there by ten o'clock.' They both nodded and Hal went on to the Lenore General Store. The old man was minding the place and Hal paid his tab, fourteen dollars and twenty cents. They hardly said a word. He rode back to the ranch.

* * *

Hal met Slade just after nine o'clock at the big rock. He figured it was at least eight miles north and two west of the ranch buildings.

'See any of those yearlings on your ride up here?' Slade asked.

''Deed I did. About two miles back. Must have been fifty of them.'

'Good, let's ride. We take them two at a time from different parts of the herd. Ten head and two horses leaves a trail a blind bookkeeper can follow. They check this part of the range often?'

'Not much. I'm doing the ride around the far reaches of our ranch.'

A half hour later they yahooed two steers out of the loose bunch of cattle and headed them north and more west. After a three-mile ride they came to the small canyon against a smattering of small hills.

They herded the steers into the canyon, then dragged some brush nailed to two-by-fours across the twenty-foot opening. They turned and rode back to the yearlings. Hal talked Slade into taking three on the next trip and then three more on the third ride.

Hal grinned. 'That should do it. I've got to get back to the north edge of our

104

range and finish my line rider job. You be careful with those brands.'

'Don't worry. Know my job. Been doing it now for almost three years and not one complaint from the ranchers.'

Hal waved and rode north. He had made a note on the second page of his notepad about every animal there was, Then he rode the rest of the far range and noted what he saw.

He veered to the east more when he saw the main road into Jackson. He continued, marking down what he saw in the final five miles into the ranch. It was almost dark when he rode into the corral and unsaddled his horse. He found Matt in the living room talking with Ginny.

'Good, you're back,' Ginny said. 'Worried about you getting lost.'

'Nope, made it. Didn't see anything unusual. A few brood cows and calves up farther north from the main bunch, otherwise all looked normal.' He gave Matt his notebook.

'Ponchy probably saw you come in.

He'll have a late supper for you. Thanks, Hal. Go get something to eat.'

Hal nodded and headed for the kitchen, his face breaking into a grin. One more nail in the coffin. He had Slade back on his side and soon they would show some movement in the grand plan.

Matt watched him go. Something different about him. He had barely looked at Ginny. She had said hello to him but Hal had just nodded and then talked to Matt. Matt wished his father was at home so they could talk it over. He didn't expect his father back for a week. Until then he would be especially watchful of Hal Westover.

★   ★   ★

That same night, Slade had stayed with his eight yearling steers until almost dark, then roped one, tied it up, and cut off the Bar-H brand. He led it toward town. He tied the animal up at a tree at the edge of town the butcher used for

106

the butchering. Then he went a block away to butcher-man Loomis and told him he had work to do. Loomis was a thick-set Irishman and he grinned.

'The usual price of twenty dollars?' the meat man asked.

'Nope, price went up. Now twenty-five. You can afford it. You'll sell fifty dollars worth of steaks off just one side.'

Loomis grumbled, put on his rubber butchering boots and went to his killing tree and went to work.

Loomis had given Slade twenty-five dollars in greenbacks, and Slade thanked him and headed for the Laughing Lady Saloon.

10

On Friday Matt watched as the ranch routine settled down after the trail drive. They had spotted a herd of six wild horses near the river and he rode out with ten men to try to catch as many of them as they could. They at last roped all six of them and led them bucking and bolting back to the small corral. Then came the job of gentling them, trying to get them to trust a man and eventually to accepting a bridle and saddle. They still had some cutting to do on the young male calves so Matt sent out a team to get that task done.

That same Friday night Gregory arrived on a rented horse out of Jackson. He'd come in by stage.

Matt told him about his confrontation with Slade that proved nothing but he was still suspicious. Gregory told them about his ride in more than a dozen stagecoaches of various makes to get back to Jackson.

'Those stages are the worst form of transportation ever invented,' Gregory said. 'I'll be black and blue for weeks. Next time I ride one I'm taking along three pillows and a padded suit.'

They all laughed, having had some experience in stagecoaches.

That night in private Matt told his father about Hal. 'He's changed since the trail drive. He follows orders without a lot of complaining, he hasn't been fighting with Ginny, and he seems to get along better with the rest of the hands. If he was in on that rustling try with Slade, I still can't see how he would profit. Then again, maybe it was like Hal said. Slade knew Hal would be on the drive.'

They talked it over for a while, then gave up and went to bed. Just before he went to sleep, Matt realized that tomorrow was Saturday and the day of the Jackson Fandangle. He more or less said he would go. Yes, he would go. He would try to buy Francine's picnic basket. It was a tradition at the ranch to work just half the day of the fandangle and then the crew was free to go to town. The festivities got going about three o'clock.

* * *

Not much was accomplished Saturday morning. Matt and Gregory worked out the sections to be checked when they started the herd count on Monday morning. They would put eight teams of two cowboys in the eight different areas and count every steer, yearling, brood cow and calf on the ranch. It was a huge undertaking.

By eleven o'clock Matt had on his new fandangle shirt, his new pair of jeans and had polished his black cowboy boots. They had a quick dinner from Poncho, who also was going into town.

* * *

Ten men from the Bar-H rode into town about two o'clock. Matt tied his mount to a rail and moved down the street. Across from the Laughing Lady Saloon the street had been scooped and swept clean of dirt down to the hard pan for dancing.

Matt wandered down the street along the booths. There must be twenty of them. Women in the booths were selling food and lemonade and other snacks. Matt stopped at the horseshoe pitching contest. Every man who wanted to compete brought his own set of two shoes. They were not fancy, most new and the regular kind nailed to the horse's hoofs. Matt had once been good at throwing them. He watched a pair of men throwing. The taller man he didn't know hit a ringer for three points and reached the twenty-one goal and won the match. The shorter man spotted Matt and called out.

'Hey Matt. Your turn. Take on Curley here. He thinks he's good as hot maple syrup.'

Matt shook his head and walked on past. A short way down the street he spotted the cake sale and hurried over to the booth. Francine saw him coming.

'Selling any cakes?'

'Half gone already. I even bought one myself. How would you like a slice of a double chocolate with chocolate frosting?'

'My favorite.'

She brought it to him on a paper napkin and he took a big bite. That's when the shooting started.

'That's the rifle marksman contest,' she said. 'You going to try it?'

He shook his head. 'I retired. What does your supper decorated basket look like?'

'Not supposed to show you,' she said and laughed. 'But everyone does. The money goes toward starting a city library. Won't that be wonderful?'

She went behind a small table that held a dozen cakes and brought out her basket. It was a bent willow basket a foot deep and a foot square. It had a large red bow on the top and a red ribbon around the center.

'Should be easy to spot,' Matt said. 'Now where is another piece of that chocolate cake?'

She laughed. 'You just had one.'

'I never stop with one chunk of cake. Any more?'

Francine giggled. 'You are something. I should just sell you the whole cake for a dollar.'

'That much?'

'Sure, we need the money for the library.'

He finished the second piece of cake and watched while she sold two cakes, then waved.

'I better check out the rifle contest. Ponchy always enters. He's the best shot on the ranch.'

'You come back. Oh, I like your shirt.'

'Good, a special lady picked it out for me.'

She almost blushed, turned it into a smile and waved back.

113

He waved again and walked up the street to the area cordoned off for the rifle shooting. It was at only fifty yards, with the bullets going through the targets and into the side of a small hill.

More than fifty men crowded around the shooters. There was a line of contestants. He spotted Ponchy, the second man back in the line. They shot at paper targets of the traditional three circles with the center one only three inches wide and blacked out. Each shooter had ten shots. The bull's eye counted five points. The second circle was two and the outer area one point.

When Matt got to the contest he found Ponchy in a shoot-off for first place after a tie. He watched. Ponchy put his rounds in the center the first six shots then had a two. The crowd murmured. His next two shots hit the bull. He had a total of forty two, two points behind Red. He took his time before the last shot. He needed another bull's eye to win. He sighted in. Somebody in the crowd yelled and

Ponchy flinched but didn't fire. He relaxed then sighted in again and fired.

'Bull's eye,' the score keeper from near the target called out. 'Ponchy wins by three points.'

Red Jones was not happy but shook hands with Ponchy.

'Hey, you shoot good, Red. So let's split the ten-dollar prize.' Everyone cheered.

Matt hurried over and shook Ponchy's hand. 'So you finally beat Red. Good of you to share the prize.'

'Red shoots good,' Ponchy said. 'You try that spicy fried chicken?'

Matt hadn't and Ponchy led him to it. Matt bought two drumsticks.

'Yeah, good, Ponchy. You'll have to fix some chicken this way for us at the ranch.'

Matt wandered around the various booths and bought a new string tie with a red stone set in it to go with his new shirt. He got back to Francine just as she sold the last cake.

'Where have you been? I almost sold

the half a cake you're eating. How about two more pieces?'

'Don't want to spoil my supper,' he said. He grinned and watched the pretty girl. Today he wasn't at all confused or shy around her. Good.

'We just have time to close up the booth before the box auction,' Francine said. 'Can you give me a hand?'

They dismantled the small booth, stacked the boards, and canvas, and then walked over to where the supper boxes were being assembled in front of the Laughing Lady Saloon. A crowd was beginning to form.

Francine smiled at Matt and reached for his hand. 'Hey, don't make a mistake and buy the wrong basket. Mine is the one with the big red bow.'

11

Matt noticed that Francine's basket was covered with a piece of cloth as she carried it toward the auction center.

'Why?' he asked, pointing to the cloth.

'So no one will know which basket is mine,' she said. 'Except you.' She smiled then giggled and a touch of blush showed on her neck.

She left him at the edge of the tent where all the baskets were being placed. A moment later she was back.

'Now we find a place to sit down and wait for the auction.'

A group of musicians had assembled in front of the tent where a small platform had been built. The music was loud.

'I like this song,' Francine said. 'Can't wait until the dancing begins.'

'I'm warning you, Francine, I'm not

much of a dancer.'

'Oh? I remember you did quite well last year with the Braithwaite girl.'

'Well, maybe. But I probably forgot what I did.'

'You'll do fine.'

Before long the music stopped and a man in a black suit, white shirt, and a black top hat came on the platform.

'Evening folks. I'm Harry Watson, your auctioneer. Not used to doing this, so bear with me.'

A pretty little girl about ten brought out the first basket and the bidding started. One dollar was the minimum bid. The first basket sold with one man bidding at a dollar and a quarter. The bidding ground on. Seldom was there more than two or three bids and the top basket carried a price of three dollars and fifty cents.

'How many baskets to sell?' Matt asked.

'Maybe twenty-five or so. Oh, here comes one with a big red bow.' Matt bid a dollar and a half. The auctioneer looked at the crowd of about a hundred people who sat and stood around.

'Do I hear two dollars?' the auctioneer called out.

'Two dollars and a half,' a voice came from across the way. Matt looked but couldn't see who made the bid. He waved his hand. 'Three dollars,' he said.

'Four and a half,' the same voice said. Matt still couldn't identify the speaker.

'Five dollars,' Matt said.

The auctioneer looked across the crowd. 'Sir, I have five dollars. Do I hear five and a half?'

'Five and two bits,' the voice said.

'Six dollars,' Matt boomed.

The auctioneer looked at the other person. Now Matt knew who it was. Slade. He didn't know whose basket it was. He was simply bidding up the price to spite Matt.

The auctioneer looked again at the other man. 'I have six dollars, going once, going twice.' He paused. 'Sold for six dollars. Sir, please stop at the cashier and then pick up your basket.'

Matt was pleased. He had won. The six dollars didn't matter. He squeezed Francine's hand and went to pick up the basket.

There was no park with grass where they could eat. Instead they found two chairs outside the hardware store and put the basket between them.

Francine opened the basket and fixed him supper on a blue-edged china plate. There was fried chicken, mashed potatoes and gravy, fresh peas, a cucumber salad, fresh-baked roll, and strawberry jam.

'You raised strawberries this year?' Matt asked.

'Of course. I always have a garden behind the house and water it all the time.' She watched him. 'Hope you like chicken.'

''Deed I do, Francine. Indeed I do.'

Before they were through eating, the band struck up again and they finished eating quickly.

'May I have this dance?' Matt asked. He could. Matt had told the truth. He wasn't much good at dancing. But it was enough that he could touch her, hold her hand, put his hand on her back, and swing her around. He wasn't always in time to the music, almost stumbled now and then, but Francine didn't seem to mind. She hummed along with the music and her smile was radiant.

Once someone tried to cut in. Matt turned and saw that it was Slade.

'No way, you cattle rustler. Get out of here. You lost the basket bidding. So you lost the dance. Get out of here.'

Slade scowled, started to say something, then decided against it, and stepped away.

'You two don't like each other?'

'Could say that. He was the other bidder on your basket.'

'Oh, I see. But it must be more than that.'

'Tell you sometime. Right now I've got to concentrate on not stepping on your feet.'

They danced and danced, doing the

group sets and the line dancing. Then at last they found chairs and dropped into them.

'This has been a remarkable day and evening,' Francine said. 'I'll always remember it.'

'Me too,' Matt said. 'When can I see you again?'

'You want to come courting?'

'So I'll have to ask your Pa?'

'That's the best way. He won't be a problem.'

'He going to church tomorrow?'

'Of course.'

'I'll try to see him right after church.'

She smiled and held his hand. 'I really liked your arm around me. We can do that when we're dancing.'

'I liked it too. Looks like the dancing is over.'

'I couldn't do another step,' Francine said.

'About time I walk you home.'

'I'd like that.'

It was there again; his feelings surged for this girl. Yes, he did want to court her, somewhere in the future he would marry her. Yes, down the trail somewhere.

'We'd better go,' he said. He carried the basket and held Francine's hand. 'Sorry about Slade. If he bothers you, let me know.'

'He won't be a problem. If he is my Pa will run him out of the store at the end of his shotgun.'

The Lenore home was two blocks from the store. It stood two storeys tall, a frame house painted white with blue trim. Two rose bushes grew near the front porch.

They stood for a moment in the darkness of the porch. He caught her shoulders and reached down. Her face came to meet his and they kissed softly, parted then kissed again with more urgency.

'Oh, my,' Francine said. 'Oh, my. I better go inside right now.'

'Yes, that would be best. Francine, I really enjoyed tonight, this afternoon, the supper, all of it. I'll be back. I'll talk to your pa as soon as I can.'

Her smile lit up half the town. 'Good. I'm so glad.' She turned and hurried into the house.

'Wow,' he said softly. 'I've got me a girl.'

12

Matt missed talking to Francine's father at church that Sunday. He had a sick cow on his hands that ate up most of the morning. It turned out the cow wasn't all that sick and nothing contagious. He got back to the ranch house just before noon.

Tomorrow was the herd count. He and his dad had to get the planning done. They went to the dining room and spread out a big map Gregory had made years ago. It showed every section of their range.

They marked it up in pieces until they had eight areas. Two cowboys would go into each area and count every critter they saw.

This count was the second most important work for the ranch next to the annual roundup. By four o'clock they had the hands assigned to the various sections and small maps drawn to show them exactly the boundaries they would work.

'Where's Hal tonight?' Gregory asked Ginny at the supper table.

She looked concerned. 'Said he wanted to go into town for a while to get in a real poker game for a change.'

'Kid has too much money. Not that we pay him all that much. He gets paid as a hand like any other. He said once that he still gets cash every month from his pa.'

'Not much we can do about it,' Ginny said.

★   ★   ★

The next morning at sunup, eight pairs of riders left the ranch heading for various parts of the range. Gregory had assigned Hal to an area near the ranch and to the south where there was a smattering of brood cows and calves, but not the main herd. Bob was teamed with Hal, and Gregory decided to tag along and watch them work.

★ ★ ★

A half hour later the three riders were near the Little Blue in a cluster of chinquapin oak, poplar trees, and brush, making it hard to get a good count. They had just left the brushy spot when a rifle shot blasted into the quiet Texas prairie.

'What in tarnation?' Hal shouted.

Bob wheeled his horse around just in time to see Gregory shot out of the saddle and slam to the ground. His big powerful black snorted, whirled, and pranced away.

Bob was on the ground near Gregory in a few quick steps and cradled the older man's head on his lap. Gregory's eyes were closed.

'He's still breathing,' Bob said. 'Looks like he got hit in the upper chest. Looks bad. Hal, ride hard for the ranch and hitch up that buck-board.

We've got to get Mr Hardy into town to the doctor soon as we can.' He changed his mind. 'No I'll go. You stay with Mr Hardy.' He pulled his six-gun and fired three shots in the air. 'Somebody will be here in a few minutes. Make him comfortable. But don't give him anything to drink. Here, hold his head off the ground.'

Bob got back on his horse but before he rode ten feet, Matt came galloping across the range.

'I heard a rifle shot, then three pistol shots, what the dickens . . . ' He looked down and saw his father on the ground, blood on the front of his shirt. 'Bob get the buckboard, fast.' Matt rode to his father, vaulted from the saddle and pushed Hal aside. 'Good, he's still breathing,' Matt said, holding his father. Gently he opened his father's shirt, saw the exit wound and pulled off his bandanna, folded it, and pressed it on the bleeding spot.

He looked at Hal. 'You see anybody? Hear a horse riding away? Anything?'

'Just the shot, Matt. Then I saw Dad fall off his horse. Did somebody shoot him on purpose?'

'You can bet the ranch on that, Hal. Not many hunters this time of year looking for deer or antelope. Sure you didn't see anybody?'

'Not a shadow. Could it be somebody from the Circle D? Maybe Mr Dunwoody himself?'

'No chance. Dunwoody is sneaky sometimes, but he's no backshooting killer. Wet your kerchief from your canteen, then fold it and hold it on Dad's forehead. He's still unconscious.'

'Who?' Matt worried. He didn't know of any real enemies his father had. But someone tried to kill him. He could die yet. Matt looked at the wound. It missed his heart, but must have hit part of his lung. That could be deadly. He checked his breathing. Slow and shallow. Not a full breath. He felt his father's pulse on his wrist. It was still there but he couldn't tell how strong or how often.

'Where is Bob with the buck-board?'

'Should be here soon,' Hal said. 'About ten minutes back to the ranch then harness it up.'

Matt scoured his memory to try to think of any old enemies his father might have had. Certainly no furious husbands. His father had not messed around with other women after his wife died almost fifteen years ago. Still, it had to be somebody.

'Did the shot come from the woods over there?'

'Near as I could tell,' Hal said. 'It all happened so fast, the shot, then Dad falling to the ground.'

'Ride over there and see what you can find. It'll have to be a spot where a shooter could get a good aim for us here. Go.'

'Yeah, good idea. I'll take a look. Maybe an expended brass shell casing from the rifle.'

'Maybe, go now.'

Just as Hal rode off, the buck-board came slamming over a slight rise, the horse heading straight for them with Bob using a whip. He skidded the rig to a stop six feet away, tied the reins, and jumped out.

'He still alive?' Bob asked.

'Right. Hope you brought some blankets.'

He had. They lifted Gregory gently and moved him into the flat cargo area behind the high seats. Matt continued to hold his father's head and shoulders in his lap.

'OK, to town but take it easy until we get to the road. Then go a little faster. No sudden bumps or jolts.'

'Right,' Bob said climbing into the high seat and slapping the reins on the horse's back.

Matt figured they were already about a mile from the ranch house so five more miles into town. Twice during the ride Gregory Hardy opened his eyes, stared at Matt but didn't really focus, then drifted off again. He didn't try to speak.

Matt held his father gently, trying to

prevent the inevitable jolts and bumps along the dirt road. He didn't think the drive to town would ever end.

At last he saw some buildings then the houses and business sections. Bob pulled the rig up directly in front of Dr Ed Clausen's office.

The two men carried Gregory into the medic's office. The man took one look at Gregory and waved them into an inner room with a high table. They lay him on it.

'What happened?' the doctor asked.

'Bushwhacked,' Matt said. 'We didn't see who did it.'

'Help me roll him over,' Dr Clausen said. They did, then the medic rolled him back.

'Good, the rifle round went all the way through. Must have missed his spine or he'd be dead by now. Looks like it clipped the top of his right lung.'

'Milly, I need some help in here,' he called. 'You two get out of here. I have a lot of work to do. I'm going to try to save Gregory's life.'

Bob drove the buck-board down a cross street, parked it, then came back. He and Matt sat in the doctor's outer waiting room.

★ ★ ★

An hour later, the doctor came out wearing a blood splattered white apron and wiping hands on a clean white towel.

'OK, your father is a lucky man, Matt. The bullet must have missed his lung by a millimeter or so, went under his clavicle and missed his heart. He's still in shock. Didn't lose that much blood. I've patched up the two wounds, stitched them and put on some medication that will help them heal. He's awake and asking for you. I want to keep him here overnight. I've got a night nurse who will watch him and change his bandages if they show he's bleeding. This way.'

Matt had never been in the doctor's office before. They went into a room that looked like a bedroom, with a bed and dresser, two chairs, and a window. Gregory lay in the bed with his head on a thin pillow. He scowled.

'Who shot me?'

'We don't know, but we'll find out. I'm reporting this to the town marshal. He'll tell the county sheriff.'

'Doc tells me that I'm too ornery to die.'

'Dad. You're staying here tonight. We'll be in tomorrow afternoon to get you back to the ranch.'

Milly came in. She wore all white and shooed them out of the room. 'He needs to rest now and sleep. We'll watch him careful.'

'Will he need a nurse out at the ranch?' Matt asked.

'Doctor will decide that tomorrow afternoon. Now get along.'

Matt talked to Marshal Olson who shook his head.

'Used to be a nice quiet little place around here. What happened?'

'Doesn't take much to mess up

134

things,' Matt said. 'Mostly one or two bad cases who make trouble and want something without working for it. I'll check that patch of woods but doubt if I'll find anything. Keep in touch.'

⋆ ⋆ ⋆

It was almost noon when they got the buck-board back to the ranch. Matt had trailed his horse along behind it going to town and coming back. At the ranch Matt told Ginny and Ponchy what had happened. Ginny cried and Ponchy swore. Then Matt and Bob both mounted and rode down to a copse of oak and poplar where they figured the bushwhacker must have been.

They checked every spot where a shooter would have an open shot. On the next to last one, and only about forty yards from the strike point, they found an empty brass cartridge.

Bob turned over the brass. 'Has to be a forty-three and three quarters caliber from a Henry rifle. Most of them shoot the same round. Not a lot of them around.'

'So, let's find out who owns one,' Matt said. 'First let's look at the other side of these oaks and check for a trail leading out. Any bushwhacker would be in one mad rush to get away from this spot.'

It only took them ten minutes to find the trail. A big horse with a long stride made deep prints in the dirt and grass. Matt checked them, squatting down beside them and looking at the route they took.

'He headed for that swale over there. It's got some hickory brush and live oaks that would hide him for almost a mile. By then he could cut back to the road into town and cover his tracks with all the other horses and wagon wheels.'

They followed the tracks and they came out on the road into Jackson about four miles away.

'No sense in going any farther,' Matt said. 'He's hiding his tracks. All we know is that he's riding a big horse with a long stride. Not a lot of them around this part of Texas.'

They turned and rode to the ranch. As they unsaddled and put their horses in the corral, Matt looked at Bob. 'Tell Ivan I want to see him in the office.'

13

As soon as Matt had come into the house, Ginny met him.

'How's Dad?' she asked. He could see the tear stains on her cheeks.

'Easy, easy. Doc says he should be alright. The bullet went all the way through his upper chest, missed his lung and heart and collarbone. Didn't lose a lot of blood but shock almost got him. Should be able to bring him home tomorrow afternoon.'

'Great. Good. I'm so glad. I've been worried sick since Bob told me Dad had been shot. You're sure that he's doing well, not just trying to make me feel better?'

'No need to do that. Doc was pretty sure that he would be fine in a few weeks.'

She smiled for the first time since he had come inside. 'Well, good. I think I can eat now. Ponchy has been saving supper for us.'

Now that it was Tuesday morning, Matt knew exactly what he had to do. Last night he had told Ivan to take Bob and finish the count on that section they had missed when the shot came. The rest of the men had finished their counts.

Matt had breakfast and headed for town. He was on the prowl to find all of the big long-gaited horses in there. Shouldn't be hard. He'd start at the livery. Old Kentucky would know most of them. Old Kentucky wasn't that old, maybe fifty. He claimed he was old when he passed thirty. He knew the mounts in town and lots of them from surrounding ranches. He made half his income from nailing on horseshoes. At the Kentucky Livery stable in town, Old Kentucky grinned when he saw Matt.

'Ain't it about time I pay the Bar-H a visit to get some new shoes on them mounts of yours?'

'About, Kentucky, but not quite.' Matt told him what he was hunting but not why.

'Hail to Betsy yes, we got maybe six or eight scratchers who can leg it out. Course most of them are on the ranches.'

'Any in town?'

Kentucky sat down on a bale of straw just inside the stable doors. He scratched his arm and then one leg. He pushed back his dirty-brown short-brimmed hat and shook his head.

'Truth be known, young Hardy, they is about half the folks in town with a little stable shed out back of their house where they keep a horse or two. I don't see them very often. Don't ride much so a set of good shoes can last a year.'

'So how many really big mounts? I'd say seventeen hands at least.'

'That big? Well there are three I can think of. The hardware man, Frank Albertson, has a big gelding roan I'd give a pretty penny for. Don't ride him much. Used to race him Sunday afternoons until the church folks made us stop it.'

Matt took off his low-crowned brown Stetson and wiped his forehead. 'Right, I've got him. Who else?'

'Why you so consarned interested in big horsepower?'

'Can't say right now.'

'How is your Pa? Heard he got bushwhacked yesterday.'

'Yes he did. Doc says he's doing good. Should pull through. Might get to go home today. Now who else owns a big horse?'

* * *

'Big horses. Yes. In town. The city councilman, Lenore over at the general store. He's got a huge mount I never see. So, could be that the bay stallion the town marshal owns could count.'

'That's not much help, Old Kentucky. I'll be back. You think on it.' Matt was almost to the door when he turned.

'Oh, you know what kinda mount

141

Slade Watkins rides?'

'Not a chance. He never brings any horse in here. Can't help you there.'

Matt waved and rode back to the center of town where he walked the three blocks of businesses, checking all of the hitching rails. He saw no horse that he would count as being big.

He mounted and rode the alleys behind the stores. Quite a few horses were tied up there but no big ones. He went down streets and the back of houses but again he saw no big mounts.

Matt pulled out an inexpensive silver pocket watch tied to a loop on his belt with a thin rawhide. It was almost noon. He had wasted the whole morning. He was famished. He headed back to town to the Texas Café near the Lenore General Store. He thought of asking Francine out to dinner, but it was too close to noon to be proper. Instead he went into the café.

He had a plateful of beef stew and a piece of cherry pie. The tab was forty cents. He paid it and left. He went outside and looked at the General Store. Why not? He walked down to the open door and went inside.

Francine wasn't behind the counter. Instead the somber-looking Councilman Duncan Lenore stared at Matt. Matt had talked to him many times in the store but now he felt like he didn't know the man. He was not smiling.

'Mr Lenore, I'm Matt Hardy.'

'Know who you are,' he said in a monotone voice showing no sign of emotion.

'I've come on an important mission,' Matt said.

Lenore perked up a little. He nodded. His eyes took on a new interest.

'What might that be, young Hardy?'

'I'm extremely fond of your daughter. I think Francine likes me as well. I want to come courting her. May I have your permission?'

'You go to church, young man?'

'Not as often as I wish I did. Lots of

times ranching must be done on Sunday.'

'Like yesterday when you were supposed to meet me?'

'Tried to, but we had some sick animals we had to care for.'

'I see. Long as you court my daughter I want to see you in church every Sunday. That agreeable to you?'

'Yes sir. Absolutely.'

'Very well. You may come to the house on Sunday afternoon, after church and until five o'clock. Oh, we'll have you as our guest at Sunday dinner at two o'clock.'

'Yes sir. I understand. I'll be at church Sunday morning at eleven o'clock. Thank you.' He turned to leave and a figure darted out the door leading to the storage room. Francine was shrieking in delight.

She rushed up to Matt and held out both hands for him to grasp. Her face showed a brilliant smile, her eyes dancing.

'Oh, thank you, Father. You've made me the happiest girl in all of Texas.'

Mr Lenore cleared his throat. 'Well, I can see that. Yes indeed I can see that. We'll see you Sunday morning, Mr Hardy.'

Matt let go of Francine's hands. 'Yes, sir, you surely will. Thank you. Goodbye, Francine.' He turned and hurried out the front door. His knees were shaking and he was afraid he would fall down. He leaned against the front of the store. He had done it. He was going courting. He could hardly believe it. He stood there for a minute or two, took one last look at the store, then hurried down the street to Dr Clausen's office. He said afternoon. It was afternoon.

Milly greeted Matt when he came in the door.

'About time you got here. Your Pa ain't the best patient. He's been calling for you most of the morning.'

'So he can go home?'

'If you got a buck-board or buggy. He certainly isn't going to ride a horse home.'

145

'Buggy? He can sit up all right for two hours?'

'Been sitting up and yelling at me most of the morning.'

'Can I see him?'

She led the way into the room where Matt had left his Pa the day before. He was fully dressed and sitting on the bed.

'About time,' Gregory said.

'I'm here, Pa. Going to go rent a buggy and then we can get you home.'

'About time.' He grinned. 'Good to see you. You catch the bushwhacker who shot me?'

'Not yet, Pa. Working on it. I'll be right back.'

Dr Clausen stopped him in the outer room.

'He's looking good. No additional damage from the bullet I could see. He can go home but keep him in bed or a chair for at least a week. If he takes bad, get him back in here pronto. Sending some bandages and salve to use on the wounds. Change them every two days. Now go get that buggy.'

14

On Wednesday morning, Matt tried to settle down to getting the ranch back on track. He had brought his father home in a rented buggy the afternoon before and sent it back to the livery by a ranch hand. Gregory Hardy turned out to be a difficult patient as Milly had said. Ginny had spent most of the evening reading to him. He at last went to sleep about ten o'clock.

Matt sat at the dining-room table that morning with the count sheets of paper from the eight zones of the ranch laid out in front of him. He had always been good with figures and now he added up the categories of animals. When he had the totals for the four classes, he checked the figures against the count from last year. They had an increase of ten per cent in all categories except one. That was in the range bull group. They planned it that way.

The range bull group was one male larger since they had bought a prize bull from an outfit down near the border.

He put the books away and went in to tell his dad about the totals.

Gregory reacted to the brood cow total. 'Should have a thousand or more new brood cows coming due from two years ago,' Gregory said. He scowled, winced when he moved, but tried to cover up the pain. 'Think we're getting rustled on a regular basis and we have no way to check?'

'Might be. But there is no way we can patrol thirty-nine thousand acres of range land to watch for rustlers. Especially if they are taking only eight or ten steers at a time.'

'Yeah, you're probably right. Still something to think about like putting a pair of night riders out there along the west and south edges of our land. Might just catch somebody driving a beef toward Jackson.'

Matt snorted. 'We might try that. How long has it been since we sold any beef to the two meat markets in town? I can't remember the last time. Might not hurt to ask some of the other ranchers. Those guys have to get beef from somewhere. They always seem to have a good supply.'

'Sounds like a good idea.' Greg groaned as he tried to sit up in the bed. 'How much longer I got to stay trapped in this bed?'

'Five more days the doc said. Then you can sit up in the living room for a week.'

'Too long. Too chicken-plucking long.'

'I'll check out the butcher's tomorrow and talk to any riders I see from other ranches. Now you get some sleep. A few catnaps wouldn't hurt.'

'Damn doctors.'

'Yeah. But sometimes we need them.'

Ginny came in with cookies and lemonade.

'Hey there, shot-up person and father of mine, how did you sleep?'

'Like a frog on a big lily pad in the lake.'

'That sounds good. You nibble on some chocolate chip cookies and I'll read something to you. What would you like to hear this morning?'

'That thing you was reading last night. How much longer I got to stay penned up in this bed?'

Ginny looked at Matt who held up five fingers. He grinned and left the room.

Now what, Matt thought. Not a lot to do on the ranch this time of year. Just keep the stock grazing and hope for some rain in the middle of August, which was coming up in a day or two. A trail drive really took up two months of the summer. But it was worth it.

He went out to the corral and found three riders working at taming down the wild horses they had brought in a few days ago. Four of them were mares with two stallions. The stallions probably wouldn't work out. Most cow ponies were mares.

One roan mare had been gentled enough to take a saddle and bridle. She fought against both but after a few rounds of the corral she seemed to accept them.

That afternoon in town Matt talked to the men at the two meat markets. One of them said he bought a steer maybe once a month and went to a different ranch each time in a rotation. He bought fewer in the summer when the meat would spoil. The second butcher was less forward and Matt figured he had something to hide, but Matt wasn't sure what it was. He might visit him again and check the hides of his butchered beef.

Matt walked down to the livery stable. Finding the guy who bush-whacked his father was still first on his agenda. Maybe the livery man would have some new ideas about the shooter's big horse.

15

Matt rode out to the edge of town where the Kentucky Livery Stable backed up to a small fenced holding area of about five acres. He'd seen this barn and sheds for years but never really took a careful look. Now he did.

The main barn was showing signs of wear and tear. It had never been painted and now the boards were gray and weathered. A second-storey hay mow door sagged a foot off center and the adjoining sheds were more ramshackle than he remembered. Old Kentucky was getting older and not taking good care of the place. Matt dismounted, tied his horse to a six-foot hitching rail at the side of the barn, and went in the wagon-wide door to where Old Kentucky sat in an old rocking chair. He had a bottle of beer in one hand and a half burned-up cigar in the other. He waved the stogie.

'Hey, Matt. Twice in a week seeing you. Things going slow at the Bar-H or are you sparking that Lenore filly?'

Matt grinned. In a town this size everyone knew all there was to know about everyone else. Old Kentucky pointed to a three-legged milking stool and Matt sat down, his long legs stretching out in front of him. He didn't use a milk stool much.

'Got me a problem,' Matt said.

'I'm just the *hombre* to fix it,' Old Kentucky said with a cackling laugh. He tossed Matt a bottle of beer. 'Serious worry?'

'Same one. Who shot my Pa, and where is that large horse the bushwhacker rode? You think anything more on it?'

'Some, but got me nowhere. Oh, you asked me about what mount Slade is riding. Still don't know. He doesn't leave it here. Must be in some town man's small stable. Used to rent a horse here time and again but last six months

I haven't seen him.'

'Thanks for the beer and the advice. See what I can dig up at the Laughing Lady.'

In the saloon he looked to see if Slade was anywhere around. He wasn't. He talked to two of the fancy ladies but neither had seen him for a couple of days. He had a beer and wandered round the four poker games in progress. The men didn't talk much. The bar was the better place and he heard some gossip about the saddle-maker's wife but didn't believe it. Nothing else of any value was said. He went outside and rode up and down the three blocks of Main Street watching the horses tied at the rails. No sign of any tall, powerful animal that could have made those bushwhacker's trail marks, leaving the patch of woods out where his dad was shot. He rode the rest of the town, checking houses with small barns, and stables, but again, no sign of a large horse.

Back at the Bar-H Matt rubbed

down his mount, watered her and turned her into the corral. Hal was throwing a lasso at a barrel and not doing all that well. He had to learn sometime. Matt tried to show him how to do it the right way and Hal flared up ready for an argument. Then suddenly he cooled.

'Yeah, you're right, Matt. Let me try it a few dozen more times.'

Matt nodded and went into the house. What got into Hal? He was acting almost normal. Where did the quick temper and surly attitude go? He shrugged and got Ponchy to make him a two-slice chicken sandwich. He'd missed dinner.

16

For most of the afternoon Matt kept thinking about his father's attack. He kept thinking about Slade Watkins but he had no real evidence. After supper he had a talk with his father in his bedroom. He seemed almost normal but he was angry about being shot and kept asking who had done it. Matt had little to tell him.

When Matt came out of his father's bedroom, Ginny motioned for him to follow her. Her face was serious and frowning. She stopped him down the hall well away from Greg.

'I don't like the way Dad is looking. Don't you think he's a little pale?'

Matt nodded. 'Come to think of it, he does look a little down. Is he complaining?'

'No, you know Dad. He could be at death's door and demand that he got to open it himself. If he isn't better tomorrow, we should have the doctor come and look at him.'

'We'll watch him close in the morning. Then if he don't look good, we'll send Hal into town to bring the doctor back.'

'Good, that's what I was thinking. I'm not a nurse but I think something is going wrong in that wound. I hear him groaning sometimes when he moves. I had a time getting him up the stairs to his bed.'

'Sorry I wasn't here to help. We'll look him over good tomorrow morning.'

* * *

They did the next morning. Then they got together in the kitchen and talked.

'Looks worse today. I think he has a little fever. I just used the back of my hand but he's warmer now than normal, I'm sure.'

Hal came up and listened. He

nodded. 'I noticed it last night. He's hurting. Want me to ride in and bring back Dr Clausen?'

The three of them looked at each other. Matt and Ginny nodded.

'I think you better do that, Hal. Tell Doc Clausen that Dad has a low fever, is hurting and having trouble moving around.'

'Yeah, seems like the right thing to do. It's about ten o'clock now. Get in to town about noon. With any luck I should have the doc back here by two o'clock.'

Ten minutes later, Matt and Ginny watched Hal ride off toward town. Then Ginny hurried back to Greg's bedroom. She had wet cloths she put on her father's forehead to try to cool him off. She wiped down his arms and chest with more cold cloths and it seemed to help.

'Ginny, what are you doing? I'm not hurting so much now.'

'You have a low fever. I'm trying to get it down. Just lay still and let me cool you off.'

Matt watched a minute, then went downstairs. It was worrisome but not serious, he decided. Doc Clausen would have something to give him to bring down the fever and make the pain go away. He went out to the corral to see how the breaking of the new wild horses was coming along. They could always use some new mounts.

★　★　★

Hal grinned as he rode. He was in no rush. There was lots of time. He figured this would be a good chance, maybe the only one for some weeks. He wanted it to move ahead faster than that.

In town a little after one thirty, he tied up at the rail in front of the doctor's office and went inside. Milly nodded when she saw him.

'How is Mr Greg doing?'

'Need to talk to Doc Clausen. Is he in?'

'He was all morning. Now he's running between two houses here in town waiting for two babies to be born. You know babies can take their time or maybe come lickety-split. One is a first child so that one will be a time. Mr Greg not doing well?'

'Ginny says he has a low fever and lots of aches and pains. Want the doc to come out this afternoon if he can.'

'Not a chance on God's green earth, Hal. Like I said, he's on baby watch. Then tomorrow he's got six appointments in the morning and two in the afternoon. Seems like everyone is getting sick at once.'

Hal shook his head. 'Don't sound good. How about if we put Dad in a slow buggy and bring him into town?'

'That would be best. Especially if it doesn't look too serious. Best we can do, unless you want to ride back home and bring him right back here this afternoon or evening.'

Hal shook his head. 'Nope. Think that tomorrow morning would be best. We'll try to get here about ten o'clock.'

'Fine, Hal. I'll put it down in the

book. See you tomorrow morning.'

Once outside Hal let a huge grin spread across his face. Yes, it was going to work. He looked up and down the street. He'd try the Laughing Lady first. He had a couple of hours to find him. Hard telling where he would be. Too early for the girls. Maybe some poker. Slade loved poker. Hal hurried down the street to the saloon.

★   ★   ★

It was evening by the time Slade found the man he wanted. The stranger had come into town the day before and Slade took note. Now Slade and another man sat at a table in the Lost Horse Saloon playing cards. It was a barrel bar. The stand-up bar was made up of two two-by-twelve-inch planks laid across two fifty-gallon barrels. Sawdust covered the floor, and there were only two poker tables. This time of day there were three men at the bar and two more playing poker. It was the

161

worst bar in town and Slade had picked it on purpose. There were no chips on the table and a pitcher of beer sat between the two players. The second man was about five eleven, under twenty-five, with sandy brown hair, a full beard and moustache, and small eyes, deep set, that were dark-blue with flecks of copper. His name was Quirt. Slade didn't ask his last name. His frame was solid, a little heavy, he wore jeans and a red shirt with no kerchief, and a low-crowned grey hat. He had no gun belt.

'Hear that you can use a long gun pretty good,' Slade said putting down a face card against the two down cards in a stud poker hand.

'Tolerable. If I can see it, I can hit it.'

'Should have had you along on the last two jobs I worked,' Slade said. He glanced up at the trail-worn face that looked like it hadn't been washed in a week. There was something deadly and wild in the eyes, and a casual don't-give-a-whit in his attitude.

'Turns out I'm no good with a rifle. Seems like I can't hit the broadside of a bucket of milk six feet in front of me.'

They both laughed.

Slade put down the second card on the stud hand. Neither one paid any attention to the cards.

'You have any problem shooting at a man-sized target?' Slade asked.

Quirt polished his deadly crooked grin. 'No, not as long as he ain't moving.'

'You available most any day?'

'Long as I have a few dollars for a room. Bone tired from sleeping on the ground.'

'When you get into town?'

'Yesterday.'

Slade slid a twenty dollar double eagle gold piece across the table on top of the stud hand.

'Shit, looks like you won again, Quirt. You be at the Johnson Hotel and I'll get in touch with you there tomorrow. Be ready an hour before daylight.'

'I can do that. I'm liking this already. Never did like to stay in one town for more than a few days.'

'Won't take that long.' Slade dropped his voice even lower. 'You take the shot and ride like crazy out of the country. No one will try to follow you. The man in question will be coming into town to see the doctor tomorrow morning. It's six miles back to his ranch. I've got a good spot all picked out with lots of cover and a get-away route that will work like a greased pig in a wrestling match.'

'You be along?'

'Take you out there just before daylight and set you up. The target will be the only passenger in a buggy. Might be a man on a horse along. Take him out as well if you need to.'

'Two will cost you double.'

'I can cover it. You make sure that you put the old man down and dead. Hit him with four slugs if you have the time. Then ride like a demon down that gully.'

'I want half my pay, a hundred dollars, when we ride out in the dark.'

'Yes I'll have it with me. You get second hundred when we meet at Adobe Spring. It's three miles south of town on the main road.' Slade rubbed his face with one hand, then looked at Quirt with a scowl.

'Do your job and do it right. Don't worry about the horseback rider if one is along. Better yet, don't even try for him. Make certain you get the old man, then cut and ride like the wind. If something goes wrong and you don't kill him, come anyway and tell me that. I'll still pay you. But I want to know for sure one way or the other. Understand?'

'Yeah. I look like a dummy to you?'

''Course not. Just want to be sure this time.'

'You missed last time?'

'Hit him but not a killing shot.'

'Usually I do one shot and one kill,' Quirt said. 'Not that I'm bragging. Just the cold dead truth.'

Slade bunched the cards and left them on the table. Both stood and left the saloon separately. Few men came in and fewer stayed. Chance of anyone remembering this meeting were zero to none. Slade went out the door, stretched and headed for the café. All this talk about killing old man Hardy gave him a monster appetite.

* * *

Hal rode into the ranch about four that afternoon and told them about the doctor and his two babies.

'Said to bring him in first thing in the morning,' Hal said. 'Doc has a dozen appointments tomorrow but he'll check out Dad as soon as he gets there.'

The two groaned.

'Best Doc can do,' Hal said. Then he began working on some story so he could get away from the ranch early in the morning, or late tonight, so he could meet Quint. This time it was going to work.

He looked at Matt. 'You want me to go along?'

Matt shook his head. 'No need. I'll have Ivan drive the buggy and watch Dad. I'll ride alongside and keep an eye on Dad. If he's having any problems, I'll tie my mount on the back and ride in the buggy.'

'Sounds good. Hey, I've been watching several deer down in that grove about a mile south. Ponchy said he could use some venison. Think I'll get an early morning start while it's still dark and go down there and try for a nice sized buck.'

Matt nodded. 'Yeah, do that. We'll get into town fine. Nothing you can do in there.'

'OK. Wish me luck. I got my mouth all set for some good venison steaks.'

17

Matt rode slightly ahead of the buggy as Ivan drove out toward Jackson and Dr Clausen's office. They were about two miles from the ranch buildings and Matt watched for ruts and holes in the road that would create a heavy jolt to the unsprung buggy's frame.

On the far side of the buggy he saw a small stream and a flush of trees and brush. It reminded him of the grove of trees near where his dad had been shot. He scanned the brush then looked back at the road.

A heart-beat later he heard a rifle shot and jerked his gaze back to the trees. He spotted a wisp of smoke near some brush and had already whipped his Winchester from the boot. He slammed four shots into the brush as fast as he could work the lever, then spurred his mount back to the buggy.

Ivan had stopped it and was leaning into the seat.

Ivan screamed.

Matt rushed up, kicked off his horse, and looked in the buggy's seat. His father lay where the bullet had thrown him against the far side of the seat, an ugly reddish black hole in the side of his head, and blood and bone fragments splattered on the other side of the seat.

Gregory Hardy was dead.

Matt bellowed in agony, jumped back on his mount and grabbed the Winchester again as he kicked the horse in the sides, aiming her at the copse of brush and trees. He fired twice more into the brush, then crashed into it, through it, and saw a mounted rider two hundred yards ahead riding fast down a small ravine the stream must have dug out.

Matt stopped and sighted in on the rider. He tried to fire again but was out of rounds. He plunged down the ravine after the killer. He wasn't going to let this one get away. Not a chance in the whole state of Texas.

He rode like a mad man, pushing the horse into a ground-eating gallop, flat out after the rider ahead. He was a little closer now and was gaining. Twice he saw the man ahead turn and look behind but he didn't try to use his rifle.

They flashed through trees and brush and at times Matt lost the rider. Then the growth thinned and he found him again. Not more than a hundred yards ahead. He was closing.

The killer was out of the trees then and riding hard toward town, which had to be at least four miles away. Matt wanted to reload the Winchester but knew it would be impossible while galloping and keeping up the chase.

He was nearing the end of the trees and brush when he heard a rifle shot close by. At the same time he felt his mount falter, then stumble, and suddenly he was thrown forward over the mount's head and jolting into the dirt and grass. He skidded on his shoulder, rolled over, and flailed out his hands to stop himself. He looked for his horse. It was down, its feet threshing, tearing at the ground, and she gave off a scream that he had heard only from dying horses. She gave one more scream, her legs stopped moving, and he knew she was dead.

How?

Who?

There must have been two killers. One to shoot his father, one to prevent anyone from chasing and catching the killer. He crawled over to the horse. She was one of his favorites. She was dead.

He kept low and looked around. He could see no tell-tale smoke from the burnt powder of the rifle round.

Matt looked down the gully to where it leveled out into the open prairie and saw the killer gradually fading from sight. He was away. Matt's only hope was that he had hit him with his first rifle shots.

Matt sat there beside his dead horse for a few minutes. Then he stripped the saddle off the mount, took off the bridle, and slung both over his shoulder.

When he came out of the trees, Ivan saw him and drove the buggy off the road to meet him. Matt took another look at his father and shuddered at the damage the heavy slug had done. Somebody was going to pay. Was going to pay with a lot of pain and agony and suffering until he couldn't stand it and would beg for a killing shot.

'He get away?'

'Yeah. A second one killed my horse. Both of them got away.'

Matt stood beside the buggy and looked at his father again. He reached out and held the limp hand that was already starting to cool. He looked up at Ivan.

'From now on, you are running the ranch. I'm working full time hunting those two killers. Let's get Dad back to the house. Send a rider into town and have the marshal take a message to the sheriff. Send a rider if he has to. I'm coming back on a horse and following those tracks. They must go into town.'

★   ★   ★

Two hours later, Matt realized that the killer's tracks were not heading for town. They angled more to the south. The only thing down there Matt could think of was Adobe Spring. It used to be a small rancher's place but he had given up two years ago and gone back to Michigan. The spring was still there. Now it had a windmill on it and a large water tank. It was part of the Crazy L ranch.

Halfway there a second set of prints joined the first. The second shooter, the horse killer, had caught up with the bushwhacker. So they were in cahoots. Now he wondered why the second one didn't shoot him out of the saddle. He pulled up. He was too far behind them and it had been too long a time. They had at least two hours head start. It had taken some time to get his Dad back to the house, console Ginny, and get a new horse saddled and ready to ride. He also reloaded the Winchester and pushed it in the boot. He'd be ready, but he wasn't sure he would find anyone. Both of them had far too much of a head start.

He sat there a few minutes looking down the double set of hoof prints and thinking it through. He stared at the trail again then turned and headed back to the ranch.

★ ★ ★

Ivan leaned against the corral as Matt rode up. The cowboy put out a cigarette and took the saddle off Matt's mount. Neither man said a word. There was nothing to say.

Ivan put the mount into the corral and the men walked toward the house.

'They had too much of a head start. The shooter met the killer down the trail a ways, but there was no chance I could catch them.'

'Ginny is really broken up about it. She says it's her fault because she insisted that Mr Greg be taken into town today.'

'I'll talk with her.' He slapped one hand against the other. 'I come back to why. Why would someone want to kill Dad? And if they had a reason, who was it?'

'Been trying to think of the same things. Don't seem like your pa had any enemies. None at all.'

'Who would know we would take Pa into town this morning?' Matt asked.

'The killer would know Mr Greg was shot before. He might need to see the doctor again. Somebody might have set up an ambush and waited for a day or two on the chance your pa went to town.'

They talked a while longer, then Matt headed for the corral. He climbed to the top rail and sat there looking out over the farthest reach of the Bar-H. This was his favorite thinking spot when things got terribly hard. It hadn't really hit him yet. His father was dead, dead and gone.

Death had never had much of an effect on him before. He was young when his mother died. Since then there hadn't been much contact with death.

Dead and gone.

The words suddenly had more meaning to him.

The top rail by the post that anchored the corral gate was sturdy. The rail was hard enough that he couldn't sit there for long. This time he ignored the pain and scowled at the rangeland.

Who in all of Jackson would want his father dead so badly that he risked two bushwhackings? He couldn't come up with a shortlist. He couldn't even come up with a single name of a man or woman who would be so furious with his father that they would kill him. Not a blessed one. He had no place to start to try to find the killer. And why two people? The second shooter must have been to be sure that no one could give a close chase to the killer.

No name.

No motive.

Nothing.

Could Hal help? He had some not too bright and not too law-abiding friends from his wild days in town. He just might pick up some idle talk. But why? Most shootings like this would be for money, to pick up a few thousand dollars the target had with him, or could get, or whatever. Matt was totally confused. It all came back to the same question he couldn't answer.

Who would want to kill Greg Hardy?

He vaulted down from the top rail and headed for the ranch house. Ginny. He should be thinking about Ginny. He knew she would be devastated by this.

Inside the house, Matt went upstairs and found Ginny lying in bed fully clothed, with a half-dozen damp linen handkerchiefs piled on the floor beside her. Her eyes were red, cheeks stained with tears, and her hair was a rumpled mass around her shoulders.

She looked up when Matt came in, the big question brimming in her eyes.

'Why?'

'I have no idea, Ginny. Not a glimmer, but I'm going to tear this county apart until I run down the crazed bushwhacker. He's going to pay for what he did.'

Matt sat on the side of the bed and Ginny sat up and put her arms around him. He held her as her sobs came, racking her slender body time and time again. It was five minutes before the sobs tapered off to gasping and shudders.

'Ginny, ever since our trail drive I've felt something wasn't exactly right here at the ranch. I didn't know why or what then, and I don't now. But looking back on it, it's possible that the rustling try for our herd was part of a larger plot to shoot at Dad. There were several shots into the camp and one man hit. It just might have been the same person or team shooting then that shot twice at Pa back here at the trail drive.'

She wiped wetness from her face and frowned as she looked at her older brother.

'Wasn't Slade Watkins involved in that rustling try? Didn't Hal say it was his voice?'

'Yes, but Slade said he was in Fort Worth during those days. No way we can prove he was on that raid.'

They sat there; at last she eased back, and sat on the bed beside him.

'Dead and gone,' she said. 'Never meant much to me. Closest I came to it was when I was twelve and one of our dogs killed my pet bantam rooster. I cried for two days. My pet was dead and gone.'

Matt stood. 'Ginny, get some sleep. I've got to go into town and report this to the marshal who will tell the sheriff. This should bring the sheriff over here. I'll make funeral arrangements. We'll bury Dad here on the ranch up on that rise behind the house right beside Mom. I'll get the preacher and undertaker to come out in two days. I'll take Ivan along with me so we can talk as we ride and lay out what needs to be done around the ranch. He's going to be in charge until I run down these killers. I'll probably stay in town for a few days digging around trying to get a lead on the killer.'

★ ★ ★

Two hours earlier that same fatal morning, Hal caught up with Quint a mile from Adobe Spring and saw that he had been wounded.

'Bad?' Hal asked.

'Bad enough. Caught me in my thigh and the slug didn't come out.'

'Unless you want me to dig it out with a skinning knife, you'll have to see a doctor,' Hal said.

'Yeah, a doctor would be good. The doctor, tonight after dark and under my gun. Then I tie him up and ride as far as I can get before sunup. You bring the rest of my money?'

'You sure he's dead?'

'Absolutely certain with that head shot. He's down and dead for sure. I'm charging you another hundred since I got wounded. No arguments.'

Hal thought about it a minute as they rode on toward Adobe Spring. He nodded. The price was small for the huge fortune that now was assured for him. He looked over at Quint who was hurting.

'Yeah, yeah. You get the extra hundred. But I want to be positive that after Doc Clausen gets finished with you, you ride out of town and get as far away as soon as possible. No offense, Quint, but I hope that I never see your face around Jackson again.'

'Hey, me too. I want to get patched up, have my money, and ride away without attracting any attention. Got no time for a necktie party. Soon as I find a town with a stagecoach I'll buy a ticket. Might go over to Dallas. Never been there. I'll save some cash. Yeah, think I'll try out the women in Dallas.'

Hal had angled them away from

Adobe Spring and back toward Jackson. Now he could see some smoke from buildings in town. Ahead a quarter mile he saw the swale and trees he had remembered.

'We'll stop up there in the trees. You can wait there for dark and not be seen. Then when it's dark you go into town. Doc Clausen's office is two doors down from the Laughing Lady Saloon. Just pound on the door and he'll come. He and his family live in the rooms in back of his office. So he's easy to find.'

Hal looked at his fancy pocket watch. 'A little after noon. I'd say we did a good morning's work. Let's get in the shade up ahead.'

In the shade of the trees, they dismounted and tied their horses. Hal reloaded his rifle with new rounds and put it back in the saddle-boot.

He took out his wallet and removed a stack of twenty-dollar greenbacks. He counted out twenty of them while Quint watched.

'Oh, yeah, that's what I like to see.

When I get rich and famous I'm going to have me a huge stack of twenty-dollar bills I can peel off from any time. Oh, yes, there's never anything like money.'

Hal had Quint sit down and took some strips of cloth from his saddlebags.

'Gonna tie up that bullet hole best I can. Don't want you bleeding to death on me. Leastwise it will get you through the rest of the day and a two mile ride on into town.'

He worked for five minutes wrapping the pad in place he had put over the wound. When finished, Quint pulled up his pants. There were blood stains on the jeans but no one would be watching for blood after dark.

'OK partner. You're all set. Have a nap and drink out of that spring. It's pure enough. Used it several times.'

'Where you headed?'

'Playing the part of the mighty hunter. That's how I got away from the ranch house early. Told them I was going after a deer. Now I better meet up with a six-point buck or I'm in trouble.'

'You'll get one. You're a lucky son of a gun.'

'Hope so.' He mounted and rode away back toward the Bar-H. He took a detour to ride into those heavy woods where he had seen the herd of deer.

* * *

It was nearly six in the evening when Hal rode into the Bar H ranch buildings. He had a six-point buck draped over the rear of his mount and tied on.

Hal let out a wild rebel yell as he came up to the corral.

Ponchy came out of the cook shack and Matt stepped out of the kitchen.

'Looks like you got one,' Ponchy said. 'We'll be eating venison tomorrow.'

Ponchy waved Hal over to the A frame that they had set up for butchering.

Hal stepped down and untied the

buck and helped Ponchy hoist the deer up to the top of the A frame.

'Would have been home sooner, but I wounded this critter and had to chase him five miles before I could get another shot.'

Matt looked at the animal. 'Good shooting, Hal. I had forgotten that you were right handy with a rifle.'

'Been known to win the fandangle contest from time to time,' Hal said.

'We have some bad news,' Matt said. He went on to lay out just what happened that morning and his attempt to track down the killers.

'Must have been two of them,' Matt said. 'Put me on foot so no way I could track them.'

Hal was shocked and surprised right down to his boots. His hands fluttered. He shook his head a dozen times. 'No, no, no. He was recovering nicely from that first shot. Then another one. Another bushwhacking.' He hung his head and tears worked down his cheeks.

'It's hard to believe. He was doing so well. Bet Ginny is taking this hard.'

'She is. You might help her get through it.'

'Yes. Yes. I'll go in right now. No, no, no. It shouldn't have happened.' He shook his head again and turned toward the house.

Matt watched him go. He didn't understand Hal's sudden anger and evident pain and loss to hear about the death. Maybe he had misjudged the man.

'Hal, we don't know if this second shooter was the same one who did the first shot. It could have been somebody else. What we have to do is figure out who in this county had a serious hatred for father. Then we'll have a starting spot.'

Hal frowned for a moment. 'Yes, you're right. I know a lot of the rougher types in town. Maybe I can dig around and see if anybody is talking about it. You know, bragging what a good shot he is.'

Matt nodded. 'Yes, good idea. Somebody might have been hired to do this. If so somebody might be spending a lot more money than usual. Check it out.'

'Right after I have a long talk with Ginny. She's a strong woman. She'll be able to get through this. But anything I can do might help.' Hal turned and ran for the house.

Ponchy had hung the deer by the rear hoofs and slit its throat to let it bleed out. He went over to Matt.

'I'm surprised by Hal's reaction to his father-in-law's death.'

Matt rubbed his face. 'My thoughts exactly.'

18

The next morning Matt and Hal rode into town.

'I'll talk with some of my not-so-upstanding friends who might have heard something,' Hal said.

Matt nodded. 'Do that. Might be some saddle bum around who made some extra money. I'll go see the marshal first, then make arrangements for the funeral.'

They made it to town about ten o'clock and Matt headed for the town marshal's office. It was in a failed store and had a home-made jail cell. The marshal came to his feet from a chair from behind a battered desk. He was a medium-sized man, balding at fifty-five, and with a touch of hesitancy in his actions that showed up on his flat but large-nosed face.

'Morning, Marshal Olson. Somebody

shot my pa dead on the way into town yesterday. Want you to get word to the sheriff over in Jasper.'

The marshal scowled and stood. 'Damn shame, Matt. Known Greg for fifteen years. Good man. Hate to see any murders near my town. Sheriff's case. I'll send a man over there this morning. What a loss to the community. Any suspects?'

'Shot him from ambush. Must have been two of them.' He told the lawman what he did and how he lost his mount.

'Heard he got shot once before. Sent a report to the sheriff but didn't hear back. Think he's out of town.'

'You seen any hard-case saddle bums in town lately?'

'None that got in any trouble. Usually that's the only time I see them.'

'Had to be somebody who knew Dad. Took them two tries but they killed him. What I want to know is why and then who.'

'Keep my ears open, Matt. But bushwhackers are always hard to find and hard to convict.'

'Know that. You just keep looking.'

Five minutes later, Matt talked to the town's preacher who did his soul saving at the Community Church. Most of the time he was the man who ran the hardware, tinware and saddle store three doors the other side of the Jackson State Bank.

The preacher was a dour little man Matt had never seen smile. Everyone called him Preacher. His last name was Edwards but almost nobody used that name.

'Some sad news, Preacher. My pa was shot and killed yesterday coming into town.'

'Oh, my. I'm so sorry. What can I do?' His face blanched and he fumbled with the tools in his hands.

'Do a funeral for us out at the ranch tomorrow about two o'clock. Can you do that?'

'Land sakes, yes. Of course. I'll tell some people. Nobody knows about it yet?'

'Just came into town. I'd appreciate it.'

Preacher finished fastening the sides of a six inch diameter length stovepipe together and set it aside.

'Yes, sir, Matt. I surely will have a good service for Greg. He was one of my favorite people in this area. I'll tell some folks and get things started. Tomorrow at two.'

'I'll take care of any expenses,' Matt said. He shook hands with the cleric and went outside.

He found Harry Chance in his small shop at the edge of town. He was the undertaker, grave-digger, and coffin maker. He also was a good carpenter and could help you build a house or barn or do it all himself. He was tall and thin with sandy hair, a big grin and arms and legs that went on for miles. He had tried ranching, but gave up after five years. Now he was settled in his new enterprises and after five more years was feeding his family and making ends meet.

'Harry, I need your services.'

Chance looked up, curious.

'It's my father. He was shot and killed yesterday morning.'

'My condolences, Mr Hardy. Where will the funeral be?'

'At the ranch, tomorrow at two o'clock. Can you do it?'

'Yes, of course. For you. I'm so sorry for your loss.'

'Make it a nice tight pine box, Harry. I don't want the winter rains seeping in.'

'Yes, sir, Mr Hardy. One of my best. I'll bring it out in the morning and get everything arranged.'

Matt's next stop was the Lenore General Store. Francine was behind the small counter. Her face lit up like a sunflower in spring.

'Matt, great to see you. You missed last Sunday.'

'Sorry. Couldn't be helped.' He told her about his father and her face fell, she blinked back tears.

'Shot him from ambush?'

'Yes. This was the second time.'

'I'm so sorry. He was a good man. I always enjoyed seeing him when he came into the store. He was a perfect gentleman.'

'Thanks.' He sagged against the counter. 'I don't even know what day this is.'

'It's Wednesday.'

'Thanks. Funeral tomorrow at two o'clock out at the ranch. Hope you can come.'

'We'll close up the store and all three of us will be there.' She watched him, a frown growing. 'Matt. Is there anything that I can do? Just anything?'

'I don't know. Thanks for asking. Afraid I'm in a bit of a fog right now. Everything has happened so fast. I'll be staying in town tonight. Going to try to smoke out whoever shot Dad. I figure he must either be here, or he was a hired saddle tramp who took off for California right after the shooting.'

'Matt, why would anyone want to hurt your father?'

'Question I've been trying to answer. I've muddled it over ever since the first shooting. I can't think of anyone who hated Dad that much. Can't think of a single enemy he had.'

'The marshal probably won't be much help.'

'Out of his jurisdiction. He sent a rider to tell the sheriff. He should come or send a man in a day or two.'

She caught his hand that lay on the counter. 'Oh, Matt. I'm just so terribly, terribly sorry.' She hesitated, looked at the back room where her father must be. 'Would you like to stay tonight at our house? We have a spare bedroom.'

He looked at her, his face a storm of emotion. At last he shook his head. 'No. Thanks for asking. But I better stay in the hotel.' He squeezed her hand, wishing he could hug her for about an hour. 'Well, I guess I should be going. Want to talk to everyone that I can.'

She held his hand tightly, not wanting to let go. At last she let his hand slip away, her eyes almost leaking tears. 'You come back and talk to Father. He'll want to hear it from you.'

Matt nodded, not sure how much time he'd have to talk to everyone he could see in town. He'd try.

He walked up and down Main Street, going into every shop and store. He stopped people on the street. Now and then he met someone who knew about the death. They offered their condolences but had no idea who might be behind the killing.

He walked past the saloons, the stores and the doctor's office. At the end of the street he pushed into Old Kentucky's Livery.

'Heard. Outrageous. Thought we were getting a little civilized around here. Guess not.' He tossed Matt a warm bottle of beer. 'Sit and let's talk. Who in wild sarsaparilla juice would want to shoot your pa?'

They talked about it for ten minutes.

'You say you got no fast shuffles or surprised looks or fast exits when you talked in the saloons? That would have been my best bet. Some low life who drank or gambled all day and could make a quick payday with his rifle.'

'Or maybe a saddle bum who just rode in and somebody grabbed him and rode him out of town before any one could remember him.'

'Somebody. So you think some town clown must have been behind the shootings?'

'Only reasonable way to think,' Matt stood and tossed the empty bottle back to Old Kentucky. 'You take care, Kentucky. You hear anything you let me know.'

Matt walked the other side of the street. He hit two saloons but there was no surprise. Most there knew about the bushwhacking. He did get one guy who ran out fast but he was heading for the outhouse in the back of the saloon.

He worked the rest of the shops and stores. Two were new to him. No luck. When he finished the strip he went back to the Lenore General Store. Mr Lenore himself was at the counter giving out change to a woman who picked up her purchase and left.

Duncan Lenore came around the counter and patted Matt on the shoulder.

'I heard. Terrible. Shouldn't be happening around here any more. Understand about Sunday. You take the time you need.'

Francine came out from back when she heard his voice.

'Talked to my ma when she was in a while ago. She insists that you come for supper about seven. We close the store at six now. You can come, can't you?'

'Be pleased if you could have supper with us, Matt. How about it?' Duncan Lenore looked expectant.

He agreed, then went back to talk to the marshal.

'Not much I can do, Matt. I sent a man riding over to Jasper to bring the sheriff. He'll probably be here day after tomorrow. Not much he can do either without some suspects.'

'Can you make a round of the

saloons with me? I'd like to yell at them again. Having you along might be a help.'

'Yep, I can do that. Let's go.'

On the way to the first saloon, Matt stopped at the Jackson State Bank and talked with Otto Westover who sat behind a large walnut desk. Otto was Hal's father and a friendly, jolly person — not at all what you would expect of a banker.

'Matt, I'm so sorry about your father. When I heard I checked over his account with us. The ranch account really. It's all in order.'

'No outstanding loans, separate funds, any stocks, anything like that?'

'No, your father believed in cash. It's there and all in order. I know that he also has an account in a Fort Worth Bank.'

'Yes, that's right.'

'You should talk to lawyer Ingles. I know your father had a will drawn up about a year ago. I've had to put a freeze on the ranch account since your father was the only one who could sign checks.'

'Yes, I understand. Thanks.'

Matt had stopped by the lawyer's second-floor office on his rounds but the man was out. Now he and the marshal went up the steps and found Ingles at his desk.

Ingles smiled with a slightly wolfish tinge. 'Matthew, good to see you. Sorry about your loss. When I heard I looked up your father's will. Yes, he has one and briefly it leaves everything in equal parts to you and your sister. All of the ranch, animals, bank accounts and all monies of all kinds.'

'What's the procedure?'

The lawyer smiled again. 'I make a motion before the judge when he comes around and you and Ginny sign the papers and it's all yours. No long legal hassle.'

'When will the judge be here?'

'In two weeks. Oh, the bank. I'll advance you five thousand dollars and you can open a new account at the bank. Then when the bank money is unfrozen you can have it transferred into the new account, or change the signature needed on the old account to yourself.'

'Mr Ingles, I appreciate it.'

Ingles laughed. 'No problem. Of course I'll charge you about fifty dollars interest on the loan, and then another fifty for presenting the will to the judge. That's normal charge around here.'

'Sounds fair. Hope to see you at the funeral.'

They left and Matt and the sheriff walked into the Last Chance Saloon. About twenty men were at the stand-up bar and ten poker tables.

Matt had worn his pistol today. He drew it and put a round into the ceiling. The chatter stopped abruptly.

'Men, I'm out skunk hunting for the polecat who bushwhacked my father yesterday. If any of you know anything about it, or have heard anything, come on up and talk with me.'

19

Matt had bellowed out the challenge to the men in the small saloon. They all had turned to look at him when he fired the six-gun shot into the ceiling. Nobody said a word. Some of them looked at each other.

'Come on. You men aren't all idiots or mute. I asked if any of you knew anything about my father's killer. So speak up.'

One man toward the back stood up and swayed a little. He held a beer bottle.

'Matt. Knew your dad. Cotton-picking shame that he passed that way. Liked your old man. But I don't know nothing about the shooter.'

Matt stared at each man in the saloon. A few looked directly at him then away. If anyone here knew anything he figured he wouldn't say a word. He saw Hal at one of the poker tables but didn't show any sign of recognition. Maybe Hal would have more luck with this bunch than he did.

'OK then. If any one of you wants to talk, I'll be out in the street for five minutes. Come see me.' He and the marshal went out the front door.

Matt shook his head. 'Afraid that's the response I'm going to get from the men in all of the saloons. But I've got to give it another try.' He looked at his pocket watch attached to a belt loop on his pants by a thin rawhide bootlace. It was a little after two o'clock. Lots of time before supper at the Lenores' house. He and the sheriff waited for five minutes outside the saloon but no one came to talk to them. They headed for the next saloon, the Laughing Lady.

★ ★ ★

Hal waited until Matt had left the saloon then he looked at the other five men at the poker table. It was a nickel limit game.

'Yeah, he's talking about my father-in-law. Freaking shame that somebody blew his head half off.' He looked at each of the men. One after another they shook their heads. He slapped his hand on the table. 'I figured you guys wouldn't know anything about it. Let's play some poker.'

As the afternoon wore on, Hal moved to two more saloons where he played some low ante poker. He was in no mood to risk big money. He got no hint from any of the men about any bushwhacker. He skipped the Laughing Lady. Not many of the low-lifes in town drank or played poker there. None of the men he talked to had heard of any saddle bums coming through asking about gun work.

At the Last Horse barrel saloon he saw Slade at the bar. He went up beside him, got a mug of beer, and whispered to him, 'Your hotel room in half an hour.'

Slade lifted his brows in silent agreement. Hal went back to the poker game with his fresh mug of beer.

★ ★ ★

A half hour later, Hal knocked on the door of the room Slade had called his own on the second floor of the Johnson One Hand Hotel. Slade let him in and wore a big grin.

'So, when do I come to work at the Bar-H?'

'Easy, steady. We're not all the way home yet. Made a good move but we have one more huge problem before I can take over. Don't get impatient. Told you it might take six months. That was only two months ago. Lots of time. Just keep out of jail, no gunfights, and you'll do fine.'

Slade laughed. 'Yeah, OK, boss. Best job I've had in years. Long as you keep paying me the twenty dollars a week I'll hang in there. Got me another one of those yearlings last night. No problem.

Roped it and led it right up to the slaughter house.'

Hal scowled. 'Hey, take it easy on them steers. Won't do us no good if you get hung for being a rustler. Don't matter none if it's one yearling or a herd. That trap door drops just the same.'

'No worry there. I'm careful and crafty.' He took a bottle of whiskey off a small dresser and grabbed two glasses. 'Figure we need to drink to progress. Stole the glasses from the café.' He poured two shots of whiskey in the glasses and they tipped heads back and threw down the drinks. Hal coughed and spluttered.

Slade laughed. 'Got to learn to drink, Hal. You always was like a little girl when it came to whiskey.'

'Hey, knock that off. I got more problems than that on my mind. Hey, I've got half a ranch to run. Don't know how Matt is going to react to this. Might take some time. So we just sit tight and see what develops.'

Hal gave Slade two twenty dollar gold pieces for the next two weeks then went back to enjoy some supper at the café before he tried the poker tables again. It had been a good two days of work.

★ ★ ★

Chicken supper at the Lenore household was a fine meal with mashed potatoes and giblet gravy, fresh green beans, fresh-baked bread and new-churned butter, big cups of coffee, and strawberry preserves. The Lenores had their own cow in a small pasture out back of their house and a large vegetable garden. Mrs Lenore was an expert gardener.

'Mrs Lenore. What a wonderful meal. I'll have to have you give our cook Ponchy some pointers. Maybe you could open a cooking school.'

She blushed and looked down at her plate. 'Well, thank you, Matthew. I do appreciate it. Now, it looks like we're through. Francine, you don't need to help me clear. Why don't you and Matthew go into the parlor and have a talk.'

'Yes, Mother,' Francine said with thanks in her voice.

Matt stood quickly, eased Francine's chair back from the table so she could stand, then they went into the parlor. It was stylishly furnished with a hand-braided rug on the floor. Matt marveled every time he looked at it. It was cloth of many colors braided into inch wide lengths, and then the long strips were hand-stitched together into a circle. It had started in the center with a two inch wide fold. Now the circular rug was almost twelve feet across.

Francine saw him staring at the rug.

'Yes, isn't it wonderful. My grandmother started it fifteen years ago. Mother finished it after Grandma died. It was only eight feet across for years.'

They talked then about the town, about the fun they had at the fandangle and the bidding for the supper basket.

For a moment, Matt didn't realize that Mrs Lenore wasn't in her usual chair across the room. They were alone. He caught her hand. She looked up at him surprised then glanced over at the vacant chair and smiled.

'Oh my,' she said squeezing his hand. He leaned in, caught her around the shoulders, and pulled her to him in a soft hug. Then he kissed her cheek and eased back.

She looked up at him, her smile so bright he thought the sun had burst into the parlor.

'Oh my,' she said. 'Yes, that was delightful. I think Mother trusts you. Isn't that marvelous?' She edged back a few inches from him and smiled again. 'Now you be nice.' Her smile glowed. 'Now, like Ma said, we talk.'

They talked then about everything.

'Did you know that I want to be a schoolteacher?' she asked. 'I've done my eighth grade work and I'm taking some classes from a school in Fort Worth by mail. They say I can pass my high school work and get a teacher's credential in two more years.'

'I didn't know that. You wanted to do this for a long time?'

'Ever since I was ten, Ma tells me.'

'I asked about a higher school here in town, but they said we don't have enough kids to go. We need to have a larger population. I don't know where the nearest nine to twelve grade school is.'

About an hour later they ran out of things to talk about. Mrs Lenore had come into the room once to find a magazine. She smiled at them but didn't say anything and left shortly.

When Mrs Lenore left Matt reached over and kissed Francine on the cheek. She didn't pull away. Instead she turned her face to his and kissed his lips. Matt felt a jolt go through him as her lips touched his. Then she leaned back and the tingling slowly went away.

Francine smiled and caught his hand. 'I liked that, Matthew Hardy. I liked that a lot.'

Her father's voice came from the dining room.

'Mr Hardy, I think that courting time is over.'

Matt squeezed her hand and they both stood and walked into the dining room.

Both her parents were there.

'Mr Lenore. I'm not sure about Sunday. I'm going to ride over to Bent River and probably on to Jasper if the sheriff doesn't come out. Tomorrow is the funeral so I'll go the next day. Doubt if I'll be back by Sunday.'

'Understand, Matt. Understand you have to try to find the man who killed your father. If I can do anything, you let me know.'

Matt said he would, thanked Mrs Lenore again for the meal and hurried out to where he had left his mount tied in front of the house. He rode to the center of town, tied up his horse and walked the street.

He talked to everyone he saw on the boardwalk asking about his father. By that time it was nearly ten o'clock and most people had gone home or were drinking in the saloons. He scoured the boardwalks for another half hour, then gave up and took a room at the Johnson Hotel.

Tomorrow would be a hard day. The funeral. He would be up at dawn and ride to the ranch. He had to get ready for visitors. He'd use the benches from the cook shack and chairs from the house. If he had time he would make some new benches. The rest of the people would have to stand. It would be a short ceremony. He had asked that of the preacher. The undertaker and grave-digger would be there early. Matt would have three of the ranch hands help with the digging.

Tomorrow would be one of the hardest days of his life.

20

The funeral of Greg Hardy began
promptly at two o'clock behind the
main ranch house where there were
two large live oak trees that provided
shade. More than twenty buck-boards,
buggies, surreys and horses nested in
the area in front of the house.
Forty-two people had arrived to attend
the funeral. All were dressed in their
go-to-meeting best clothes, suits and
white shirts and long dresses. Most sat
on benches from the cook shack's
dining area. The rest sat in chairs that
had been carried from the house. All
fourteen ranch hands came in a group
and stood behind the rest of the
mourners. The cowboys were all
washed, combed, and wore the best
clothes they had.

Preacher Edwards began the ceremony with a hymn. Rock of Ages.

Most of the people there knew the words to the first stanza. He stopped them after that verse.

'We are here today to honor and pay our respects to a valued member of our community, Gregory Hardy. Several of you have asked to speak and we will hear you.'

Matt knew what he wanted to say, but when he stood in front of the people, he forgot most of it so he was brief.

'He was my father and I will always miss him.' He turned and sat down.

Ginny tried to talk, but stood there a moment, shook her head, and sat down.

Three people from town spoke including Mayor Johnson. Then Preacher took over and talked for ten minutes about God's plan for every soul and how Greg had been called to heaven before any of them wanted him to go.

Matt heard little of what he said. The full weight of the fact that his father was dead had at last settled down on him like a thousand pound load of rocks.

They sang another hymn that few of the people knew the words for. Then Preacher nodded at the six men who were to carry the casket up the slight rise to where another live oak stood shading the grave of Matt's mother.

Matt helped carry the heavy pine coffin and set it down beside the open grave that his men had dug the day before. When the mourners had walked up the hill to the grave site, Preacher Edwards lifted both arms.

'Lord our God. We pray for the immortal soul of our brother Greg Hardy who has soared into heaven to stand beside you. Ashes to ashes, dust to dust. We commit his mortal remains to the earth and we pray for his soul. Amen.'

Four men lowered the casket into the ground on ropes then pulled the ropes out. The preacher looked at Matt and offered him a shovel. Matt turned and shook his head. He couldn't think straight. But he knew he could not put dirt into the grave, he couldn't cover up his father. He turned and walked quickly down the hill, past the ranch house, the big barn, and the corral. He stopped a quarter mile along the road to town and sat down.

Matt Hardy cried.

★　★　★

Behind the house under the two live oak trees, Ponchy had set up tables and the benches. One table was stacked with food for the after burial reception and traditional social. The fare included fried chicken, roast beef slices, turkey breast, roast venison, ham, four kinds of cheese, crackers, buns and fresh-baked bread, canned peaches, apple-sauce, raisins, dates, and dried apples. Guests were provided with china plates from the house, smaller china pie plates, and when those ran out there was a stack of tin plates.

Matt sat by the road for ten minutes. He thought of his father, the good times, the troubles, the victories, the trail drives, teaching him how to shoot, and a hundred other good times with his patient father.

Then Matt Hardy cried again.

★ ★ ★

Ten minutes later, Matt wiped the tears off his face, brushed back his hair and went to the feast. He couldn't eat a thing.

★ ★ ★

Two hours later the last carriage had left. Matt had positioned himself near the rigs and shook hands with all who had attended and thanked them. They murmured their condolences again and drove away. When the last one had left, Matt went into the house and collapsed into a big chair.

A short time later Ginny came in and sat beside him. She put her head on his shoulders. Neither said a word. They sat there in silence until the sun went down.

As it started getting dark, Ponchy brought in a pot of coffee and two cups along with some small cinnamon rolls he knew were Matt's favorite. He lit a lamp and left without a word.

Matt pushed up from the chair, poured two cups of coffee, and handed one to Ginny. They both sipped the brew without enthusiasm.

Matt rubbed his face. 'So what now? I've heard it said by people who have lost a loved one that life must go on.' He winced and shook his head. 'I don't understand that kind of thinking at all. One life is over. One man has lived out the skein of his years. So why then do we need to go on? I don't understand.'

Ginny put down her cup on the small table nearby and held Matt's face with both of her hands.

'Big brother. I know what you're saying, but I don't agree with you. Yes, our father has moved on from this life to the next. He is *muerte* as our

Mexican friends would say. But his memory is not dead. What he has built here and left in our hands is not lost. Life must go on. I agree. To me that means that we must move ahead, we must make progress in all things, and we must do it to honor our father. We must save what he worked so hard to achieve, to improve our stock, to develop a new breed of cattle that are heavier, will produce more meat and will sell for much more at the market place. That was one of father's biggest dreams.'

She stopped and moved her hands. She wiped away tears from his face with a cloth handkerchief from her sleeve.

'Yes, we must mourn. We must mourn and at the same time remember what a good man our father was. How he built this ranch from nothing to its present size and importance in the county. We must do this to show that we loved our father, want to create a better life for our workmen, and to keep our own lives growing and developing.'

Matt stared at his younger sister. Never had he heard her talk so much or get so serious, or delve into deep matters of life and death. He was impressed. He caught her hand.

'So, just what does all this mean to you and me? What do we do tomorrow and the day after that and the days and years after that?'

She frowned slightly. 'Matthew, I know that you have a fire-burning hatred for the man who killed Father. I know that tomorrow you will ride to Bent River and search for the killer. I do hope that you take someone with you.' She looked at him and Matt nodded.

'If you find no leads there you said you would ride on to Jasper and talk to the sheriff. This, I know, is what you must do to help temper the fires of your anger and fury. At the same time we have a ranch to run, you and I. I'm suggesting that we keep Ivan as our foreman and ranch manager. Do you agree?'

'Yes he's been doing the job for most of the past year. We'll make it official and give him a big increase in his pay. If he wants to get married, we'll build him a house here on the ranch.'

They kept talking. Soon the rolls were gone. Ponchy brought in a fresh pot of coffee and more rolls. Matt had told her about the papers they would have to sign, about the judge making the will official, and how the bank funds had been frozen but that their lawyer had loaned them money to keep functioning with until the judge arrived in about two weeks. He was on a circuit and came when needed or every three weeks or so.

The second pot of coffee was dry and the plate of cinnamon rolls empty when Matt checked the time on his pocket watch.

'Almost ten o'clock, baby sister. I think it's past my bed time. I want to get an early start on a survey of the south range.'

Ginny looked up. 'Any problems, or just checking?'

He kissed her cheek, grinned at her concern and headed for his bedroom. At the living room door he turned.

'Ginny, you're right. We do have to move on, to keep this ranch growing and prospering. Thanks for helping me see that.'

Then he went upstairs and into bed. He fell asleep almost at once.

21

Matt overslept.

He never overslept. Matt awoke to hear the bawling of the milk cow pleading for more of the fresh hay they had brought in for her. He looked at his pocket watch laying on the night-stand beside his bed. It was just after eight thirty. He had planned on doing a good survey of the stock this morning.

He pulled on his jeans and shirt with snaps, pushed into his boots, and grabbed his low-crowned black hat. He ran into the kitchen where Ponchy had been waiting for him.

'Morning Mr Matt. What can I get for you?'

'Morning, Ponchy. Overslept. Bacon, three eggs — scrambled, fried potatoes and onions, toast, some of that strawberry preserve, and a gallon of coffee.'

Matt thought of riding to Jasper. The sheriff hadn't come or even sent a deputy. After talking it over with Ginny, he decided the seventy-two-mile ride would not produce any benefits.

That was when Matt realized that the next day was the last one of the month. For the past year or so he had been riding into Jackson and drawing out cash for the payroll. He knew his dad had kept cash in the safe in the den but he never knew how much. It wasn't one of Matt's favorite tasks. But it had to be done. He'd get an early start and be there when the bank opened at ten o'clock and be home shortly after noon. The will had been approved and all the legal papers signed by Ginny and him at the bank so it was a routine withdrawal.

Matt and Ivan took the survey ride later that morning and saw nothing out of the ordinary. All looked fine. They rode the circuit and back to the ranch.

It had used up most of the day. He and Ginny went over the ranch books and tried to figure out how they were doing. They finished and Matt did some reading before he went to bed.

Matt had left the Bar-H just after seven thirty the next morning and didn't push his mount on the ride into town. Once in Jackson, he had a cup of coffee at the café as he waited for the bank to open at ten. He had another ten minutes. He mentally totaled up how much cash he would need. He would need to check the Lenore General Store bill, get enough for an allowance for Ginny and to pay the cowhands. He figured the usual withdrawal of seven hundred would take care of everything.

When the bank opened he made a withdrawal from the new account the lawyer had opened for him then went to the general store. Mr Lenore was there. The bill was for twenty-eight dollars and eighty cents. Matt paid it, told him about being up to his elbows in work. He knew it was Saturday.

'Hope to come to church tomorrow,'

he told Mr Lenore, then slipped away and headed back toward the ranch.

He was a mile from town when he realized that he wasn't at all afraid of being robbed. Dozens of people must know he took the payroll out on this day each month. During the past eight or ten years of making this money run, neither he nor his father had ever been held up. He moved along at a brisker pace than when he came that morning. He should be home well before noon. Come to think of it he was hungry already.

Matt tensed as he came to the creek where his father had been bushwhacked and killed. He slowed and looked both ways along the line of brush and small trees that hovered around the winding stream. Then he kicked the mount into a gallop and hurried a quarter of a mile beyond it before he slowed.

He knew it was dumb but he decided on the spur of the moment to make the dash. Now he grinned. There had been nothing.

It was nearly a mile later when a dry

draw angled off from the road that he heard a shot and at once was slammed off the horse with a hit on his left shoulder. He managed to drag the rifle out of the boot as he fell. The horse jolted in fright and a moment later took a head shot and fell down, dying as it crashed into the dirt of the road.

Two more rifle shots narrowly missed Matt and he crawled behind the dead horse for protection. He had his rifle but no target. He lifted up once and jolted back down just before a rifle round clipped the side of the horse over his head and whined off into the distance. His left shoulder hurt like a branding iron had just kissed it. He pulled off his neckerchief and tried to stop the bleeding. He couldn't do much with one hand but managed to slow the blood as long as he held the folded-up cloth over the wound with one hand.

Two more rifle shots came and Matt grunted in pain as he lifted the rifle over the dead horse and fired off a return round. No way he could hit anything. He slid toward the horse's rump and peered around. He could see the ravine and where the gunman and his horse were almost hidden by the dirt banks. Then to Matt's surprise, the rifleman ran down the open ravine and in a rush, charged across the open road thirty yards west toward the ranch.

Matt figured the gunner was trying to circle around him and shoot him in the back. When the rifleman was shielded from Matt's position, Matt surged up and ran across the road and into the two-foot-deep ditch on the far side. He peered over the grass and weeds and spotted the shooter's horse in the ravine.

Matt wished he could lift up and run for the horse, but the rifleman would spot him and kill him before he got there. He sighed and did the only logical thing he could think of. He sighted in on the horse and shot it in the head. It went down pawing at the dirt. Matt shot it once more and it was dead.

Now he and his bushwhacker were both without horses and the odds were even. Matt lay there in the protection of the ditch thinking it through. The shooter was on the side toward the ranch. Matt was closer to town which he figured was about three miles away. Was his best bet to head for town, or to try to gun down the bushwhacker? A rifle round from behind him and up the road slammed into the dirt just in front of him. Decision time.

Matt rolled out of the ditch, sending shooting pains through his shoulder, but he was up and zigzagging down the slight slope toward the ravine where the dead horse lay.

He heard two more rifle shots but no lead hit him. He dove into the ravine which was about ten feet deep. He was now shielded from the gunman. He set off on a jog down the ravine toward the west. Jackson was over in the distance somewhere.

The ravine became deeper as it ran down grade. At a small turn, Matt stopped.

He went around the bend, then went to his stomach, eased up to the bend, and watched up the slope behind him. A man with a rifle ran in dashes and stops coming down the ravine. Matt brought up his rifle and sighted in on the spot he figured the man would run toward next — a stack of rocks three feet tall that the winter rains had washed out.

Matt waited. A trickle of sweat beaded and rolled down his forehead and soon dripped off his nose. He wanted to brush it away but held his sight on the spot he had picked and his finger on the trigger.

Now. The man moved, leaping from the cover and charging forward. At the first sight of him, Matt fired. The round was low, cut into the man's left leg and sent him sprawling in the dirt. He rolled to the left, dropping his rifle then slid into a ditch in the ravine deep enough to hide him. He reached out, grabbed his rifle, and pulled it in before Matt had made up his mind to shoot again.

Matt considered it. The man was

crippled. Matt knew he could circle around, stay on the high ground, find a spot and kill the bushwhacker. He shook his head. He had killed a man on the trail drive and he couldn't think straight for two days. He had no desire to kill this one. At least he was no threat. He would have a hard time hobbling into town. Matt turned, jogged down the ravine, and made another turn so he knew he was well out of sight of the gunman. Then he concentrated on holding the rifle and trying to keep the kerchief over his bleeding shoulder. Now that the rush of adrenalin was fading, his arm again hurt like he had been freshly branded. He tried to beat down the pain and slowed to a walk. He was still two miles from town. He had to make it before he passed out from bleeding too much.

A ride. He needed a ride into town. He left the fading end of the draw and turned to the right to find the road to town. It was two hundred yards away. Not a lot of traffic on the road but somebody might be coming along.

At the road, he went through the shallow ditch and stood there looking both ways. Nothing. He walked toward town. It was still over two miles away. His shoulder still drilled pain through his system. He gritted his teeth and kept walking.

A quarter of a mile later he heard a horse coming behind him. He stopped, turned, and saw a rider come at a walk. The closer the man came, the easier it was to figure it wasn't a Bar-H rider. Then he recognized one of the men from the Circle D, the Dunwoody ranch just north of them. He held up his right hand with the rifle pointing at the ground.

When the rider came closer, Matt called out.

'Hey, I need some help here. Some bushwhacker hit me in the shoulder. You probably saw my dead horse in the road back there. Can you give me a lift into Dr Clausen's office?'

The man on the horse grinned.

'Looks like you got yourself shot up bad as your horse. You're Matt Hardy, right? Seen you around. Put that rifle in my boot and I'll get down and give you a hand up into the back of the saddle.'

★   ★   ★

Twenty minutes later, Matt sat in Dr Clausen's office and watched the sawbones do his work.

'Slug went on through, Matt. Lucky. I hate to have to go in and dig out that lead. Seems like you Hardy folks have been getting shot a lot lately.'

'Right, Doc. Wish I knew who was pulling the trigger. Might have a clue. I shot the bushwhacker in the leg, left one I think. If a man with a rifle bullet in his left leg comes in, you call the marshal.'

'Yep, I can do that. Any idea who?'

'Not a single idea, Doc. None at all.' Matt watched the doctor working on his shoulder. He washed it out with some foul smelling antiseptic, put some stitches in the exiting hole, lathered both wounds with some salve of some kind, and bandaged his shoulder. Matt could barely lift his arm.

'Fine, Matt. Finished. No work for you for a while. Come in here in three days and I'll take a gander at it. Should be fine.'

Matt put his shirt on. 'Remember to watch for that shot-up leg guy.'

The doctor nodded, took the five dollar gold piece Matt gave him, and Matt headed for the livery stable.

★   ★   ★

Kentucky nearly laughed himself hoarse when he saw Matt.

'Another Hardy gets himself shot? Consarn it if that don't beat all. You want what?'

A few minutes later Matt rode away with a saddled mount and headed for the side of town halfway between Dr Clausen's office and the road east. The shooter should come in one way or the other.

* * *

Matt waited there until nearly dark. He had found a small tree he tied the horse to and then hunkered down in the shade. Two riders came in on the road. Nobody came cross country aiming for Dr Clausen's back door. At dusk he gave up and rode back to the Bar-H. He still had the seven hundred dollars that he had put inside his shirt before he left the bank.

* * *

Ginny, Ponchy and half the hands were watching for him. They looked at his shot shoulder and it took him ten minutes to explain what had happened.

Ginny hugged him.

Ponchy asked him what he wanted to eat.

Ivan scowled and said this bush-whacking was going to have to stop.

The cowboys frowned, talked among

234

themselves, and went back to the bunkhouse.

'We're out of beef,' Ponchy said. 'How about half a fried chicken, mashed potatoes and giblet gravy?'

Matt said that would be fine.

'About time we kill another steer or maybe a yearling,' Ponchy said. 'Waste about a third of one in this summer heat. Be all right if I send a quarter up to the Dunwoody ranch?'

Matt said that would be a great idea, then went in and washed up, put on clean clothes and tried to relax. He had given Ginny the greenbacks. She made up envelopes for the ranch hands' pay and for Ivan and Ponchy.

'There's a hundred there for you. Figured you might want to start getting some baby things.'

She kissed him on the cheek and ran into the office.

22

Hal had told Ginny that he needed a day off and rode into town that morning after Matt left to play some poker and do some drinking. That was what he told Ginny.

Now he sat two miles from town near a small creek and two hundred yards from the East Town Road. He watched to the east and waited. Hal was not noted for his patience. He was amazed at himself for being so patient while his plot played out for him to take complete control of the Bar-H ranch. He sat up, put down the flask of whiskey, and stared to the east. He should be coming along soon.

In town, he had seen Matt making a call at the Lenore General Store. He would be paying off the charges made at the establishment during the past month. He had ridden with Matt a time or two on the payroll run and he knew the routine inside out. He scanned the draws and slight rises of the Texas high prairie. Nothing. Not a coyote or fox or rabbit stirred. Neither did a man on a horse. He gave a sigh, treated himself to another shot from the whiskey flask, and settled back down. He should be close enough to hear the gunfire, at least one shot, which was all he hoped that he heard.

Hal checked his gold-filled railroad pocket watch. It had cost him over a hundred dollars. It showed precisely twenty minutes after ten o'clock. At four miles an hour, Matt's mount should be two miles from town by four thirty. Another ten minutes. He stood near a blush of green brush and trees, hiding him beside the small stream and looked eastward again.

Nothing.

He settled back down and took another shot of the best whiskey he could buy in Jackson.

Two minutes later he heard a rifle

shot. It came from the east at what he knew was roughly three hundred yards away. He tensed. Then there were two shots, then two more. One more rifle shot cracked through the dry Texas summer air.

Then silence.

More than one shot was not good news. It meant that Slade had missed on his first shot and that Matt was still alive. Hal looked east again toward the ravine they had picked out but he couldn't see it from beside the stream. He sat down. He had to wait. Nothing else he could do. He hadn't brought along a rifle. Going to town to play poker he wouldn't need one. Somebody might have noticed if he had a rifle and wondered. He couldn't afford anyone questioning him.

Two more rifle shots. Then silence again. He wished he knew what was going on. He had a sinking feeling that Slade had missed again and that Matt Hardy was not dead. He sat down in the grassy shade and took another pull from the flask. Almost empty.

He wasn't sure how long it was before one more shot tore through the quietness. Now he was getting nervous. He pulled his horse deep into the brush and trees so it couldn't be seen. Then he settled down in the dense thicket but at a place where he could see out.

He studied the land to the east. Yes, there it was, the end of the ravine that Slade would have used for cover. Not a creek this time of year, now a ravine with banks high enough for protection. If Slade missed, he might be coming out this direction to escape from Matt. He knew that Matt carried a rifle on his money run.

Hal drained the flask then checked his watch again. It had been twenty minutes since he heard the first shots. What in the world was going on?

A moment later he saw movement at the mouth of the ravine. Then he spotted a man moving across it, evidently angling toward the town road. He squinted to be sure. It was Matt and he held a cloth against his left shoulder. He had been wounded but wasn't dead. Hal pounded the ground with his fist. Why did he hire that idiot Slade again? This was three times he had missed his target. The third time was not the winner.

He watched Matt work his way over to the town road and look both ways. Then he began to walk toward town. Evidently heading for Doc Clausen's office. What the devil did he do now? Why was Matt walking? Maybe his horse got killed. Yes, probably. So where was Slade? What if his horse was dead as well and he was walking? Would he wait for Matt to clear the area then head for town?

Hal saw Matt get a ride on a horse then Hal left the trees and brush. He led his horse behind the cover of the trees toward the ravine. Slade might still be there. He might be walking.

By the time the cover of the trees ran out, Hal could no longer see the town road or Matt. Hal got on his mount and rode up the ravine. He had gone only half way when he came on Slade. He was using his rifle as a crutch as he hobbled downstream. His left pants leg was crimson and black with blood.

When Slade saw the rider coming, he sat down and raised his rifle.

'Hold your fire, idiot,' Hal shouted. A few moments later Hal stared down at the wounded man. 'You missed him again,' Hal snarled.

'Not my fault. New rifle. I never got a chance to zero it in. Shoots way to the left.'

Hal dismounted and looked at the leg. Slade had tied it up with his kerchief but it still oozed blood.

'You can't walk, can you ride?'

'Absolutely. Be ever so thankful for a ride.'

★ ★ ★

They had ridden almost a mile before Slade roused enough to ask where they were going.

241

'Don't worry about it, Slade. You just concentrate on not falling off. We can't go back into town. Matt will be at the doctor's office, or been there and left. He'll for sure know he wounded you and tell the doc to call the marshal if you show up with a shot-up leg.'

Slade groaned. 'Yeah, makes sense. We'll wait until dark, go in and get leg fixed, then kill the doc.'

Hal snorted. 'Slade, you have all the good ideas.'

*　*　*

An hour later they came to another small creek, well south of Jackson. It held a good growth of small trees and brush. Hal rode into it and dismounted. Then helped Slade to the ground.

'We hole up here for the rest of the day?' Slade asked.

Hal tied his mount to a tree and nodded. 'Yeah, Slade, we're going to hole up here.'

Slade moved on the grass in the

242

shade and groaned. 'Hal, you got any whiskey? Leg is killing me.'

'Fresh out of whiskey, Slade, but I can end the pain.' Hal pulled out his six-gun and thumbed back the hammer to full cock. 'Slade, you failed me three, no four, times. No chance that I want you as my ranch foreman. We're going to end our partnership right here and right now.'

Slade looked up, surprise flooding his face. 'Hey, what are you saying? I missed him, yeah, but I'll get the sidewinder next time. You said there was no rush. What the hell you talking about?'

'Talking about you, Slade. You were supposed to kill the old man on that cattle drive. You missed. You were supposed to nail him on the range when he was counting cattle. You were supposed to finish him off at the creek when he was going to town. I had to hire somebody else to kill Greg. Now you mess up here again today and get yourself shot. You're not reliable, Slade.

I can't put up with you any longer.'

Slade's face went slack. The truth had broken through to him.

'Oh, God in heaven, help me. This mad man is going to kill me. Strike him down. Do it now.' Slade picked up his rifle and started to swing it toward Hal but he was too slow.

Hal shot him in the left eye, saw his head jolt backward, and blood and brains and bone splattered the ground behind him. He slammed to the ground, dead before he came to rest.

Hal pulled Slade's wallet from his pocket, took off his gun-belt, and picked up his rifle. There was nothing left on the body to identify Slade. The wolves and the buzzards would make short work of his face and body in three or four days. Chances were nobody would find the body until it was totally unrecognizable. He sighed. In a way it was too bad. Slade could have been a big help. Didn't turn out that way. So he became a liability. He knew too much about what Hal was trying to do.

That would never do. Slade might have got sloppy drunk and bragged to half the town what he had done.

Hal pushed the rifle in the saddle-boot, looped the gun-belt over the pommel and mounted. Then he looked in the wallet. Six dollars and an old letter. He would get rid of all of it on the way back to the ranch. He'd ditch the pistol and rifle in a creek somewhere far away. Nobody would be able to tie them to Slade. The man rode out of town one morning and simply never returned. Almost no one in Jackson would miss him or be sorry that he was gone.

★　★　★

It took Hal almost two hours to ride back to the Bar-H. He knew that Matt might be home. Hal would have to slip in as quietly as possible. He'd confide to Ponchy that he lost so much at poker that he didn't want to eat in town. Ponchy would fix him dinner or supper.

He set his jaw and added a firm scowl. No sense in trying to hire someone else to kill Matt. He would do it himself. That way he was sure the job would be done, and then he would own the Bar-H and all its lands and cattle. He'd be a rich man. Later he would figure out how to take care of Ginny before she gave birth.

23

The next morning Matt awoke with a groan. His shoulder hurt like he'd been stepped on by a range bull. Then he remembered the bushwhacker. He groaned as he got up. His shoulder wasn't working right, his arm felt like it had a ton of rocks holding it down. Gradually he made his arm work. Just putting on his shirt was a chore.

'Great,' he said out loud. This was Sunday and he had promised he'd be in church and courting today. He had to do it if it killed him. Which it wouldn't. He took off the work shirt and put on a white one. Then struggled into his black suit pants. He'd have Ginny knot his tie.

He at last got his shoes on but tying the laces was impossible.

Downstairs Ginny frowned when she

saw him. 'You getting ready for church?'

'Right, and then courting and Sunday dinner at the Lenores' house. Can you give me a hand?'

Ginny wanted to go with him to church, but then realized that she would only be in the way at the courting. She insisted that he take a buggy so he didn't have to ride the twelve miles. She tied his necktie and shoe laces. Then patted his good shoulder.

'Be easier on your shoulder in the buggy,' she said. He at last gave up and let her have her way. She went out and had a horse hitched to the buggy.

★   ★   ★

Halfway to town he realized that Ginny had been right. Even a good breakfast and three cups of coffee hadn't made him feel much stronger. But he had to go. He had to keep up the courting. He got to church ten minutes early. His bandaged shoulder was hidden by his black suit coat, but he didn't have a lot of control of his left arm. He mostly kept it at his side. He sat just behind the Lenore family at church. Francine looked back and gave him a huge smile which he returned. He stood for the hymns, listened to the sermon, and he was ready for the service to end. On the way out he greeted friends and then found the Lenore family getting in a buggy.

Mr Lenore shook his hand.

'Glad to see you, Matt. Heard you had some trouble on the road home yesterday.'

'A little, but I'm still alive. First time I've been shot. Hope it's the last.'

They talked a minute or two, then Matt got in his buggy, and followed the Lenores to their house. Mrs Lenore had the dinner almost ready before they went to church. Now she warmed up the beef roast and the mashed potatoes and gravy and the rest of the food and had it on the table by one o'clock.

The dinner was delicious and he complimented Mrs Lenore. She almost blushed, bobbed her head, and thanked him. After dinner Francine and Matt retreated to the living room where she insisted that he tell her about how he was shot the day before. He did, leaving out most of the trouble.

'And Doc Clausen fixed you up, bandaged your shoulder and all?'

'He did. Now, let's talk about something else. You said you'd like to be a schoolteacher. How are your studies going?'

'Oh, so fine. I'm enjoying them. I get lessons in the mail and then do the work and mail them back. I get five or six lessons at a time and mail them back when I finish. It will take a long time. But I'm determined.'

He had been thinking about that. So now he said it. 'What if somebody swept you off your feet and married you. What would you do then?'

'Oh, well, I'm not sure.' She frowned, shook her head, and then smiled.

'Never thought much about that. If it happens, then I would decide what to do. The education won't hurt anything one way or the other.'

That satisfied Matt. He moved on, asking her about the new dress she was sewing.

'Love to sew. I make lots of my own clothes. I get a magazine that has all kinds of patterns in it. Lots of the latest styles from Chicago and New York. It's the most fun I have. Mother and I are making a quilt. She says I can have it when it's done. It's called a double wedding ring. I'll show it to you after a while. It's on a big quilting frame up in the spare bedroom.'

They went on talking about everything. She asked him about the ranch and how things were going.

'I imagine that you're running things now with Mr Hardy gone. Is that a really hard job?'

He explained to her that he had been doing a lot of the managing of the ranch the past two years when his father was feeling ill.

'So now it's just a little more of the same thing. Only I know now that I don't have anyone to confer with about the big decisions.'

'Wow, that sounds really hard. I don't know what I would do if father got sick or something and I had to run the store. I'd be totally lost.'

'I bet you would do fine. But let's hope that your father stays healthy for thirty or forty years yet.'

At about three o'clock Mrs Lenore came in with fresh-baked peanut cookies and lemonade.

'Mrs Lenore. How did you know that lemonade is my favorite drink? Thank you so much.'

'Just took a chance. Enjoy.' She paused a minute, smiled at them both, then left.

Matt had to move closer on the couch where they sat so he could reach the cookies.

'Ma left us alone again,' Francine said. 'I know she likes you. She's never made lemonade for a young man courting before.'

'You've had courters before?'

She smiled. 'Wish I could say six or eight. Actually only one and he only came once and Father told him not to come back. He wasn't very nice. I think he and his family moved out of town.'

'Good. I hope that I'm the last suitor that you have. How about another cookie?'

A half hour of talk later the lemonade was gone and most of the cookies. Matt moved over closer and caught her hand. He felt a little jolt when she squeezed his hand. Then he reached in and kissed her on the lips. She gave a little sigh and kissed him back. Then they eased apart. He watched her.

'Francine. I really don't want you to be swept off your feet by some six-gun-toting young buck on a prancing white stallion and carrying you off. I want you to stay right here so I can come courting every Sunday no matter how bad I'm shot full of holes.'

She reached in and kissed his cheek.

'Matthew Hardy, if you don't come every Sunday I'll just stay at home and cry my eyes out. I have feelings for you, Matt. I want you to know that.'

'Francine, I have feelings for you as well. Strong, very strong feelings.'

They had moved apart then and a few minutes later Mrs Lenore came in.

'Well, looks like you do enjoy my lemonade, Matthew. Now I think courting time is over. We'll look forward to seeing you next Sunday at church. Then you'll come to dinner of course.'

Matt said a herd of wild horses couldn't drag him away to keep him from church. He stood and touched Francine's outstretched hand, said goodbye to Mr Lenore, who was deep into reading the Fort Worth newspaper, and then walked out to the buggy.

Now Matt was sure of it. He was going to ask Mr Lenore next week for Francine's hand.

★ ★ ★

An hour and a half later, Matt drove the buggy into the Bar-H ranch and was met by Ivan who seemed to be waiting for him and nursing a big corncob pipe.

'Made it both ways,' Matt said. He stepped down from the buggy but had to hold on with his right hand.

'You all right, Mr Matt?' Ivan asked.

'Been better. Think I'll curl up around a big supper and then find me a nice comfortable chair. Ginny was right. I shouldn't have gone into town.' He shrugged. 'A good night's sleep and I'll be raring to go tomorrow.'

24

Matt had his big supper, a snooze in his favorite soft chair and went early to bed. But, when he awoke Monday morning, he could barely move. His arm hurt more now that it had when he was first shot. He tried to turn over in bed and have another sleep, but he touched his arm to the mattress and let out a groan of intense pain.

Sweat beaded his forehead. He tried to relax, to will the pain to go away, but it didn't work. It took him another half hour to sit up in bed and push his legs to the floor. He wore the pullover cotton shirt with short sleeves that he usually slept in and short underwear. He looked at the jeans and blue shirt with long sleeves that lay on the chair beside his bed.

He snorted. Not a chance he could

get the shirt on with those sleeves. His jeans, maybe.

It took him fifteen minutes to get his jeans and his house shoes on. Then he took himself firmly in hand and stood. For a moment he thought he would fall flat on his face but he stayed upright by reaching out for the wall.

He made it down the hall as far as the steps. He took one step down and then sat on the floor. Ginny came out of the living room and saw him there. She rushed up the stairs.

'I knew I shouldn't let you go to town yesterday.' She had her fists set on her hips and her dark eyes flashed. 'Now, Mr Matt Hardy, you have your choice. You can go back to bed for the rest of the day and let me ply you with home remedies, or you can let me and Ponchy help you down the steps to the sofa in the living room where you will stay the rest of the day.'

Matt tried to grin at her, but it came out crooked and he was sure he was a fright to behold.

'The living room, and get my blue shirt off the chair.'

She called to Ponchy who came out of the kitchen and when he saw Matt sitting on the steps he hurried up. Ponchy guided him down the steps, half-carrying him, being careful not to touch his left arm or shoulder.

Once settled on the couch Matt thanked Ponchy and Ginny.

'You're going to stay right there until I'm sure you don't have a fever or an infection,' she said. 'I'll bring you some magazines you never have time to read. Maybe even one of those strange dime novels about the Wild West.'

Ponchy frowned at Matt. 'Now for breakfast. I'll bring you what you should have to keep up your strength. You will eat it.' He turned and hurried into the kitchen.

★   ★   ★

Ginny and Ponchy pampered and ordered him around that way for the next three days. On the fourth day he took control again. He was up at dawn and got his arm into a shirt and his pants on. He even pulled on his boots. Downstairs, Ponchy was surprised to see him.

'Three flapjacks, bacon, coffee and some of that left-over apple cobbler. Then I want three sandwiches I can take along on an all day ride. Get it all fixed as soon as you can. I want to be out of here before Ginny gets up and I have to argue with her.'

Ponchy grinned. 'Sounds like you're feeling better Mr Matt. Right away with breakfast.' He paused. 'Oh, Mr Matt. Should I make those three sandwiches for two? You are going to take a rider along with you?'

'No, Ponchy just for one. Now hustle.'

★   ★   ★

It was just a half hour later when Ponchy tied a flour sack with the lunch things on the back of the saddle, including some apples and raisins and two canteens of water. He stepped back, worry showing on his tan face.

'I surely hope that you will be careful, Mr Matt. Let me roust out one of the hands to go with you.'

Matt chuckled. 'Ponchy you've babied me enough the last three days. Now I'm able to dress, to ride, and to shoot if I need to kill a rattler. So rest easy. I'll be fine.'

Ponchy stood there, eyes down and the frown growing as Matt rode away.

'Mr Matt. I surely hope that you will be safe and come home to us.'

*   *   *

Matt rode out to the north. He planned on going almost to the ranch north line and then working west, swinging toward town and checking over the cattle that often wandered up that way. Sometimes the grass was a little better up there and lasted longer in the heat of summer.

He had gone a hundred yards when he lost some of his bravado. His arm still hurt. The doctor said it would for a month or more but it was healing. They had been to town the day before for a dressing change and a look over. Now he realized that he would have to walk his mount most of the way. The jolting ride of a gallop would leave him gasping for breath as the pain increased with each bounce.

★   ★   ★

An hour's ride north had covered about four miles and he veered to the west. He saw some yearling steers in a little draw and watched them carefully. None was down and none seemed to be hurting. He went on north of them and found a dozen brood cows with their calves working to the west. All looked in good health.

His arm was hurting more now, and he unbuttoned one fastener on his shirt and pushed his left hand inside so it acted as a sling for his arm, protecting his shot shoulder. That helped. As he rode on, he wondered if this was a fool's errand. Maybe he didn't have to make this final check to be sure that his stock was safe. Hooves on the ground were the way to find out. He scowled and shook his head. No. He had to do the check, do it himself so he could be sure that his herd was clean of the disease.

On a small rise he turned his horse and looked over the land he had just covered. Nothing moved but a few cattle. He squinted and checked again. His eyes were sharp and he could sometimes see what others could not. But he saw no rider and no trail of dust. For a moment he had the feeling that there was someone back there. Nonsense. Who would it be? If it were someone from the ranch, he would be riding hard to catch up with whatever urgent news he had to tell Matt.

Now he did a series of half mile

zigzags to cover more territory so he could see more cattle. Everywhere he looked he found animals that were up and grazing or moving, and that appeared to be well and healthy.

Good. Part of the reason he came.

He had just started his slanting forty-five degree angle to the north-west when a shot slammed through the pristine Texas summer air. The round whined off a rock twenty feet to his right. He spurred his horse ahead and then to the left and then again to the right making himself a tough target to hit. The sound of the rifle shot had come three, maybe four seconds before the slug hit, which meant the gunman was some distance away.

Just ahead to the left lay a small ravine with a twenty foot wide copse of poplar trees and brush. He spurred his mount to the trees and made it just as another rifle round ripped through the leaves above his head.

Matt slid off his mount, led her to the

far side of the brush, and tied her. Then he pulled the lever action Winchester rifle from the boot, pocketed two boxes of extra shells and eased back to the front of the little woods. He bellied down in the weeds at the edge but stayed where he couldn't be seen. He watched the view of the downgrade in front of him.

It went downward for a quarter of a mile before it faded into another draw and small hill. He scanned the whole area.

Nothing. No rider, no horse.

He looked again, this time peering carefully at one small section at a time. Clearing it and then moving to the next small section. It took him ten minutes to clear the whole area he could see.

Nothing.

Then he saw movement. He checked that section again and saw the edge of a man's hat and torso above the side of the small draw.

A rider moving slowly up the draw toward him.

Why? Who? Was it the same bush-whacker he shot up four days ago?

He waited and watched. At no time did the rider make himself a target. Down this small draw there were two more little clumps of brush and a live oak or two. They grew only because in the rainy season this draw would be a small stream, providing nourishment for the growth there due to a small pooling of the water until it evaporated in the summer heat or soaked into the thirsty soil.

The ravine took a slight turn to the left down about two hundred yards, and there for a brief moment he saw a rider spurring his mount across a twenty-rod open space between the turn in the ravine and the second growth of green brush and the darker live oak tree. He got only a brief glance at the man but could see that he wore all black and he rode a black horse.

Matt watched and waited with his rifle loaded with a round in the chamber ready to fire. He studied the clump of green a hundred and fifty yards down slope. The horse and rider had not left the cover. Matt lifted the rifle and aimed at the greenery. His left hand and arm had trouble holding the rifle steady. A pain shot through his shoulder and he lowered the weapon.

Just great. He wouldn't be doing much sharp shooting today. Matt kept watching the splotch of brush and live oaks. No movement. The shooter must still be in there. Matt knew he could put four or five rounds into the brushy area but that would give away his own position. He waited.

To Matt's surprise the brush parted and a horse with the black-dressed rider charged out, heading for Matt's cover. The rider was low in the saddle to make a small target. Matt lifted the Winchester to get off a shot. The first was way low as his shoulder burned like fire and his hand wavered on the stock. He tried again as the horse charged forward. His next shot was closer but again his arm sagged, ruining his aim. No chance to hit the rider. He'd aim for the horse.

This time he rested the rifle on a branch and aimed carefully. His round hit the horse in the head and it went down hard, throwing the rider off. The rider was only a hundred feet away now and he began snapping off shots from his rifle at Matt's hiding spot. Matt tried to follow him with the rifle, but as soon as he swung it to the side, it fell off the branch and his left arm refused to hold it up in a firing position.

Matt tried holding the weapon against his leg. But the attacker was zigging from side to side and Matt couldn't follow him. When he was twenty feet away, Matt drew his six-gun, but before he could fire the gunman dove into the brush and trees fifteen feet away but hidden in the thick brush.

Matt fired one round into the brush where the rider had vanished but heard no cry of pain.

'Drop it, Matt. I've got you centered in my rifle sights and you so much as twitch, you're a dead man. You hear me?'

Matt knew the voice. He shook his head. 'Hal, it's you, isn't it! It's been you all the time ever since the trail drive. You want to own the Bar-H badly enough to kill again for it?'

'Drop the six-gun, Matt. And the rifle. Then stand up and turn around.'

'Shooting me in the back, Hal? Bad form. Won't go down good with the county sheriff.'

'One more time, Matt. Drop the weapon.'

Matt did and a moment later Hal, in his black clothing, came out of the brush and kicked the revolver away.

'How's the shoulder, Matt? I figured you wouldn't be able to shoot good with that wounded arm.'

'Why, Hal? The ranch?'

'Yeah, sure, the ranch. This place is worth maybe half a million dollars. Easy half, maybe a million. Set me up for life.'

'How you going to explain me being

dead?' Matt asked.

'Easy. Ponchy told me you'd left all alone. I was concerned and came to help you. I got here a little too late. There's about two hundred head of brood cows just over the rise. Amazing what eight hundred hoofs will do to a body when it gets trampled. So sad. You just couldn't get out of the way.'

'Never work, Hal. Those broods are fat and sassy. You'll never get them to stampede.'

'Keep hoping that, Matt. You're staking your life on being right.'

Matt watched Hal, but the man stood a safe distance away and held the six-gun.

'Let's move, Matt. You walk and I ride your horse. It's just up this ravine and over that rise. Then I'll introduce you to the vicious, stampeding herd of brood cows.'

25

On the way to the herd, Hal had taken
a detour and stopped at his dead horse.
He took something from his saddle-
bags, transferred it to Matt's horse's
saddle-bags and then remounted.

'Had to come over here and get some
surprises,' Hal said as his only explanation.

Ten minutes later Hal had led Matt
in front of a herd of two hundred and
fifty or so grazing brood cows. Most of
the calves with this group had been
weaned and wandered away. From his
saddle-bags Hal took out sharpened
sticks an inch thick and a foot long. He
produced a hammer and a quantity of
twine.

He made Matt lie down on the
ground and spreadeagled his arms and
legs. Then he drove a stake into the
ground near each of the limbs. He tied

Matt's hands and feet to the stakes with the twine. Matt lunged to get away once but Hal put a shot six inches from his foot and Matt settled back to the ground.

'Simple little matter, brother-in-law of mine. You lay here and the brood cows stampede over you. I try to rescue you but all I can find is your trampled, dead body. Real shame. You shouldn't have gone out alone to check the herd.'

'Nobody will believe you,' Matt said.

'They'll have to. Ponchy will vouch for me going out to help you. Just got here too late.' Hal stared at Matt from where he sat on the ground. 'You don't know how long I've waited to do this. We tried on the trail drive, but Slade missed. Then he failed to kill your father during the cattle count near the grove. He was just not a good shot. I had to go out and get a good shot to take care of your dad on his way into town in the buggy. I've got to say, it was my fault I didn't kill you with that rifle shot from my horse with you on the road. But I've never been very good shooting a rifle from a horse.'

'I did suspect you a time or two, but decided that even you couldn't be that cold-blooded. Why tell me this now?'

Hal chuckled. He was enjoying this. 'Why? Bragging a little bit. Rubbing your stupid face in it. Making up for all of the insults and degrading work you've made me do. So what? You'll never live long enough to be able to use any of it.'

Matt turned his head and looked at the grazing brood cows a quarter of a mile up the slope from him.

'You don't have a chance to stampede those broods. They look fed and contented.'

Hal laughed. 'Matt, you are stupid to let me get this close to killing you. But that's in the past. You can bet your life there's going to be a stampede in about ten minutes.'

Matt had been testing the twine tying his hands to the stakes. They were driven too deep into the ground for him to pull out. His right hand seemed looser tied than his left.

'So long there, cowboy. Meet your brood cows up real close.' Hal laughed again and mounted the horse and rode off toward the herd.

Matt concentrated on his right hand. Pull and then push, pull again. Looser. Pull again. The tough twine couldn't be broken but it had been tied looser around his right hand. Slowly he worked the twine looser. He then pushed the loops of twine up the stake toward the top. If he could just get it loose enough he could get one loop over the top of the stake and get his right hand free. He was sweating with the effort. The pain in his left shoulder paled in the rush of emotion. He won at this or he died. He had no idea how Hal would try to stampede the placid cows. He just might do it. Matt knew he had only a few minutes left to get free.

Matt heard the first explosion two minutes later. He had just pulled the first loop off the stake at his right hand. More explosions. Two or three more.

Yes, they would stampede a herd. Sticks of dynamite would send the animals in a wild panic and they would race away from the unknown danger. Frantically he undid the twine on his left hand with his right. Then bent and pulled at the strings on his feet. A moment later he heard the ominous rumble of hoofs pounding on the hard Texas land. He looked up. The cows were a hundred yards away and coming fast. No chance he could outrun them or get away to one side.

He jerked the bindings off his feet and stood. The first cow came charging almost at him. He jolted away to find two more bearing down on him. He couldn't avoid them. He couldn't run as fast as they were. How could he survive?

Then the picture of branding came to him. How they had to grab some of the young steers by the horns and twist their heads to the side until they fell down. Could he get a grip on one of these brood cows?

A big cow brushed past him almost knocking him down. He surged ahead running with the animals. He looked behind him. A two-year-old brood bore down on him. She was smaller than the rest. He let her come even with him, then put on a burst of running speed, kept up with her and, as he had so many times, grabbed the cow's horns and hung on. He ran as fast as he could alongside the cow. He couldn't quite keep up and felt himself being dragged now and then but he held on like his life depended on it.

It did.

His left shoulder stabbed him with a thousand slashing knives as the pain rocketed down his arm and into his back.

Matt held on.

Gradually he sensed that the animals were slowing. He found he could now keep up with the pace of the cow he held by the horns. The herd slowed even more. Matt realized that he had lost his hat and his holster flapped at his side without his six-gun in it.

Ahead he could see the leaders slowing even more, then walking and slanting off to both sides in search of new graze.

The stampede was over. He grinned. He was still alive. But Hal was determined to kill him one way or the other. The worst of it was that Hal still had two rifles and two handguns.

Just ahead of the grazing cows, Matt saw a small gully and worked that way to the west. He ran to it hoping that the cows would serve to hide him. With luck, Hal would be looking elsewhere. He made it into the green patch, bellied down in the dirt, and crawled up so he could just see over the top of the clay bank. The cows had all stopped running. Far to the back he saw Hal on the horse. He was working back and forth across the trail of the stampede. Matt snorted. The killer was searching for a man's body, for Matt dead under the thousand sharp cattle hoofs.

Matt watched him trying to figure out what to do. He could hike down the swale and keep on going back toward the ranch. There were enough small hills and ravines so he could have cover from Hal's searching eyes most of the time. With luck he could make it back to the ranch before Hal found him. But if the man on the horse searched far enough, he would have better odds at finding Matt.

Matt watched the sun sink lower. It had been well after noon before Hal had spotted him and caught him. By now it must be past four in the afternoon. Something told Matt to wait until dark. He doubted that Hal would give up his search. The darkness could be an ally for Matt, he knew.

By this time, the brood cows were clustering and moving slowly up the slopes toward the fresher graze. Matt saw Hal working the ground again, searching for a body or some body parts. Matt figured that Hal was a half-mile away.

When the rider turned his back on Matt in his search pattern, Matt sprinted for a dozen brood cows moving slowly to the north toward Hal. By bending over he could stay below the backs of the large brood cows. He moved with them.

An hour later the sun had dropped behind the hills and dusk settled in. The cows began to look for a spot to settle down. Most of them kept clumped together. Matt thought about the four weapons Hal had. Matt stumbled over a dry cow pie and almost fell down. That made him remember how they used to throw the dry ones at each other. Dry they were as hard as rocks but could be made to spin and sail a long distance.

As the cows knelt down, Matt had to squat and then lie down with them to avoid being seen. He was within two hundred yards of Hal who still rode the horse. He at last gave up his search for body parts and rode over another hundred yards to a smattering of brush and some live oaks. He was settling in for the night. That gave Matt some ideas.

Matt worked closer to the copse of trees and brush, staying among the bedded-down cows. When he was thirty feet from where Hal was making a small fire, Matt spotted the horse ground-tied so it could move around and munch on the sparse green grass at the water seep. Matt found two good-sized cow pies he could throw. When Hal had his back to Matt, Matt stood and threw the two cow pies, sailing them toward the horse. One hit the horse in the side. It bleated in pain, shied to the side, then trotted away from the brush.

Hal was on his feet at once chasing after the mount. He had to run off more than a hundred yards in the dark to catch the frightened horse. When Hal was well away from the fire, Matt charged into the site. He'd spotted the two rifles that Hal had left by the fire. Matt grabbed them and ran back into the darkness among the sleeping broods.

Hal shouted at the horse and evidently caught it somewhere in the darkness. Soon he led the mount back, tied it securely to a tree, and slumped to the ground near the fire. A moment later he must have noticed the rifles missing. He gave a bellow of rage and stood looking into the dark countryside.

Matt put a shot into the fire, scattering it.

'Give it up, killer. Drop your gun-belt on the ground, then go flat on your face well away from the weapon.'

'No way,' Hal screamed. 'How in the blazes did you get away from that stampede?'

Matt didn't answer. He'd had enough of Hal Westover. He sighted in carefully and put a round through Hal's right leg. Hal screamed and jolted backwards but still in the firelight. Matt charged in, kicked the second six-gun from Hal's hand and pushed him back on his stomach.

Hal brayed in fury. 'How did you get away?'

As he talked, Matt tied Hal's hands tightly behind his back, then tied his ankles together.

'Get away? You're not much at tying knots. I got loose, bulldogged a young brood and ran with her on the stampede. You should try it sometime.'

*   *   *

Later that night Hal went to sleep. Matt didn't. He stayed up until daylight. He knew what he was going to do. He had decided he couldn't just kill Hal in cold blood. He was Ginny's husband. He would take him into the ranch, then into town, and charge him with three murders. Ginny was strong. She would understand, and be able to watch Hal be hung after his trial.

*   *   *

A cold wind had blown in overnight. Matt smelled rain. They sure could use it. At daybreak he saw the ominous clouds moving toward them.

'Wake up, Hal. You've got ten miles to walk back to the ranch. You'll have a noose around your neck and your hands will stay tied behind you. Let's go.'

They had moved less than a quarter of a mile toward the east when the first spatters of rain came. Matt checked the clouds. They were angry. He watched the herd of brood cows he had hidden among before. They were stirring, smelling the rain. Matt looped the noose around Hal's neck and cut loose his feet.

'Let's move, killer. You walk, I ride.'

They were only a hundred yards on the way when a series of six or seven sharp lightning bolts riddled the clouds and darted toward the ground. Matt turned to look at the herd of cattle. Not again, he thought. Not another stampede. But it came. The broods started bawling and charging away from the lightning. They thundered forward and Matt figured he and Hal were a hundred yards to the right and out of the path of the bellowing animals. Then another pair of lightning bolts slashed through the clouds and into the ground to the left of the herd. The leaders jolted to the right.

Now the 250 heavy brood cows were storming directly at Matt on his horse and Hal on foot. Matt yelled at Hal.

'Run for it. We can get away to the right side.'

They ran, Matt holding the horse to a pace that Hal could keep up with.

The cows were running twice as fast. Matt shook his head. They were losing ground. Soon one of the front-running animals pounded past Matt. Hal screamed and jerked the rope out of Matt's hands and charged toward the east.

'Not that way,' Matt bellowed. But Hal didn't change his headlong streak toward safety. Matt knew at once that

Hal didn't have a chance of making it. Matt hesitated only a moment, then kicked the horse in the sides, angled around one running cow and spurted ahead of the pack heading more to the right and away from the broods.

One of the big reddish cows with three-foot-long horns brushed against Matt's leg, then fell behind. Matt rode hard and three minutes later he had outdistanced the herd which was gradually slowing. He circled around back toward where he had last seen Hal. He was afraid what he would find.

* * *

Almost three hours later, Matt met two Bar-H riders who had seen him coming and rode on into the ranch with him. He didn't say a word and they didn't ask.

Near the front door they stopped. Ginny came out of the house and ran to the body draped over the back of Matt's horse. She stared at the battered, hardly recognizable face, touched her forehead with a pale hand, and collapsed just as Matt caught her.

★   ★   ★

Two days later they had the funeral. It was private with only the family, the preacher, and undertaker there. Ginny had looked at Matt and asked him one question.

'Stampede?'

He nodded. She knew about the lightning storm that had soaked the ranch the day Hal died. She understood what lightning could do to a herd of cattle.

Matt went on managing the ranch. He never said a word about Hal's traitorous and murdering behavior. He knew that Ginny would meet a good man, a real rancher type who would merge in with managing the ranch.

Matt continued his courtship after church every Sunday and soon he took Ginny along to church with him. She visited friends in town until Matt was ready to take her home in the buggy.

Three months later Matt married Francine, who came to live at the ranch, giving up her idea of becoming a school teacher.

Ginny's baby arrived right on schedule, a seven-pound perfect little girl.

Matt beamed, even knowing that now he had three females in the house to contend with. He would manage. He did.

THE END

We do hope that you have enjoyed reading this large print book.

Did you know that all of our titles are available for purchase?

We publish a wide range of high quality large print books including:
Romances, Mysteries, Classics
General Fiction
Non Fiction and Westerns

Special interest titles available in large print are:
The Little Oxford Dictionary
Music Book, Song Book
Hymn Book, Service Book

Also available from us courtesy of Oxford University Press:
Young Readers' Dictionary
(large print edition)
Young Readers' Thesaurus
(large print edition)

For further information or a free brochure, please contact us at:
Ulverscroft Large Print Books Ltd.,
The Green, Bradgate Road, Anstey,
Leicester, LE7 7FU, England.
Tel: (00 44) **0116 236 4325**
Fax: (00 44) **0116 234 0205**

Other titles in the
Linford Western Library:

KILL SLAUGHTER

Henry Remington

When a California train is robbed of $30,000, and two Pinkerton detectives are killed, bounty hunter James Slaughter rides to investigate. But a cloud of fear hangs over the railroad town of Visalia, and even the judge is running scared. Beaten up, jailed and framed by the sheriff's deputies, Slaughter survives assassination attempts — but is hit by still more trouble as a vicious range war erupts on the prairie . . .

LAWLESS GUNS

M. Duggan

Imprisoned for murder, innocent Luther Larkin feels only resentment towards the town of Black Bear Crossing and its lawman. When an unexpected confession sets Luther free, he finds himself drawn back to his boyhood home — and pretty soon trouble seeks him out. Nor is he the only one who has been drawn back to Black Bear Crossing: deranged killer Donald Ricket has a score to settle with the town, and only Luther stands between him and his goal . . .

CRAZY MAN CADE

Amos Carr

'Crazy Man Cade' has done it all: foiled a robbery, stopped the beating of an elderly man, halted a kidnapping. But his life is changed forever when an Arapaho brave walks into his camp to tell him that Cade's oldest friend is dying. A perilous journey and a bloody battle ensue and, not being one to settle down, Cade is faced with a choice: will he deny his attraction to one of the Indian girls and ride away from his old friend, and the possibility of a new life?

Dionysus to Hercules:
*   "That's the reason I've come here*
and dressed like you – so you can fill me in,
in case I need to know, about this place ...
who welcomed you down here, who'd you meet
that time you went down after Cerberus.
Tell me about the harbours, resting places,
bakeries and brothels, water fountains,
the cities, highways, all the detours,
the local customs and the fine hotels,
the ones with fewest bugs."
> 'The Frogs' by Aristophanes (translated by Professor Ian Johnston, Vancouver Island University)

"Man is only breath and shadow."
ἄνθρωπός ἐστι πνεῦμα καὶ σκιὰ μόνον
> Sophocles, Fr. 13 (Ajax the Locrian; Stobaeus, Anth. 4, 43, 52)

Preface

I left Alexandria in 322 BC in search of a lost soul. History would say that my husband, Alexander the Great, had died in Babylon – but I'd saved him. However, something was missing. He felt it keenly, *"Like wind blowing through a cracked cliff"* – another of his Macedonian maxims that would fall through the cracks of posterity. He consulted an oracle, and the oracle told him his soul had been stolen by a druid: a thief of souls. I was the only one who had trouble believing this. Everyone else was convinced, so Alexander, my son Paul, and I headed north to the Land of Snow and Ice[1] to recover his soul. We travelled through Gaul, then hitched a ride up the coast on a trading boat with an Iceni girl, Phaleria.

Meanwhile, back in Egypt, Plexis, Alexander's and my lover, discovered that the druid who had stolen Alexander's soul also wanted our son, Paul. On his way

---

[1] There were no *float-vid-maps* back then – just the known kingdoms or tribes and vague directions. *'Come and visit sometime. I'm an Iceni and live on the river Iken in a red house with lots of mint in the garden. You can't miss it.'* Needless to say, people often wandered like Moses in the desert.

1

to warn us, Plexis was attacked by the druids and badly wounded, but he managed to find us in the far-north village of Orce. Apparently, the druids were fixated on saving their world by using Paul to change time. Since Paul should never have been born, it was feasible that a group of fanatics with Stone Age beliefs could alter the future.

The druids tracked us to Orce, and we barely escaped capture. Our choices were to flee by sea with our trader friend, Phaleria, or go inland where Alexander felt his soul had been taken. In the end, we decided to head inland, towards the Land of the Eaters of the Dead. But the druids were right on our heels.

Chapter One

The attack came just as we had stopped for a rest. Five men surged out of the darkness and swooped upon us. They were dressed in grey robes and wore strange bronze helmets with masks. The scuffle was short. My husband, Alexander the Great, was a superb swordsman; his admiral, Nearchus was even better, and Demos, once a soldier himself, was taller and stronger than any of our attackers.

I hid under the seat of the wagon, clutching my son Paul in my arms. For a few minutes, there was noise and confusion as the men fought and Paul's dog, Cerberus, barked. The horse shied, but Axiom held the reins firmly. He also held a sword, and if anyone had tried to leap into the wagon, Axiom would have killed him. As it was, Demos found an opening and thrust his sword into one man's throat. Seeing that, the other men ran away.

Afterwards, Axiom wrapped the slain man in a shroud. 'I think I'd better go back to the sanctuary in Orce.'

'But why? Now the druids know we're here and not on the trading boat.' I was confused. 'What good will it do to go back?'

3

'Everyone in the village believed that Plexis was dying. When I deliver this body, I'll say it was his. Then I will tell everyone in the village that you've left with Phaleria on her boat. Perhaps the druids will not be completely fooled, but they will want to make sure. They may split up.' Axiom spoke firmly, and we knew he was right.

'Only five druids attacked us,' said Demos. 'Yet there were dozens aboard the dragon ship. Where are the others? If we *can* split them up, it will make it harder for them to get Paul.'

'They didn't see him, he was under the seat with me,' I admitted. 'You're right, Axiom. Maybe they'll think Paul is on the trading boat with Phaleria and will follow her.'

'Here's money for the inn. You'll want to stay there until we come back.' Alexander gave Axiom his purse.

We looked at each other. Axiom had wise eyes. That's what I was thinking as he took the small, heavy pouch of coins. He had always been with us. I couldn't remember a time when he hadn't been there. His first gesture in the morning was to make a fire. Then he would pray, and then he would eat breakfast. He smiled crookedly. He could read my thoughts so easily. 'I'll be safer than you, My Lady.'

'I'll go with him to make sure he gets back to Orce,' said Alexander.

Demos had spoken up. 'I will go with him too.'

There was a short discussion about who would go where, with whom, and why. Then Plexis, Paul, and I hid in a thick copse of trees while Nearchus and Yovanix stayed to guard us. Alexander and Demos went with Axiom to make sure he made it back to the village.

One thing was certain; Alexander and Demos would be tired after the night was over. They hadn't stopped jogging after the cart, running through the forest, or fighting.

We lay on a thick bed of pine needles, with our warm cloaks over us. Paul started to shiver. He looked ill. 'What's the matter?' I asked.

'I can't stand it,' he said, his voice breaking. 'Because of me, everything is wrong. The druids want to kidnap me. I don't understand why. And Father is in danger because of me. Everyone is in danger. I'm so sorry I ran away. I should have stayed at home.'

'No,' I said. 'The druids have been searching for you since you were born. The only place you were safe was in the Sacred Valley of Nysa. But Roxanne made sure you didn't stay there. She brought you to Babylon. None of this was your fault. If you had stayed with Plexis in Alexandria, the druids would have killed everyone in the house to get you. They would have killed Chiron and Cleopatra.'

Paul was crying softly. 'But what about Father's soul? How can we get it back if the druids are chasing us? And who took it, anyway?'

I soothed him as best I could. 'I think I can answer your last question. When we were in Babylon, just before your father was supposed to die, an envoy came from the kingdom of Gaul. He must have been a druid. He had long hair and wore a grey robe. Most of the Gauls have short hair, did you notice? And they are clean. This man was dirty, he rarely washed, and I think he was a soul thief. When your father lay dying, he stole his soul.' I paused, remembering that day. 'Usse, Millis, and I were in the throne room. Alexander lay on his bed, which had been moved there so his generals could see him. The Gaul came in and chanted something, then put his hands on Alexander's chest. Usse rushed over to stop him. We had no idea what he was doing, but the man just picked up the staff that he'd put on the floor, and left. I don't know what happened. I have no reasonable explanation, and I don't know how Voltarrix managed to get Alexander's soul. To tell you the truth, Paul, I don't know if I believe any of this. But your father is convinced his soul has been taken.'

'How is that possible?' Paul asked. 'Isn't your soul attached to your body? Did the man cut it out? Did he have a knife?'

'No, he didn't, and no one knows what a soul looks like or where it is.' I shook my head. 'I never learned about souls from my family or from school, but I've read about them. In most stories, souls are what make men and gods different. Gods have no souls, but we have them because it's what animates the clay the gods used to craft our bodies.'

'But if Father's soul is missing, how is he still alive?'

Plexis spoke up. 'You can remove a person's soul, but it still belongs to that person and animates him. I learned this in Alexandria after the druids' attack. The Thief of

Souls can pass it to another person, but the soul will always belong to its original body. But if your father should die, Paul, then his captured soul can animate another person.'

Paul was silent for a while, thinking about this. 'Are there any stories about this from your time, Mother? Can you tell us one?' He shifted and pulled his cloak tighter around him. 'Please, tell me a story with a stolen soul in it.' He had the same faults as his father. He loved to command people. He never asked, he ordered, and even if it were done with a 'please' and an engaging smile, his expression said clearly, 'do it and do it now.'

I sighed. I was raising another Alexander, and one at a time in the world was enough.

There was only one tale that came to mind. 'Once upon a time there was an evil necromancer named Dr. Frankenstein,' I began.

'What in Hades' name are you telling the boy?' gasped Plexis, when I got to the part where the hunchbacked assistant, Igor, was heading off to dig up some bodies in a graveyard.

'A story!' I said crossly. 'Is anyone else going to complain?'

'Well, if you really want to know, I'd prefer something a little lighter, seeing as we're heading towards a place the natives call Land of the Eaters of the Dead. Plexis spoke in a whisper.

'Are you scared?' I asked Paul.

He just nodded, his eyes like two blue saucers.

'OK. It wasn't such a great idea after all,' I said. The

7

wind suddenly rustled the boughs of the pine trees making strange shadows in the night. Paul disappeared under his cloak, and Plexis heaved himself up on one elbow and peered into the gloom.

'It was an interesting tale,' said Plexis, 'but I wish you had waited until everyone came back.'

'It *is* scary here in the dark,' I agreed. 'How's your arm?'

'Hurts. But it hurts like an arm that's been broken twice and is finally starting to heal.'

'Well, you should know what that feels like,' I said, half joking. His arm had been broken *more* than twice, and I could remember a time when his collarbone had been broken four times in a row.

He didn't reply. Instead he hitched himself up a little straighter and his eyes narrowed. Then he lay down again, but instead of resting he pressed his ear against the ground. Paul and I had been around soldiers long enough to know when to be quiet. After what seemed like a long while, Plexis lifted his head and stared at us. 'I hope we're well hidden.'

I could tell he was worried, his movements were slow and careful, and it wasn't only because of his wounds. We *were* well hidden; at least I was sure of that. Alexander and Demos had taken great pains to hide us.

The wind was blowing in gusts. Sometimes the trees would lean over and hide the moon, other times all was still. An owl hooted softly nearby. Plexis cupped his hands around his mouth and hooted back. We held our breaths, and then the branches parted and Alexander poked his head through.

'I heard you coming,' said Plexis, a note of satisfaction in his voice.

'The owl wasn't me,' said Alexander curtly. Plexis swore. I grabbed Paul and we huddled next to Plexis. The branches hadn't moved but Alexander was gone. I braced myself for the inevitable sound of metal clanging on metal. The attackers had found us, and this time there would be more of them.

Plexis looked at me bleakly. He would have preferred to be out there but was in no condition to fight. He'd already been hurt in a previous attack by the druids following us, and it was a miracle he was alive. I wondered if he shouldn't have gone back to the village with Axiom. But I had the strongest feeling that he had to stay with us. I'd learned to trust my intuition. The last premonition I'd had saved our lives. I reached over Paul and took Plexis by the hand. 'Don't worry, we'll be on our way soon.'

'I hope I won't slow you down,' he said.

'Don't be silly. Even wounded you are stronger than Paul or me. Don't worry so much. You'll heal fast, you always did.'

'I know, but I'm getting old.' We sat up, straining for some sound or a clue as to what was happening outside the thicket, but all we heard was the wind in the trees.

Paul gave a soft snore, and I realized he'd fallen asleep.

Then Cerberus barked. The dog had been hiding with Yovanix. If the attackers had wanted to sneak up on us, it was too late. I heard a man shout something in Celtic, and the clash of fighting.

The conflict was over quickly yet, to me, it seemed to last an eternity as I sat in the dark listening. There were yells, but they didn't come from the men I knew. Alexander fought in silence. I pictured him with his mouth drawn in a tight line, his eyes fierce. Demos was a bear, growling between slashes, and Yovanix was an untrained ex-slave, but he had a large sword and he used it the best he could. Nearchus was the best sword fighter, and he only swore once. Plexis sat without moving, but I could feel his frustration. His good hand clutched a sword. It would not be easy for anyone to reach Paul and me.

The sword Plexis had was bronze and very old, even for those times. It had belonged to his great-grandfather who'd used it in the wars against the Persians; Plexis had taken it to India and back. Bronze often shattered in a fight, since it was more brittle than iron, but this sword had lasted for more than a century; it would probably end up in a museum in another three thousand years. When I'm nervous, it helps to think about things like that.

When the skirmish finished, Alexander came for us. My heart slowed its frantic pounding when I saw he was unhurt. Well, almost. He was nursing an angry cut on his forearm. When he lifted his hand from the cut, blood welled out. Demos wrapped Alexander's arm with a strip of cloth to stem the bleeding.

Plexis lay back and put his good arm over his face. We were all exhausted. Dawn was minutes away and no one had slept since the day before. Nearchus and Yovanix fell asleep sitting with their backs against a tree. Demos lay down and he was soon snoring loudly. Cerberus snuggled up to Paul, who hadn't woken up. Alexander and I looked at each other. He was haggard.

'What happened?' I asked.

'There were seven of them,' he answered. 'We didn't kill anyone this time. They faded away. They're testing us or maybe just letting us know we're being followed. I'm not sure.'

'But they wounded you.'

'They were good,' he said reflectively. 'Not soldiers, but swordsmen. I'm not sure I've ever fought better. They could have killed Yovanix whenever they felt like it. They were just playing.'

I looked at his arm. 'Some game,' I said angrily. But he just shrugged. He got to his feet and went to the far side of the copse. He parted the branches and peered out. 'Do you see anyone?' I asked.

'No. They won't bother us. Why don't you sleep?'

'I want to keep you company.'

He smiled then. His teeth shone in the half light of dawn. 'Your eyes are nearly closed already,' he said. 'Lie down. There's no more danger; I'm keeping watch. And when Nearchus wakes up, he'll watch. Then I'll lie down by your side.'

I closed my eyes. I meant to tell Alexander that I wasn't sleepy and that I'd wait up with him, but when I next opened my eyes, the sun was sparkling through the boughs of the pine trees. Alexander was sleeping deeply beside me. A fire crackled merrily in a small stone hearth, and Paul was carefully poking dry branches into it.

I sat up slowly. Alexander murmured and snuggled deeper into his cloak, but didn't wake up. I watched him for a moment. He looked so young when he was asleep. All the lines of worry and tension disappeared. His hair lifted off his temples in tight curls before becoming long and wavy. It was down to his shoulders and he had started tying it back with a leather thong. He preferred it short, but he would only let Brazza cut it. I had an urge to run my finger down his face, starting with his broad forehead, over his proud nose, his lips, his stubborn chin, then down his neck to his chest where a jagged scar shone whitely. But I didn't. I let him sleep. He needed it. Instead, I pulled his cloak higher and tucked it carefully around him. I lifted my head and met Nearchus's gaze.

'Do you want a hot drink?' he asked quietly.

Thankfully, I took the steaming cup of chicory and sat next to him. He looked as tired as Alexander. Two deep lines ran down his cheeks making his mouth look harsh. However, he wasn't a hard man. He was quiet and introverted; normally he could hide his feelings better than anyone else of that time. But fatigue let his guard down, and what I'd seen in his eyes had been worry. And if he was worried, I should be too.

I cast a glance at Demos, sitting next to Paul, and at Yovanix who was sleeping deeply. There were only four men capable of fighting now. Demos didn't look particularly worried. However, appearances can be deceptive. The way he stayed so close to Paul belied his calm exterior.

Plexis woke up with a grimace. His arm pained him, and Demos spent a good part of the morning carefully tending the wound.

Yovanix woke up with a start. He looked around for a few seconds, as if he'd forgotten where he was. Then his shoulders slumped and he ran a shaky hand over his face and through his hair. Without a sound, he folded up his cloak and joined us around the fire. His face was crumpled with fatigue and his eyes were red, but he didn't look worse than anyone else. He took a cup of chicory from Nearchus with a shy nod, then sat next to Cerberus, busy worrying his fleas. The hound would often break off his scratching and look around. His black nose would twitch, but he didn't bark. I felt more secure knowing he was there; he would bark and give us time to grab our swords before an attack. At least I hoped so. I looked at the enormous puppy. He was still growing, much to Alexander's dismay. His fur was rough and grey and his eyes yellow. I thought he looked like a wolf, and Alexander said he looked like a pony he once had, only taller. Paul didn't care what he looked like. He had a dog, his own dog, and it didn't matter to him that the dog ate twice as much as he did.

And speaking of eating. I looked into the bag that held our food supplies. It was empty. An onion rolled around the bottom and there were a few crumbs, but that was it. In last night's scramble, most of the food we'd managed to bring with us had either been lost in the

13

forest or had been forgotten in the cart. I put my face in my hands. I'd also lost my own bag with my cotton and my toilet case. I didn't know what depressed me more: no more shampoo and soap, or no more food. Our belongings now consisted of the clothes we wore and our cloaks, whatever the men had with them in their leather pouches, five swords, and one large, round shield that Paul carried everywhere. Much to Alexander's dismay, Cerberus used this as a bed. But nothing could stop the dog from curling up and snoozing on it. Otherwise, Paul kept the shield clean and polished, so Alexander, who had given it to his son, only cast occasional disapproving glances at the gangly puppy.

Then there was Plexis. He was sitting up, but couldn't move without wincing. What had I been thinking? I'd insisted on bringing him along instead of trusting Axiom to care for him in Orce. We could have been safely tucked on board Phaleria's ship right now instead of huddled in a tiny clearing in the middle of a primeval forest.

Chapter Two

When he awoke, I braced for Alexander to say something about Plexis and the safety of the ship, but he didn't. Instead he rolled over, stretched, yawned and sat up blinking. His face was dappled in yellow sunlight, and his hair had pine needles stuck in it. He grinned ruefully as he plucked them out.

'I feel much better,' he said in a normal tone of voice.

We all stopped what we were doing and looked at him. Not that we were doing much, but just the strain of listening for any further attack required constant effort. Plexis paused from cleaning his teeth, Paul stopped grooming Cerberus, and Nearchus, who'd been polishing his sword, glanced up in surprise.

Demos frowned. 'You've slept most of the morning,' he said. His voice wasn't reproachful, but it did sound a bit puzzled. 'Aren't you worried about an attack?'

Alexander grinned. His smile was wide, and if I didn't know better I would have thought he was completely stoned. Sometimes he got that same smile when Usse gave him the hashish he used for medicinal purposes. He shook his head slowly. 'You've been on guard all morning? Protecting me?' There was something in his voice. I sat back on my heels and studied him carefully.

'What do you know that we don't?' I asked in a level voice. My nerves were pretty well frayed, and so were everyone else's. When Alexander started to chuckle, I saw Nearchus's hand tighten on his sword.

Alexander saw it too because he stopped and frowned. 'Think,' he said reasonably. His eyes met Plexis's and he started smiling again.

Plexis grinned too, and settled back onto the tree trunk he'd been leaning on. The tenseness left his face. 'They *want* us to go north,' he said.

'Exactly.' Alexander shrugged. 'As long as we're heading in the direction they want us to go, they'll leave us alone. Why were they so worried last night? Because they weren't sure where we were going. How many forks were in the road? My bet is that we've passed most of them. As long as we go north we'll be fine.'

'They're not chasing us then,' said Demos.

'No, they're herding us.' It was Yovanix. 'They know exactly where we are and where we're going.'

'And the more tired and weak we are when we get there, the better,' I said snappishly. 'All that's fine, but what should we do about it?'

'Well, until we're rested, nothing,' said Alexander. 'They had ample chance to kill us and they haven't yet, so I think we're to be kept alive. For now at least,' he added thoughtfully, taking a pine needle from his hair and studying it.

'I feel terrible, I'm sorry,' I said softly.

'For what?' Alexander looked surprised.

'For leading you into this mess; if it weren't for me we'd be safe on Phaleria's boat.'

'And Phaleria and her crew would be feeding fish at the bottom of the sea. No, we made the right decision. The dragon boat is swift. They would have caught us and forced us northwards one way or another. All they have to do is follow along and prod us when we start to go off track.'

'And the men in the dragon boat?' I asked.

'Were to keep us from escaping by sea.' Alexander paused. 'It's not an ideal situation. We don't know how many are following us and how many were lured into following Phaleria. Hopefully, Axiom will give us some respite with his story. I'm not counting on it, though. We'll have to make plans. For now, we must rest and get our strength back. They won't attack us.'

'Why?' Demos frowned. 'We were outnumbered. Why not just attack?'

'In Orce, there were too many people around. And they've split up.' I said thoughtfully. 'They can't risk injuring Paul or Alexander. They need them. Am I right?' I asked Alexander.

'I believe so.' He tousled Paul's hair. 'Never fear, Son. The oracle said I would find my soul in the north, and that's where we're headed.'

We looked at one another. The sun was sparkling in little pinpricks of light as it filtered through the immense pine trees, and the air was a cool greenish colour and smelt like fresh pine cones and pine needles heating

17

slowly in the sunshine. It was hard to feel threatened in a place like this. Maybe Alexander was right.

Afterwards, he and Nearchus went hunting while Demos and Yovanix stayed to guard us – although we trusted Alexander's instincts. It made sense. The druids had known for some time where we were headed; it wasn't a mystery. The only thing that might have stopped Alexander had been Plexis, so they'd tried to kill him. Luckily, he was tough. Then they watched to see what we'd do. When we headed inland, it had surprised them into showing themselves, but they had faded away when they were sure we were heading in the direction they wanted.

What exactly *was* waiting for us in the north? A Paleolithic tribe of people called the Eaters of the Dead, a thief of souls called Voltarrix, a bunch of druids who thought Paul could twist time, and a lost soul. No wonder I was nervous.

I pushed a lock of hair out of my eyes. Paul was whittling a piece of tender pinewood into a semblance of a dog under the watchful guidance of Yovanix, who could carve anything from a block of wood. Paul's face still had the smooth, round cheeks of youth. His eyes narrowed as he concentrated on his carving.

'O *"Child of the pure unclouded brow and dreaming eyes of wonder!"*,' I said, then stopped. The poem was too close to my own time. It made me feel the chasm that separated me from everything I understood and exaggerated my feeling of helplessness. And I didn't usually feel so helpless. I was pretty tough. Not many people, having been abandoned in a time not their own, would have survived. But I had. Was it because I'd been raised by two utterly ruthless people, or was it something in my genes that made me grit my teeth and go on when most people would have given up in despair? I didn't know. So far I'd managed to survive, and I suppose I could keep on surviving. However, I'd also learned the difference between mere survival and living. For the first time since I'd been stuck three thousand years in the past, I was frightened of the unknown.

Alexander came back with a large rabbit. He soon had it skinned and stuffed with a mixture of onion and some greens that Nearchus had picked. I knew almost nothing about edible plants. Even Paul knew more than I did. I could tell the difference between a silicon mini-microprocessor made in Germany and a biotechnical chip from China, but that wouldn't help me now. Most of my schooling was useless here, although my knowledge of the future *had* helped save Plexis and had certainly saved Alexander. But we'd stepped off the timeline when I saved them. We navigated in unknown territory and, as it said on an ancient globe, *'Hic sunt dracones'* – here be dragons. Did Alexander realize how dangerously close we were to alerting the Time-Correctors to our situation?

I lowered my lashes and looked at my husband. He still had all the power and grace he'd possessed ten years ago when I'd first met him on the banks of the Euphrates. He had been twenty-three then, just starting on the amazing journey that would take him halfway across the known world and set him up as the greatest conqueror the world had ever known.

For a few years, Alexander had been the catalyst in a change that had rocked the world. For the first time East met West. A breach had been created that was like a sudden opening in a dam that let water come surging through. Only, instead of water, it was new ideas, trade, philosophy, science, and religion that flooded the world. Now every historical time-line would have a mark with Alexander's name next to it. Thirty cities would carry his name to the future. His legend would be translated into every language on the globe. He would be present in four major religions, as a demon, a saint, a hero, or a mystery. His tomb would remain undiscovered. And that was just in the future.

People still turned and followed him with their eyes when they crossed his path. They didn't know who he was, but he had something about him, a glow that even a blind healer had felt. When she first met him she had touched him with a hand that shook. 'It can't be,' she'd kept saying softly. Then tears had poured down her face. 'What I would give, just for a minute, to be able to look upon your face,' she'd murmured.

It had shaken me. Since his faked death, I had grown used to having him for my own without the hundreds of generals, soldiers, satraps, and other people constantly begging to see him.

Decisions. His whole life had been full of decisions and plans. He'd started an adventure and swept us all after him like the tail of a comet. Everyone had relied upon him. They had turned towards him for everything short of breathing, and I often wondered at the strength of his shoulders to carry an empire. But he carried it as easily as he breathed.

Half the world had called him 'king' when he was thirty-two years old – and then he'd died.

He knew I was watching him. He always felt the weight of my gaze. He told me it was like a cool touch. However, he only looked at me for the space of a smile, then bent back over his work.

I was shaken because I had realized how vital he was to us. We still relied on him and followed him blindly. I wondered, in that second, just how much we were responsible for his melancholy. We smothered him with our love, our devotion, and our inability to separate ourselves from him.

We rested for a day and a night, eating rabbit and drinking cold water from a nearby stream. Nearchus speared fish for our breakfast. After eating, we moved on. Our stomachs were full, but so were our minds. Everyone was thinking about what Alexander had told us. We were being followed, herded as it were, to the land of the Eaters of the Dead.

Plexis walked the slowest, so he set our pace. When his arm hurt too much to go on, he sank to the ground and that's where we made camp. At first he drove himself, but then Alexander managed to persuade him that there was no rush. After that we rested more often, and Plexis slowly got his strength back.

I liked walking through the forest. The tall pines were

far enough apart to make large corridors. The pine needles made a springy carpet. It was too early in the spring for ants, so we could sit anywhere and relax. The weather was clement until the third day.

We sat under a lean-to, expertly made by Yovanix, and watched as the rain fell through the trees. Some drops made their way through the roof and fell sizzling into the fire – or icily down our necks. Our conversation lagged. No one knew what lay ahead, and we were apprehensive. No, let's make that *terribly* apprehensive. It showed in the way Nearchus kept polishing his sword, the way Yovanix jumped every time anyone said his name, or the way Paul couldn't get to sleep at night.

'I'm afraid that there will be another sacrifice,' he told me, as we huddled out of the rain. 'I won't go through another one.'

'Neither will I,' I told him.

'I dream about it almost every night as it is,' he said glumly. 'It's not a nightmare any more, not really anyway, but it still frightens me. And I don't think I could stand seeing another man killed in front of me.'

'I'm sorry,' I said softly.

'Don't feel bad. It's enough having Father feeling bad about everything. He's not himself any more, it worries me.' He was whispering now, his voice tickling my ear. The rain was making a pleasant patter on the roof of criss-crossed branches above our heads, and I was feeling sleepy.

'I miss Chiron and Cleopatra,' I said softly.

'So do I. It gave me an awful shock to see Papa, is he

better now?' Paul always referred to Plexis as 'Papa'.

'He'll be fine. He's been wounded worse, you know. Why, once he spent three days in a coma. When he woke up he didn't remember a thing about the battle.' I shook my head. 'He had no idea where he was. He was persuaded that we were still in Bactria, although we'd been in India for months by then.'

Paul made a face. 'I never saw India.'

'Maybe someday we'll go back. Your father loved it there,' I told him. Our whispers were as soft as the rustle of the branches in the rain. The sky was growing progressively darker. I yawned. It wasn't the night; it was simply a storm moving across the sky like some slouching beast. Lightning flickered in its black belly, and thunder growled at us. The men put more wood on the fire, and we huddled around its warm brightness waiting for the rain to end. I fell asleep waiting.

A pine needle tickling my nose and the high trilling of a songbird woke me. I opened one eye, then another. The silence was odd. It was rare that I woke before everyone else. Usually there was someone sitting guard, keeping the fire going if there were a chill, or doing some quiet chore like mending clothes or polishing swords. However, there didn't seem to be any movement around me. It didn't worry me overmuch. The quiet was peaceful.

I could see the sun filtering through the trees. It was promising to be a beautiful day. I sat up as silently as I could, intending to slip out of the shelter and attend to my needs. The men were sleeping soundly. Paul stirred as I stepped over him but otherwise didn't move. Even Cerberus only dug his muzzle deeper under his master's arm and went on dreaming.

Once out in the open, I stood up very straight and took a deep breath of fresh air. If you've always lived in the modern world, and never had the chance to take a trip back in time, then you can never imagine how sweet the air was before the invention of fossil fuels. In my day, the earth was surrounded in a faint haze of pollution. Here, there was nothing but the faint scent of wood smoke. Otherwise, the air was as clean and pristine as the beginning of the world. The water was clean, the air was clean, the ocean was full of fish, and wild animals still roamed the forests.

As a matter of fact, there was one right in front of me.

Nothing too scary, just a large, grey wolf. He was sitting in a clearing staring at me, and something in his yellow gaze was reassuring. He was not hungry, and his eyes seemed to tell me that he was just curious about the pale, two-legged beast shuffling noisily through the forest. It was *his* forest. He lived there. We were just passing through, but he had been born beneath the towering pines and would live his whole life there before dying beneath the very same trees. We were his guests for the short time we stayed there.

There was a swift stream nearby, and I washed myself. I was very careful to leave everything just as I'd found it.

The wolf had vanished silently. I suppose he was somewhere close by keeping an eye on us. The thought that maybe it was a druid flickered like a spark through my mind, but three thousand years of civilization put the spark out as if I'd dumped a whole bucket of water on it. Absurd. People don't change themselves into animals. They simply can't. It is impossible, going against all the laws of science and nature. Matter doesn't change into other matter. The wolf was a wolf and that was that.

Of course, I'd come across a monkey claiming to be a druid. He could write in Greek on a wax tablet and pluck silver coins out of purses, but even that could be explained – by thin layers of wax, by patient training. I didn't for an instant believe the monkey had really once been a man.

Or did I? I sat at the water's edge and stared at the flowing stream. Small green leaves floated in eddies. I plucked one and nibbled it. Watercress was one of the edible plants I was capable of recognizing. I sighed for no particular reason and glanced up at the sky, visible through the canopy. Sunlight dappled my face and arms. A trout splashed in the stream, startling me. I wished I knew what was going to happen next. I had the frightening feeling that I was cut off from the world. I hated the way we were being herded along towards an unknown destination. There had to be a way to escape, or at least turn the situation more towards our advantage.

What frightened me the most was that a group of powerful men had stolen Alexander's soul somehow and had decided to change the future by using Paul to unite the tribes of Gaul. If that happened, the Gauls would defeat the Roman Empire. Progress would be stopped.

The druids were leery of writing and still made human sacrifices. If they succeeded in their plans, history, as I knew it, would be erased, along with Alexander, me, and everyone we knew and loved.

Chapter Three

I walked back to the shelter and was disconcerted to find Plexis sitting alone in front of the fire. As I arrived, he motioned to me to sit next to him and to be quiet. I obeyed. I'd been in the army too long to hesitate an instant.

We sat in silence for an hour. The fire in front of us crackled merrily, and the wind picked up making the tree branches whisper. Then Plexis smiled at me and said softly, 'We're on our own now. Alexander has decided to split us up into three groups.'

I just stared at him. Finally, licking dry lips, I asked, 'Where are the others, and why?'

'Nearchus and Yovanix are in the first group. They have gone ahead. Paul, Alexander, and Demos are perhaps an hour's march behind them. You and I will bring up the rear. We're to wait another hour and then follow. The idea is to separate the people watching us.'

'But we'll be separated too!' I was agitated. The idea didn't seem to make any sense to me. 'There's safety in numbers,' I said.

'Hush. Listen. Alexander wants to give us time that's all. We're buying more time. Our pursuers know I'm wounded, so they won't find it strange to see us lagging. He thinks that after a while the people who are watching us will concentrate on Paul and him, leaving you and me alone. If we are not being watched, we can act if need be. Do you understand?'

'Not really,' I said nervously. 'How will we know when we're left alone?'

'I think we'll know within a day or two. Today I'm going to pretend to take a turn for the worse and we're not going to go further than the stream. Tomorrow we'll start out as usual, but we'll go slower and slower, and Alexander will take care to leave marks for us to follow. I think there will come a time when we'll be left alone. They will assume we're following.'

'All right. I suppose it's as good a plan as any.' I sighed and then shivered. 'I'm hungry. Did they leave us some food?'

Plexis shrugged. 'No, but Nearchus left a fishing spear. You can go get us some lunch.'

'If you're going to rely on me, I'm afraid you'll starve to death,' I said. However, nothing ventured, nothing gained. I went back to the stream and stood for an hour on the bank, spear poised, waiting for an unwary trout.

We ate watercress for lunch.

By teatime, my stomach was growling. Plexis and I walked a mile or so into the forest and saw the signs Alexander had left us. He'd carved arrows on trees by peeling the bark off, pointing the way we should go.

When he changed tack he left another mark. Plexis could follow the faint marks left on the ground, he didn't really need the tree carvings, but I couldn't follow their tracks.

'Are you sure they went that way?' I asked, peering at a thicket.

'I'm sure.' Plexis was laconic. He didn't need to pretend to be wounded. His wound was extremely painful; I could tell by the way he walked. He set his feet down carefully and cradled his arm with his good hand, wincing whenever the ground got too rough.

'Will you be all right?' I asked, for the hundredth time that day.

'Fine.' He sank to the ground. 'Well, maybe not fine.' He looked up at me and I swore under my breath. His face was drawn with pain.

'Can you try and find some arrowroot?' he asked. 'We can eat that for dinner. I think I'll rest here. I'll try and make a fire later.' He leaned back against a tree and closed his eyes.

'Don't worry, I'll get us some dinner,' I said bravely.

I was gone for two hours. The light had faded when I made my way back to the deep thicket. I'd found arrowroot and dandelions, and in a shallow stream I'd managed to capture six crayfish. Plexis had begun to build a fire, so I fetched some firewood and wild cabbage leaves. When I was returned, Plexis fashioned a pot from the leaves and we boiled the crayfish in that. The meal was meagre. Afterwards, we wrapped ourselves in our cloaks and snuggled together. Worn out with pain and hunger, Plexis fell asleep quickly. I stayed awake to feed the fire, then lay down next to Plexis.

I woke up at dawn. Nights were getting shorter; I'd only slept about two hours. The fire had died down to a bed of cold, grey ashes. The air was chill, but my cloak kept me warm. There was not a sound to be heard. The birds hadn't started singing and the wind had died. Carefully, I eased out of the thicket. There was a stream nearby; hopefully I'd have more luck fishing this morning.

Breakfast for me was clear water. I took a cabbage leaf and made a cup, drinking deeply, then I washed, sitting in the freezing stream just long enough for my legs to get blue in the icy water. I dried with my cloak then dressed. My clothes were getting grubby, but I wanted to wait for a hot day before I washed them. I hung my cloak on a low branch to air and broke a twig from a birch tree. As I cleaned my teeth, I walked slowly upstream looking for a likely spot to fish. When I found a deep pool, I took Nearchus's spear and tried to gaff some trout. I could see them, swimming lazily in the water, sometimes they would leave the shade of the bank and the sun would speckle them gold and green. My stomach hurt, I was starving. After twenty fruitless stabs into the water I sighed, put the spear down, and started to search for arrowroot. Instead, I found a clump of dogtooth violets. I dug up their roots, rubbing the mud off them with my fingers. Maybe we could boil them and call them lunch?

Plexis joined me sometime later. He still looked

30

peaked, but he managed to spear three large fish. He was an accomplished hunter, and if he'd been feeling better, we would have had more than enough food. Then he sat and watched as I cleaned them and started the fire.

Plexis had your basic fire-making kit in his leather pouch: a piece of pyrite; some flint; and cotton soaked in alcohol. I whacked the stones together trying for a spark. I didn't do this often, so it took me forever to make the fire. Once, I smashed my thumb and dropped the stones, swearing heartily. Plexis was shocked at all the bad language I'd picked up. I told him it was from Nearchus.

Finally, a spark burst into flame. Plexis carefully fed it pine needles and bits of fluff until the fire was big enough to handle dry sticks. I sat back, sucked my wounded thumb, and wondered when matches would be invented. Probably not for a while.

We grilled the trout and boiled the roots. The meal was delicious, but I think, at that point, I would have happily eaten raw fish and muddy roots.

'Let me see your arm,' I said to Plexis when we'd finished eating.

He nodded and carefully shrugged off his tunic. The wound on his forearm was healing well, but the torn biceps was swollen and painful to the touch. I boiled water in a cabbage leaf pot then washed the cut with the hottest water he could stand. Afterwards, I boiled his bandages while he rested in a patch of watery sunlight.

'We'll stay here today,' I said to him. 'I want to keep putting boiled water on your arm, maybe that will help. I wish Alexander were here. He always has a clove of garlic or two tucked away.'

'Garlic?' Plexis smiled. 'I have garlic. Do you want to use it to clean my wound? Rather a waste, don't you think?'

'No, I don't think so,' I said crossly, taking the garlic from him, peeling it and crushing it into the hot water. 'It will help disinfect your wound.'

'Disinfect". Is that another of your words from the future?' He flinched while I washed his arm. To distract him, I asked if he wanted a story. 'Yes, please. The one about how you were sent here. You never did explain it to me.'

'Because it's too complicated. The mechanisms of the voyage are impossible to explain to a layman.'

'In other words, you have no idea how it works.' He grinned, then hissed as I probed a bit too deeply.

'Sorry.'

'Am I right?'

'You're right.' I finished bandaging his arm and sat cross-legged in front of him. 'I have no idea how it works. However, I do know that it works on three levels, atomic, magnetic, and spatial. There's also a phenomenon related to temperature. When you voyage in time your body is first frozen, the atoms separated, sent into a magnetic beam, and projected through time and space. When your atoms arrive in their programmed time-location, they first reconstitute themselves, then they thaw, and you wake up in another time.'

'Aren't you worried that your atoms will put themselves together in a different arrangement? That

32

you'll end up as a goat, say, instead of a person?'

I was startled. 'No,' I said slowly. 'Atoms are put together in an immutable pattern. You can pull them apart, but they bounce back to the same position they were in before. That's why water can freeze, become solid, then thaw out and still be water, and not become oil, for example.'

'I see.' Plexis said. 'So, in your time, can atoms be taken apart and rearranged? Can you create other things besides water with water atoms?' His questions were always tricky.

'We can. In my time, scientists have discovered many different ways of using atoms, either in their natural state or in artificial combinations.' I broke off and frowned. I wasn't sure just how much to tell him.

'And one of the ways they use the atoms is for weapons, is it not?' Plexis peered at my face. His eyes were searching. He could see right into my heart.

'That's right.' I shook my head. 'But I don't want to talk about that, please? It's like, like …'

'A sacrilege? In this time and place?' Plexis's voice was gentle.

'Yes. That's what it's like. It's worse than a rape. It's worse than anything you can imagine,' I said bleakly.

'Then tell me another story. In the three thousand years that separate your time from mine, there must have been countless storytellers who wove their tales. Are there any you love the best? Can you tell me one that I'll understand and love the way you do? Do poets still recite adventures like Homer did? Do they still tell stories to entertain, or have all the poets died and the stories vanished?' His voice wavered.

'They haven't vanished. I'll have to think though; I love so many stories.' I sighed.

He reached over and touched my cheek lightly. 'Tell me you love me.'

I looked up at him. His expression was serious. I smiled and tucked a stray curl back behind his ear. 'Of course I love you,' I whispered.

He looked at me through long lashes. 'I love you too, Ashley of the Sacred Sandals, and I have a confession to make.' He paused. 'When you were kidnapped, so long ago in Arbeles, it was I who arranged it.'

Arbeles. The word was like a stone thrown into a pool of water. The ripples spread, and I remembered the panic of my abduction, the four days of fear spent in the bottom of a wooden boat heading for an unknown destination. Then the desolation of a year in my temple prison in a silence that no one would break, even when my son was born and stolen from me.

I closed my eyes and found I was trembling. I looked down at my hands. They were gripped together, fingers twisted, knuckles white. Even now, even ten years later, the memory felt like a nightmare.

'Why?' I finally asked. I didn't dare look at him. I was afraid to. My gaze was as frigid as an arctic winter – and that was when I was happy. Right now it would freeze the atoms in his eyeballs.

'Look at me,' he said.

'Please, Plexis, don't make me ...'

34

He took my chin in his good hand and tipped it back. 'Look at me, Ashley. I did it because I was afraid. I was afraid that you were a minion of Hades, and …'

'I mean, why tell me now?' I kept my eyes squeezed shut.

'Look at me.'

I opened my eyes. He was staring at me, his face solemn. 'I'm telling you this because I want you to know. There's no other reason than that.'

'Because you think you're going to die?'

'A confession?' He raised one eyebrow. 'Maybe, who knows.' His voice had gone so quiet it was as if he were speaking to himself. I had to strain to catch his words. 'Perhaps I am afraid of dying after all. I suppose it's not something one gets used to, although I've died twice already, haven't I?' He turned his gaze to me. 'I told you because I had to. Because I love you, and I can't keep it a secret any longer.'

'Does Alexander know?'

'No. Nobody except Olympias and me.'

'I'm sorry,' I whispered.

Now he was surprised. Whatever reaction he expected, it wasn't that one. 'Sorry? Why?'

'Because I know Olympias.' I reached over and took his face in my hands. My eyes were filling with tears so his face was a blur. 'I always suspected it was you,' I said. 'But I didn't care after I got to know you.'

He didn't speak. After a minute he disengaged himself and he got up. When he left the circle of fire I saw that night had fallen. The darkness swallowed him, but I let him go. Privacy is something we all need at one time or another.

I fed the fire, watching as tongues of flame flickered among the branches. Sparks flew off the resinous wood in red showers, and I remembered all the other times I'd sat in front of a fire at night. The memories I had of electric lights were fading. Soon I would be unable to recall the glow of a neon tube or the blinking, coloured lights on a Christmas tree – or the cold, white light in the Institute of Time Travel and Study sending room. I had stared at that light for an hour while my blood slowly froze and my atoms were registered and disunited, their matrix sent spinning through time in a magnetic vacuum.

I could remember that now, but perhaps in a few years it would fade. I closed my eyes, the images sharpening in my mind. I saw the nurse bending over me with the glowing needle and could almost feel the shock as she inserted it into my arm. She looked at me with eyes almost as cold as my own and she said, 'Soon you won't feel a thing.' Someone behind her had laughed and said, 'That won't change anything for her.'

At the time it was true. The only thing I was feeling was apprehension. I was going back in time to meet a man I'd been in love with ever since I'd first read about him in my history class. Love? Maybe not love, but certainly infatuation. I was consumed with a burning curiosity about someone who had swept through the known world and irrevocably changed it. He could change people's lives after meeting them for just a moment, and I wanted to find out why. I needed to understand the emotions that he conjured. *I wanted to feel.* I wanted to come face to face with a raw passion, because in my time none of that existed. What the nurse had said about me was true. I had no feelings for anyone.

Of course, I said nothing about that on my admission. I stayed well within the clinical, detached scientific approach the Time-Senders required of all their Chrononauts. I'd won the contest and had been sent back in time.

Then I'd been trapped here; kidnapped by Alexander the Great who thought I was Persephone, the terrible Queen of the Dead. He saw me in the freezing, magnetic time-beam and he thought I was being taken back down to Hades' realm. Every Greek knew that Persephone hated it down there and wanted to be saved. He thought he was doing me a huge favour. He also thought I'd be so grateful, I'd help him conquer Persia, vanquish Darius, and then we'd rule together from his favourite city: Alexandria near Egypt.

Things didn't quite work out that way. For one thing, I wasn't the goddess he thought I was. I was *far* from grateful – I was terrified. And before I could fully explain who I was and where I'd come from, I'd been kidnapped once again and held prisoner in a place called Mazda in the temple of Gulu, the Assyrian goddess of healing. The memories of that time were painful. I'd discovered I was pregnant and had my first child, Paul, surrounded by silence. No one would speak to me. Paul was taken away when he was ten days old, and I nearly lost my mind.

I learned the hard way about emotions. I fell in love with Alexander, but I didn't dare believe he'd love me in return. I fell in love with my infant son, but he was wrenched from my arms. When my baby was taken from me, all the pain and anger I'd kept bottled up inside burst out. A psychologist could probably explain it better – say I'd been traumatized and suffered short-term memory loss. Whatever it was, I have no recollection of anything until three months later, when an earthquake razed Mazda.

Was Paul really protected by the moon goddess? When his life was in danger, an earthquake destroyed the temple where I'd been imprisoned and I escaped to Babylon, where the priestess told me I'd find my baby. He was meant to be a sacrifice for the hungry god Marduk. However, Darius found out about Paul and took him, and another baby was put in his place. I made it to the temple in time to save the baby from the sacrifice. Marduk's jaws closed on nothing and they broke, crushing the high priest.

There, in Babylon, I met Alexander again. A year had gone by, a year where he thought I'd been taken back to Hades and that he'd never see me again. Time had changed Alexander as well. He had become colder, harder – and when he found out about Paul, he was even more obsessed with Darius, because Darius had taken our son and had fled to Persepolis.

Why was I torturing myself? All those years spent trekking across Asia, searching for our child while

Alexander conquered Persia, were terrible years. Darius had been killed, silly fool that he was, and Paul was taken east, always eastward.

For five years we searched for our son. In the beginning, Alexander had simply wanted to consolidate his hold on Persia and return to Alexandria near Egypt to rule his kingdom. Instead, he dragged his entire army to the Sacred Valley of Nysa in India to find Paul. And then we had to leave him behind.

How can a mother contemplate abandoning her child? Even now the memory was a pain so sharp it brought tears to my eyes. But I had left him there. I thought he would be safe. I would not have been able to protect him from Alexander's enemies, nor from Roxanne, after Alexander's death. My son would be safe, I'd thought, in the beautiful valley where I would find him when the adventure was over. It would end when Alexander died. Then I was sure I'd be able to slip away, return to India, and find my son.

I hadn't counted on love. I never dared hope that Alexander would love me, but he did. My love was so great that I braved the Time-Senders and saved him from his death, smuggling him out of Babylon one sultry night after freezing him in the magnetic beam and killing the parasites that were in his blood.

Paul was with us now, and Plexis was here. Plexis, who had looked upon me first as an enemy, then as an ally, and finally, as a lover. My lover, who'd organized my kidnapping because he was sure I was a spy from Hades, or worse, Persephone the Terrible, the Queen of

39

Ice and Darkness, with a frozen and empty heart.

I put another branch on the fire and my eyes followed a shower of red sparks as they leapt skywards. I thought of Plexis. It surprised him when we fell in love. We complemented each other. We were two halves in love with the same whole, Alexander.

I didn't mind. I'd shared Alexander with his three other wives, and I knew what it was like to be in love with a legend. Plexis and I fell in love with one another, and even now I had trouble separating the two men in my mind. They were both mine, I was theirs, and we were a family. A family made up of three adults, three children, freed slaves, and Nearchus. I smiled in the darkness. The warmth of the fire was kind to my bones. I felt content here in the great woods, surrounded by the night and alone. Almost alone.

I never heard Plexis coming. He appeared in the circle of firelight and sat beside me. I reached for him and he leaned into me.

'I've been thinking,' I said. 'About everything. Everything that happened and everything about us. And do you know what? I can't explain any of it. It simply happened, and I was swept along as if I were a leaf in a stream. Nothing I planned happened the way I thought it would. Everything I ever knew, or thought I knew about life, death, love, and hate turned out to be wrong. Do you want to know something else? I don't care. I really don't care.'

'It's the magic of Alexander,' he said softly. 'I have been thinking as well, and I've decided that anything that's ever happened to me was because Alexander wanted it so.' He was quiet for a moment, then he added, 'Except you. I wanted you for myself. And now I have you, and I can't bear the thought of losing you.'

I was startled. 'Why would you lose me?'

'I don't know. Because of the kidnapping. Because of Olympias. I know her too, and I understand what you meant. A woman who uses her son to gain power is a woman without a soul. I was her minion, wasn't I? I followed her orders and we hurt you.' He broke off and stared at the fire. 'When I was dying I dreamed of her. Perhaps that is why I needed to confess, or perhaps it is simply because I wanted to cleanse my soul. You make me feel clean and new again. It's a power you have. The ice in your gaze purifies me.' He sighed. 'When I stayed behind in Alexandria, I didn't think I would miss you so much. But I did. Each day without you was sadness, each night I spent alone was emptiness.'

I said nothing; one side of my mouth quirked in a smile, but I knew he was sincere. 'I longed to see you too. Alexander and I spoke of you often, and every time we saw something new we discussed how we were going to explain it to you.'

'Truly?' He grinned, pleased, then blinked and glanced back at the fire.

'Truly.'

'So you forgive me for causing you such pain in Arbeles?' When he blinked, tears slid down his cheeks.

'Of course I do.' I sighed. Time had ways of changing everything, but one thing seemed as immutable as my

41

atoms: the love I had for Plexis and Alexander. Two men for whom I would give my own life. When Plexis reached his hand under my tunic, I shivered with delight. Our lovemaking was slow and careful because of his arm. He lay on his back on the soft moss and his eyes were black in the firelight. There were silver streaks on his face, traces of tears, but I loved him more for them. I loved him more for his fear, and for his pride, and for the way he tipped his head back and cried out when the waves rushed over us, sweeping us along like leaves upon a fast moving stream.

We were helpless, ultimately, in the presence of love. It almost made me start believing in fate.

Chapter Four

We managed to lose the druids who herded us. Or rather, Plexis shook them off our trail. They were now in front of us. When he realized we were alone, he sat on the forest floor and shook for an hour. He had been concentrating for days, hiding our footprints, doubling back, making false leads, and making sure it looked like we were blundering after Alexander's obvious path. The path he continued to leave for us carved into the trunks of pine trees. Plexis contrived to let the men following us pass, and now we were on our own. We were no longer being watched, and we could go where we pleased. The relief was almost sickening in its intensity.

I thought he was ill and it frightened me. Then he told me what he'd done and how he'd managed it, and I put my arms around him and laughed. We had a chance to save our companions.

'Are you finished laughing at me?' His voice was low.

'Yes,' I giggled. 'Can you stand up?'

'I think so.' He chuckled softly. 'I feel as light as the breeze. It's the relief, isn't it? Look at my hand, I can't hold it still.'

He was right. I took it and held it tightly. 'What do we do next?'

'We have to find out where they're being taken, and we have to see if we can help them. It's not over yet. The druids are in front of us, but that doesn't mean they've forgotten us.'

'It does mean we're not as important to them as Alexander and Paul.'

'That's right. We're not essential to their plans.'

'What plans?'

He looked at me out of the corner of his eye. 'I think you know what they are trying to do,' he said.

'I know what they want, but I don't know how they're planning to go about it,' I said.

'Me neither. Rituals are different here. The druids are a strange group.'

'Did you ever study their religion with Aristotle?' I asked, curious.

'I studied the Etruscans with Aristotle, not the Gauls. He only spoke of them briefly. Supposedly they believe that your soul can go into another body.'

'Reincarnation?' I was amazed.

'No, not exactly. It takes a certain type of druid to remove the soul from a dying man's body. They call that druid the 'Thief of Souls'. Ashley! What's the matter?'

I couldn't speak for a while. Plexis's words were like a punch. Finally the urge to vomit passed and I unclenched my jaw.

'Don't you know who is waiting for Alexander? Voltarrix, the one called the Thief of Souls. Do you know

44

what that means?' I asked.

'It means we'd better hurry,' he said laconically. But his face was pale, and when we looked at each other, the fear we felt was reflected in our eyes.

The deeper into the forest we went, the colder it became. Almost everywhere we looked, there were signs of the tribe whose lands we had entered. Plexis was good at spotting the lichen-covered carvings on rocks, the tree branches that had been cut a certain way, and the sacred springs with the ceremonial rocks nearby. We skirted these after seeing the first one up close. It was covered with dried blood, and a raven's wing tied to a branch above it turned and twisted in the wind.

That evening we camped in the roots of a massive fallen tree. Plexis told me how to use pine boughs to make a thick mattress and a small fire kept the chill away. We were sitting on a foot-thick mattress of fragrant pine. Fragrant, *prickly* pine. I winced as another needle poked my thigh.

'It could be worse,' said Plexis, glancing up at the sky.

'In what way?' I asked peevishly. Cramps nagged low in my back and I knew what that meant. The thought of not having any clean clothes or clean cotton pads was depressing.

'It could be raining,' said Plexis, stroking my cheek, trying to coax a smile from me.

I looked up. In the brief night, a million, billion stars blazed. The tall pine trees seemed to point at them, their tips like spires reaching towards the sky.

'Or it could be snowing, that would be worse,' I said.

'We could be surrounded by hungry wolves, and have no fire to protect us,' Plexis tossed another branch onto the greedy flames.

'We could each be alone,' I said. 'That would be the worst.'

'But we're together.' He smiled, but his eyes were serious.

'I missed you so much, we all did.'

'I know. When I discovered the druids were looking for Paul, I didn't hesitate. I knew I had to find you quickly.'

'What did you think of Gaul?' I asked, curious.

'It's very primitive. The cities are nothing like Athens or Babylon.'

'Give them time,' I said. 'The houses are very comfortable though, didn't you think? They have to be, I suppose, seeing how rude the climate is.'

'I didn't waste time sightseeing,' said Plexis. 'I was in a hurry.'

'I still can't believe you came. It was so sweet.'

'Sweet?' He wrinkled his nose. 'I don't know if I'd call it "sweet".'

'What then?'

'Heroic? Brave?'

'Brave then. Heroically brave. Thank you. And you nearly died.'

'It was close.' His face was next to mine. I leaned over and kissed him. His lips were soft in a prickle of new beard. Since we'd been travelling through the woods, he hadn't shaved. He looked distinctly barbarian now.

Plexis sighed against my kiss. His eyes were hooded. Lashes brushed against my cheek, and a stray curl tumbled across his forehead. His hair was tangled. I pulled him over and he lay across my lap. Using my fingers, I combed out his curls, smoothing his hair. His breathing deepened and evened out. Soon he was fast asleep. I watched him fondly. Then I carefully curled myself around him and fell asleep.

During the short night the fire burnt low and the chill woke us. I was shivering and my teeth were chattering. Plexis sat up and poked the embers into life, adding twigs until flames appeared. The fire soon warmed us and I felt my muscles relaxing. I held my hands towards the fire.

'What time is it?' I asked.

Plexis looked at the pale grey sky. 'We only slept for three hours,' he said.

'How long before full light?'

'Soon.'

The half-light was quiet. Dawn was minutes away.

I snuggled close to him and smiled contentedly.

'Tell me, what happens to Athens?' he asked.

'Athens?' I paused, gathering my thoughts. 'It's a very popular tourist spot. They've rebuilt a good many temples and the Acropolis is nearly intact, although it's a copy. The first one was destroyed, and then the second one, but the third one is still there. There's lots of graffiti

47

on it. You'd feel right at home,' I joked.

'And India? Is it still there?'

'Oh, it's still there. It's changed. I never went there. The world I live in is divided into two parts, East and West. They don't communicate with each other. It happened because of a war. Entire nations perished.'

Plexis looked shocked. 'Whole nations?'

'Millions died in 2050 AD. You can't imagine how awful that war was. I like it better here. Please, don't make me talk about my time,' I begged.

'But I want to know; what happened after the year 2050 AD? You say that date as if it's a curse.'

'It was.' I sighed. 'It was the start of the Third World War, a war that nearly wiped out the planet. The East was pitted against the West. Africa was totally annihilated. The fighting, for some reason, took place mostly on that continent. Then there was a famine, and a virus that killed off most survivors. Ten years later there were only a few million people left. They created the "Great Divide", and separated the world into two halves. Then they closed off communication between them. I was born three hundred years later. Three centuries of relative calm as the world rebuilt itself from the ashes. A new renaissance took place, and the West developed while the East sank into ashes, and that's how the world is in my time.'

'You lived in the West? Was your world prosperous?'

'Very rich and comfortable. And shallow, and futile, and petty and contrived. Nothing matters except wealth. People don't care what is happening to the rest of the world, and that always tormented me.'

'What is the "Great Divide"?' Plexis asked.

'It's a huge wall, surrounded by a vast no-man's land. It's a crime for anyone to try to approach the wall, and the Easterners haven't been heard from since it was built.' I shook my head. 'In the East, shortly after the Great Divide, the women started a rebellion. It was called the "Fatima Jihad" by those reporting it. Some say the women were all killed, and that's why the silence has lasted so long; because there are no more people left. Others say there are only clones, which have been outlawed in the West.'

'What's a "clone"?'

'A copy of a person made by taking a morsel of flesh and growing a whole new person.'

Plexis swallowed nervously. 'Ashley?'

'Yes?'

'You can stop talking now. I think I'm going to have nightmares for weeks. I wish I'd never asked. Isn't there anything nice about the future?' His voice cracked.

'I'm sorry.' I tipped my face to the sky and closed my eyes. 'There is music and laughter and poems. There are still banquets and children go to school in the morning and play in the afternoon. The seas have been cleaned and fish are making a comeback. The air will be clean some day, and people are more careful about population. I think that, in a few hundred years from my time, the wall will fall. People are curious, and they will want to trade or simply talk. I hope that the lesson has been learned, and that the extremists on both sides will be pushed aside. Most people are decent, if you get to know them. They stay the same throughout the ages, loving stories and songs and beauty.'

I opened my eyes. Plexis was gazing at me. How much had he understood? Far too much, judging from his expression.

'Did you feel it was a terrible time to live?'

'No. I didn't think so when I was there. Although I did feel the shallowness and the waste. It was as if Pandora's box had been opened again and everything let out.'

'Hope remained,' said Plexis.

'Hope? What is hope,' I asked angrily. 'There is no more compassion, no more common sense. That's what makes me so sad.'

'It would,' said Plexis, cradling me with his good arm, 'I've rarely seen a woman with so much compassion. Or common sense.' He cuddled me close. 'So don't think about it any more. Your future is so far away that it won't even stir the dust of my bones. We're alive, here and now. The water is sweet, the air is pure, and there are none of those exploding weapons that frighten me so.'

I snuggled against his chest. There was something reassuring about Plexis. No matter what the situation, he still had a sense of humour. Nothing was grim enough to quench it. Nothing, I hoped. I closed my eyes, then fell asleep.

When we woke up again it was late morning. A thick

mist blanketed the ground, swirling around us as we walked through it and leaving sparkling droplets of water on our cloaks. Sunlight dappled the ground. First the light was shell-pink, becoming more golden as the sun climbed higher. Around noon, the mist evaporated, and we could see everything clearly. Plexis studied the ground carefully, moving in concentric circles, looking for a clue to tell us where we were going.

'I thought for sure we'd find something by now,' he said, baffled. He knelt and carefully peered at a likely looking spot then sat back on his heels. 'A fox's track,' he said ruefully. He slapped at his head, then scratched hard, digging his fingers into his hair. 'Ouch! I think the lice here are far bigger than the ones in Persia, don't you?' he asked with a grin.

'Plexis!' I hissed. 'I'm not in the mood for jokes.' He looked crushed, so I said gently, 'besides, that's not lice biting you, it's deer flies. There are swarms around here. When it warms up, we'll be surrounded by them. And there are horseflies and mosquitoes as well.'

'That can only mean two things,' said Plexis, brightening.

'What?'

'There are big animals around, and we're approaching a wetland.'

'Big animals?' I asked, glancing nervously around. What kind of big animal do you …?'

I hadn't finished my sentence when a huge moose surged out of a thicket, crashing noisily through the underbrush. I gave a shrill scream. I'd never seen such a huge beast. It was at least three metres high. However, the moose had no interest in us. It vanished into the forest, disappearing faster than its size seemed to warrant.

'An elephant!' cried Plexis. 'I just saw an elephant with black hair and horns on its head! Amazing! Alexander will never believe me when I tell him about that!' He shook his head. 'But it had no trunk. Its nose was rather long, to be sure, but it had tiny ears and slender legs. If it hadn't been so big, I would have thought it was a deer.'

'Actually, that was a moose,' I said. 'It's the largest member of the deer family, if I remember correctly.'

Plexis was thrilled. 'A moose,' he said reverently. 'Just wait until I tell Alexander. He hasn't seen one yet, has he?' He frowned in the direction the beast had taken. 'For once I want to be able to amaze him.' He dug a parchment out of his belt and made me explain a moose. I couldn't draw, but Plexis could sketch remarkably well. After just a glimpse he had a clear image of the animal, but he made it look like a cross between an elephant and an elk. I told him to make it skinnier and to widen the antlers. When he'd finished, he had a nice drawing of a large bull moose. He was pleased. 'A moose,' he kept muttering to himself.

He picked mushrooms as he walked. I knew nothing about fungi, so I let him do the gathering. It was something everyone at that time did almost without thinking. If they saw something edible, they would squirrel it away in their pouch. The soldiers in

Alexander's army had done that while they marched, and Plexis had been a soldier for more than ten years. When we stopped for the evening, we built a fire and cooked the mushrooms and roots that Plexis had dug up during our march.

I noticed Plexis was moody. He picked up a stick and prodded the fire, then put it down, nearly burning his foot. Then he spilled his dinner on his lap. I thought at first it was because of his arm, but when I asked him he shook his head and sighed. 'I'm worried,' he admitted. 'The others have vanished.'

'What do you mean, "vanished"?'

'I can't find a trace of them. I have no idea if we're still on the right track. At first I thought they'd skirted the mountains, heading due north. Now I'm not so sure. Moreover, I'm wondering if we shouldn't turn back. I want to find their trail.'

'What does it mean? Are we lost?'

'Lost? Of course not. I can find my way back to Orce.' Then his handsome face clouded. 'But I'm beginning to think they were "vanished" on purpose. I think that our plan backfired. The druids have separated us.'

'But, why?' I asked, frightened now. 'Why would Alexander try and lose us?'

'Not Alexander. The people who were following us.'

'They haven't tried to harm us,' I said, uneasily.

'Perhaps they are afraid of you.' He spoke slowly, the weight of his thoughts behind his words.

'That's silly,' I said.

'It wouldn't be the first time people feared you. I don't know what these druids believe, but perhaps they have an underworld, and a king of the underworld, and you are supposed to be his queen.'

'Persephone the Terrible,' I said, giving my title. I nibbled on a mushroom, but worry took away my appetite. 'Will we be able to find them soon?' I asked.

Plexis grinned. 'I can find them.' When he sounded so sure of himself, I believed him. 'We'll leave at first light. Come with me now, I'm going to set some snares. Hopefully we'll have a rabbit or two for dinner tomorrow night.'

'And hopefully we'll be on their trail again,' I muttered.

Breakfast was rabbit and mushrooms, lunch was rabbit and wild onions, and dinner was boiled vegetables and broth made with the rest of the rabbit. Plexis didn't waste a thing.

We covered roughly five parasangs, which was the Persian unit of measurement Alexander used on his marches. They were worth just over five thousand metres, so that meant we hiked about twenty-five kilometres through the forest. Then finally Plexis picked up a faint trail.

He smiled at me and in the violet evening his teeth shone white. 'I've found them.' There was a definite note of smugness in his voice. 'They're ahead of us, and the druids are covering up the trail.'

'How did you find it?' I asked.

'The signs Alexander leaves for us have been erased

54

by the druids. But I found this one. Alexander knows that we were left behind on purpose, or perhaps he simply guessed, or wants to make sure. At any rate, he has started leaving secret signs, ones we used when we were boys in Macedonia.' His voice trailed away and he sighed. 'It seems so very long ago.' He looked glum. 'Long ago and far away.'

'I love hearing stories about you and Alexander when you were little,' I said, to cheer him up.

He brightened. Stories were his favourite things, and he loved both listening to them and telling them. 'Did you hear about the time I visited him in Pella?' he asked.

'When he got Bucephalus? Alexander told me about the horse, but I didn't know you were there as well.'

'Yes, I was there when he got Buci,' he said, giving the horse Alexander's nickname for him. 'Let's see, I was twelve then and Iskander was thirteen. Bucephalus was a full-grown stallion. A trader had brought him to Philip's court to sell him. The price was steep, but the horse was exceptional. They took him out to the field and, one by one, Philip's grooms tried to ride him, but they were all thrown. Philip declared he didn't want the horse, that he was far too expensive for a wild horse, and ordered the trader to take him away. Then Iskander spoke up.'

Plexis's voice grew dreamy. 'He was such an intense boy. I can see him now, standing in front of his father with his hands clenched and his eyes blazing. 'I can ride him! Let me have the horse, Father!' he cried.

'And Philip guffawed. "What? You? You'd better run

55

back to your books, son, this is a real horse not one of your daydreams!".'

'He said that?' I frowned. I knew they didn't get along, but that seemed harsh.

'Philip used to accuse Iskander of being a sissy. He hated the fact he was always reading. Philip couldn't read three lines of Greek. I think he was jealous. Iskander was as handsome as a young god, whereas Philip was crooked with scars and bloated with drinking. He was missing an eye as well. His face could frighten brave men. Anyway, Philip was sure that Iskander was going to disappoint him. You'll never believe me, but Iskander hated going to war with his father.'

'Oh, I think I can believe you,' I said dryly.

'So, there was Iskander, standing in front of his father, challenging him. Philip was taken aback, then he grew angry. "Go ahead and mount the horse then, boy! And if you break your neck, it will be as the gods wish. But hear this. If you fall, you will pay me the full price of the horse." "And if I ride him, he's mine!" Iskander retorted coolly. "*If* you ride him!" Philip burst out laughing again. I was standing nearby. I didn't dare get involved. Iskander was my friend, but I was frightened of Philip. He had a fearsome temper and a heavy hand. He used to beat Iskander. He thrashed him if you want to know the truth. Well, Iskander took the horse from the groom and led him to the centre of the field. I could see him talking to the beast, and soon Bucephalus pricked up his ears and started to listen. Alexander was slight for his age but strong and wiry– despite having a penchant for books,' added Plexis with a wry grin. 'He'd also noticed the horse shied at shadows, so he turned him around until he was facing the setting sun and the shadows were behind them. Then, in one fluid motion, he leapt onto the horse's back. Bucephalus snorted and pranced, but he didn't see any shadows and Iskander was light on his back. Bucephalus let Iskander ride him, and I think Philip was more angry than proud at that moment. Plus, Iskander was a terrible winner; you know how he is. He couldn't help gloating. It's in his nature. He trotted Bucephalus around the pasture, and then he cantered. He was showing off. I was pleased for my friend, but Philip was livid. He paid the trader the full price for the horse and then stormed off to the palace. And Iskander got another thrashing that night.'

'Why?' I was shocked.

'Oh, no reason, really, except that Philip was a brute and Iskander didn't have any respect for him. His father could have thrashed him from one end of Pella to the other, and Iskander would still look at his father with that superior air he has, and Philip would lose his temper and strike him. I used to beg Iskander to show some respect, even if he didn't feel it, but he couldn't. Iskander could never hide his true self. He was always so sure he was right, and that everyone else was wrong, and Philip felt the same way. It made the atmosphere unbearable sometimes. However, it never cowed Iskander. I think that Philip knew he could never break his spirit, and that's why he sent him to study with Aristotle. In his own way, Philip loved Iskander, and he knew he'd kill him if he didn't send him away.' Plexis shrugged. 'Love can show itself in different ways. Philip was incapable of making a tender gesture, but he *was* able to save Iskander's life.'

'Do you think Alexander realized?' I asked.

'No. Certainly not at the beginning. At first, he thought school was just another torture his father had invented for him. Then he grew to know Aristotle. Soon he loved school. He wanted to study everything. He learned things like a sponge sucks up water, thirstily, always asking for more. He wanted to know everything about anything. When Aristotle couldn't answer him, he would get angry! It was funny sometimes. The questions he asked, the utter intensity of his regard. He read voraciously. He wanted to be a doctor, an engineer, a scientist, and an astronomer – everything but a soldier; but that's what his father wanted. Philip recognized his genius and wanted to turn it towards war.'

'Alexander was an incredible leader of men,' I said cautiously.

'I think that for one of his smiles, I would follow him to the ends of the earth,' confessed Plexis. 'And most everyone felt the same way. He was brilliant, and his sheer audacity combined with genius won him battles no one else could have won.'

'And he knew it,' I said.

'And he knew it,' agreed Plexis, grinning broadly.

'Did Alexander kill his father?' I asked.

Plexis drew in his breath. 'Don't ask me that,' he said. 'I was not in Pella at that time, and, despite the rumours,

I never believed Iskander capable of killing his own father.'

'Unless he thought that Philip wasn't really his father.' I chose my words carefully.

Plexis stared at me. 'If you're suggesting Olympias succeeded in convincing Iskander his father was Zeus, you can forget it. That never happened, no matter how hard Olympias tried. Besides, what difference would it make now?'

'I'm not sure. But I think something is tearing Alexander apart, and I often wonder what it is. I want to be able to help him. He may think he can do everything on his own, but he can't. I'm frightened for him,' I said simply. 'And I love him.'

Plexis looked at the ground, then up at the sky. 'Well, that makes two of us then,' he said.

Chapter Five

A human skull, polished white by the wind and rain, sat on top of a stone. Bright green fungi streaked it, and a bizarre orange mushroom grew from the top of the skull.

'How did *he* die?' I asked, peering out of the undergrowth at the macabre relic.

'Probably not on purpose,' said Plexis grimly. 'He has all his teeth and they look to be in good condition. A young man, I'd say. I'd bet he was killed with a ceremonial stone axe.'

'How can you tell?' We were whispering, hiding in a dense thorn bush.

Plexis didn't want to get any closer to examine it. 'Someone might be standing guard,' he'd explained. 'I can see a large hole in the temple from here.'

I squinted, but all I could see was that orange mushroom the skull sported like a weird hat. 'Do you think we're far from the village now?' My voice was little more than a sigh. I was thoroughly frightened.

'I'm not sure, but I think this must mark the druids' boundary. We'll back up and circle around. I want to see just how vast their territory is and if there's a secret way into their village.' He started crawling backwards and I followed him. My heart was pounding painfully. When I blinked I sent tears down my cheeks. I was experiencing a primeval fear, I told myself sternly, trying to get a hold of myself. It was perfectly normal for modern man to be frightened of his ancestors. Because I'd finally realized who the Eaters of the Dead were.

Time is a strange thing. Just as the Time-Senders couldn't send someone back more than five thousand years, so man can't really imagine any greater passage of time. Words like two million and ten thousand blur together and form a block of time, a sheer mass our minds cannot grasp. As a time traveller I had more of an idea what time was like. And to tell the truth, it frightened me.

Ten thousand years ago, the Mesolithic age was in full swing. Mesolithic man used fire, buried his dead, and made spear-throwers, and bows and arrows. He sewed his clothes, he painted masterpieces on cave walls, he carved statues, and he had started to form permanent settlements. All that took two million years to accomplish. Two million years of time moving hardly at all, forming a solid, frozen block of time.

Then suddenly things started to move faster. Was it the climate? Time melted and flowed like the glacier ice being freed from the grip of cold.

Roughly five thousand years ago, the Neolithic age began. People domesticated livestock, grew crops, and settled on farms and in villages. Tribes spread all over the known world. Five thousand years ago in Mesopotamia, the Sumerians began to develop writing. It was a great leap forward. From caveman to modern man; the change was like a bolt of lightning. Civilizations began, as did history as we can comprehend it.

Strangely enough, it is almost as if our collective memory only started five thousand years ago. Before that is only cold and darkness and a primeval fear that shakes our bones.

Neolithic man replaced his ancestors, the Mesolithic man, around that time. Why and how is a mystery. No matter how hard the Time-Senders tried, they could never get past the barrier of five thousand years. It was as if a solid wall really did exist. Every single time-traveller sent back further than five thousand years disappeared without a trace.

I had my own theory about that. The incredible number of years that made up the Stone Age was too dense. It was literally a block made of two million years that held time immobile. Two million years. Twenty thousand centuries. Two hundred thousand decades. Too many years for the mind to grasp. An eternity filled with cold and darkness, when people huddled in caves for warmth and barely kept the spark of humanity alive. The Time-Senders would do anything to be able to study cavemen.

I was about to do that. I had the conviction that the Eaters of the Dead were no more than a Mesolithic tribe living in 'modern' times. And I was terrified.

Plexis was as scared as I was. It made him doubly wary about canvassing the area. We spent five days creeping around the outskirts of their territory, getting to know the terrain, the routes leading in and out of the valley, and planning our escape. I was anxious to find Paul and Alexander, but Plexis wanted to be careful not to get caught. So I fretted silently, my nerves making me sleepless and jumpy.

On the fifth day, we climbed an outcrop of rock overlooking the village. It was built in the deepest part of a narrow valley. Through it tumbled a swift brook, about three metres wide. Sheer cliffs rose on either side casting the valley in nearly perpetual shadow. Huts made of wood and bone covered with leather seemed to be the most common dwelling. Three longhouses made in the Viking style formed a three-sided square in the middle of the village. A pasture on the flank of the hill held a large flock of goats and sheep, and I could see pigsties built next to the huts. The village seemed deserted that night – everyone was sleeping when we first spied on them. But Plexis silently pointed out shadows standing hidden in doorways and behind trees, and I saw that the village was being guarded.

There was an open space next to the stream, with a stepping stone bridge. Just outside the village stood a circle of roughly hewn megaliths. The stones were black and seemed to swallow the pale light of the moon and the flickering torches set around them. They looked malevolent.

In the centre of the village was an open pit lined with slabs of rock. All this we could see clearly because there were four torches, one at each corner. In the pit were

Alexander, Paul, Yovanix, and Nearchus. We couldn't see Demos. Plexis swore under his breath. He was sure it meant that the big man had been killed.

I tried to stay more optimistic, but I couldn't understand why they would keep Demos apart from everyone else.

We watched for a while, then we eased backwards out of sight. We ate our dinner cold, hidden up on the ridge, then curled up in our cloaks and slept. We needed to see what would happen during the daylight hours.

Plexis was awake long before I was. Or else he hadn't slept at all. He looked haggard, the strain of his wounds and fatigue lining his face and tightening his mouth. I ran a rueful hand down his cheek, and he managed a smile. We didn't speak. We were afraid someone would hear so we communicated with gestures. Silently, we ate breakfast and cleaned up our campsite, and then we started off towards the village. Plexis led, I followed, stepping lightly in his footsteps, trying to move as quietly as he did.

When we took our place on the outcrop again, we were doubly careful not to be seen. Like snakes we wormed onto the flat rock, staying under the cover of a thick bramble. Flat on our stomachs we inched forward and then peered down into the valley below. We were perhaps a hundred metres from the outskirts of the village and at least that high above it. We stared at the strange scene below.

People appeared to be divided into groups according to sex and age, and they were all working. I could see

64

young boys sitting near the stream fishing. They were dressed in leather pants and sleeveless woollen tunics. The girls were working in the doorways of their huts scraping hides or sewing. They wore long, plain dresses made of leather or wool. Older women were weaving in the shade of the cliff near a large tree.

The people were a mixture of sizes and shapes. Some were tall and blond like the Valerian tribes. Others were short and dark of skin and hair. I'd never seen a tribe like that, and I was perplexed.

The fishing was soon done. Now I could see the boys lifting traps from the stream and shaking them out. They were full of crayfish. When they were finished, half of the boys went to tend the goats and sheep while the other half went into the forest to gather firewood.

I noticed there were no men except for the druids guarding the village. They stayed in the shadows of the houses, not moving – except one. When I saw him, my breath caught in my throat and I shivered. Voltarrix! I recognized him from his long, blond braids, his sharp nose, and the Celtic torque around his neck. He strode to the pit, and I could see Alexander's face as they spoke to one another. We were too far to hear what was being said or even read their lips. Alexander seemed agitated, and my heart started to thump.

'Why are you scrunching up your face like that?' whispered Plexis, concerned.

'I'm wishing a thunderbolt,' I answered.

'Why?'

'That's the man who killed Millis, the one the Gauls

call the Thief of Souls.'

Plexis glanced at the sky, a cloudless expanse of pale blue above our heads. 'I don't think Zeus will send one.' There was real regret in his voice.

Then Voltarrix turned his back to the prisoners and marched away. He wore the grey robes of a Celtic druid, and as he walked through the village everyone stopped what they were doing and made a quick sign with their hands. They appeared to be frightened of him.

Voltarrix motioned to the other druids, and they stepped out of their hiding places and followed him. He was coming towards us now, heading towards the circle of stones, his loose robes flapping.

The standing stones were nearly beneath us in the centre of a large clearing. I had hated the sight of them last night and I hated them this morning. Nevertheless, I inched closer to the edge of the rock to study them. They were really an odd colour, I decided. Black, but a strange blackness, as if they'd been painted with thick tar. Then as I looked, the stones began to shiver.

I uttered a gasp and Plexis turned to see what I was staring at. I felt him flinch, and his hand crept over my arm and he gripped my wrist so tightly I felt my bones grind together. I was incapable of uttering a single sound.

The stones were shuddering. They vibrated like living things. Then suddenly, sickeningly, just before I thought I'd faint with fear, a huge black cloud of flies lifted off them as if a thick, black, skin peeled off and disintegrated in the air with a sound we could hear from our perch.

I closed my eyes, my stomach heaving. Underneath the flies, the stones were encrusted with dried blood. Blood that attracted the flies; they stayed on the rocks unless something disturbed them. They'd been disturbed by the druids.

Voltarrix walked towards the stones with measured steps, ignoring the billions of flies that darkened the clearing. The others formed a giant circle around him. When he reached the very centre of the stones, Voltarrix stopped and stood motionless for a long time. Plexis and I were utterly silent. It was quiet all around us. A queer silence descended upon the whole valley. All we could hear was a deep buzzing. Then the air seemed to swell and crystallize around us. My ears hurt and I shook my head. Plexis made a frightened sound deep in his throat and gripped my hand tighter. Voltarrix stared around him, swinging his head back and forth slowly as if scenting the wind.

I had the sudden intuition that he was looking for Plexis and me. *I knew it.* I also knew we were well hidden. My breath caught in my throat, and I closed my eyes in a superstitious effort to keep myself invisible. A raven cawed loudly overhead and I pressed myself into the ground. I didn't dare move. Next to me Plexis had stopped breathing. The strange sensation of a vacuum grew and the roaring, buzzing noise became louder. All of a sudden, the breeze rustled the trees over our heads and the birds started singing again. The air whooshed back to normal with a 'pop' that nearly stunned me. My fingers released their grip on the ground. A small branch dug into my cheek. I wondered for a brief second if I'd peed in my pants. My fear had been so overpowering, I was drenched with sweat. A drop rolled down my temple and cheekbone, coming to rest at the base of my throat. We didn't dare move until the druids had gone, and even then we waited a good hour before peeling ourselves off the ground and worming back into the undergrowth.

Plexis was shaken. 'What was that?' he finally managed to croak, but the question was rhetorical. I had no idea, and he knew it. It took us twice as long to get back to our campsite.

I wanted to take a bath. I was just about ready to take off my clothes, bury them in a deep pit, and go naked. I was wondering how I could fashion a skirt and a shirt from pine needles. I felt terrible. My hair was sticky, my face was muddy, and my hands were caked with dirt. I won't bother to describe the rest, you might be eating. Plexis wasn't much better. He looked like a barbarian.

I had a sudden fit of the giggles, thinking about presenting him to my mother at that minute. His hair was tied back neatly with a thong, but his beard had a bramble caught in it, his face was streaked with dried mud, and his hands and forearms were black with muck.

He stood up and stretched, scratching his chest and winking at me.

'Why are you laughing?' he asked.

'I was just thinking of my mother's face if she saw you. I would absolutely love to be able to say, "Mother, I do formally present you to my lover,

Hephaestion." ... what is your full name, by the way?' I frowned. 'We weren't together in Massalia, with all the paperwork, so I didn't get to hear you present yourself to the customs official.'

'My name?' He knitted his brows together. 'Hephaestion Sophocles of Attica. Rather a long name, don't you think?'

'I think it's nice. Was your father Sophocles, the playwright?'

'No, no relation, unfortunately. My father was Sophocles, the lawyer. He died when I was young; I don't remember him well. I had a brother and a sister,' he said, divining my next question. 'My mother took us all to live with her family when my father died. I was the youngest, and a handful, which was why I was sent to Athens to school at a very early age. It was also because ...' He broke off and stared at me moodily.

I knew the look in his eyes; I got it too, whenever I spoke of my past, which was actually three thousand years in the future. I sighed. Things were complicated enough. 'You don't have to say any more,' I said gently.

He shook his head, chasing away the demons. 'No, it's all right. I was five when my father died and six when we went to live with my mother's family. And I was eight when my uncle seduced me. I think I was a handsome child, and the Greeks love beauty.' He smiled, but his eyes were sad. 'I loved Athens. I loved the school. And I especially loved the attention men paid to me. If I hadn't missed my father so much, perhaps it wouldn't have happened. However, I did miss him. And by my fault my brother was killed.'

'Alexander killed him,' I said, 'Not you. It was his fault, not yours. And he's yet to forgive himself.'

'I know. Even though I forgave him, I forgave him completely. But I'll never pardon myself. I was young and foolish, that is true. However, nothing can bring my brother back or take away my mother's pain. She lost her firstborn son, and the worst of it was she knew it was my fault. When I came back home she wouldn't receive me. I was only fifteen and I had nowhere to go so I travelled for a while. Aristotle let me stay with him and his wife. I went to Macedonia but not to see Iskander. Then his father died, and I heard he was looking for finances for his new army. I wrote to him, and told him what I'd done. I'd taken all my mother's money and invested it in his army. If he lost a battle he would ruin my family. It was a childish strike against the young man who'd killed my brother. I did it out of sorrow and rage – and regret, because I still loved him. He'd been my best friend for so long that I couldn't imagine life without him.'

'But you did see him again.'

'I did. In Arbeles, after his second victory over Darius. You were there as well. The minion of Hades who frightened Olympias.'

'Was that who you went to see in Macedonia?' I asked.

He flinched. 'Yes.'

'Revenge is sometimes harder to give than to receive,' I said slowly. 'If you used Olympias for your revenge, then it must have been bitter indeed.'

70

'I did it for love, not revenge. I went to Macedonia intending to make up with Iskander, to apologize, something – I don't know. Olympias was there. She thought I was handsome and she was tired of her brute of a husband. It's all very painful to speak about, so I hope you'll forgive me if I just say I didn't stay long. I was sickened by everything that was happening to me. Sometimes I don't know why I'm still alive. I thought about suicide, but the hope of making up with Iskander kept me going.'

I blinked away stinging tears. 'I'm glad you're not dead.'

'Me too. I have you, and Chiron, and Iskander. It's too much for me some days. I still don't feel as if I deserve any of it. But I try, I try to deserve you all.' He looked at me from under his long lashes. Even filthy and uncombed, he kept his sensual beauty. I could easily see why men and women would want to seduce him. His mouth was made for kisses, so I kissed him softly.

'You are a sweetheart,' I said 'And nothing that happened was your fault. You were young and easy prey for corrupted adults. They should have been severely punished, not you. Your mother was grieving, but I'm sure she loved you still.'

'No, she did not.' He shrugged and tried to smile but the pain was still sharp in his eyes. 'She died before I could speak to her about the whole thing. The worst was, she adored her brother. He managed to convince her that everything was my fault. He claimed I was the one who'd seduced *him*. That I was only eight made no

71

difference. I was "born decadent", as he explained it. He managed to make it sound so very plausible.'

'Whatever happened to him?'

'I killed him.' He said this so simply, it sent shivers down my spine.

'How?' I managed to whisper.

'When my mother died, I went to Athens. It was just before I met you and Iskander again in Persepolis. My family refused to see me. I wasn't allowed to go to the funeral, and when I tried to see my sister, her husband threatened to have the magistrates throw me out of the city. I was in Athens to see Demosthenes. You can imagine the scene. I had to speak to him about the embezzlement scandal, and at the same time explain why my own family wanted me out of Athens. Demosthenes was accused of stealing half the money from the army's payroll. It was a fortune, more than a fortune actually; and I'm sure Demosthenes did steal it.'

'But, why? Why you? Why did you have to speak to Demosthenes?'

'I was a lawyer, didn't I ever tell you? I wasn't born in the cavalry. I received a note, a rather curt note from Iskander himself, asking me to go and see about it. It was the first time he'd contacted me since, well, since you'd been kidnapped, and I was feeling guilty again. As you can imagine.'

'I suppose.' I tried to keep my voice level.

He shot me a pained glance. 'I'm sorry about that. Well, I went to Athens and my mother died the day I arrived. My uncle made it seem as if I'd killed her. It made no difference to my family that she'd been ill for a long time.

'When I saw my uncle, something snapped. He ordered me out of the house, screaming that I was no longer welcome, that his sister and my brother were dead by my fault. My own sister spat at me, and I was dragged out of the house by the servants. That night I waited in the dark until the funeral feast was over. And I stabbed him. No one saw me, but I think I was past caring. I don't know why I did it. The strange thing is, I never felt any regret. He'd destroyed my life, so when I killed him it didn't seem wrong.' He shuddered. 'Even now, all I can think of is his cape. Since I'd invested my money well, I was rich, but I'd sent it all to my family and they lived like princes. My uncle's cape was made of the finest wool and was dyed black. It must have cost a fortune. He lived off my money, and he *dared* refuse me entrance to my mother's funeral?' His voice was rising and I saw his shoulders start to shake.

'Hush.' I wrapped my arms around him and held him tightly. 'Why don't we speak of other things? All that is in the past, years and years behind you. You're not the same person who I saw in Persepolis. You've changed. We all have. The boy you once were is gone forever.'

'No. The boy is still inside me. I feel him when I'm frightened.'

'We all do,' I said. 'Honest. Whenever I try and talk sternly to myself, it's my mother's voice I hear. We're all stuck with our past, but we just have to put it in its rightful place, behind us. With our past behind us we can look towards the future.' I was rather proud of my little speech. I waited for Plexis to congratulate me, but he stared moodily over my head and sighed.

'I stabbed my uncle in the back. It's when something is behind me that I fear it the most.'

Chapter Six

That evening we ate our dinner raw. Plexis didn't want to make a fire, he was afraid we'd be discovered. I remarked that anyone standing downwind of us would find us in five minutes, but he shook his head.

'We'll wash when it gets dark,' he told me, biting into a raw mushroom.

I wasn't looking forward to swimming in an icy stream in the middle of the night, but I couldn't go without washing one more day. I was nearly crying with filth. Plexis, being Greek, loved cleanliness as much as anyone, except perhaps the Egyptians who were fanatical about keeping clean. However, men seem to be able to handle dirt better than women. I thought it was horribly unfair, and told him so.

He grinned and covered my shoulder with a handful of soft, wet, sand. 'Here, rub this on your skin, and then you can rinse off and you'll be clean.' In the dark his eyes gleamed.

I scooped up another handful of wet sand from the streambed and scoured myself all over. The sand was cold, but it was fine and it cleansed well. 'How's your arm feeling?' I asked him, scrubbing hard.

'Better - really.' He didn't blink when he said that, although I knew it was a lie. He couldn't use his arm any more. It hung at his side and if I touched it he flinched. I thought there was an abscess that was keeping it from healing, but there was nothing I could do until I got some decent surgical instruments and could boil water.

I washed, then took our clothes and washed them. They were clean, but wouldn't be dry by morning. Nights only lasted a half an hour now, and even then they weren't very dark. The summer solstice was approaching rapidly. That was the day set aside for the ceremony. I paused in my washing and stared at the sky. The edges were starting to pale already, dawn was coming. Plexis made a soft splashing sound as he slid into the water.

I helped him wash, being careful not to hurt his shoulder. He stood still while I scrubbed, his eyes scanning the bushes around us. Ever since his story, he'd been distant. The hurt had bubbled up to the surface and it would take time to bury again. I understood, or hoped I did. He was a complex man. He rarely let his thoughts show. I'll admit, the first time I set eyes on him I thought he was probably the most handsome man I'd ever seen. I'd also thought him difficult and unfriendly when I first spoke to him. He took time to get to know. Not like Alexander, who wore his personality on the outside. Alexander, whose face wore a hundred expressions a minute, whose eyes spoke volumes and whose smile could charm the most virulent of enemies. Alexander, who was prisoner in a stone pit.

My hands fell to my sides and I uttered a frustrated

sob. How could we save them? Plexis might be the most handsome man I'd ever seen, but he was wounded. He only had his ancient, bronze sword with him. I was the one carrying it half the time. Plexis knew what I was thinking. He always did. He should have been a psychic; he could pick up thoughts as if they were radio waves. My thoughts must have wounded him, but he just took me in his arms and held me close. 'Don't worry,' he said.

We hung the clothes to dry in the middle of a thicket, then cuddled up together and tried to keep warm. I was miserable, Plexis was hurt, and things hadn't seemed so awful since I'd been kidnapped in Arbeles.

Of course, when the sun's shining and you're feeling clean, almost dry, and well fed, things look brighter.

The sun was hot that day and our clothes dried quickly. Plexis speared three large fish and we grilled them while there was still mist on the ground to hide the smoke from our fire. Afterwards, we wrapped the leftover fish in a large leaf to take with us and made our way carefully towards the village. Plexis didn't take the same trail twice so it took us two hours that day. I was chafing at the slow pace but knew we had to be careful. The only way we could help the others was to stay free.

I paused under the skirt of a large pine tree while Plexis scouted the area in front of us. He could move without making a sound. I was always amazed when he disappeared into the underbrush without a 'swish'. The tree I was hiding under was short but very dense. It would have made a perfect Christmas tree. I could picture it decorated with tinsel and twinkling lights, with a little white angel on the top, her wings made of real dove feathers.

I sighed softly and turned my attention back to the direction Plexis had gone. When he reappeared, motioning me towards him, I crouched down and crawled on hands and knees, as quickly as I could, down the little path he'd opened up. Thorns caught at my hair and nettles stung me, but I didn't mind – too much. Plexis followed behind and carefully plucked my hair from the briar bush. In his hand the long, silver thread looked almost like a spider's web, or tinsel. I made a face. Why was I thinking of Christmas? Was it because the whole village was being decorated, as if for a fête? Today everyone in the village bustled with activity, mainly twining flowers into crowns and wreaths and hanging them on doors and windows.

The men were still in the pit, and I could see them moving around so I knew they were still alive. It gave me scant comfort. There seemed to be even more druids today, and Voltarrix was wandering around. He didn't appear to have anything else to do besides occasionally glancing into a huge caldron hung over a bright fire. I wondered if I could shoot an arrow far enough to kill him, but since I had no bow and no arrow the question was not even moot.

Plexis put his mouth next to my ear and breathed, 'It would take a six-foot-long bow and a four-foot arrow shot by someone with Demos's force to hit Voltarrix, and even then you couldn't be sure to kill him. We're too far away.' I just turned and stared at him. Sometimes he was downright spooky.

The sun climbed high and then started to descend. It would hardly set tonight. Plexis and I shared the rest of the cold fish and some vegetables he'd picked in the forest. There were berries too. Summer was coming; I nibbled on a tart raspberry and licked the juice off my fingers. Plexis watched me and I saw his eyes darken.

'Not here, not now,' I said to him. It was his turn to widen his eyes.

'I didn't say anything!'

'Your eyes change colour when you're aroused,' I told him.

'Really?' He thought about that for a minute. 'How interesting. What colour do they change to?'

'Dark amber. They get darker. Shhh, look. Something's happening.'

He turned his attention back to the village, and we watched as two druids helped an old woman out of her hut. They placed her onto a litter and carried her over to the pit.

'What is going on?' I asked, but Plexis only shrugged.

The old woman got to her feet and leaned over the edge of the pit. She reached down, and I saw Paul's bright head. To me it looked as if they were shaking hands. I frowned. 'An odd place for an introduction,' I murmured.

Then the old woman tottered back to the litter and was carried back to her hut. She disappeared through the doorway and Plexis and I stared at each other, baffled.

'Your eyes change colour too,' he informed me, after

an hour had gone by and nothing of interest happened in the village.

'Oh? From what to what?'

'From ice blue to frosty blue.' He was looking mischievous.

'Oh, ha-ha. Can we please think of a plan to help them?'

'Well, I have thought of a couple.'

'You have? Why didn't you tell me?'

'I wanted to make sure. I've been watching for a few days, and I'm pretty sure of one thing.'

'What's that?'

'We're not alone in the forest. There are several other groups scattered around. I'm even certain that others are watching the village besides us. The only problem is, I'm not sure if the others are "good guys" or "bad guys", as you say. I don't know who they are or why they're here. I can only guess. The first option is that they are on our side, which means enemies of this tribe, coming to attack. The second is friends of the village, either looking for us, or keeping a permanent, secret watch for enemies.'

'So what do we do?'

'We find out who and where they are. And what they're doing.'

'How?'

'Well, you're not going to like this … I go off to spy, you stay here – and whatever you do, don't move before I get back. If I don't get back by noon tomorrow, you make a tough decision. Either you go straight to the village and give yourself up, or you abandon the others and you go back to Orce.'

'You're right, I don't like it. Can't you think of something else?' I asked.

'No. Do you have any ideas?'

I'd given it a lot of thought. 'Well, the pit is in the middle of the village, but it doesn't seem to be heavily guarded. There are a couple of men in the village who are not druids. They must be slaves. They chop wood and carry water. Otherwise, the village is made up of children and woman. I did wonder if they were the druids' wives and children – but I don't think so. They seem frightened of the druids. In the evening, everyone gathers in the middle longhouse to eat dinner. I was thinking we could sneak down quickly while they eat. It's the only time the guards aren't at their posts.'

'No. The problem is the view. You can see from here that there is an open space that leads to the pit from the standing stones. It's a ceremonial walkway. Everyone can see the pit from the village, which is why it's not guarded. And, besides, I suspect there are lookouts we haven't spotted.'

'What about at night, when everyone is asleep?'

'There are sentries posted around the village, and there are only two of us. And I'm in no condition to fight.'

'So you think you'd better see who the others are, those who are spying on the village too?'

'And hope they can help us, yes.'

'When do you think the ceremony will take place?'

'I think, in four days.'

'Great.' I stared bitterly at the village and at Voltarrix bent over his caldron. 'If only he'd fall in and boil to death,' I hissed.

'I was wondering something,' said Plexis, frowning.

'What?'

'I'll tell you when I get back. I'd better get going. I have an idea where to look and I want to hurry. Don't forget to stay put. You have some food in the pouch and water in the flask. I'll see you soon. Don't worry.' He leaned over and kissed me hard on the mouth. For a moment, we held each other. I could feel his heart thumping strongly against my chest. Then he disengaged himself and slid out of the thicket. I didn't hear a sound. It was as if he'd disappeared into thin air.

I rolled over onto my back and put my hands over my face. If Plexis were right, they were safe for four more days. Then the summer solstice would arrive, and my husband would be killed. His soul would be put into my son's body, and the druids would have the leader they needed to overthrow Rome. A new world would come into being, one where the Romans had no foothold in Europe, and where the old gods, the druids, and the Celts would rule.

What would that mean to history, I wondered? Would the Romans then concentrate on the Middle East and Africa? Would Africa emerge then as the new power, instead of Europe? Would Roman roads, cities, organization, and laws make Africa a totally different place than the one history knew? How would it affect the spread of Christianity? Would the religion known as Islam never come into being? Would Europe remain in the grip of the bloodthirsty old gods for a long time, slowing the arrival of modern civilization and the discovery of the New World?

The Time-Senders would have a terrible time of it, I decided, trying to unravel the change. They would end up erasing a whole section of time, starting with the years following the death of Alexander and ending with the domination of Rome. That would mean we would all be erased: myself; Paul; and even the people around me. It would be an incredible outpouring of energy and it would cost the Western Hemisphere trillions, but they would do it. They would have to, in order to put Time back on its track. I sighed. The consequences of a successful summer solstice ceremony were serious. Say that tongue-twister ten times, fast!

I rolled over again and watched the village. The sun burned my back. It was very late in the afternoon and still bright. I watched the pit, but no movement could be seen. After lunch everyone napped. Even the guards sat down in the shade of the nearest tree and lay their spears on their knees. A few women wandered over to the stream to draw water then went back to their huts. The sun made their hair flash bright gold in the sun. One woman went to the pit and leaned over it. She asked a question then lowered a bucket of water. So the prisoners were well looked after, at least. When it was hot they were offered water often during the day.

I thought about that for a minute. Then I got up and

started to make my way down towards the village. Plexis would probably kill me, but I was tired of waiting. I might as well be killed now, by strangers. Besides, I didn't think anyone would notice another blonde woman giving water to the prisoners; the guards hadn't even glanced at the scene. I wondered where I could find a bucket. That seemed to be my only problem. That, and nettles.

Chapter Seven

Tall pine trees grew on the cliff, so I had no trouble hiding as I slithered down. However, once at the base I was confronted by a briar patch, and after that, a forest of nettles. The village was surrounded by a massive hedge of these, separating it from the forest.

The brambles were loaded with white blossoms promising a heavy crop of blackberries later that fall. The villagers must come often to pick them, because I found narrow paths in the bramble thicket. Carefully, I pushed back the prickly branches and managed to pass through, losing only a handful of hair and getting scratches on my arms, legs, and face. The brambles were thick but not impenetrable. The nettles, on the other hand, were a daunting, stinging barrier. I thought maybe I could bend them aside and creep through. I didn't know much about nettles.

I sat in the shade of a giant bramble bush, sucking my sore hand, wondering if the stinging would subside enough so that I could start breathing again. Tears leaked from my eyes. The nettles were two and three metres high, bright green, and covered with deceptively soft-looking leaves. I needed a machete to get through, thick gloves, and long pants–none of which I had. No, wait. I had an antique bronze sword which had belonged to Plexis's grandfather. I could use that to cut a tunnel through the nettles. I turned around and wormed my way out of the brambles. The sword was on top of the cliff – of course.

A long while later, my arms covered with painful welts, my face drenched with sweat, and with blood trickling from various scrapes and scratches, I had managed to cut a narrow passage through the nettles. I crawled on my hands and knees, keeping low and disturbing the plants as little as possible. I'd discovered the stems were just as painful as the leaves, and nettles stung right down to their very roots. Their roots were deeply embedded and they grew in clumps. I tried to uproot them, but hundreds of plants shared the same root system.

It was getting late. Exhausted, I rested on my stomach trying to quell the urge to scream. I wasn't sure what to do. I ended up wriggling out of the nettles back to where I'd started. I sat under a bramble bush and tried to catch my breath. It was not quite a failure. I'd cut a tunnel nearly all the way through the bloody nettles, and I could finish tonight while the village slept.

With that thought in mind, I turned around and bumped into a man.

Immediately, a hand clamped over my mouth and a voice hissed in my ear, 'It's me, Demos. What in Demeter's name are you doing?'

Demos! My joy and relief made me giddy. I nearly

laughed aloud. I turned and gave him a hug. Not easy in the middle of a briar patch. 'I'm going to go to the village tomorrow to give some water to the prisoners; no one will notice. I'll tell Alexander we're here and planning on rescuing him.' I whispered.

'You don't think he already knows that? Why risk your life to tell him something he already knows? Think, woman! If you get caught, they'll know we're out here and come searching for us. Now follow me and be quiet. Here, give me that sword. Plexis is going to kill you.'

'I hope he won't kill me too painfully.' I started to joke, but stopped when I saw his expression. 'Why should he kill me? All I did was go down the hill when he told me to stay put.'

'He won't kill you for disobeying him, he'll kill you for using his sword to cut plants. By Ares' wrath, he'll probably chop your head off for that.'

'Cute,' I muttered. 'You try and make a joke and you get your head bitten off.'

'*Or* he'll bite your head off.' Demos grinned.

Clambering as silently as possible, I followed him back up the steep cliff. I was mortified to see that Demos, despite his large size, could move almost as quietly as Plexis. And as quickly. He reached down, grabbed my wrist and hoisted me up the last five feet to our hiding place. We crawled into the deep thicket and I slumped to the ground, sprawling on the moss. I was filthy, my mouth was parched, and I thought I'd probably die from the nettle stings. Demos gave me the goatskin flask I'd left behind. The water was warm and smelled of goat, but it was divine. I drank and drank, pausing only long enough to gasp for breath.

When I'd finished drinking, Demos eyed me and smiled. 'Plexis won't kill you. He'll think you've been punished enough.'

I shuddered. Nettle stings had left huge welts all over my body, and my face was so swollen that I could hardly see. The pain was pretty much constant, and now, far from the village, I finally gave in to the hurt and started to sniffle.

Demos patted my shoulder, making me wince. 'Tch, tch. It's not that bad. Besides, I think you have the right idea, but the wrong reason. We don't crawl into the village to help them drink – we sneak in to help them escape. Plexis had the best idea.'

'He did? You saw him? Where is he?' I asked.

'Shhh. He's around. Probably with the others; but I think we'll stay here for now. It's safer.'

'What others?' I was agitated. 'But, but … may I take a bath? The stream isn't too far away.'

'No, no bath. Sorry. The others … oh, didn't I tell you? Axiom came, and he brought an army.'

I just stared. Finally his words sank in. 'An army?'

'Well … a small army,' said Demos carefully.

'A small army?' I repeated, stunned.

'A very, *very* small army. But it's better than nothing.' He grinned, showing gap teeth, and spread his hands, showing nine fingers. He had almost as many battle scars as Alexander.

'But, how, I mean where did he find them? Where did

they come from?'

'Oh, I'm sure you can think of the answer to that yourself.'

I frowned in thought. Finally, I guessed. 'The villagers from Orce? And Roman soldiers from the trading boats?'

His broad grin answered my question. 'And Phaleria,' he said. 'She insisted on coming. Titte, Kell, and Vix came along too. She left two crewmembers behind to watch the boat.'

'The boat is all right?'

'No, not her boat. The dragon boat sank it. It's a good thing Iskander told her to unload all her goods before she led them out to sea.'

My head was spinning. Too much sun, pain, and relief were making me dizzy. Demos was here, and so was Axiom and a small army. 'But how did you convince the Romans to come?'

'Well, they're not exactly fighting for free. We had to pay them, for sure. They're mercenaries, hired by the boat captains to protect the cargo. But, for a price, they will follow us. I bet they were getting bored. They can't wait to storm into the village and rape and pillage.'

'That's not very nice,' I said, thinking of the people I'd been watching for days. 'Can't you tell them to just rape and pillage the druids?'

Demos looked at me incredulously. 'Rape and pillage druids? Do you think that mercenaries are going to fight for the right to do that?'

'No,' I said dryly, 'they're fighting for pay. You tell

them that the first one who rapes or pillages doesn't get paid. Is that perfectly clear?'

Demos raised an eyebrow. 'I'll tell you what; you tell them. All right?'

'All right,' I said smugly. I spoke Latin. I'd show him. *Huh*.

I imagine I made quite a sight, standing in front of the Roman mercenaries telling them they mustn't rape or pillage. I spoke in my best Latin, a language I'd painstakingly learned in school. I had made good grades, so I expected to be understood.

'Excuse me,' said one, pointing his finger in the air. 'Excuse me, I say. What are you telling us? That we can't have any fun?'

I'd gotten through to one. Good. I smiled brightly. 'That's right. You'll get paid richly. You don't have to rape anyone.'

'What if I ask first?' The soldier was frowning. Obviously he hadn't quite caught on. I sighed. Part of the problem was the accent. In my school, no one was really sure how ancient Romans had sounded when they talked; and they used a lot of slang. The soldiers in front of me spoke several different dialects and none of them was in my schoolbook.

'You don't ask if you can rape someone – you just don't do it, that's all.' I said patiently.

I didn't think I was reaching them. Another part of the problem was my appearance: nettle rash and scratches covered arms and legs; my face was still swollen; and dirt caked me from head to foot. As I spoke, I plucked a stray nettle leaf from my tangled hair. I flinched, swore, and sucked my fingers. The soldiers were impressed.

Demos had told them that I was the daughter of the goddess Demeter. Consequently, the Romans were in awe of me. They had never seen a real goddess, so my appearance didn't shock them too much – they thought I was in disguise.

The villagers from Orce, who'd also come for the rescue, were with Plexis and Axiom getting a crash course on warfare, while I was in charge of the Roman mercenaries. It was not an easy task. I sighed and started again.

'Now listen, guys, there's to be no stealing, no killing children, no raping women and, if you *can* manage, take prisoners, and try to kill as few as possible.

'Ahh! Slaves!' cried one soldier. 'Now we understand. You need slaves, so we keep them alive. You know,' he continued, lowering his voice, 'if we castrate them right away they're much more docile.'

I shuddered. We were getting nowhere. I wondered how Plexis was getting on with his students. Apparently, Plexis was having as much trouble as I was.

'Watch out!' A scream came from the thicket behind us and the soldiers, professionals, threw themselves flat on the ground. An arrow whizzed over my head and thunked into the tree behind me, missing me by inches. The bushes parted and a man peeked through.

'Uh, sorry about that,' he said sheepishly, trotting over and retrieving the arrow from the tree. 'I'm having difficulty aiming this thing.'

The fact the arrow didn't hit me convinced the soldiers I was divine, which was fine by me. They listened with rare concentration as, one more time, we went over the tactics of not killing. And they mostly agreed about the rape part, although one soldier insisted he would ask first, and if the girl said 'yes', well …

I wished I could see Axiom and Plexis, but since they'd arrived we'd been put into groups and scattered throughout the forest. I had insisted on lecturing the Romans, so I was with Demos. He sat with his back to a large pine tree, watching me with a huge grin on his face.

When I thought they had the gist of my demands, I dismissed the soldiers and sat down wearily next to Demos. 'Do you think I can go for a wash in the stream now?' I asked him.

He glanced at me and then shrugged. 'I don't see why not, but I'm staying right here, and so are the soldiers.'

I nodded happily – a bath, at last.

The stream was about hip-deep, and surrounded with moss-covered rocks and ten Roman soldiers standing guard. Mindful of their rape fantasies, I took a bath with my tunic on. Well, it needed washing anyway. I scrubbed my hair, my face, my clothes, and my body with handfuls of soft sand from the bottom of the stream. When I rinsed the sand away, I felt much better. The cold water soothed my nettle rash, and I'd managed to rub most of the grime out of my hair. My tunic was pretty much ruined though. I squeezed the water from it and looked at it ruefully. It was knee length, not sweeping the ground, and practical for walking through the forest. I loved its deep green colour, another reason for wearing it in the forest, and the dye, being of the best quality, hadn't faded. However, the cloth had suffered: thorns had torn it; branches had ripped it; and a rent had nearly removed one sleeve. Underneath, I wore a light cotton sleeveless shift I'd bought in Egypt. It had been pearly pink but was now oyster shell-grey.

When I finished bathing, the soldiers finished standing at attention and resumed polishing armour, sharpening swords, and making arrows.

I went back to the tiny clearing and paced back and forth, driving Demos crazy with my questions.

'What will you do?' I asked.

'Wait and see what happens.'

'Why?'

Demos frowned. 'Because Axiom said that a large delegation of druids arrived in Orce just before we left, and they're heading this way.'

'Why let them through? Why not storm the village and surprise them at night?'

'Because they will be wary and on their guard. We have to wait until they are involved in the ceremony before attacking. We will know then how many of them there are, and we will be able to surround them.'

'Do they know we're here?'

'No, I don't think so. They might think you and Plexis are out here with a few more people from the village, but I don't think they'll expect the Romans.'

'Why did the villagers from Orce agree to come?'

'Because the Eaters of the Dead have been taking their children. The villagers want to recover their family members, if they're still alive.'

'Oh.' I frowned and thought a while. 'Why didn't they do that before?'

'They were afraid.' Demos spoke shortly.

'Of what? The village isn't very big, and the people aren't that numerous. I saw the Eaters of the Dead. They're short and have dark hair but they don't look dangerous.'

'No, you saw the people from Nordica. The Eaters of the Dead don't live in the village. They only come out on special occasions.'

'Where do they live? What occasions?'

'They live in caves in the mountains far behind the village. And they come to the ceremonies to eat the dead. And the villagers of Orce have tried to find them, but every time a hunting party sets out they never return.'

I shut my mouth. Demos was looking at the sky. I shivered despite the hot sun. For a while we didn't speak. Demos used a reed to sketch a map in the dust at his feet, chewing now and then on the end of his reed and frowning. He was a mountain of a man and even sitting down he looked forbidding. He'd been a tactician in Darius's army, and according to Alexander, one of the best.

'If anyone could have defeated me it was Demos,' Alexander had told me one night. 'But Darius, silly fool, didn't believe him. Worse, he ordered his death as a traitor. Luckily, Demos escaped the prison.'

'Luckily for you, Darius didn't listen to him!' I'd said.

'Perhaps.' Alexander had given an eloquent shrug. 'It would have made the fight more interesting.'

I shivered again. History hinged on little details like that. If Darius had listened to Demos, Alexander would likely have been stopped at Issus, the first battle against Darius, and pushed back to Greece. Perhaps the war would have ended there. Persia would have stayed Persian under Darius, and Greece and Macedonia would have merged and become one under Alexander.

Alexander the Great would simply have been Alexander, ruler of Greece and Macedonia. He never would have spread Greek culture east as far as India, or have founded the cities of Alexandria; cities with parks, temples, gymnasiums, libraries, civic amenities, swimming pools, and hydraulic and sewer systems. Greek art and philosophy would have stayed put, trade would have been limited, and the great kingdom of Alexander would never have existed. All because of a difference of opinion between Darius and Demos.

Other little things could have changed history, but perhaps not as radically as that quarrel. Radical changes like that concerned the Time-Senders. Small changes are often absorbed into the normal flow of events or are part of an existing trend towards change.

However, the Romans were vital to the history of the world. I had to make sure that they were not beaten before they even started. Somehow, we had to get Alexander and Paul out of that pit.

Demos reached over and clapped my shoulder with his massive hand, nearly pushing me off the log. 'Don't worry,' he said. 'We'll save your son and husband.'

I blinked quickly, then smiled up at him. 'I'm trying not to worry, honest. But I can't help it. I'm afraid of Voltarrix. He's dangerous. He knows how to fight. And I have a feeling the other druids know, too. Voltarrix wouldn't call ordinary druids north to help him. He must know we're here and he's waiting for us. He has something planned; I only wish I knew what it was.'

Demos was silent. He stared at his map again and scratched out a line with the pointed end of the reed. Finally he said, 'Our plan has nothing to do with surprise. As you said, he most likely knows we're here, although I doubt he knows how many we are. However, we can act quickly; maybe that will be to our advantage. We want to rescue the prisoners and set the villagers free – perhaps Voltarrix doesn't realize that.'

I was confused. 'What do you mean? Why else would we be here?'

'To rape and pillage?' He grinned. 'You were right about one thing, the other druids are warriors. And they look dangerous. Maybe Voltarrix thinks we're here to kill the druids.'

'Has the group Axiom spotted arrived in the village yet?' I hated to be so far away. Demos had set up our camp in a marshy area a good two-hour hike from the outskirts of the village. There was a stream, to be sure, but, judging by the quantity of mosquitoes buzzing around, we were close to a swamp as well. The air hung as hot and muggy as an old muslin curtain in a Turkish bath.

I slapped at a biting insect and rubbed another handful of lemon balm over my arms and legs, filling the air with the sharp scent of lemons. Lemon balm grew in clumps, it was plentiful, and the leaves were velvety and easily crushed. However, the scent didn't last very long and the soft leaves left bright green streaks. Well, good for camouflage, I supposed.

Demos didn't seem bothered by mosquitoes. Nothing seemed to bother him. He sat solid and still on the log, looking down between his feet at the map, scratching his rough beard and muttering now and then.

One thing I'd forgotten to ask him. I cleared my throat. 'Charidemos?'

'Yes?' He turned to me, a question in his dark brown eyes. We didn't usually use his full name.

'How did you escape? I mean why …?' I broke off, flustered. I didn't know how to phrase my question.

'Why did I abandon Paul, you mean?' His eyes were serious.

I sighed. I wished I weren't so transparent. 'I know you would never have left him if he were in danger. But how did you escape? It was hard enough for Plexis and me, and we were not being watched very closely.'

'I pretended to die. Alexander and I got in a huge fight and he stabbed me. It was a good act. Copious blood and guts of an animal did the rest. I hid in the shallow grave that Alexander, "in a fit of remorse", dug for me, until the coast was clear.'

I swallowed. 'A grave? He stabbed you?'

'No, he didn't really stab me, and the grave was carefully engineered to let me breathe. I did have a hard time getting out. It's a good thing I'm strong,' he said without bragging. 'I waited two days and then sneaked back to Orce. I didn't see you and Plexis. But then again, I didn't expect to. He's a crafty woodsman. He came upon us without anyone hearing. Even the scouts were fooled. I had to thrash two of them, just to set an example. But I honestly don't know anyone who could have spotted him.'

'How did Axiom managed to convince the Valerians to fight?'

'The people of Orce have no love for the Eaters of the Dead. They fear them above all other men. However, they are too few and too disorganized to fight them, and, like I said, their last forays were all disasters. When Axiom asked for their help, at first they said "no". Then he turned to the Roman soldiers and Phaleria emptied her treasury to hire them. With the soldiers on our side, it was easier to convince the people of Orce to come with us. And there was the weird-woman, of course.'

'What did she do?' I asked.

'She is the chief of the village, in case you hadn't realized. She called a meeting and told the men to fight. She made them sound like awful sissies. You should have seen her; she pointed at each one as if she could see him, and called him by name. It was eerie, I got chills just watching.' He shivered.

'I imagine so! She made them join Axiom's army.' I

shook my head. 'I wish I could have seen that. Axiom has saved us all.'

'Well, the fight hasn't started yet. Maybe we'll lose and end up as slaves, or dead.'

'That's the spirit,' I said.

He grinned at me. 'I know.'

Chapter Eight

We ate lunch: cold vegetables and meat that the Romans had with them. The meat resembled the sole of a leather shoe. It was dried, smoked, too tough to chew, and the Romans informed me they brought it on all their campaigns. I remarked that if they wanted to keep up the morale, they'd do well to imitate Alexander's army and bring good cooks. The soldiers said that food was unimportant; discipline and hard work kept up the morale.

They were serious. A more serious bunch of guys was hard to imagine. They marched straight, stood straight, sat straight, and slept lying in straight lines. They built straight roads. They were hard workers and disciplined. They were tough and highly trained.

When Julius Caesar invaded Gaul, Roman soldiers accomplished incredible feats of engineering. For example, in one week they built a wall fifty kilometres long and dug a ditch around it two metres wide and two metres deep. Then they cleared a big area in front of it and stuck thousands of pikes in the ground to keep men on horseback away from the wall. Around the wall, every hundred metres, they built towers for armed sentries. The ninety thousand Gauls who'd taken refuge in the fortified town of Alesia had no chance of escape. Julius Caesar's fifty thousand soldiers fought off the two hundred thousand men who came to free the Gauls. The Northern men were defeated in a huge bloodbath, and Julius Caesar went on to conquer Gaul with his disciplined, hard-working, highly trained soldiers.

Alexander's fighters had been tough and disciplined, but the Romans put them to shame. Well, except the Spartans. The men from Sparta were so tough they often died because they just didn't know when to give up. More Spartans had been lost in the wrestling matches than on the battlefield. The words, *'I give up'*, were not in the Spartans' vocabulary. The words, *'It's impossible'*, were not in the Romans' vocabulary.

I watched the Roman soldiers for a while, but they tired me out even doing nothing. I wondered why I worried about the druids. After all, they couldn't be better warriors than these soldiers, could they?

That afternoon we crept towards the village. We walked in single file as silently as possible. Scouts moved along ahead of us and at our flanks, but I couldn't see or hear anyone. It was like being alone in the forest. As we approached the village, Demos started imitating bird calls, and some of the soldiers answered back exactly like birds singing, *'it's a lovely day and all's well in the forest'*. I had to admit it was a nice touch. Birds sang, warbled, and chirped all day, but if they noticed intruders, they became silent. This way, if there were any druids on guard at the edge of the forest, they wouldn't be forewarned.

Demos and I slithered to the edge of the cliff and peered down. He'd chosen this vantage point because, he reasoned, Voltarrix wouldn't expect us to come down such a sheer rock face. It was open and unprotected.

I looked down and my heart lurched. I think that if Demos hadn't clapped his huge hand on my back just about knocking the wind out of me, I would have screamed.

We were on the side next to the standing stones. The megaliths were still covered with millions of flies. They looked as if they were vibrating. Only now, there was a double circle of druids around them.

Big druids, tall druids, thin druids, and short druids, all carrying iron spears and swords. They were armed to the teeth, and they were standing in two concentric circles around the stones. Each druid's face and chest were painted with ochre. Around their shoulders were wolf pelts with the heads still attached. They wore the heads like hoods, and gaping jaws nearly hid the druids' faces. Necklaces made of sharp teeth gleamed around their throats. The pelts were huge; some of the tails dragged on the ground. I started to understand where the legends of the shapeshifters came from.

There must have been at least a hundred druids. My heart was beating so hard it shook me. My chest hurt and tears blurred my vision. In the very middle of the circle was Alexander, and he looked more dead than alive.

He was hanging by his wrists from a gibbet. His body

was streaked with blood, and flies swarmed around him in a dark cloud. His head had fallen forward so that I couldn't see his face. Every rib showed, and I wondered if he'd been fed in the pit. Then I reasoned they'd starved him in order to weaken him. The druids wouldn't want to tangle with a fit Alexander. I shuddered and clenched my teeth to keep the bile down.

I have to stay strong, I have to stay strong, I thought sternly to myself. For Alexander's sake, if he were still alive, and for Paul. I took shallow breaths and watched. I was hoping for some sign of life. The slightest twitch to show me he was breathing, but he didn't move – and neither did the druids.

It took me a while to realize Demos was swearing quietly under his breath.

'What is it?' I managed to ask him when I'd unclenched my jaw.

'They're waiting for the Eaters of the Dead. Until then they will guard him.'

'Is he still alive?' My voice broke and I hated myself for it. 'Be strong,' I whispered angrily in English, 'Just be strong.'

Demos covered my hand with his massive one. 'Yes, he's still alive. They can't kill him until the moon and the sun share the same sky. It won't happen until midnight tonight. By then I hope we'll have a plan.'

'What? You don't have a plan?'

'No. Do you?'

I stared at him, but he was serious. I turned my head, peering through the leaves, trying to catch sight of the

Roman soldiers, but they were too well hidden. 'Can we use the tunnel I cut through the nettles?' I asked hopefully.

'That's for you. You're going to use that tunnel. When the fighting breaks out, grab Paul and go straight up the side of the mountain and back to the camp. Plexis will be waiting at the place where you usually watched the village.'

'He's not fighting?' I asked, forgetting for a moment about his arm. 'No, I'm sorry, don't answer that. I'll do as you say.'

He nodded and turned his attention back to the druids.

The sun rose higher. I couldn't look at Alexander. Each time I did I had to clench my fists in order not to scream at him, 'We're here! Don't give up hope!' I must have whispered it once though, because Demos told me that Alexander knew we were there. I can't say that it gave me any comfort.

When the sun was high enough, Demos said that our allies were getting into position. I strained my eyes and ears, but all I heard were the liquid notes of bird calls and the rustle of leaves.

It was summer, the summer solstice to be exact. Today the sun would not set, and the moon would join it in the sky at midnight. At that hour, the moon and the sun would stare across the standing stones at each other in perfect alignment. The shadows of the stones would criss-cross, forming sacred symbols on the earth. Then the druids would feed the stones. Carved from the limestone cliffs in the south, they were porous and thirsty

104

in the hot sun – the stones drank blood. When the ceremonies were over, the Eaters of the Dead would come out of their caves in the mountains and accept the sacrifices made for them.

At least, that's what Demos told me, as we lay in the shade watching the villagers prepare for the ceremony.

It was a very long and complicated process. Voltarrix was in charge of everything. He showed where the pits were to be dug for the fires and supervised building a tent by the stream for the purifying baths. A large fire was built next to the tent, and armloads of fresh herbs were tossed onto it filling the air with a pungent smoke.

The smoke billowed around the camp and rose into the air. Soon we could smell it. It was bitter and made my eyes water.

The village children put the goats into their pasture, took three pure white kids out from the herd, and led them away. These would be sacrificed along with a white bull tied to a large wooden post near the standing stones.

The bull was content; a pile of hay was at his feet and hundreds of flowers strewn around him. He munched on the hay and flowers, unaware of his role in the proceedings. The three kids baa'd plaintively for their mothers. The children wove garlands of flowers and put them around the goats' white necks.

Flowers were everywhere. Each hut had a wreath on its door. Each woman had a necklace of blossoms, and the men had crowns made of yellow flowers. The children made daisy chains, twisted flowers into their hair, and wore them around their necks, ankles, and wrists.

More druids materialized. They came from the valley following the stream. I counted fifty of them. They weren't armed. They were dressed in long robes, had long beards, and carried staffs with green leaves on them. When they arrived in the village it was a sign for everyone to hasten with their chores. All at once, everyone was rushing about. Wood was carried to woodpiles, animals were herded into their pens, and last minute bouquets deposited in strategic spots around the village. When all was ready – pits dug, wood stacked, caldrons set to boil, knives sharpened, and flowers arranged – it was time to bathe and dress.

I watched as the women lined up according to age in front of the bathing tent. They each held a clean, folded tunic in their arms. Two women carried the old woman on a stretcher, but she was left alone in the tent to purify herself. When she finished, two women went back inside and carried her out. I didn't notice any difference in her appearance.

Then the women, one by one, disappeared into the tent and reappeared a few minutes later with wet hair and a fresh dress. They had discarded their leather clothes for beautifully woven robes.

I was interested, and asked Demos why they hadn't changed before. He told me that the woven clothes were used only during the festivities. As today was officially the height of summer, they could change out of their casual wear and welcome in the solstice. I imagine they were happy to do so. It had been hot and the leather must have been sweltering.

The women wore long dresses. Intricate designs were embroidered on them in the Celtic style. Little girls wore short dresses with pretty patterns. The colours were beautiful – deep yellow, red, sky blue, or dark blue. When the women finished, the tent was taken down by three men and another tent was erected. Then it was the men's turn to wash and purify themselves.

The women gathered in a circle and started to chant. Children seemed free to do as they liked, but I noticed that none of them approached the druids or went near the sacrificial animals any more. Before the purifying ceremony they'd petted the goats and made them garlands. Now they stayed away from them.

The women sang, but appeared nervous. I noticed that one or two were even crying, although they wiped their tears away quickly. I could tell from their expressions that they were upset. When I pointed this out to Demos he shook his head.

'I think I can guess why.' Demos pursed his lips but wouldn't elaborate. 'Get ready to move. When the men finish purifying themselves you must go into the valley. Don't try to get to Paul until we enter the village, is that clear?'

'Perfectly.' I nodded and crawled away. I eased from the edge of the precipice and crept down the narrow path. I was careful to walk as quietly as possible, stopping now and then to listen. I stayed on the faint path and soon found myself on the shelf of rock where we'd first spied on the village. Plexis was there. He was

107

watching the village with a rare concentration, and when he turned to greet me I saw the traces of his tears.

'Don't worry, he's tougher than he looks,' I said quietly.

'I know, but it pains me to see him like that. He hasn't moved. I'm so worried,' he said. 'My arm is useless; I can't even go down there to save him.'

I took him in my arms and held him tightly. He tucked my head under his chin and I pressed my cheek against his throat. He'd shaved, I noticed. Axiom must have brought a razor with him.

A razor. 'Plexis, ' I whispered. 'Where is your razor?'

'In my pouch.'

'Give it to me.'

Plexis didn't ask why. He opened his leather pouch and carefully pulled out the iron razor. It had a short handle, a blade as wide as my hand, and was easily as sharp as a modern atomized ceramic razor. It was wrapped in a piece of soft leather. I unwrapped it, held it in the palm of my hand, and sliced a neat cut in my skirt.

'It works,' I murmured.

'Well, of course it does. I never knew a better razor-sharpener than Axiom. He's always kept Alexander's blades perfectly honed.'

'I have to go now,' I said.

'Be careful. I'll wait right here for you and Paul.' He leaned over and kissed me on the lips.

I sighed deeply. 'Wish me luck, Plexis.'

He almost smiled. 'Go now. And save Alexander.'

The trip down the mountain was easy. I had already

done it once, and I was careful to keep low to the ground and stay behind deep cover. I watched where I put my feet, avoiding dry leaves and sticks. If I hadn't known someone like Plexis, I would have thought I'd done a good job, but compared to him I must have made a racket. Luckily, the women were singing and covered the noise of my descent.

They chanted so loudly that I could have shouted all the swear words I only muttered in my head, when I accidentally grabbed a clump of nettles. I thought them very loudly though. One of the druids frowned mightily and swung his head from side to side. I figured he was like Plexis – he could pick up thoughts as an antenna picks up radio waves. I immediately brought to mind the trees and plants around me, crushing a handful of wild thyme in my hand and inhaling deeply. I tried to imagine I was a rabbit, hopping around looking for food. The druid grew even more suspicious, stepping out of line and looking over the women's heads in my direction.

I was hidden in a little bush. It was small but dense. I was roughly thirty metres away. The land sloped steeply downwards. The vegetation became thicker and thicker until it met the hedge of nettles. The nettles kept everyone at bay, including the druid. He stared suspiciously into the forest, but I made my mind as blank as possible. Finally, he went back in line.

Voltarrix had noticed though, and he went to see the druid himself. He was watching everything, I thought bitterly.

The two men spoke briefly, and then Voltarrix turned

and faced me. He held himself absolutely still. But now I was onto him. I crushed some more thyme and breathed deeply, flattening myself to the ground, waiting for the air pressure to change around me. I don't know how he did it. How can anyone concentrate enough to create a sort of vacuum?

I'm sure he had some simple explanation for it, and I'd understand it as clearly as he would if I tried to explain to him just how a floating crystal video worked in my time. Three thousand years of scepticism and incomprehension separated us. I was a sceptic, but the air changed around me just the same.

My ears rang and my head felt as if it were full of helium. I dug myself deeper into the soft earth and took fast, shallow breaths. I was closer to him now, so the feeling was more powerful. The women felt it too, because one began to wail and a child screamed in fright. Soon all the small children started to cry.

This must have caused Voltarrix to lose his concentration. The last time he'd done this trick, I remembered he'd been practically alone in the village. Now the air whooshed back with the familiar 'pop', and my heart slowed to normal. The children were still crying, and I stole a glance at Voltarrix.

He was looking angrily at the group of women and children huddled together. The smaller ones had all run to their mothers and were seeking refuge in their arms, but the women were acting strangely. Instead of comforting them, they were pushing them away and speaking to them urgently. I was close enough to hear, but because I didn't speak their language, I didn't know what they were saying.

I soon found out. Voltarrix, after one last piercing look in my general direction – although not straight at me, which made me think he hadn't been able to use his powers as well he'd have liked – pointed at the women and barked some orders.

Immediately an icy silence fell over the group. Even the sobbing children seemed to understand the gravity of the order, because they stopped crying and stood still, some still hiccupping miserably.

In the quiet, Voltarrix's words fell like an axe.

'You,' he said. 'And you and you.' I divined the meaning of his words. He pointed as he spoke, and the children he pointed at stared at him with round eyes. Their mothers flinched as if they'd been struck. Three druids, their wolf-skin capes flapping around their bare legs, broke away from the circle and strode over to the three children. Without a word, they seized the children by their arms and dragged them away. The children struggled and cried in high, piteous voices, but the men held tight.

The women screamed, tearing at their hair and clothes and ripping their flower necklaces off. I felt a wave of heat rush over me. The children were being led to the place where the bull and the three kids were waiting. They were sacrificial victims as well.

Once before I'd seen children sacrificed, but it had been in a place far away and the memory had mercifully faded to a blur. This was here and now, and the three children were not more than five years old.

Two were boys, dressed in yellow tunics with copper bands around their arms. They were twins and held onto each other, eyes wide with terror. They didn't cry, but their mouths trembled violently. The other was a little girl. Her hair was full of flowers, her face was streaked with tears, and she held her thin arms out to her mother and screamed and screamed.

Chapter Nine

I felt faint. I was certain I'd pass out, so I pressed my head to the earth and tried to breathe deeply, but my chest was too tight. Desperate, I reached over and grabbed a briar branch. The thorns made me gasp, but I got my breath back. Then I made my way down to the edge of the nettle hedge and carefully parted the leaves, looking for the tunnel I'd worked on. I didn't have to worry about making noise. The women were wailing right on the other side of the nettles, and the noise they made covered any rustle that I might make.

I slithered through the tunnel, getting stings and welts again, but the pain was welcome. I needed it to keep me from shivering into a faint. Shock was making my hands and feet icy. The burning pain worked. By the time I'd made it to the women, I was as clearheaded as I'd ever been.

'Psssst!' I said nervously. This was either going to work or it wasn't. 'Psst!!'

One of the women heard me and broke off her wailing. She shook her head slightly and looked into the nettles. When she saw me she opened her mouth to say something, but I put my finger to my lips in the international all-through-time sign to be quiet. She nodded, her eyes wide. Then I motioned her nearer. When she was close, I asked in a whisper, 'Does anyone here speak Greek?'

I could only speak Greek with these people. I knew no Celt, or Keltoi, as they called it back then. 'Find a woman who speaks Greek!' I commanded. 'Please!'

She didn't speak Greek, but she got the gist. She moved back into the group and made her way to another woman's side. This woman was older, perhaps forty, and she looked darker than the usual Valerian. She eased over to me. When she saw me her eyes grew very wide, but she didn't give me away either.

'I want to rescue my son and husband,' I said, without preamble. 'And if you help me I believe we can rescue the children, defeat the druids, and free all of you. The people of Orce have an army hiding in the woods.' I was exaggerating a little about the army, but I meant it about trying to rescue the children.

'Who are you?' she asked, her eyes narrowing suspiciously.

'Some call me Persephone, daughter of Demeter,' I said, putting swagger in my voice. Now I knew how Clark Kent felt when he opened his shirt and let the big red 'S' peep out.

She stepped back as if I'd struck her. For a second I thought she would scream and call the druids to me, but I'd misjudged her reaction. Her eyes filled with tears and she leaned towards me again. 'We will help you,' she said, her voice breaking with emotion. 'Tell us what to do.'

'Continue singing as usual. Can you get me a dress? I'll join you. Do the druids know every one of you by sight?'

'No, they don't know us. They come once a year for the ceremony. They kill three children and three men. It has been so for generations. Afterwards, they call the Eaters of the Dead to come. We must feed them, otherwise they will kill us all.'

'I don't understand. The druids *call* the Eaters of the Dead? Who are they? Where are they?'

'Voltarrix is their master. He controls them. They come out of their lairs when they smell the blood. If they are hungry, they sometimes come at other times during the year. However, they always come for the summer solstice. *Always.*' She shivered.

'Perhaps it would be best to leave before they come,' I said.

'Many have tried, but The Eaters of the Dead live in the forest and know it by heart. They hunt like wolves, and if you flee they run you down. No one has ever succeeded.'

'There are enough of us to fight against them and win this time,' I said.

She shook her head. 'I don't know. I will give you a dress. We can only try. We have been slaves here far too long.'

'Why didn't you try to fight them before?'

'The druids are armed. If we rebel, Voltarrix said he will turn us into goats.'

'Oh.' I frowned. 'Do you think he can?'

'He can stop time,' she said seriously. 'That's what he does the best.'

Stop time? I doubted that. But he was dangerously close to changing time. I waited for the woman to fetch me a dress. She came back with one hidden under her clothes. She sat with her back to me and passed it to me through the nettles. I had a rough time dressing in the thicket. When I finished I was burning with nettle rash, but I was wearing a lovely blue robe with green and yellow trim. I crawled out and knelt next to the woman. Immediately, several others came and surrounded me, absorbing me into the group and hiding me from sight.

Hardly any of them spoke Greek, only two or three, but it was enough. I explained in a low voice what was happening, and they spread the word as casually as possible that there was going to be an attack. When that happened, they must grab their children and rush up the mountain slope away from the village.

Some women broke off their chanting and stared at me with wide eyes until the cleverer ones elbowed them sharply. None of them made the slightest move towards the druids, so I imagined they were all glad to be planning an escape.

Most women knew the legend of Persephone, and I suppose I looked like someone who'd just crawled out of the underworld through a thicket of nettles. In all likelihood, that's what the real Persephone would have done.

The woman who'd given me the dress eased over to

116

my side and spoke without looking at me. 'We know that human sacrifices are an abomination to you, but the druids and the Celts have bloodthirsty gods. I was born in Athens as a slave and sold to a Keltoi. He took me to Orce and married me. One day, while I was gathering nuts in the forest, the people of the reindeer stole me. They took me to their village, but soon after, the Eaters of the Dead came and massacred the tribe. They took two other women and me as slaves and brought us to this valley. Voltarrix, the druid, comes once a year. He is the master for the Eaters of the Dead.'

'How terrible,' I said softly.

'I have prayed to Zeus every day for three years to deliver me. Today he has sent you, Demeter's daughter. My prayers have been answered.'

'I hope so,' I said nervously. I glanced into the forest. Where was everyone?

The sun was sinking.

To me it seemed as if it were falling towards the horizon. I wanted to push it back up into the sky, to slow it down. Its edges shimmered and turned blood-red.

I searched, but I couldn't see Paul. He was still in the deep pit with Yovanix and Nearchus. My eyes were drawn back to my husband, and I shuddered. Alexander still hadn't given any sign of life. Then a drum started beating. The sound came from all around us; it echoed off the tall cliffs on either side of the valley and filled the air with a deafening throbbing. The women turned to face the druids. In front of us, lined up on the other side of the standing stones, were the few men from the village. They wore their finest clothes; brightly embroidered tunics over yellow leggings and sandals. Everyone slowly kneeled, eyes wide with fright.

'What's happening?' I asked, kneeling next to the Greek-speaking woman.

'Voltarrix is going to sacrifice your husband. His death will last forever, and when his soul has had enough of suffering, Voltarrix will capture it in your husband's blood. The person who drinks that blood will then inherit the soul.' Her voice was so low I could hardly catch her words, but I heard enough.

'Alexander said he felt as if his soul were already gone.' I said to the woman.

'But it is still his own. A soul can leave a body and still belong to that person. However, if he dies slowly enough the soul can be captured. Voltarrix can make death last for hours.'

'I have to save him,' I said brokenly. 'Alexander!' I was halfway to my feet but the woman pulled me down.

'No. The druids are armed with sacred iron. They will kill you before you can pass the outer circle. There is nothing you can do, even as a goddess. Time obeys Voltarrix.' She spoke harshly, gripping my arm hard enough to bruise. Sacred iron, I knew, meant it had come from a meteorite. The people of that time thought it was a gift from the gods. I closed my eyes and breathed a prayer to any god within hearing to spare my husband.

Nothing I had ever experienced prepared me for what happened next.

The sun came to rest on the edge of the valley. On

one end of the valley the shimmering sun hung like the bronze shield the Greeks used. Paul had a shield like that. It used to be Alexander's but Apollo had ordered him to give it to his son. Paul had it now, if he hadn't lost it.

On the other end of the valley, the full moon glowed fat and silver, casting its own pale light. The shadows lengthened, met, criss-crossed, and vanished. Voltarrix stood next to Alexander and raised his arms.

The air crystallized around us, all sounds were lost in the vacuum. I heard an eerie clicking. Voltarrix raised his knife and cut Alexander's throat.

Time stood still.

It was as if someone pushed the 'Pause' button on the floating vid display. The air hardened into solidity. Everyone around me was caught, frozen, in a moment of time that Voltarrix had somehow stopped. Everyone was caught, except me. I found myself running towards Alexander. It was a purely reflexive action; my legs had launched me before I could think. All I could feel was rage and sorrow.

Chapter Ten

As I ran, I caught sight of someone else. It was Paul. He clambered out of the pit and dashed towards his father. His mouth was open in a silent scream. Everyone else was turned to stone.

I was moving, but it was a struggle. I felt as if I were in a dream. I was running, but it felt more like swimming. I breathed in great gulps.

A red line was forming on Alexander's throat.

He was looking at me. His lips were moving but too slowly for me to understand what he was trying to say. He was caught in the same frozen moment as everyone else. Everyone was a prisoner except for Paul and me. Even Voltarrix was trapped like a fly in amber.

He hadn't expected Paul and me to resist. He had no way of knowing who we really were, and what rules governed us. His eyes slowly widened in shock.

When I reached Alexander, after what seemed like an eternity of running, I used the razor to cut the ropes holding him upright. I saw what I needed to know. Alexander was caught in time, he didn't move, but the ropes fell slowly as if they were floating through thick honey. My actions created their own reactions.

Alexander's throat was cut. Voltarrix was holding a copper bowl in his hand. He wanted to collect the blood.

I finally understood what he did, and how he did it. He was moving. Slowly, to be sure, but he could force himself to move. His sacrifices would last for ages. The victim died for hours.

The strange thing was that time had no effect on our thoughts. My thoughts worked as rapidly as ever, perhaps even faster because of the panic gripping me.

Voltarrix held a knife in his other hand, and it was moving. He wanted to finish the sacrifice, but Paul was too quick. Paul held a shining shield – the one his father had given him – and he thrust it at the druid. The knife's stab that was meant to slit Alexander's belly open was deflected by bronze.

My hands flew to Alexander's throat, and I wrapped cloth I'd torn from my dress tightly around his neck. The edges of the wound gaped, but there was no time to spare. Before the blood splashed down his chest in a scarlet wash, we had to get back up the hill.

I screamed words at Paul. My voice came out weird and twisted, slowed by the forces of time and the strange vacuum we were in, but he understood what I needed. We sat Alexander on the shield and placed his arms around our necks. He was helpless to move, but using the shield as a seat, we could carry him. We lifted him and set off at a run towards the group of women standing like statues. When we passed through the double ring of druids my breath caught in my throat. I could feel their anger and their power. They wielded their minds like weapons at us. Their thoughts rained upon us like blows, then we were through the outer circle and they ceased.

My heart was hammering so wildly I thought it would explode. Black spots danced in front of my eyes. Everything was unnaturally silent; all I could hear was my breath whistling in my throat. My feet hitting the ground made no noise at all, and everything I touched felt strange, as if I were a ghost.

Voltarrix was staring, incredulous. His features twisted with rage and he started to raise his arms to the sky. It was slow, so slow. The knife in his hand described a shining arc towards the heavens. His muscles and tendons stood out like cords in the fierce effort he made to move. His eyes were as red as the bloody sun and glowed eerily.

Paul and I ran through the nettles, but even they were caught in time. They didn't release their venom and we received no stings. It was like pushing through a grove of brittle silk. Leaves beneath our feet swirled like slow water. Stems we pushed back stayed in that position, weirdly out of shape. Grass bent and stayed bent. We left a gaping trail through the undergrowth, but I could feel neither stem nor leaf. Nothing left an impression on our skin. Even the weight of the shield with Alexander upon it, was like a feather. Out of the timeline, in a sort of parallel world, we were almost superhuman. Nothing touched us, and we were as strong as Titans.

At the base of the cliff, we lay Alexander across the shield. His torso fit on it, his legs and arms dangled from the sides. I climbed up first, reaching down to catch the round edge of the shield and heave Alexander up. Paul scrambled past me, and then I pushed while he pulled. The ground beneath us felt elastic, even the rocks were springy to the touch. I could dig my fingers into the granite. It gave like rubber.

We kept going upwards, alternately pushing and pulling, and our progress was equal to the power of Voltarrix's arms. We were halfway up the hill when I glanced back at him. His arms were straight out at his sides, his eyes blazing with madness. After that I stopped looking back. He frightened me too much.

The earth beneath us began to tremble. Paul slipped, but I caught the shield and held on. It had a thick, rolled edge, just right for getting a good grip. Alexander lay upon it like a white statue. His eyes were closed, the skin around his mouth and nose was crusted with dried blood. I had no idea what he'd suffered before we rescued him. I only hoped we weren't too late.

One last heave, and he was sliding onto the ledge where Plexis lay, frozen in time.

Then Voltarrix's hands met above his head.

There was a clap of thunder that flattened us to the ground. Blood spurted from our noses, ears, and from Alexander's throat. However, I was ready. So was Plexis. He couldn't move, but he could think. When the thunder subsided, I spit out a mouthful of blood and shouted. He didn't waste time asking questions.

As soon as time was released, Plexis tore open his sewing kit. He was always mending something. His needles were always threaded and ready, neat in their case. Now we used them to sew up Alexander's neck, holding the wound closed, wiping his blood away with the backs of our hands. It was soon done. Voltarrix hadn't cut any major blood vessels; death was to have come slowly. Thankfully, the cut was shallow.

Plexis stared in stupefaction. 'I never saw that before,' he said finally, referring to the stitches. They didn't exist in his time. Wounds were cauterized with white-hot metal.

He'd watched me start and then he'd taken over, sewing with the small, neat stitches he always used and knotting carefully after each one. Afterwards, he'd slumped to the ground, his head next to Alexander's. They looked like two cadavers covered in blood.

I leaned over the ledge and started to shake. It was all too much. The shock was making my head spin. My hands were ice. I trembled violently. I hung onto the edge and I stared down in the valley where everything was utter pandemonium.

A swarm of women and children were fleeing up the path I'd made. In a moment we'd have fifty people upon us.

The Roman soldiers and the men of Orce were fighting the druids, and the fight seemed even. I caught sight of Demos, towering above the rest, and Nearchus, his golden hair flashing in the ever-setting sun. The druids were like wild animals with their painted bodies and wolf-skin capes. They had iron swords and shields, and the sound of clanging metal was like bells ringing and ringing. It was deafening. As I watched, a druid lost an arm to a heavy swipe by Demos. The sight made me feel faint. I took a deep breath and turned to my son. He was sitting with his legs drawn up to his chest, his hands clasped hard around his knees.

'Are you all right?' I asked.

'No.' He shook his head, making teardrops fly. 'I'm so afraid. I hate Voltarrix. He killed my father. I saw him kill my father.' He was trying to make himself as small as possible. His voice was thin as wire.

'Your father is not dead, and Demos will kill that horrible man,' I said, moving towards him slowly, carefully. I moved slowly because I didn't want to startle him. He was in shock. His whole body was cold and his hands and feet were marbled white and blue.

Carefully, gently, I draped a wool blanket around his shoulders. 'You're free. And you helped save your father. We're all together, look around you. Plexis is here and I'm here. Your father is here. He'll get better, I swear to you. The wound was awful to see but it wasn't deep. It will heal quickly.' I spoke in a soft whisper, rubbing his back and shoulders, finally gathering him in my arms and letting my tears wet his hair. 'Oh Paul, my little Paul. You've grown so big. Look at you,' I drew a ragged breath. 'You're nearly as tall as I am. Oh Paul, my sweet Paul. I love you so much.'

He stopped shivering and his arms crept around my neck. 'I won't go back to the pit. I'd sooner die. Promise me we won't go back.'

'I promise.' I spoke fiercely.

'Cerberus is dead.' His voice broke and finally he

began to sob. Huge racking sobs that shook his whole body.

Cerberus was his hound puppy. My face twisted, thinking of how much my son adored his dog. 'Paul, hush, hush baby. I'm so sorry. Poor Cerberus. Please don't cry. Wipe your eyes. We have to leave. We have to leave now. Somehow we have to get back to Orce with the people.'

'What people?' Paul asked in a small whisper.

'These people.' The women started clambering over the ledge. They said nothing. Their faces were blank with shock and fear. Most had red welts from nettles, some held children. I saw the twin boys clutched tightly in their mother's arms, and the little girl, saved from the sacrifice, held tightly by her mother.

The people climbed onto the ledge and stopped to face me. One by one, they knelt at my feet, pressing their foreheads to the moss. They touched Paul on the shoulder, they bowed to Plexis, and then they walked silently past Alexander's body, reaching down to touch him on his hair, his cloak, or his feet.

Alexander was still unconscious, but his chest moved slightly with each breath. He was lying on the shield, his purple cloak tucked around him. Plexis washed his wound with marigold water and bound it with a clean strip of cloth. I thought Alexander's neck would heal if it didn't become infected.

Paul and I were still shocked. The women from the village didn't look much better. Everyone was pale and tearful. Plexis took over. He stood up and gathered his cloak around him.

'We're leaving now before the fighting is done,' he said. 'We will walk in single file. Carry your children, walk as quickly as you can, and make no noise.'

I stood up on unsteady feet and looked down at my husband. I had no strength left. I couldn't lift him again. My hands, when I grasped the edge of the shield, slipped off. Tears rolled down my cheeks. Then a hand touched my shoulder.

I looked up, and through a blur of tears, saw Phaleria. She was hard to miss with her bright copper hair. I smiled then, though my tears fell even faster. I hugged her hard. She held onto me. Her strength was so reassuring. When she'd managed to calm me down, she smoothed my hair from my face and grinned. 'Don't worry, we'll carry your husband,' she whispered. My shoulders slumped with relief.

Plexis watched us, an unreadable expression on his face. I looked away, shaken. I'd seen him look like that once before, in India, when Alexander had been struck by an arrow in the chest. I longed to reassure him, to tell him it looked far worse than it was, but I had no more energy left. Besides, I knew I would never be able to sound convincing. I was terrified.

A tall woman nodded at me. Two other women were lined up behind her. Without a sound, they bent down and picked up the shield., Holding it between them, they carried Alexander as they followed Plexis.

I trailed just behind them, behind me was Paul. After us came mothers with young children in their arms, and bringing up the rear were four women armed with light spears.

They were all Valerians. The other tribe, the smaller, darker people, with high cheekbones and slanted eyes, faded into the forest and took a different route. They were heading north, to their own territory. Before leaving, they bowed to me and touched Alexander reverently, as if he were something holy.

We walked five hours without stopping. Plexis kept a steady pace. Before we were too tired, we halted at the side of a stream. The women didn't waste time asking questions. One started a fire, two went to gather wood, and three went fishing with the spears they carried. Several others disappeared into the underbrush. One dug a latrine pit, and another started digging for edible roots. They all knew exactly what they had to do. The children were just as well disciplined. They used the latrine, washed in the stream, and sat down quietly and stayed out of the way. A row of seven children, ranging in ages from about nine months old to six, sat with fingers in their mouths, staring at Paul, Phaleria, Alexander, and me.

Well, I was used to it. I smiled at them and received wide-eyed looks in return. Then I knelt next to Alexander. He was still unconscious. I tucked his cloak warmly around his shoulders and sat back on my heels putting my hands over my face. It was wet with tears and sticky with blood. With a sigh I got up and went to the stream to wash. Alexander needed rest. I wanted to boil water to sterilize bandages and make nice, hot soup.

When I finished washing the best I could in the shallow brook, I wandered back to the camp. Fish had been caught and several women, including Phaleria, were preparing dinner.

I sat next to Phaleria, busy cutting fish into little pieces.

'What happened?' I asked.

'When?' She tilted her head to the side. 'Right after you left that night?'

'Well, yes.'

'We sailed out to the open sea, pursued by the dragon boat. They caught up with us easily, although I did manage to lead them a merry chase through some islands off the coast. When I was sure we could no longer flee, I surrendered and let them come aboard.' She grimaced. 'I thought that once they saw we didn't have Iskander or Paul with us, they would leave.' Her hands flew, chopping up the fish. When she was done, she tipped the meat onto a large leaf. The woman next to her skewered them on a slender branch and set it over the fire.

'But they didn't.' I watched as she picked up another fish and expertly gutted it.

'No, they sank my ship.' There was real regret in her voice, and I stared at her in consternation.

'But that was the ship you grew up on! It was your home!' I cried.

'I know.' Her pretty mouth twisted. 'We were taken aboard the dragon boat, who knows why. They should have thrown us overboard, but they didn't.'

'They *should* have tossed you overboard?' I stared

129

some more.

'Well, yes. Because as soon as their guard was down, we attacked them and threw *their* bodies into the sea.' She shook her head. 'They thought I was just another helpless female.' Her mouth twisted again, but this time it didn't look so pretty. 'They *actually* thought they could rape me!'

'Phaleria!'

'Well, I showed them.' Her voice was grim. Luckily there were only seven of them, and six of us. A fair fight.' She shook her bloody knife in front of her face, scowling, then went back to preparing the food. The fish she was holding was gutted and sliced up in no time.

'I'm glad you won,' I said.

'Me too.' She shrugged. 'When we got back to the fjord, the other half of the druids had already left to hunt you, and more were coming in by sea. We hid the dragon boat and went by land to Orce. I spoke to the wise woman. When she heard that the great Iskander had been kidnapped, she ordered the villagers to go after him. Axiom managed to buy a small company of Roman guards, and they led us.'

'They would,' I said with a wry grin. Then I realized what she'd said. 'You called him the great Iskander,' I said uneasily. 'Why?'

'Maybe you think I'm as blind as the wise woman?' she asked, reaching for another fish.

'I didn't say that …'

'She told me,' said Phaleria matter-of-factly. 'Don't worry, I won't say anything to anyone. How many people would believe it anyway?' She held the last fish on the ground in front of her and flicked off the fins, scales, and head with deft motions of her knife.

I looked over at Alexander, lying still as death on the ground. 'No one, if they saw him now. But when he's fit, I think anyone would believe it.' Phaleria leaned forward to catch my words, spoken in a mere breath.

She nodded. 'You're right. When he's well, he emits a sort of radiance. I saw it right away. I think if he'd asked me to sail off the edge of the earth I would, just for one of his smiles.' She finished cutting up the trout and wiped her hands on the grass.

I nodded; most people felt that way about him. 'There are people who know who he is. Yovanix overheard Demos talking with Nearchus and Alexander about their battles. And the wise woman guessed, though how she did so is beyond me.'

'She says he is golden,' said Phaleria, with a shrug. She smiled thinly. 'She said the same for your son, for Paul. She said she wants to see him when he gets back to Orce.'

'She was so sure we'd rescue him?' I asked.

'She is a wise woman. She sees places we haven't been to yet.'

I had just about had it with wise-women who sensed auras and druids who twisted time. Thinking about that raised goose bumps up and down my arms. I suppressed a shudder. 'Well, he's no longer the Great Iskander. He's just Alexander, and he's hurt. He needs to get back to Orce as quickly as possible.'

'Great Iskander or not, he'll have to make the voyage like the rest of us, through marsh and forest, over mountain and plain. And hope the Eaters of the Dead don't catch us before we're ready to fight again.'

'Who? The Eaters of the Dead? Why?'

'Because,' she said grimly, 'they will be following us.' She held her knife tightly in her hands, then, with a frown, wiped its blade with a piece of torn cloth.

Chapter Eleven

Alexander woke up and tried to sit, but he was far too weak. His hands flew to his throat and he touched the bandage we had put there. His face became even paler than before, but he didn't faint. Instead he took a deep breath, experimenting, and then he whispered, 'Thank Zeus', before smiling at us.

I smiled back, and then flung myself on him, holding him so tightly he could hardly breath.

'Ashley,' he whispered.

'How do you feel?' I asked, not letting go.

'Shaky. Dirty. Hungry. Weak. My neck hurts like Hades. What happened?'

'We'll tell you later. I've heated some water. Do you want me to wash you?'

He grinned. 'You women are always giving baths to the heroes in the stories, aren't you?' He was referring to my preference for *The Odyssey*, a story we used to read aloud to each other.

'Either that or weaving with our looms,' I said with a dazzling smile. 'Oh, Alex, I was so worried about you.'

'I'll be fine after you wash me and shave me.' He fingered his uneven beard. 'I can't see myself, but I imagine I must look fairly barbarian.' His voice was still a broken whisper.

Plexis helped me, and soon Alexander was clean, shaved, and propped up against a tree. He swallowed his fish soup carefully, grimacing when his throat muscles moved. The stitches held, although a thin ribbon of blood trickled down his chest. I waited until he had finished the soup. Then I examined the wound. It was still clean, not inflamed. I washed it carefully with boiled water and marigold, then bandaged it again with a clean cloth. Alexander wanted to see the stitches so we held up Plexis's mirror. His eyes grew very wide and he turned white.

'By Arachne's web, that is a terrifying sight,' he whispered nervously. 'Who would have thought of sewing skin together?'

'You would have preferred us to cauterize it perhaps?' It was Plexis, a teasing note in his voice. He looked almost as as ill as Alexander though, and his hands shook.

Phaleria strolled over, twisting some cabbage leaves into a bowl. She caught sight of the stitches and the leaves she was holding slipped from her fingers. Her face drained of all colour, and she hastily made signs to ward off evil as she backed away. 'It was true, I didn't imagine it,' she gasped. 'He was dead; the druid did cut his throat. I saw it, I saw it, but I thought … by Lug, I thought I had just imagined …' Her voice climbed skyward and several women looked at her curiously, but they didn't speak Greek.

134

I quickly covered his neck with clean linen and got to my feet. 'Don't be afraid, it's only stitches,' I said, trying to make my voice sound reassuring. However, Phaleria looked at me now with the same expression everyone wore when they found out I was supposed to be Persephone the Terrible, Queen of the Underworld, the Queen of Ice and Darkness. And the look she gave Alexander was so full of awe it was positively overflowing. The Great Iskander indeed. How many times had he been resurrected? Three thousand years later there was still no rest for him. Twice, time-travellers had been to see him. That was unheard of. No one was visited more than once. However, I'd managed to convince the Institute of Time Travel and Study to send me to him. And look what happened. I sighed and pressed my forehead to my knees.

'Are you all right, Mother?' Paul sat down by my side, taking my hand in his.

'I think so.' I smiled. 'I was just thinking about the first time I saw your father.' My voice was wistful.

'When he captured you?' Paul always loved that story. He lay his head on my shoulder and snuggled close. 'Tell me again.'

'I arrived here in the past dressed in the fine linen robes of a Mesopotamian priestess. I was supposed to pose as an onirocrite. That was part of the plan to get Iskander to talk about what he wanted to do, because no one ever understood why he'd decided to conquer Sogdia, Bactria, Lydia, and go all the way to India when he'd already beaten Darius. He was already king of

Macedonia, Greece and Egypt; they thought it should have been enough.'

'He wanted to unite East with West,' murmured Paul, half asleep.

'And we wanted to find you, our child of the moon,' I said softly.

'When you met Father you fell in love, and he captured you.'

'I guess that's what happened, although I didn't realize it at the time. I only knew he was special. I was under his spell, so I didn't fight as much as I could have when he dragged me out of the Time-Tractor beam.'

'He said it made a blue light all around you, and that you were silver with frost. His soldiers screamed in fright and wouldn't go near you, but Father threw down his sword and reached into the cold crying, 'I shall save you from Hades, my Lady Persephone, and you will be my oracle!" Paul chuckled quietly, then yawned.

'I wasn't really Persephone,' I said, stifling my own yawn.

'Hmm. Father said he was surprised you turned out to be mortal.'

I hugged Paul. 'Well, that was how I met him.'

'Then you were kidnapped, and when I was born, I was taken away from you. We were separated for seven years.' Paul's voice turned fierce. 'If I ever find out who did that I'll … I'll …' He broke off, his fists clenched. His vehemence didn't surprise me. Paul had spent the first four years of his life as a hostage, taken from one end of Persia to the other by our enemies. He'd been too young to truly understand, but it had been a solitary, precarious existence.

'Sometimes things happen, and they seem one way at the time,' I said carefully. 'Then years go by, and you look at them differently. You see the whole picture not just the details. You were kidnapped, and that was one of the elements that led your father to India and made his legend what it is now and what it will be three thousand years from now.'

'It was a horrible thing to do. I suffered for years because of it. I had no parents, I was all alone except for Maia, and then she died,' he said, his eyes brimming with tears.

Maia had been his Sogdian nurse. She'd taken care of him from when he was four until he was nearly ten. She'd been his guardian and had died on the way to Babylon. 'I can't change your past, Paul. No matter how hard it was, you must try and forget. It is in the past, and it cannot be put right, so you just have to learn to live with it. Perhaps someday you will be able to step back and see that it was just a small part of a great whole, and you will understand.'

Paul looked unconvinced, but exhaustion made his mouth tremble, so I put his head on my lap and stroked his bright hair until he fell asleep.

I looked over at Plexis, sitting protectively near Alexander. His head was slumping forward with the effort of staying awake, but it would never occur to him to lie down and sleep while there was danger. Every once in a while he'd stand up and stay perfectly still, listening and looking around in every direction. Then he'd sit back down, slowly, as if his muscles hurt, and take Alexander's hand in his. What would Paul think if he knew it was Plexis who'd arranged my kidnapping?

I didn't know, and it worried me. He was too young. He would feel betrayed. He hadn't had the time to be able to look back and see the whole picture. He wouldn't be able to see, because he was the bright golden thread running through the tapestry of the tale.

We rested until the sun climbed past midday. When it was late afternoon, Plexis ordered the women to cover all traces of the campsite, and we left in the same formation as before – Plexis leading and Alexander lying on his shield with Phaleria and another strong woman carrying him. I walked in front of Paul, and the rest of the women and children followed close behind us.

Phaleria carried Alexander with even more care. Sometimes she'd glance at me and try to smile, but her eyes flickered nervously. I sighed. I would have to have a nice long talk with her. We walked until the sun was a low, red disc in the sky. Then we set up camp.

We had gone through a marshy land, skirting the flank of the mountain where the going would have been rougher. The bog was disagreeable, even if it was easy to navigate. Millions of bugs swarmed around us: horseflies, deerflies, mosquitoes, and midges. All were intent on sucking our blood. We pulled up handfuls of lemon balm leaves, rubbing them over us. We wore woven crowns and necklaces of fragrant plants. It didn't work. Believe me. Nothing worked. I wrapped a linen cloth around my head because the most aggravating flies were those that buzzed around my ears and bit my scalp hard enough to leave bleeding holes. Even so, midges slipped through the cloth and settled in its folds, nibbling happily at my skin.

We were all exasperated by the bugs. Children were crying fretfully, everyone was tight-lipped and haggard, and even Alexander had begun to wriggle, making it harder for the women to carry him. Then I slipped and fell with a resounding splash into a deep puddle. I staggered to my feet, absolutely covered with sticky mud. It dripped off my fingers and nose, matted my hair and glued my eyes closed.

'Agh!' I gasped. 'What happened?' I swiped the mud away from my eyes and peered around. Everyone had stopped and was staring at me as if I were the Bog Monster. I spit a mouthful of mud and sneezed. Then I stood still for a minute. 'You know what?' I said to Plexis.

'What?' he asked, eyeing me dubiously.

'My bug bites feel much better. As a matter of fact,' I said, watching as everyone swatted and slapped. 'They have ceased to bother me.' I bent down and picked up a handful of mud and smeared it on the back of my legs, which were still clean and still under attack. 'There, that feels better.' I sighed. The mud was cool and soothing. It felt wonderful.

I coated Alexander's skin with mud, being careful not to get it anywhere near his wound. Then everyone had a dip in the mud hole, the children enjoying it thoroughly.

When we moved on, we looked like a group out of a horror movie. I could imagine the title – *The Attack of the Mud People*. I didn't care. It was such a blessing to be rid of the flies. They still buzzed around us, but in lesser numbers. They were stymied by the thick mud on our skin. As soon as it dried and flaked off we covered ourselves with more mud. In the swamps there was plenty.

Chapter Twelve

We camped as soon as we reached dry ground. It was just on the edge of the swamp, though, so we didn't bother to wash off the mud. I'd never slept with a coat of mud before. It was most uncomfortable, drying, cracking and pulling my skin, but there were fewer bug bites, and I actually slept deeply for a few hours.

In the morning, I unstuck myself from the ground, crawled out from under the sheltering branches, and stretched in a shower of dried mud flakes. I examined the crackled effect of the mud on my arms and legs and rubbed an itchy bit off the end of my nose. The mud turned to a soft grey dust. I brushed most of it off with the back of my hand.

Melodious bird songs came from the marsh but that was the only sound in the air. I was surrounded by silence. It was a mysterious silence, wrapped in a light fog and sealed with the rays of the sun's first light.

The sun hadn't really set, so one couldn't say it had risen. It was hiding behind a thick, pink mist. Fog hung low over the marsh, hiding the tops of the hazel and hawthorn, and making the taller larch and blackthorn trees appear to float in eddies of opal cloud. I advanced to the edge of the clearing and peered down.

We were camped between the edge of the marsh and the beginning of the mountain's steep flanks. The land rose abruptly, and the stream we'd been following suddenly splashed at our feet in a small cascade. On each side of the waterfall grew thick clumps of fiddlehead fern. We ate our fill of them for dinner. The stream led us to a grove of tall pine trees, and we stayed there for the night. Well, for the half-light, half-dark hours that marked the middle of the night. It was hard for me to judge how late or early it was any more.

Right now, it was time to wash off in a crystal clear pool at the base of two large, moss-covered rocks. The water was icy, straight off the mountain, but it felt invigorating. I scrubbed the mud out of my hair and body, and was rewarded with clear, glowing skin and shiny, clean hair. The mud had done more than just keep the bugs at bay. It was a complete beauty treatment. I washed my clothes and hung them on an ash tree to dry. Then I shook my cloak out and draped it over me, Greek-style, using a long thorn to pin it closed. I wondered where I'd lost my fibula. I had a gold one from Persia that I'd used to keep my cloak fastened, but it had fallen off somewhere in the pine forest. Perhaps someday it would be found and an anthropologist would conclude that the Persians had traded with the Valerians.

Pausing, I admired the mist obscuring the swamp. I loved the way it moved – almost like ethereal water in soft eddies and curls around the huge willow that marked the end of the marshland. Now we would be heading uphill, through the narrow pass I could see between the high peaks. Then we would trek through the great pine forest that stretched all the way to the coast. However, I didn't dwell on the journey – instead, I headed back to our clearing, wondering what we'd eat for breakfast. My stomach was growling.

I was not the only one awake. Plexis still hadn't slept. He was sitting next to Alexander, slowly coaxing a flame from a heap of grey ashes. Two other women were awake; one was nursing a small child and the other was quietly gathering dried wood for the fire. Phaleria was sleeping, curled up in her cloak, and so was Paul – only his hair was visible from under his cloak. He looked warm, though, hidden under a sweeping pine branch.

Almost everyone lay half hidden under massive pine trees. The branches reached out several metres from their trunks, forming a sloping roof. Underneath, layers of pine needles carpeted the ground, making a soft, springy – albeit prickly – bed.

I sat next to Plexis and put my arms around him. He smiled and nuzzled my neck. 'Good morning,' I whispered. 'Do you want to sleep now? I'll take over the watch.'

His mouth twitched. 'I'm not tired.'

'You haven't slept in two days,' I said, tracing the line of his jaw with my hand. I twirled a lock of hair around my finger and let it bounce back. He was irresistible. Whenever I saw him I wanted to … well, let's just say he had an enormous amount of sex appeal. Even as haggard and exhausted as he was now. The circles around his eyes only made him look sexier.

He gave a soft laugh. 'All right, I'll sleep. But first I want to start this fire again; I let it burn down last night. Afterwards I want to bathe, and I want to see about getting food for everyone. If I can snare a few rabbits we can eat them tonight.'

'I'll help you.'

'Do what?' Plexis asked, gathering a handful of pine needles and poking them in the fire.

'Bathe, what else?' It was Alexander. His voice was stronger. He stretched carefully, wincing at all his hurts, and then managed to sit up by himself. 'I feel as if I might live,' he said, and he sounded surprised.

Plexis nodded. 'You sound better. You look better too. But you need to rest and get your strength back.'

'That's right,' I said wisely. 'You're not out of the woods yet.'

Alexander had heard me use that expression before, but Plexis hadn't. 'Of course he's not,' he said. 'We're *all* still in the woods. And we'll be here for quite a while, too.'

'She means I'm not better yet,' said Alexander, eyeing his friend. 'You look terrible. Why don't you go have a bath and get some sleep? Wake Paul, he's capable of setting snares, and I'm sure Phaleria can spear us some fish. There must be at least one or two women with us who can gather vegetables and fruit. Tell them to hurry.'

'He might not be out of the woods,' said Plexis, 'but he's getting much better. When he starts giving orders,

144

you know he's back to normal.' He couldn't hide his relief, and his face was illuminated with a huge grin.

I saw Alexander's eyes become hooded. Plexis did that to everyone. I didn't think it was what Alexander needed at the moment, so I took Plexis by the arm and said, 'Let's go, I'll help you wash.' Before we left, Plexis woke Phaleria and told her she was in charge of breakfast.

She nodded, sitting up and stretching and plucking pine needles out of her copper hair. 'Don't worry, I'll manage.' She rubbed a clump of mud off her chin and scratched her nose. Even covered with dust and with pine needles poking out of her hair like porcupine quills, she looked capable of doing anything.

I took Plexis down the game path leading to the small pool I'd discovered earlier. Plexis shrugged off his tunic, still favouring his arm. When he was undressed, he took handfuls of soft sand and scrubbed himself all over. Then he plunged under the water.

'Oh, that feels good,' he said, standing in the hip-deep water and shaking his head, making the water droplets fly off his curls. He looked like a faun, or some water sprite. The mist lifted and the sunshine filtered through the trees, dappling his skin with green. He sank back into the water, swam a few strokes, then he stood up in a patch of warm sunlight, tipping his head back. All around him was a deep green darkness, the water at his hips swirled clear as jade while his shoulders and head were illuminated. The silence around us was broken only by the trilling of a bird in the mossy oak growing by the

145

pool. I watched my lover, my heart both glad and apprehensive.

I knew I had to tell him sometime soon, but the time had never been right. I wasn't even sure if now was the time, there were still too many uncertainties, but he caught my mood. He waded over to the rock where I was perched and leaned his good arm upon it. 'What is it?' he asked, cocking an eyebrow.

'What is what?'

'Don't play that game with me. You have something you want to say. I can tell.' He leaned closer and kissed me. 'I feel so much better now,' he murmured.

'Now that you're clean or now that you've kissed me?'

'Now that we've saved Iskander and Paul.' His hazel eyes were serious. 'What is bothering you? Is it the Eaters of the Dead? I know they will be on our trail, but I'm not worried. Before the day is out, we'll have met up with Demos and Nearchus and what remains of the villagers and the Roman soldiers.'

'And if the druids won?'

'Then we'll meet up with them, and we fight to the death. Whatever happens, will happen. Why worry about it? It will be as the gods wish.'

'I forgot how religiously backward and superstitious you are,' I said.

He looked at me quickly, then saw I was joking. 'Tell me,' he said again, gently.

'I think I'm pregnant.' I said, lowering my eyes.

'Mine?' he asked.

'Yours,' I agreed.

'Are you glad?' He tilted his head to the side, a mimic of Alexander.

'Of course.' I smiled. 'You know how much I love babies, and Alexander was begging for another.'

'Perhaps not mine,' he said.

'Don't be silly,' I said tenderly, and I kissed him again.

He nodded and looked down at the water, but a smile tugged at his mouth. 'Well, that was fast,' he said, a note of teasing in his voice. 'We only made love twice since I was wounded, and look what happened.'

'I'm never late, not the even by a day,' I said. 'And I haven't bled for two weeks now; I'm fifteen days late. I'm sure it's yours.'

'I'm glad, so very glad.' He put his good arm around me and pulled me close.

He was standing in the water; I was sitting on the moss-covered boulder. I smiled and wrapped my legs around his hips, pulling him closer, feeling his hardness, and moaning as he slid into me. For the space of a moment we didn't move. The water lapped against the boulder, the breeze rustled the fragrant pine branches, and I felt a rush of heat in my belly. I closed my eyes and let the tightness grow. My breath grew short. Plexis trembled, then started to move.

I leaned back on my hands, arching up to meet him, pulling him into me with my legs, urging him on. The feeling grew more and more urgent. It was blooming like a flower in my breast and belly, opening up and engulfing me. I let my head fall forward on Plexis's shoulder. A cry escaped me, a strangled, animal cry. He wrapped his arm around me and thrust harder and harder. Waves of pleasure washed over me, submerging me. My legs tightened and my belly convulsed. I moaned again, all sense of time and place faded away in a climax that shook me.

Plexis uttered a cry and bucked against me, holding me tightly to him, his thighs pressed against mine. Then he moaned and stood still, breathing hard. His heart pounded against my chest and his arms trembled.

Afterwards, Plexis crawled into a grove of soft ferns. He fell asleep immediately. I smiled as I watched him sleeping, his face in repose. When he was awake, his expressions were always so carefully guarded. His nose, which had miraculously escaped being broken despite ten years of battles, was straight. I longed to touch him, to trace the pure line of his jaw and throat. Instead I kissed his lips, but he didn't stir. Then I drew his cloak around him and eased out of the grove. He needed to sleep. I had to see Alexander.

Alexander had tended the fire and it was a crackling blaze. He saw me and nodded. 'Plexis sleeping?' he asked.

'Yes.' I sat next to him, curling my feet underneath me and leaning lightly against his shoulder.

Alexander looked at me gravely. 'I asked Phaleria to fetch some water from the stream,' he said. 'She'll be back in a moment. Do you want to tell me now or do you want to wait?'

148

'Am I so transparent?' I asked, and I felt a blush stain my cheeks.

'No, but I know you too well, and something's unsettling you. Is it good or bad news?'

'It's a good inconvenience,' I said, and I told him. He reacted as I'd expected, flashing a joyous smile and giving me a soft kiss.

'A baby,' he said, his voice vibrant. He loved children. He loved them when they were tiny and helpless, he loved them when they were toddling around, grasping the hems of cloaks to stay upright, and he loved them when they started to talk. He loved them when they were almost as tall as he was. His eyes would glow with pride whenever he was with Paul, or when he spoke of Cleopatra or Chiron. And when he thought of Mary, the baby who'd died in Samarkand and whose memory still made me keen with sorrow, he would cry.

Alexander understood. He gathered me in his arms and held me close. I trembled against him. I was frightened suddenly for so many reasons. I was afraid of losing the baby, I was afraid of losing Alexander, who was far from well. I was frightened because I knew that soon we had to move on, and that sooner or later the Eaters of the Dead would find us. I hoped that Demos and Nearchus had defeated Voltarrix, but I was far from certain. Yet, I was happy at the same time. I was with the two men I loved, Paul was with us, and we were all safe, at least for the time being.

I drew away and wiped my eyes, smiling shakily at Alexander. 'Thank you,' I whispered.

His surprise was comic. 'For what?'

'For staying the same and for not changing. For being yourself, always Alexander.'

His mouth twitched. 'I am always Alexander,' he agreed, tilting his head to the side and smiling at me. 'And you are a pregnant woman prone to easy tears and laughter. I shall have to get well quickly. Knowing that there is a new baby coming, will help me immensely. As a matter of fact, I feel better already.' He touched his neck. 'The sewing itches, but the hurt is less than a burn. A strange way of healing wounds, to be sure, but one I prefer over a hot iron. I would like to see it done – but not on myself,' he added quickly.

I laughed and kissed him. At that moment Phaleria arrived and cleared her throat nervously. 'I have water,' she said, 'and we have food.' She hardly dared look at Alexander; the sight of the stitches had unsettled her. Moreover, I had suddenly changed, from being a lowly slave from a Persian harem (which is what she thought I had been) to Persephone, the Queen of Hades, who brought the Great Iskander back to life. I sighed. What a reputation to live up to.

Breakfast consisted of cattails and fish. I heated water and bathed Alexander, washing his hair and shaving him carefully. When I finished, I checked his neck. I was pleased to see that the stitches were holding and the huge cut was healing. It still looked dreadful, and Paul, when he caught sight of it, looked like he was about to be ill.

'Lean over, put your head down.' I said to him.

He gulped. 'I won't faint, but it looks painful. Does it

150

hurt?' he asked.

'Well, yes,' Alexander turned his head from side to side, experimenting. 'It hurts. However, I think it is healing. It feels very strange, actually.' He frowned. 'You look terrible, what's the matter?'

Paul's face convulsed. 'Your neck. Oh, Father, I thought he'd killed you.'

Alexander held still while I wrapped a new bandage around his neck. Then he motioned to Paul to sit next to him. The tall boy crept over to his father and they sat together. Alexander put his arms around his son's shoulders. 'I'm not dead. Just as your mother said, the wound was fearsome to see but not deep enough to cost my life. She sewed it closed. I wonder why none of my army doctors thought of doing such a thing. It is better than being seared with a hot iron.'

I think that you'd best stick to the heat,' I said. 'It kills the germs, and in this time there are no antibiotics.'

'Ah, those weapons that can kill the invisible creatures.' Alexander nodded sagely. 'I suppose you're right. My other wounds healed well enough with the cauterizing irons.' He twisted his shoulder and examined a scar that ran down his arm, then looked at his thigh, where a wild boar had gored him. 'The scars are wicked looking though.'

'The one on your neck will fade to nothing, if it doesn't get infected. Be careful not to get it dirty,' I said.

Alexander smiled at Paul. 'I have some excellent news.' Before I could protest, he announced, 'You will soon have a new brother or sister. Isn't that wonderful?'

Paul started to smile, but then his face grew curiously blank. 'It is wonderful,' he said, looking at me.

'What's the matter?' I asked, touching his shoulder.

'I'm sorry, Mother, but I just keep thinking about the time you were kidnapped and what happened then.'

'What happened was that you were taken away from me,' I said gently.

'Yes, exactly. And I didn't have the chance to grow up with you, or with Father.' His voice was vibrant with passion. 'I missed having a mother. I was always alone, and moving all the time.'

'I'm sorry. I missed you too. I felt as if there were a hole in the centre of my chest. However, I always believed that I would find you and that we would be reunited, and that's what happened. That's what matters to me now, not anything that happened before.'

'What about you, Father?' Paul asked, his voice curiously hard. 'Would you take revenge on the person who kidnapped me?'

Alexander didn't answer right away, and when he did his words were measured. 'When I found out Darius had taken you, I pursued him all the way to Bactria. Then I chased Bessus, who took you to Sogdia. There Bessus was betrayed by his own followers and killed. His cousin, Spitamenes, thought to use you to secure the crown. However, he too was betrayed. He sent you to the Valley of the Gods where an ancient prophecy said you would be safe. When your mother and I found you, we knew that we could not take you with us.'

'I know that,' Paul said, 'and I understand. You

thought you were doing the only thing you could to protect me, but you didn't answer my question. Don't you want to avenge my mother's kidnapping? Wouldn't you want to punish the person responsible?'

'She's been punished enough,' said Alexander softly, and I realized that he still thought his mother had been the only one responsible.

Paul looked startled. 'She? It was a woman? Who would do such a terrible thing? Who would dare?'

Alexander smiled sadly. 'Someone who thought that it was the only thing to do at the time. Don't ask me any more, Son, I am growing tired.' His voice was nearly gone, and he was slumping with fatigue.

'I just wanted to know if you cared,' said Paul, his face flushed. 'It sounds almost as if you don't.'

'Paul!' My voice was sharp, but Alexander shook his head painfully.

'I do care,' he said, 'deeply. I wanted to kill the person. I swear.' Then he lay back on his pallet and pulled his cloak around him, falling asleep in an instant. I got to my feet and backed away. I tasted blood in my mouth and realized my nose was bleeding. I put my hands to my face. They were shaking as well.

Paul stood up with the same fluid movement his father had and took me by the shoulders. 'What is it, Mother?' he asked, concern in his voice. 'Did I bring back too many bad memories? I'm sorry.' His face was both terribly young and strangely adult. I wondered why I'd never realized it before.

'No, no, it's not that at all.' I looked at him and tried

to smile. 'Paul,' I whispered. 'We must talk. Plexis ...' I got no further. Paul was staring over my shoulders and his face suddenly hardened into a marble mask. I gasped. I'd never seen that look before, it was completely alien and it frightened me. Before I could react, Paul pushed me aside and snatched up Alexander's sword that was carefully placed against a tree.

'Murderer!' he screamed, 'murderer!' Then he lunged, blade flashing, at someone who was slowly coming out of the undergrowth.

The sun was in my eyes, so I couldn't see who Paul was attacking. I was still thinking of his rage and our discussion about my kidnapping. Plexis was on my mind. I stepped forward, intending to grab Paul's arm before he hurt himself. Plexis was wounded, I remember thinking. Paul could hurt him. I saw the bright flash of highly polished metal and I sidestepped quickly, my hand outstretched to grab my son's shoulder. Instead, the blade caught me on my side, sending me reeling into a tree.

I tried to catch myself, but I was stunned and fell in a heap. There was a strange silence in the woods. All of a sudden the air was heavy and hot. I felt nauseated and dizzy. I wondered what had happened. Was it noon already? Where was I? I sat up slowly and looked around. My head was ringing; blood was pooling on my lap. I stared up at Paul. He looked at me with an expression of pure terror. I never saw anyone look so horrified.

'Don't worry, it's just my nose,' I started to say, Then, strangely enough, the world tilted and I fell sideways.

Behind Paul stood Demos, and I wondered, before fainting completely, why Paul wanted to kill Demos. Then everything vanished.

Chapter Thirteen

When I woke up, my head felt odd. I was shivering with cold, despite the fact that I was wrapped in blankets and propped up in front of a roaring fire. There was a chill in my bones that ached horribly, a cold so intense it was unbearable.

Demos was sitting in front of me. I smelled something disagreeable and wondered what it was. I also wondered why I'd woken up. I'd been having a dream, although I couldn't quite recall what it had been about. Then a searing pain bloomed in my body and I screamed. My voice was completely shattered and I realized that the sound of my own screams had woken me. There was a lull in the pain. It had been so severe I'd gone blind for a second, and when my eyes next registered the light, Demos was gone. The pain was gone too, which was a blessed relief. Only a strange cold remained. I wondered what was going on. I didn't remember anything then. Not the conversation with Paul, not the sword, not even Alexander's promise to kill the one who had kidnapped me – Plexis.

I blinked, puzzled. I couldn't understand. The fire was blazing, yet I was still cold. I tried to look around, then realized that I was being held tightly and that's why I couldn't move. Two strong arms were around me, pinning me against a hard chest. Then Demos came back into view and he said to the person behind me, 'It's over, Nearchus, you can let go of her. I think she'll be all right.'

Nearchus? He was here too? I was suddenly filled with joy. Demos and Nearchus were here; they had fought the druids and they were still alive! They must have won! I twisted around, intending to say something, but a terrible pain shot up my side and I moaned.

'Shhh, it's all right, My Lady. Don't try to move. It will hurt for a while, but it will not bleed again.' Nearchus spoke into my ear, his voice sounded strained.

'What happened?' I glanced around me. Now I could see faces. Alexander, very white, leaning against a tree. Plexis was there too, not looking much better. Next to him was Paul, his face devoid of colour or expression, as if he were made of wax.

'It was an accident, My Lady.' Demos squatted in front of me and brushed a lock of hair out of my eyes. It was bloody, I noticed. My hair, my clothes, everything was soaked with blood. Was it mine? Bits of memory came tumbling back and I flinched.

'How did it happen?' I croaked.

'Paul tried to kill me. It's not his fault, you see, I killed his dog. I'm sorry, but I had to.'

I was starting to understand. I nodded weakly. 'Blood and guts. You needed the blood. And an excuse for you and Alexander to fight.'

157

'Well, that's right.' Demos smiled widely, showing gap teeth. 'Paul swung the sword back, exactly as I taught him mind you, but you stepped in for some reason. It was a folly to do that, My Lady, begging your pardon. Why did you do that?' He was smiling but his face was drawn and tears had made tracks through the bloodstains on his cheeks.

'I thought he was trying to kill Plexis.' Relief and pain were making my head swim. 'You won? Is everyone all right?'

'We won. We lost a great many men. But the druids lost everyone.' Demos was eyeing me curiously, and he also turned and frowned at Plexis, who tightened his grip on Paul's shoulder.

'I feel strange,' I said. 'What happened to me?'

'The sword cut you from shoulder to hip,' said Demos. Luckily, it glanced off your bones, nicking the ribs and hitting your hipbone. It didn't hit any vital organs, and we managed to cauterize the wound. It bleeds no more.'

So that was the pain. No wonder Alexander used to scream himself hoarse. I shuddered. And the burn would only hurt worse later, as burns tended to do. I sighed, but that made the pain flare up. There was nothing I could do except rest and recuperate. If the wound went from shoulder to hip, I was lucky I hadn't been disembowelled.

Nearchus held me on his lap, not moving, and Axiom handed something steaming hot to Demos. It was a bowl of tea. Demos held it to my lips so I could drink. It was made with bitter herbs, and I knew it would put me to sleep. I didn't mind. I wanted to sleep; I wanted to forget what I'd seen, what my mind simply refused to acknowledge when I'd looked down at my lap. My hand was gone. Gone at the wrist. I had been reaching for the blade when it came flashing back. The blade had taken off my hand and sliced my side open. Alexander always did keep his sword razor sharp. I closed my eyes. I wanted to sleep.

My dreams were tangled and dark. I was frightened about something. I had to do something important and I kept forgetting what it was. My babies were gone, all of them. In the dark I couldn't find them. When they cried, I couldn't see where they were, and I couldn't comfort them. Nothing gave them comfort. They cried and cried, wearing me out with their thin wails. Panic had me in its icy grip. I rushed around in darkness, trying to find a way out, trying to save my babies.

I woke with tears on my face. Alexander told me we'd been travelling for two days. I'd been carried on a litter. The Eaters of the Dead had found our trail, and we were making our way through the pine forest as quickly as possible. Alexander was walking now. He'd recuperated well. Almost all his incredible vitality was coming back. He stayed next to my litter, holding my good hand.

'I need to speak to Paul,' I said. The darkness was gone. I knew what I had to do.

Alexander looked at me, his face a study in planes

and edges. It looked sharp, his mouth was drawn in a thin line, and his eyes were hooded. 'I spoke to Plexis,' he said, his voice harsh.

I drew a sharp breath then shook my head hard enough to hurt my wound. 'No, you mustn't blame Plexis for what happened. It was my fault.'

'No. I know what happened – now. He told me that he organized the kidnapping, and that he had kept it a secret all these years because he was afraid you and I would never forgive him.'

'But I did,' I said, 'I did. I won't blame him for what happened.'

'Because of him, Darius, Bessus, and Spitamenes died. Because of him, I nearly killed my own mother. And because of him, you lost your hand.' He broke off with what sounded like a curse. Then he turned to me, his face tragic. 'What would you have me do? I made a promise to my son. I swore to kill the person responsible.'

I felt faint. 'Did you ... did you kill him?' I whispered. 'Because if you did, I'll never pardon you.' I closed my eyes. I couldn't bear to see his face. He could never hide his emotions, like Plexis could. I was afraid of what I'd see. Instead I heard a soft chuckle. It was a sad sound, but it was a laugh just the same. I fluttered one eye open and peered at him.

'Do you think I could kill Plexis?' he asked. 'I killed his brother, and that nearly destroyed me. No, I love him. I could never kill him. We'll speak to Paul together. I think we can make him see that everyone can do things they regret bitterly.'

'I don't mind about losing my hand. Stop looking as if I've lost my life.' I said. Perhaps I didn't know what I was saying, I hadn't really thought of all the repercussions, but I meant it. At least I wanted to mean it. 'I have to see Paul. I love you all so much, you, Plexis, Axiom, Phaleria, and Nearchus. And Demos, who saved me. I'm still alive; we're together. Don't you see that's what matters to me?' I felt lightheaded, shaken with relief, knowing that the druids were beaten, that we were safe now.

Alexander gave a short laugh. 'You always surprise me,' he said, colour coming back to his cheeks. 'And if Demos hadn't been there, you would have lost your life. He always wanted to be a doctor. Thank the gods, he studied medicine on Kos.'

'Thank the gods,' I echoed faintly.

'He operated on Plexis's arm,' he said matter-of-factly. 'He's gaining the use of it again. It will never be as strong, but at least he will be able to use it ...' His voice trailed away and he looked at me, his face sombre. 'Why, Ashley, why? Was it a trade? Your hand for my soul? We lost so many other precious things. Millis, Yovanix, Cerberus ...'

'Yovanix? He's dead? When he fought against the druids?' I felt a stab of sorrow. Our Gaul, our friend, another one gone.

'Nearchus said that they searched for him and never found him among the dead. Yovanix was gone and so was Voltarrix. Someone said they'd seen them fighting

161

near the river. Nearchus thinks they fell in and were swept away.'

I shook my head slowly. 'Oh, Alex, I'm so sorry. Has your soul been returned? How do you feel?'

'It has been restored. I can feel now,' he said. 'I feel sorrow, sharp pain, joy to have found you again – and a sweetness thinking about the child to come. All those feelings were gone before. I was just an empty shell. Then there was a clap of thunder and everything came rushing back. I remember being in a deep pit, lined with stones, where an old woman touched our hands to see which of us would die first.' He shuddered. 'She was a weird woman; blind, and so old her hair was like cobwebs around her ruined face. Her mouth was a toothless gash, and she took my hand and said, 'This one has no soul. Let him die first, and may his death last forever. Nearchus killed her. He hated her as much as I did.'

I saw his quick shiver and reached out my hand, before remembering it ended in a tight linen bandage. 'It's over.' I said.

'No, it's not. We're still not out of the woods,' he said, trying to joke, holding my forearm gently in his hand, his thumb stroking the inside of my elbow. 'Does it hurt?'

'No, I can't feel a thing.'

'Sleep now. Sleep some more, and when we stop, I will be here. I will always be here. I promise.' Tears glittered on his lashes, but he didn't try to hide them. He never hid anything from me.

I slept then, because it was what I needed, and I slept deeply, because Alexander was beside me, and he would always be there for me when I needed him.

When I surfaced again, I felt better. My dreams faded, I didn't even know what they'd been about.

I was lying in a grove of giant ferns. They were tall and curled and waved above my head in a riot of pale, feathery green. The sun was shining through them, making a play of gold and emerald. Spiders' webs were frail silver threads floating in the breeze. Everything was surrounded by a bright nimbus of light, soft and clear at the same time. The air was balmy; it touched my cheeks in a warm caress. I stretched, wincing because the wound in my side was still sore. I must have made a faint noise, because the ferns suddenly parted and Alexander was there beside me. He held his finger to his lips. 'Shh,' he murmured. His eyes were dark with worry.

'What …?'

'We're hiding.' His voice was little more than a sigh. I nodded to show I understood. There was no sound around us. The birds had hushed. The breeze barely moved the branches above us. The ferns nodded silently, gossamer webs floating in bright silver tatters from their tips. The sun gilded everything, the ferns, the webs, and Alexander's hair. He lay down beside me and took me in his arms. He held me tenderly, gently, and I felt his ardour; it was like the glow of the sun. My hurts faded, a peaceful serendipity filled me, even more unexpected because of the fear I could feel all around us. I clung to the feeling of deep peace, I clung to Alexander and closed my eyes once more and slept for three days.

They say shock does that to you.

Chapter Fourteen

The Eaters of the Dead wore animal skins and walked as silently as wolves. They followed us, moving quietly and in deadly earnest. Nearchus killed one and we stared at the body. I'd never seen a human quite like him. To me, he looked like a Neanderthal. The cheekbones were low, the jaw heavy, and the skull sloped backwards from prominent brows. His skin was swarthy and his brown hair was roughly braided and tied back with a leather thong. Swirling tattoos covered his arms and chest, and another strange tattoo, a thin black line, divided his face in two.

We glanced uneasily at one another. The women held their children tightly and stayed far away. Only three Roman soldiers were left of thirty-five who had fought for us. They stood next to the women, weapons at hand. Axiom was with us. He'd managed to escape the massacre and found us after three days of wandering through the forest and marsh with the Roman soldiers. Yovanix was still unaccounted for. We dared not wait for him. We pressed on as quickly as possible, the strange tribe pursuing us. Nearchus had been behind us, protecting our rear. He'd surprised a scout and killed him. Now we wondered what they'd do. So far they hadn't attacked us. This might be the signal they were waiting for.

Demos examined the corpse with interest. 'I want you to see this,' he said, as he bared the man's teeth.

We leaned forward to see. At once, most of us stepped back involuntarily. It was an eerie sight. The canines were huge, overdeveloped, and as sharp as fangs. 'Do you think he sharpened them, or are they naturally like that?' Alexander crouched down by the man's face and looked. 'Very odd,' he said.

I was feeling tired again, so I went to sit in the shade of a large hemlock. I was up and around now, though still very weak. A tumble of large boulders was at my back. They led down to the stream where I could see Paul fishing with Axiom and Phaleria. He concentrated, standing on the bank, a long spear in his hand. In an instant his muscles bunched and he threw the spear into the water and pulled out a wriggling fish. The fish flashed silver and bronze, water droplets scattering like diamonds, and Phaleria grabbed it and put it in a deep wicker basket. It was almost full. Soon we would eat and move on.

Phaleria started to clean the fish while Paul went back to his pose on the bank. My son was ten now, very tall for his age and trim. The resemblance to his father was striking, from the proud nose to the shape of his body. He was well proportioned, finely balanced and strong. His hair was blonder than Alexander's, but both had fair skin that tanned easily. Paul's eyes were a deep, navy blue. They were stormy now, stirred by a tempest of emotions.

All Paul's movements were hard and stiff. Axiom went to him and put his hand on his arm. For a minute I thought Paul would shake it off, but then he seemed to slump forward. His head fell to his chest and the spear slipped out of his hands. Axiom spoke to him earnestly. I couldn't hear what he said. I was too far away, but I knew what he was trying to tell him. That it wasn't his fault. That he mustn't torture himself. That nothing was changed between us. He was trying to tell Paul the same thing I had, but Paul wouldn't listen. He was determined to punish himself. I found myself wondering if we *should* punish him; perhaps it would make it easier for him to bear. I had no desire to do so. I had no idea what to do. Paul needed to find his own equilibrium.

We had spoken together, Paul, Alexander, Plexis, and I. It was a difficult conversation for many reasons. Part of the difficulty lay in the mentality of the time. The notion of revenge and honour was woven into all the stories children learned from their infancy. In them, children learned that heroes would rather die than lose their honour. They took revenge whenever they felt slighted, and often had the benediction of the gods.

Paul had grown up listening to *The Iliad* and *The Odyssey*; two stories that were beautiful, but bloody. It was difficult for him to understand my point of view. I could step back and look. However, I was looking from further back than anyone was at that time. I had three thousand years of distance separating me from their gods and stories. Paul was different. He was also young. A child usually has enough problems coping with growing up. Paul had to cope with growing up alone as a small child, with kidnapping and murder, with the death of his beloved dog, and now he felt betrayed by everyone he'd always trusted.

Paul had come to see me when I felt better. He approached me cautiously, following just behind Alexander and Plexis, using them as a shield. We sat close together in a small clearing. Nearchus and Demos were not far away, standing guard.

Paul had trouble meeting my eyes. I think that hurt me more than the blow had. I told him this and he looked up at me, surprised.

'I'm sorry I tried to kill Demos, I wasn't thinking. It was a foolish thing to do, and there isn't a moment that goes by that I don't regret it. Can you ever forgive me?' he asked. He didn't know what else I had wanted to tell him. It threw him completely off balance when I spoke.

'Of course I forgive you. I'm sorry I tried to grab you. I thought you were going to kill Plexis, and he was wounded. Demos would have been able to take care of himself,' I added wryly.

'But, why would I have tried to kill Plexis?' Paul was sitting next to him and he patted Plexis on the shoulder. 'I love Plexis, he's my second father. You know that.'

'Because I was responsible for your mother's kidnapping in Arbeles,' said Plexis. He looked intently at Paul. 'It's something I regret doing. There's hardly a moment I don't regret it. Can you understand that?'

168

'Why?' whispered Paul, recoiling away from him.

'Because of the oracle.' Plexis spoke seriously. Paul stiffened. He understood oracles even more than I did. 'The oracle said that your mother could destroy the world. Well, it didn't say so as clearly as that, but that's what I understood. I wanted to save Iskander. I'm sorry, Paul.'

Paul looked at his feet. Two tears fell from the tips of his long lashes and trickled down his smooth cheeks. I reached forward to brush them away but he jerked backwards. 'Why didn't you ever tell me, Mother?' he whispered, his voice breaking.

'Your mother didn't know,' said Plexis. 'She thought it was Olympias behind the whole thing.'

'She was,' I said angrily. 'Stop taking all the blame for yourself.'

Plexis half smiled and shook his head. 'No. I *must* take the blame. For one thing, I'm here, not Olympias. You lost your hand because you thought you were defending me.'

'It doesn't matter any more. None of it does.' I sat up straighter and tried to chase the fatigue from my voice. 'Look at me, Paul. What happened was an accident, but it does go to show that you have to learn three things in life. You must learn to wait, to let years go by sometimes if need be. Then you must learn to step back and look at the whole picture. Lastly, you must learn to forgive. Start by forgiving yourself, then, hopefully, you will be able to forgive me and Plexis for what happened.'

Paul was shaking his head slowly from side to side.

'I'm sorry,' he said, 'so sorry.'

'I am alive,' I said. 'It was an accident.'

'I might have killed you.' Paul turned a tragic face to his father. 'You told me never to touch your sword and I disobeyed you.'

Alexander didn't smile. 'I disobeyed my own father often enough to know that it's an easy thing to do. When I did so, I was beaten for it. My father had a heavy hand. I had no love for my father and I believed he had none for me. I don't want to lift my hand against you. I will not punish you. I agree with your mother. You must learn to forgive and then to forget. Only then can you be at peace with yourself. I, too, had to learn that lesson, and it was the hardest one I ever learned. Perhaps someday I will tell you about it. But for now kiss your mother and Plexis. We are together and that's what really matters.'

Paul leaned over to me and brushed a soft kiss on my cheek. 'I'm sorry for your hand, Mother,' he said.

'It is a small thing compared to the love I have for you,' I told him quietly. 'It changes nothing. You never meant it to happen.'

Paul nodded, kissed Plexis, and left the clearing at a shambling run, too blinded with tears to see where he was going. He blundered into Demos, who caught him by the shoulders. Paul tensed and tried to escape; he was still angry at Demos, but the big man held him tightly, and after a moment, Paul collapsed against him. We could hear him sobbing in Demos's arms. Plexis turned to me, his face sombre.

'It will take a while for him to look at us the way he

used to,' and his voice was sorrowful. 'I feel as if I've taken him away from you a second time.'

I nodded slowly. 'It will take time, but they have a saying from the future, *time heals all wounds*. I think I'll just leave it at that.'

Alexander cocked his head. 'In Macedonia they have a maxim like that, though perhaps not as apt. They say, *time can make you forget when you've been cheated out of a goat, so save your proof of payment.*' He broke off and shrugged. 'Well, don't look at me like that, I didn't make it up.'

'Are you sure?' Sometimes I wondered.

'I'm always amazed at the sayings of the Macedonians,' said Plexis, looking very serious. 'I can't understand why they didn't make it to posterity. The part about the goats rings so true.'

We ate fish for lunch, and then we moved on. There was no time to spare. The days were growing shorter. Soon there would be a proper night, and that was what the Eaters of the Dead were waiting for.

I was still being carried on a stretcher. I was in no condition to walk. I'd lost so much blood that I felt lightheaded most of the time, and I was shaky with fatigue. Mostly I slept, my bed swinging back and forth gently as I was carried along. The two men carrying me were tall and strong; they made me understand that I was no weight for them at all. They were slaves stolen from Orce or the surrounding villages. Both were brawny Viking types with long braids, wide shoulders, and many missing teeth.

I woke up long enough to eat and drink. Demos and Axiom gave me bitter tea each time I opened my eyes. It was made from wild sorrel. I drank it, wincing at its lemony tartness, but it was full of vitamins.

They also made sure I got the liver of whatever animal was on the menu. I had a better diet than anybody in our group, and no matter how I protested, they made me eat.

'No, My Lady,' said Axiom sternly. 'You must build up your strength. You're expecting a child and you lost too much blood. Do you want to lose the babe?'

I scowled. 'Of course not. Stop "My Lady-ing" me. I'm Ashley and you know it. I simply want to be fair. There are women and children with us who could use the vitamins too.'

Axiom had no idea what I meant by vitamins, but he knew how to argue. 'No one wants you to die,' he said, 'least of all the women and children you helped save. They would not eat your portion, even if you left it on your cabbage leaf. They would probably pray over it then offer it to whatever barbarian gods they believe in, and a wolf would end up with it. So eat!' Axiom was a Jew and a frightfully logical one at that. I appreciated the fact that he only believed in one god. He and I were alike in that respect, although he believed much harder than I did.

I ate well, slept well, and by the end of the week felt well enough to walk. Even then, I only walked a few minutes at a time. It was a shock to find myself so weak.

I leaned against Alexander and he held my arm. He looked good. He glowed again, his eyes bright with excitement, his face alight. He didn't mind the Eaters of the Dead following us; he was spoiling for a fight. I shook my head. I would never understand men.

Plexis worked his sword arm, bright bronze flashing as he parried an imaginary thrust. Alexander saw him, and of course he couldn't resist a fencing match. The woods rang with the bright sound of metal hitting metal, clanging like sharp bells.

Demos stood back and admired their style. Plexis was quick and deadly with his blade. He used his classical training to the utmost, combining a rare elegance with a sure eye and a quick foot. Alexander had studied with the best teachers of the time, but he had his own style. It was brilliant, full of nerve and with an icy detachment that fooled the adversary into forgetting his fiery nature.

The two men circled each other warily. They knew each other too well. Plexis searched for a chink in Alexander's defence but found none. Alexander played a defensive game, contenting himself with parrying attacks with insulting ease. His fluid movements were sometimes too quick to see. Plexis tried everything. Then finally, out of breath and patience, he cried, 'All right, you win!' and tossed his sword onto the ground – carefully, onto a soft patch of moss. He flopped down next to his weapon and wiped the sweat off his brow. 'You haven't lost your swordplay,' he said, shaking his head.

Alexander grinned and sat next to his friend. 'You

haven't either,' he said. 'I was just about to give up.'

Plexis eyed him incredulously. 'I suppose you want me to believe that?' he asked. 'No, don't bother to answer. At any rate, I'm glad I'm on your side. I wouldn't want to fight against you in earnest.'

Alexander nodded. The two men lay side by side in the shade, their bodies gleaming with sweat. I saw more than one covetous look from women and men alike. They were simply fleeting glances because everyone was in awe of Alexander, and they were, frankly, terrified of me. The looks lingered on Plexis, but he was blind to them. He had always been blind to them. He had eyes only for Alexander. Alexander smiled and took his face in his hands. 'Ah, Plexis, don't look at me like that.'

'Why? The gods will be jealous?' Plexis asked, half jokingly completing a saying of the time.

'Perhaps that's what I meant.' Alexander closed his eyes and kissed him. They embraced tenderly. Nobody was startled by their embrace. People were quite demonstrative at that time, and love between men was considered the norm in Greece and Persia; women being slightly above cattle and just below camels in the great scheme of life.

Of course, I can go into quite a long speech about what people thought at that time about love in general, but it was basically the same as it has been through all time. Gold and love. The most stable values on earth.

I, for one, loved to see Alexander and Plexis together. One reason was purely aesthetic. The other was more personal. Sometimes I used to wonder if I were normal, but then I decided that I couldn't change the feelings I had for both men any more than they could change the feelings they had for each other. It wasn't a complex relationship. Everything was clear and simple. Plexis and I were in love with a phenomenon, a divine being, and no matter how hard he protested he was just a man, no one believed Alexander. Anyone who came into his orbit immediately became one of his satellites.

Alexander was not a common mortal. Axiom and I had discussed it often enough. For Axiom it was simple; Alexander was one of the 'chosen few' who come to earth every three centuries or so and are made to change the world. The gods send these people – for Axiom only one god sends them – and they are so extraordinary that they irrevocably alter the course of history.

One day, Axiom and I sat down and worked out a graph showing the people who'd had the most influence on the world. The dates coincided closely with Axiom's theory, it went like this: *300 BC – Alexander, 1 AD – Jesus Christ, 300 AD – Chandragupta; 700 AD – Charlemagne; 1000 AD – William the Conqueror, 1200 AD – Ghengis Khan; 1600 AD – Louis XIV; 1800 AD – Napoléon Bonaparte; 2100 AD – Stansilas Demitrivek; 2400 AD – N'go Kallihagi,* and so on, Axiom told me, until the end of time.

I had to agree, Alexander *had* changed the course of history. He'd almost done more than he was supposed to do. I suppose that if Voltarrix had killed him in the manner he'd planned, and if Paul had been used for the druid's purposes, things would have been wildly different. Even as it was, with Alexander officially dead at thirty-three years of age, the world would never be the same.

And in three hundred years another man would arrive, preach about love and forgiveness, die at the age of thirty-three, and change the world completely.

I sat up and propped my chin on my hand. My other hand, gone now, ached sometimes. It was odd, I could still 'feel' my hand and even wiggle imaginary fingers. I wondered when it would finally sink into my brain that my hand was truly gone.

In my time, I was so used to the grafts that replaced hands, arms, legs, and feet, that I hadn't fully realized what had happened to me. In my time, if you lost your hand, it was easy to put it back on. Bodies without central nervous systems were grown especially to use as organ and limb donors, so there was never any problem.

I think everyone was a little shocked at how unaffected I was by the loss of my hand, but as I said, I hadn't really comprehended the full extent of my deprivation. I had never told Alexander about the donor bodies. I'd never even told Usse, our doctor. I'd never mentioned the fact that one of my fingers wasn't even my own, I'd lost it when I was five years old. I had been wearing one of my mother's rings, and I'd fallen down. When I put my hand out to catch myself, the ring hooked on a small part of a metal fence and tore my finger off. I'd been in shock. I hadn't thought of taking the finger – or the ring, which made my mother furious – when I ran screaming back to the house.

My mother hadn't wasted time looking for my finger. She took me to the graft centre, and by that evening I had a whole new finger.

Well, it was gone now. It had been on my left hand and now there was nothing left of that. I sighed and looked down at the neatly wrapped bandage. Demos did a fine job of nursing. Soon the skin would grow over smoothly, and it wouldn't look so frightening. However, it could never be put back on. At least while I lived in this time. I shrugged. I simply couldn't believe it. My mind refused to compute.

That evening we were set upon by the Eaters of the Dead. We lost one man, and when the dawn came we couldn't find his body anywhere. The fight had been short and fierce. Another man lost a hand. He sat, stunned, under an oak tree and didn't even scream when Demos seared his flesh closed. My own wound ached abominably when I saw that, so I turned away. Paul was staring at me. I tried for a smile, but it wobbled across my face and I didn't think he was fooled.

He came and sat next to me, and I hugged him.

'I'm so sorry,' he said. He said that each time he saw me.

'Listen, Paul,' I began. I wasn't sure how to tell him what I was feeling, but I tried. When I finished, he stared at me with the strangest expression.

'You had a finger that wasn't your own?' he finally said. 'How horrible.'

I grinned faintly. 'Well, I don't have it any more. Stop

acting so tragic. Look at that poor man over there, under the tree. Losing a limb is fairly common here. I remember when we were in the army there were lots of missing fingers and hands. Look at Nearchus and Demos, they have nine fingers each. So don't worry. I know it's hard for you because you feel responsible, but it was an accident, and they can happen to anyone, anytime. That's why they're called accidents, OK?'

'O-K,' said Paul. He put his head on my shoulder. 'I feel so awful about everything,' he admitted. 'About Cerberus, and Plexis, and Demos. I don't know what to think any more, or who to trust.'

'You can be sure that if Demos killed Cerberus, it was for a very good reason. I can't imagine he liked doing it. He probably feels just as bad about the whole thing as you do. And as for Plexis,' I sighed. 'You'll just have to work that one out by yourself. It's true that your whole childhood was ruined because of him, but it's over. You're still alive, and safe, which you never would have been with us. I can't even begin to count the number of times Chiron was almost poisoned.' I shuddered. 'I never would have been able to protect you against Roxanne. She was diabolical.'

'Where is she now?' asked Paul.

'Somewhere in Macedonia, I think. I'm not sure exactly where, but I believe she's with your grandmother, Olympias.'

'So you're saying that Plexis saved my life?'

'Indirectly, yes. If you think of it that way, you'll see that we should thank him for having me kidnapped.

178

Remember; he had no idea I was pregnant. When you were taken from me it was all Darius's doing, and he's dead now, poor fool. So, forget about the whole thing, forget about revenge and retribution. Look ahead and know that we all love you.'

Paul frowned. 'I feel so dreadful.'

'I think it's called being a growing boy,' I said helpfully. 'Do you remember what I told you about hormones?'

'Those little beasts within me who control my actions?'

'Sort of. You're going to be full of them for a while, at least until you're grown. They'll make you overly emotional. Think long and hard about any actions you might want to take. Talk to me and whoever else you feel you can trust. Above all, don't worry. I think everything will be all right.'

'How can you say that?' He looked puzzled. 'Everyone else is on edge and panicky, and you're as calm and cool as ice.' He shook his head. 'Sometimes I think it's true, you are the Queen of Hades.'

'Ha, ha, very nice. I feel safe because I'm with your father. I've always had confidence in him. I can't help it.' I smiled. 'He's here, and you're here, and I guess I'm just happy.'

'I guess you're still suffering from severe loss of blood,' said Paul gloomily.

'Shhh, there are people trying to sleep. Why don't you put your head in my lap and sleep too? I don't think you slept much last night with the fight going on so close by. And tonight it will be worse, they say. Sleep now, my little one, and dream. Dream of Chiron and Cleopatra and our home in Alexandria. I would love to be lying next to the pool with the white stones gleaming around us and the date palms waving overhead. Do you remember how lovely it was there? Your room had blue and green walls with pictures of dolphins and an island on them. The ceiling was high, and the floor was tiled in blue and white squares. Do you remember?' I looked down at the fair head on my lap. Paul's eyes were closed, his breathing deep and even. I smiled. He might be almost as tall as I, but he was still young, and he fell asleep like a child.

Chapter Fifteen

During the day we walked quickly, staying closer together since two scouts had disappeared. Meals became frugal affairs, mostly consisting of berries, roots, and whatever was edible along our way. We camped in places that were easily defensible. Alexander and Demos took one half of the group, Plexis and Nearchus the other, and the two groups took turns sleeping and guarding.

Nights were getting longer. The sun dipped below the horizon earlier and earlier, making the twilight last longer. Strange cries echoed deep in the woods, frightening everyone. Then people started to disappear. Two scouts vanished, and then the last man in line, a Roman soldier, disappeared. He'd been walking close behind his comrade when there came a swish of bushes, and then nothing. No cry, no shout or struggle. Simply a missing person and a huge pool of blood not far from the place he was last seen.

Plexis and Alexander stared at each other. Losing the soldier was a serious blow; there were few men trained for fighting in our group, and now we were down to only two Roman soldiers. His weapons had disappeared along with him, which was another loss.

Alexander looked at the blood and frowned. 'It looks like a ritual killing. Look at this.' He pointed to a small plant that I hadn't noticed, floating in the scarlet puddle. 'That flower comes from the mountains. There are none here.' He raised his head and sniffed, his eyes closed in concentration.

'What are you trying to do?' I asked, nervously. I had visions of the Eaters of the Dead feasting on the missing soldier. It was not a nice vision, and I swayed. I'd already seen cannibalism and was terrified.

Plexis was by my side in an instant, holding me firmly by the elbow and steering me to a fallen log. 'Sit down. Don't move. I'm going to get Axiom, he'll tend to you.'

'I don't need Axiom,' I said, but he was already gone, and the woods abruptly grew darker. The pine trees leaned over my head, their sharp needles and prickly branches swooping down at me. Their shadows twisted and groped at my feet, bright points of sunlight shifted and wove. I blinked, but my vision didn't clear. I should have put my head between my knees, but it was too late. I fainted, toppling backwards off the log, landing in a boneless heap in a heavy growth of fern.

When Axiom came to get me, I was nowhere to be found. Plexis had stayed at the camp to speak with Phaleria, and Alexander and Demos looked at Axiom in puzzlement when he asked them where I was.

'She was here a minute ago,' said Alexander, glancing back at the pool of blood. 'Strange, there are no

182

footprints. Go back to camp and get Plexis, will you? He can track better than I can. Demos, what do you think we should do? Walk in a double line?'

Axiom frowned. 'Are you sure your Lady Ashley went back to the camp? How could I have missed her?'

'She must have taken another path.' Alexander looked around and frowned again. 'Try over that way. I'll take the other trail, but first I want to wash my hands in the stream. Demos, can you go back to the camp and get everyone moving? We have to get away from this place. Head towards the treeless mountainside we caught a glimpse of earlier. I saw huge boulders. I have an idea it will be easier to defend ourselves there. And send Plexis back here.'

Everyone left, and after a short while Plexis came back and started to cast around for a trail to search for the missing soldier. He found a faint one and followed it, leaving the clearing and heading away from the camp. In his hand was his sword, and he carried Alexander's shield strapped to his wounded arm. Alexander caught up to him, he'd been to the stream, and the two men continued their way together. Plexis never thought of asking Alexander where I was; he thought I was with Axiom, and Alexander thought I was back at the camp.

Meanwhile, I lay in a dead faint in the bushes, completely unaware of what was going on. When I woke up, there was no one around; night had fallen, and I was alone.

At first, I had no idea what was going on. I'd been so warm and comfortable in the ferns that when I woke up I stretched lazily and yawned. The moon hung in the sky like a slice of yellow cheese, and the pine trees seemed to be pointing at it and saying, 'Look at that!'

I looked at it briefly, then gazed around me. Suddenly I sat up in fright. 'Hello?' I said. 'Anybody here?' There was no answer, except for the soft sound of the wind in the trees and night insects chirping and buzzing. An owl hooted and I jumped. Slowly I poked my head out of the ferns and looked around. The clearing was empty. The moon's light was bright enough to cast deep shadows and was reflected in the pool of blood.

From where I was sitting, I could see that the blood was in the exact centre of the clearing. I could also see a glow-worm creeping through the moss on the top of the huge fallen log from which I'd toppled. I watched the worm for a while. My mind was frozen with panic. I was isolated in a dark forest, and there were strange noises all around. I knew that if I stayed where I was, I would be found eventually. It was the *eventually* that frightened me the most. I wanted to be found sooner than eventually.

Ever so slowly, I started to ease out of the ferns. I put my hand on top of the log and braced myself while I stood. My legs shook. I listened carefully. There was no noise. Still, a strange feeling of dread froze me in my place. I'd learned to pay attention to my instincts. I sank back down into the ferns, disappearing beneath them like a fish into green water. I pressed myself to the earth and found I could see out of a gap formed between the log and the ground. I lay my cheek on the soft moss and breathed in the sweet scent of the violets growing in purple profusion. Dried ferns made the ground beneath me soft and warm, but they crackled faintly when I moved, so I held myself immobile. I glanced at the sky. The moon was half hidden by clouds. The night was at its darkest. I thought that whatever was about to happen would happen soon. A snail crawled past, leaving a silvery, slimy trail. His head nodded a slow greeting to me, his tendril-like antennae prodding the air delicately. Then he lowered his head and grazed like a placid cow on a violet blossom.

I raised my eyes to the clearing and froze. There were shadows converging on the pool of blood. Slowly, stealthily, they eased like smoke out of the forest's darkness and coalesced in the feeble light of the moon. Shadows slunk out of the woods on all sides, and one slithered by me not a stone's throw away. I held my breath, but the shadow didn't discern my presence.

I willed myself invisible, trying to melt into the ground. The shadows moved like wolves, on all fours; they were as silent as wolves and wore grey fur cloaks with wolf heads still attached. They were not the druids, although they were wearing capes made out of wolf pelts. I recognized their brawny arms and bony faces. They were the Eaters of the Dead.

When they were all gathered around the pool of blood, they joined hands and stood up, rising from their four-legged stance in unison, their faces held towards the moon, their sharp teeth bared and gleaming. They didn't speak. Some of them carried weapons. Most had spears

185

and a few had swords. The swords were probably taken from the dead soldiers. They didn't look like an Iron Age tribe, they looked like they were still in the Stone Age – their spears had flint points.

They stood perfectly still for what seemed like hours to me. Then, as one, they dropped their hands to their sides and their leader took a human skull out of his pouch.

I thought of him as the leader for two reasons. He was taller than the others and he was wearing the pelt of a jet-black wolf. His back was to me, so all I could see of him was the wolf skin with its head like a helmet. He held the skull over his head.

The others knelt in front of him, and for the first time, they uttered a sound. They started a low moan, which rose in volume and pitch until I nearly clapped my hands over my ears. The sound caused sudden crashing in the undergrowth on the far side of the clearing. A badger had been hiding, very much like I had, and the sound frightened him out of his refuge. He quickly waddled deeper into the woods, fading into the black shadows of the pine trees. The men didn't even stir. They stopped their eerie cry as suddenly as they'd started it, and then another group of shadows eased out of the forest.

This time I was hard put to keep quiet. They held a prisoner, bound and gagged. Two men carried him slung between them like a big game trophy. When they reached the centre of the clearing they dumped him to the ground, heedless of the blood. The leader raised his arms again and the men untied the prisoner. He got to his knees, slowly. It was the missing Roman soldier. I could see that his hands were tied behind his back. A wound gaped on his shoulder, and his hair was matted with blood as well. He looked stunned and half dead. The blood on the ground had been his, and now he was kneeling in it. He swung his head back and forth, then suddenly turned and looked straight at me. Dark tears coursed down his cheeks. I shoved a fist into my mouth. Where his eyes should have been were two dark holes. The tears were ribbons of blood. My stomach heaved.

I was about to close my eyes again when, all of a sudden, the leader pulled his hood back. Luckily, my fist was still in my mouth and stifled my cry. It was Voltarrix. He was no man, I decided. He was a demon. A demon straight from Hades.

He raised the skull to the moon and said, 'Take this man, the blind god, for your feast, and make us one of yours.' I had no idea what he meant, or to which gods or god he was praying. My skin crawled with horror. Then Voltarrix tucked the skull back into his pouch and raised his arms to the sky.

The air started to thicken around us. A buzzing started in my ears, and I felt as if I were going deaf. As before, all went still. The night froze, while the stars whirled then coalesced above us into a fiery nimbus of blinding light. All sounds ceased. The men around Voltarrix became immobile. Voltarrix forced his arms to move, and with agonizing slowness, cut the prisoner's throat.

Chapter Sixteen

This time, I couldn't act. I didn't have a back-up plan or people waiting in the wings to protect me. I didn't have needles and thread, a white-hot iron, a sword, or enough energy to fight against the time warp Voltarrix used to make his sacrifices. I could only cry, scalding tears of rage and sorrow, as the man died … and died … and died … while time stood still for hours.

Then Voltarrix clapped his hands over his head, and the thunder released time. The Roman toppled forwards into his own blood and didn't move, and the Eaters of the Dead fell upon his body and devoured him.

I lay in the ferns and stared. I was frozen. Tremors of shock ran through my body. I couldn't feel my limbs. I kept thinking that perhaps I was dreaming, but my eyes wouldn't close. I had no control over my body. My nose was bleeding, and the thin trickle of blood down my chin was the only warmth I felt. The scene faded and lightened, the air turned grey, and I realized dawn was approaching.

The Eaters of the Dead realized this as well. They ended their macabre feast and faded into the undergrowth, disappearing in the direction of the shadows, fleeing the growing light of dawn. A shaft of pale sunlight made its way through the trees, filtering down past pine needles and branches, and landed on one man's arm.

He gave a frightened, snarling yelp and scrambled into the dark. I nearly sat up. A tiny pinpoint of light had touched him, and it had looked almost as if it had hurt him. A supernatural fear made my skin crawl. Who *were* these men? Were they some sort of primeval monsters? My mind failed to comprehend what my eyes had seen. I kept trying to understand and my mind kept telling me I had dreamt everything.

Voltarrix was the last to leave. He stood in the clearing and looked around him. His face was in shadow, the wolf's upper jaw jutted from his forehead and the fangs were level with his eyes. The lower jaw had been sectioned and it gaped, lying on his chest as an ornament, holding the wolf's skin closed. Evidently the druid didn't sense my presence; he seemed satisfied that no one was watching. He dropped to his hands and knees, then lifted his leg and urinated on the spot of the sacrifice, exactly like a male dog or wolf would do to mark his territory. He uttered a half snarl, half growl and left the clearing, trotting quickly. For the life of me I couldn't tell if it were still a human dressed in a wolf's skin, or a real wolf. I lay in the ferns and shuddered until Alexander and Plexis found me.

They came into the clearing and I saw them but couldn't stand or speak. I lay in the ferns and trembled, my teeth chattering and my legs jerking in little tremors.

Plexis came right to the log where I'd been sitting and looked around, but the ferns hid me completely. The sound of my teeth chattering gave me away. He stopped, listened, then suddenly plunged into the thicket where I was hiding.

'Iskander, come quickly. I've found her!' Plexis heaved me up into his arms and lifted me over the log. Alexander grabbed me. His face was drawn and grey with worry.

'Ashley! What happened?' he asked, nearly shaking me.

I couldn't speak. My mouth opened, but no sound came out. I couldn't stop shaking.

'Quick, build a fire,' he ordered.

Plexis took his fire kit from his pouch and, using dried fern and pine needles, soon had a warm blaze. Both men covered me with their cloaks and held me tightly. My eyes were drawn to the centre of the clearing, though, where nothing, absolutely nothing, was left to show of what I'd seen or what I'd thought I'd seen. Had it been some sort of hallucination, I wondered? A hallucination brought on by fear, hunger, and loss of blood? Could the shock of losing my hand finally be sinking in? I quivered, my teeth chattered, and I tried to recall everything I'd witnessed and make sense of it.

But nothing was rational any more. Suddenly the pine trees with their spiny, spiky needles seemed too tall and too disturbing. The shadows were sinister and the shrill cries of the birds hurt my ears. I whimpered in fear. Finally, the fire caught my eyes. It leapt and danced, its

190

golden tongues reaching for me. Its warmth finally started to penetrate my icy bones. Alexander stroked my hair. My muscles loosened, and I passed out.

I woke up when the sun touched the horizon and its orange rays made shafts of light between the black pines. When I opened my eyes, I saw Alexander. He was sitting next to me, looking towards the sun, its light setting his hair on fire.

'Alex,' I said softly.

'Hail,' he said. 'How are you feeling?'

I moved my shoulders and legs. They were stiff but the shaking had disappeared. 'Better. I have to tell you something, I saw Voltarrix. He's with the Eaters of the Dead. Alex, he's their leader, and I don't think he's given up the idea of killing you. I saw him, he was dressed in a black wolf skin – and then he was a wolf. I know it sounds strange. I don't know. I don't understand what happened.' My voice wavered and broke.

Alexander listened carefully, without interrupting, like all people of that time. He listened both to my words and to my voice. When I finished, he nodded. 'I suspected Voltarrix survived. Yovanix was no match for him.' His voice was pensive and soft.

'I saw the missing Roman soldier.' I stopped and stared at Alexander. 'But I can't tell you what they did to him.' My voice climbed very high and broke. Tears spilled onto my cheeks, and the horror of what I'd seen chilled me once more.

'Shhh. I don't need to know.'

'But you do,' I said. 'They're not normal. There's

191

something horribly wrong with them. They fear the sun's rays, and they wear wolf skins like the druids.'

He shivered quickly, making an involuntary sign against evil. 'I hear you. The sun frightens them then, good.'

'During the day, I don't think they will bother us,' I said.

'What about a rainy, overcast day?' Alexander glanced upwards.

'I don't know.' I squeezed my eyes closed, trying to shut out the memory of a heaving mass of men acting like wild animals, ripping apart the Roman's body with their sharpened fangs. 'Where's Plexis?'

'He went to tell the others we found you.'

'I'm so sorry. I didn't mean to faint.'

'Let me see your arm.'

'It doesn't hurt any more.'

'Does it trouble you?' He looked at me, a question in his eyes.

'I don't really know yet. So far, I haven't thought about it. My mind has been full of worry about Paul and Plexis, and you, and now the Eaters of the Dead and Voltarrix.' I smiled wryly. 'I haven't had time to think about myself. Perhaps it's a good thing. Does it trouble you?'

Alexander's face was uncharacteristically still. 'I remember what you said to me once when I was wounded, that you hated to see me hurt because my body was too fine. I thought it was a strange thing to say. But now I understand you better.'

The sun slid below the horizon, the shadows disappeared. A night bird hooted and I shivered again. 'I'm afraid of the night,' I said.

'We'll build up the fire.'

'We mustn't leave the circle of light,' I said. My heart was beating faster. I felt an icy trickle of fear down my back. 'Alex, how much time until sunrise tonight?'

'Half an hour, maybe more.' He looked at me and his face was solemn. 'It's been ten days since the solstice.'

'Only ten days? It seems like it was a year ago. How far are we from Orce?'

'Another ten days' walk. We're going slowly because of the women and children.'

'And the wounded. I feel so dreadful. Alex, I'm sorry. I seem to be saying that too often,' I said with a mirthless laugh.

'I thought I was dying,' he said then, taking my chin in his hands and tilting my face up towards his. 'I felt the knife slice through my skin, and it seemed to take forever. I heard the sound the sharp blade made as it cut my throat and I could feel its hideous coldness. I felt every fibre of my being scream in pain and terror. However, I could not move. Everyone was caught in the solid air. It turned golden, like amber. I remember watching a fly caught in that amber air, just hanging motionless in front of me.

'When you and Paul moved, you both seemed to shimmer. Your skin was silvered as if you were underwater. When you touched me, your hands were as quick flames licking my body. I was helpless, powerless, and unable to move or to speak. But I could see and feel and think. And during that eternity, I thought of all the time we'd been given, all the time we'd spent together, and each minute appeared to me encased in a diamond. I thought I was dying. I didn't realize I'd been frozen in time. All I kept thinking, over and over again was, *"I'm dying, my shade is leaving my body, and I will never see her again. I will never see Paul again, or Plexis, or Chiron and Cleopatra."* All those thoughts ran through my head. I tried to imagine everyone. I tried to picture their faces, to hear their voices. It lasted so long, those moments of agony. Then everything went black. There was a clap of thunder, and it was like waking up in a panic from a nightmare. But it wasn't a dream, was it?' His hand reached up and touched his throat lightly.

'Show me.' I had to whisper. I didn't trust my voice. Alexander just looked at me, tears running down his cheeks.

'Demos took the sewing out.'

'He did a good job.' I reached up and brushed away his tears. 'Don't cry.'

'I'm not crying.' He shook his head, then let it fall forward to his chest. 'I don't know. Maybe I *am* crying. I'm so tired. When you disappeared yesterday, I thought you'd been taken by the Eaters of the Dead. Plexis and I tracked them. We followed their trail, but they just led us in a huge circle. Each step I took was a torture. Each minute that went by without you was another agony. I died again yesterday, Ashley. I didn't realize how much I needed you with me. You are my oracle, my talisman, my lover, and my wife. I'm sorry.'

'Why are you sorry?'

'Because I haven't told you I love you in so long. I haven't held you in so long, and I never told you I needed you.'

'I need you too. We all need each other,' I said gently. 'It's called being human, I think.'

He raised his head and his mouth twitched. 'I'm waiting.'

'For what?'

'Aren't you going to tease me some more about my ancestors?'

'I shook my head. 'No, no, Alex, I'm not. You were born in the middle of a raging storm, and during your birth two eagles came and took refuge in the temple where your mother lay. When you were born your mother said she saw a vision, a blazing trail of stars over the land, marking your destiny. She told you that you were directly descended from Achilles and Hercules, and that Zeus was your father. How could you ever admit to needing anyone? How could any human fill the emptiness inside you?'

'It's filled,' he said slowly. 'It's filled with you. And all the others I've come to need.'

'I have always loved you, and I've always needed you.'

'I know that,' he said, a tiny quiver in his voice.

'Now you must accept the fact that we can die too,' I said. 'Accept the fact that we can lose hands, and fingers, and our lives. It's part of life. To answer your question, yes, losing my hand troubles me, but I will learn to live without it.'

'Perhaps.' He gave me a blinding smile. 'But you have never accepted the fact that I could die,'

'Twice,' I murmured. 'Twice you've died for me.'

'I think that's enough. I want to grow old with you and the children.' He cupped his hands on my belly. 'There is something about a baby that makes you feel immortal.'

'Can you just hold me?' I asked. 'Just hold me until the sun comes up?'

'I think I can manage that,' he said gravely.

'Then hold me, and tell me that everything will be all right; because I'll believe you if you tell me that.'

'Why? Because I'm such a great warrior?'

'No, because you're directly descended from Achilles and Hercules, and Zeus, your father, will protect us.'

'I love it when you're sarcastic,' he said, burying his face in my neck. 'It means you're feeling better.'

Chapter Seventeen

The night was only thirty minutes of darkness, but it seemed to last an eternity. Perhaps Voltarrix was up to his tricks again, stopping time, or just slowing it down so that he and his wolf pack of men could hunt. I dreamed I fell asleep in Alexander's arms. In my dream the wolves were in a hungry circle around us, jaws open, slavering and growling at us. But we were in an enchanted circle of light, and they could not touch us. Then a rainstorm put out the fire, and the wolf-men closed in. Voltarrix raised his arms and stopped time, and I saw what I must do and started to scream.

I was still asleep. It was only a nightmare. Alexander shook me gently and murmured in my ear, 'Hush, hush, it's just a dream. I'm here. Open your eyes, look, it's morning. Will you be all right now? I have to get some more firewood and breakfast. Plexis will be back with Demos and Axiom, and then we'll carry you up the mountain.'

'I'll be fine.' I suddenly discovered I was weak with hunger. When he mentioned breakfast, my stomach growled so loudly I winced.

'I'll try to hurry,' he said with a grin and vanished

from the grove.

I took advantage of his absence to wash in a small, icy stream. I shivered, and wondered why all streams had to be icy. Why couldn't I find a nice, lukewarm stream? Or discover a hot spring? Why was I always splashing with water that made me gasp when it touched my body?

I shrieked as I ducked under the water, slapped a mosquito off my cheek, shivered, and rushed back to the fire to warm and dry myself. Then I gingerly unwrapped my bandage to examine my wrist. The sword had been razor sharp, and unfortunately had caught me squarely on the joint where the delicate bones and cartilage had been no match for the heavy blade. The hand hadn't been completely severed, but Demos had taken it off. There was no use trying to save it. He'd cleaned the wound and cauterized it as he'd learned in the medical school on Kos: first the arteries, then the veins, then the skin. He'd done a good job. My wrist ended in a painful looking knob, but it would heal. The redness would fade, and I would just have to wear long sleeves for the rest of my life.

A strange pang shot through me. The thought of never having another left hand was sinking in. I tucked the bandage in my belt and plucked wild cabbage leaves. Using one hand and my left elbow, I managed to fashion an acceptable bowl, filled it with water, and put it on the fire to boil my bandages. Then I sat and poked at the fire cradling my hurt arm in my lap. I kept trying to get used to the stump, but every time I saw it, I felt sick. When the linen bandage was sterilized, I hung it on a branch to dry and waited for Alexander.

He came back with a leather pouch full of roots, a large fish, and a handful of wild berries. He had washed; his hair was dripping, his tunic clung to him, and his sandals were wet. I frowned. He didn't usually bathe wearing sandals.

'I fell in the creek,' he said cheerfully.

'I wondered what kept you so long,' I said.

'It's strange, but there are no animals left in the region. I must have walked a parasang in every direction. I saw no sign of deer or rabbit. No game birds. They've all disappeared.'

'Animals tend to hide when they feel hunted, don't they?'

'Yes, but they leave a trace. I saw nothing. Well, at least I caught a trout. Here, move over, I'll make us some breakfast.'

We grilled the trout and boiled and mashed the arrowleaf roots. It sounds frugal, but I was travelling with someone who was used to gourmet food in any situation. We nibbled on the berries while waiting for our food to cook, getting our lips and fingers purple. Alexander had salt in his pouch, a clove of garlic, and he had picked some fresh herbs, so he seasoned the mashed roots sumptuously. I ate until I was stuffed. Then I leaned back against my husband's shoulder and sighed deeply.

'That was wonderful.'

'Mmm. Maybe not as good as the dinner we had at Musicanus's palace.'

'How can you speak so blithely about a man you

slaughtered?' I sat up and frowned at him. 'I can't believe you sometimes.'

'I had to slaughter him, he attacked us. It was either kill or be killed. What would you have preferred?'

'It was the Brahmin's fault. They wanted to fight, Musicanus didn't. He was tricked.'

'Yes. Unfortunately, I didn't know that at the time. I am sorry for killing him. He was a good host.'

'He was, wasn't he?' I agreed.

'We had a good dinner there, didn't we? How many courses? Ten? Twelve? And there were musicians and magicians and snake charmers and fakirs – and those dancing girls! Do you remember?'

'Of course.' I snuggled back under his shoulder. 'You nearly peed laughing when that poor snake charmer was bitten and died right in front of us.'

'I *never* peed laughing,' he said huffily. He brightened. 'But it was funny, wasn't it? Do you recall that man who climbed up the rope? I'll never understand how he did that. The rope wasn't attached to anything. Amazing. I think I liked the peacock tongues the best,' he said, darting away to another subject. 'Or the curried lamb. Oh, and I loved the dish with the creamy coconut sauce. You know what? I'm still hungry.' He eyed the bare fish bones and the empty bowl. 'I wish we were in India. I could eat a whole curried lamb right about now.'

I smiled and snuggled deeper into his arms. He chuckled and the sound was like a purr. His magnificent jaguar eyes softened when he smiled. 'I hear the others coming.'

I strained my ears but heard nothing. Sure enough, though, after a short wait, Plexis came padding silently into the grove. Paul and Demos followed, with Axiom bring up the rear. They all fell upon me, laughing, crying, hugging me, and scolding.

I was soon floating above the ground on a comfortable litter carried by Demos and Axiom while Plexis led and Paul and Alexander walked close behind. I could hear them talking together; it sounded like Alexander was describing the banquet at Musicanus's palace in great detail. Occasionally Paul would interrupt with a question then say, with a sigh, 'How I wish I could have seen that.'

We hiked up the mountain, stopping once for lunch and once to rest. By the time the sun was low, we'd reached the others. I was glad to be in the midst of a bustling crowd. The silence of the forest had started to unnerve me. Alexander made sure that the soldiers understood that they had to stay within the circles of light, and the women and children gathered around a central bonfire. We spent the short night huddled within the flickering firelight. Flames glinted off the men's spear tips and swords as they stood ready to fight.

However, Voltarrix was biding his time.

We advanced as quickly as we dared, hoping to lure Voltarrix into an attack while we were all armed and ready, but he remained invisible. Then, on the morning of the third day, a small child disappeared. The mother's anguished wails echoed through the campsite and surrounding forest as everyone spread out to search.

Plexis found the trail and started to track the child. At first it was easy, the little boy had seen a bunny and had followed it. Both sets of prints were clear.

Then the rabbit vanished into his hole, and the boy, instead of heading back to camp, had chosen to venture into a deep thicket. There were wild berries, so the reason was obvious. Then the footprints seemed to vanish. Plexis cast around, his face a study in frustration.

'I don't understand how he could have disappeared. It looks more as if someone erased his tracks. Look, here, how the ground is smooth. Someone has passed his hand over it. But here is a print, quite clear, of a wolf. Except there are no others.' He stopped and frowned. 'I don't like this at all.'

I was standing well back, staying out of his way. But when he mentioned a wolf print, my heart lurched.

'Plexis,' I whispered. 'You must find a trail. Even if it looks as if an animal made it. Find a trail and follow it. We have to reach the child before nightfall.' I looked at the sky. There were only a few more hours until sunset.

I went to find Alexander and spoke to him urgently. He listened with a growing scowl. At first, he didn't want to agree to my plan, but I insisted, and the woman who'd lost her child was sobbing so hard that he relented.

Paul, Demos, and Alexander went with me. We followed Plexis as quietly as we could. I was alternately quivering with fear and horror. I knew what I must do. I'd seen it in my dream. What I would do would destroy part of me. I would never be the same. I would think of the consequences later. Much later.

Plexis followed a faint trail into a saddleback ridge. There, two mountains rose side by side, forming a deep ravine between them. A stream cascaded down one narrow end, splashing over boulders and mossy banks, disappearing into the darkness below. Tall pine trees grew precariously on steep inclines, looking like intrepid mountain climbers dressed in prickly green holding out their branches for balance. The trail twisted downwards, weaving between trees and boulders, leading us down, down, into the gloomy twilight of the ravine. Once at the bottom, Plexis stopped. The stream had widened, its gravelly banks overgrown with fern and nettle. The trail led into the stream and we could see where it picked up on the other side. However, we hesitated. We couldn't see through the gloom, and we didn't want to fall into a trap or let Voltarrix know we were on his heels. Raising my eyes, I caught sight of darkness behind some pine trees. I pointed silently. Alexander peered upwards then nodded grimly. 'A cave,' he whispered.

We faded into the undergrowth to discuss our plans. They were simple and horrifying.

The sun crossed over the chasm and disappeared behind the steep mountainside. Almost at once, I heard the shriek of a frightened child. I felt a rush of adrenaline. Any misgivings I had faded with that anguished cry.

Paul and I made our way up the hillside, following Plexis, putting our hands and feet exactly where he showed us. He moved like a shadow over the rocky ground, never putting his foot wrong, picking out the trail through the gathering darkness. Near the mouth of the cave he stopped and turned. His amber eyes were dark pools of fear.

'I cannot go any further,' he gasped. Sweat pearled on his brow. I could feel a change in the air. It was growing stronger. The child's cries grew higher and higher, then stopped. Plexis froze. Paul and I looked and each other and nodded. It was time. Taking deep breaths, we stepped inside the cave.

There was no light inside, but we could see the faint outlines of the Eaters of the Dead gathered in a tight circle around the child. Voltarrix was holding his ritual knife, but it hadn't begun its slow descent. The timing had been perfect. I could feel electricity coursing through my veins. There was a ringing in my ears. Time had slowed again. I moved through it, a knife in my right hand.

In my dream, I had held Alexander's sword, but it was too heavy and unwieldy for me. I had chosen a knife; dreams are not reality. Dreams are only our subconscious, sometimes telling us what our minds refuse to acknowledge. My subconscious had told me what I had to do. I moved through the darkness like an avenging angel.

And the kneeling men, the Eaters of the Dead, grimaced in frozen agony, their sharp fangs shining, their eyes glittering with anguish and fear as I pushed the knife into their throats and sawed it from side to side. I had to shut my eyes as I did it. My skin crawled with horror. I clenched my teeth to keep my stomach from heaving.

I completed the circle just as Voltarrix's knife found the child's throat, and my scream echoed through time, a shattering roar in the cavern. There was another cry. Paul leapt through the crystal air and struck the knife from the druid's hands. It fell to the ground in an interminable, shining arc and shattered in slow motion when it hit the stone.

I dropped my own knife, my heart lurching. A stray shaft of light, reflected from outside, had somehow found its way into the cave. In front of me knelt a man I knew. A young man with creamy skin and brown hair the colour of fall leaves. His teeth were not pointed. His hands were bound behind his back. His eyes were deep pools reflecting the madness of that night; I could see blood between his teeth where he'd bitten his tongue.

I bent down, picked up my knife, my fingers wet with blood and sweat, and I cut the ropes binding his arms. 'Run!' I roared to him. 'When you hear the thunder run!' My own voice was like a roll of thunder. I hoped he understood. How long had Yovanix been a prisoner? Had he lost his mind? He only stared at me blankly.

I turned then and faced Voltarrix. His mouth was frozen in a scream. I was the image of death reflected in his eyes. I had no pity for him. What would happen if I killed him before he set time back on its track? I had no idea, but if I didn't kill him now I never would. My knife plunged into his chest. Alexander had showed me exactly where to place it. The knife was held horizontally, I ran my fingers lightly down his chest, counting the ribs, finding the space between them. My mouth moved as I whispered. Voltarrix screamed silently. I shoved the blade in, and then a clap of thunder threw me to the ground.

I looked for my son, but Paul had already taken the child. He'd left the cave at a run.

I scrambled to my feet, staggering as the ground lurched again. Voltarrix was on the ground, his blood bubbling out of the wound. Alexander had told me to remove the knife, but it was torn from my grasp when the world shook, now it protruded from his chest. With a snarl, he reached out and caught my ankle.

I screamed and fought, but even mortally wounded, he was too strong for me. The Eaters of the Dead had fallen. They would not help their master again. We were swimming in blood, blood was choking me, blinding me, and burning my skin.

Suddenly a boulder fell from the roof of the cave, and the sound deafened me. The whole cave was falling in on us. I screamed again and kicked backwards, clawing for a handhold on the slippery floor, struggling through thick, hot blood. I was trapped in a nightmare. I kept screaming, straining to get away. The sound of rocks falling was like cracks of thunder.

Then a shock went through Voltarrix. I felt it like a jolt of electricity. I screamed again, but now strong arms were lifting me, and I was half carried, half heaved out of the cave. Someone had torn me from Voltarrix's grip and saved me from the mad druid.

I lost my footing and tumbled, rolling over and over

down the hill. Behind me, there was a muffled roar. A cloud of dust and stones enveloped me as the cave collapsed. Behind me, someone uttered a loud curse, then started to laugh hysterically. I landed in a heap next to a boulder and shook my head to clear it. 'Yovanix?' I gasped. Then I couldn't speak as nausea swept over me. My stomach heaved and I leaned over and vomited on the shattered ground. Behind me, I heard the sound of uncertain steps. The earth gave one last tremor, tumbling me the last few feet to the bottom of the gully.

Yovanix crumpled into me. We lay in a heap, panting and disoriented. 'Are you all right?' I asked, finally getting my breath back.

'I don't know.' He started to laugh again and it turned into a wail. He was shuddering against me, trembling so hard his head was hitting the stones. I tried to hold him but I was hampered by my wounded arm.

'It's over,' I said, 'Don't cry. Don't worry. We're here and we'll keep you safe.'

'You will?' His voice broke and turned his face to me.

I was past shock. Trauma had numbed me. I just stared at Yovanix, taking in the gaping holes where his eyes should have been, the tears of blood that ran down his face. I found I could breathe then. 'Oh, no, please, no,' I choked, and I put my arms around him and held him, just held him while he sobbed.

'I didn't know if it was you,' he said. 'I heard a god speaking, and he said, *run*. There was thunder. I heard screaming. I didn't know if it was really you.'

'You saved my life,' I said. 'You saved me from

Voltarrix.'

He couldn't speak any more, his head fell onto my shoulder and he shuddered against me. I held onto him and crooned into his ear until Alexander, Demos and Plexis crept over to us.

I looked up at them. 'He's dying,' I mouthed silently.

Alexander knelt by my side. 'No,' he said. 'No. He'll be all right, I promise.' I caught him glancing at Demos and I tightened my arms around Yovanix.

Demos took my arms and gently pulled them apart. 'Let me see,' he said softly.

'I cut his throat,' I said brokenly. 'It was dark and I couldn't see very well. I closed my eyes. Everyone was in a circle. They were gathered around the child and Voltarrix ...' I looked around. 'Where is Paul? Where's the child?'

'They're safe. Don't worry. Shhh, let me see him.' Demos nodded to Alexander and he raised me to my feet. I walked unsteadily, my body strangely unwilling to move.

There was a noise behind me, sort of a gurgle. I turned and saw Yovanix sitting up. Demos was holding his face in his huge hands looking at his wounds. Down his chest streamed fresh blood. The cut I'd made hadn't been deep, but it was deep enough. Plexis was ready though. Using the method I'd tried on Alexander, he carefully closed the wound with tight stitches, his face a mask of concentration. Yovanix squirmed and tried to speak, but Demos held him firmly, speaking to him in a deep, gentle voice, telling him over and over not to worry.

I looked at Alexander. My teeth started to chatter. I couldn't speak but he knew what I wanted. He led me to the stream. Without a word he stripped off my blood-soaked clothes and washed the gore from my body. The water may have been cold, I don't recall. I couldn't feel a thing. I put my head into the water and let the current wash my hair. I lay in the fast flowing stream and tried to clear my thoughts. I wanted very much to be able to close my eyes, but I couldn't. Each time I did, I saw the eyes of the men I'd killed. It had been like killing innocents. They couldn't move; it had been so unfair. Like stabbing someone while they slept, but worse. These men had all watched me coming at them with a knife. I was trapped in my dream, helplessly watching as my hand advanced towards the white throats all offered to me. And the knife that Axiom had sharpened to a bright razor coming closer and closer to taut skin …

I sat up, sputtering and gasping. The cold rushed over me, slapping me awake. Alexander hauled me out of the stream and half led, half carried me into the forest. We went back up the path towards the light that was growing stronger over the eastern side of the mountains.

At the top, in a clearing, a yellow fire burned brightly in the pale grey dawn. Axiom was feeding soup to a little boy sitting in Paul's lap. As I neared the fire, the child saw me and shrank back in terror. I stopped and looked at him. I can well imagine what he'd seen in the dark cave. A terrifying goddess of shimmering silver holding a glittering knife. Then the dark lines that gaped at the bases of the men's throats like sick smiles.

Paul spoke to him, whispering in his ear in his own language, and the child relaxed. I sat next to the fire, and Axiom draped a warm cloak over me. I'd asked Alexander to bury my old clothes. I could never wash the stains out of them. I clutched the cloak around me, holding its warmth to my skin, staring at the fire. I couldn't unclench my teeth. I was stupefied with the horror of what I'd done. Even my tears felt like drops of ice trickling down my cheeks.

Alexander spoke in a whisper to Axiom then went back into the ravine to help carry Yovanix out. I drew my knees to my chest and waited, staring unblinkingly at the flames.

We must have made a pathetic sight coming back to the camp. Nearchus saw us first; he was standing guard on the outskirts, his spear and sword in hand. He dropped them and rushed towards us. When I saw his face, I realized how dreadful we looked. Yovanix was stretched on a litter, his face towards the sky, a bandage swathing his throat and eyes. I was walking next to Alexander, clutching his arm, afraid to let go. I felt exactly as if I were about to fly off the face of the earth. I needed an anchor.

Paul was leading the child. The little boy was still dressed in his ragged, bloodstained tunic. Paul had tried to wash his own clothes, but he couldn't. They were still rust-coloured and stiff with dried blood. We had been drenched in it. It had dried in rivulets on our faces and in our hair. Plexis was leading the way, but his face was paler than usual. He had sewn up Yovanix's neck, then fainted at Demos's feet.

Demos didn't look so well himself. Each time he glanced my way, he made signs against evil. He couldn't help it. It was completely involuntary. But he'd seen me coming out of the cave. Alexander said it had looked as if I were flying with Yovanix clutching me from behind. I had been scarlet from head to toe, absolutely painted with blood. We'd plunged down the hill in front of a landslide and come to rest against a massive boulder, miraculously unhurt. Demos shuddered whenever he saw me now. I couldn't blame him.

What had frightened him the most had been the amount of blood. Even after ten years of fighting in the Persian army, he'd never seen anything like it. Then Yovanix had turned his ruined face towards him and the big man had just about fainted. Now he held Yovanix's hand with one hand, and he made the sign against evil with the other.

I walked and I looked closely at everything and thought hard about everything I saw, muttering the names of trees and plants as I spied them, asking Alexander to name them for me if I didn't know them. I watched the sky and the clouds. I studied the men with me, looking at their clothes and the way they moved. I tried to keep my mind busy with the here and now. I still didn't dare close my eyes.

Axiom paused now and then to gather herbs. I saw him studying me. He smiled sadly every time our eyes met. I could never smile back. I could only shudder.

Nearchus rushed towards us and stopped when he saw who was on the stretcher, but he didn't ask a single question. His eyes flew from Plexis to Alexander to me, then to the child Paul was leading by the hand. Haltingly he approached us and dropped a light hand on Plexis's shoulder. 'Hail,' he said. 'The boy's mother will be overjoyed to have her son back.'

Yovanix struggled to sit up on the stretcher. 'Nearchus, is that you?' he asked, his voice high.

'It is. Hail, Yovanix, my heart is glad to see you; I thought that you were in Hades' realm.'

'I was,' said Yovanix, his bandaged face turned towards the blond admiral. 'I *was* in Hades' realm, and Persephone the Terrible delivered me. She killed everyone, everyone, and Voltarrix as well, but not before he blinded me. "Look upon death!" he said to me, and he put out my eyes. But not before I saw the Queen of Ice and Darkness sailing through the night.'

My arms prickled. All my hair stood on end. 'It's not true,' I whispered. 'It was only me. Voltarrix had no hold on me; I don't come from this time. I had to slay them; I had to. Otherwise they would have hunted us all the way to Orce. Don't you see? I had to kill them. I didn't want to. I swear to you I never wanted to slaughter anyone!'

Yovanix kept shaking his head, and Nearchus's lips drew back from his teeth in a grimace of fright. 'What do you say, Iskander?' he whispered.

Alexander sighed then seemed to gather himself together. He had more strength than any of us. He looked at Nearchus. He raised an eyebrow and he shrugged. 'What do you want me to say? That it's true? Yes, it's true. The Eaters of the Dead are all lying in a cave with their throats cut from ear to ear, and Voltarrix is dead with my knife in his chest.' He paused and then turned to me. 'I told you to pull it out,' he said, and his old grin was back. 'By the gods, Woman, now I have to wait until I get back to Gaul to get myself a new knife.'

Nearchus's mouth twitched and then he smiled. 'You moved through time again?' he asked, and he looked straight at me. His dark blue gaze was no longer fearful. 'No, My Lady,' he said, divining my thoughts. 'I have known you too long and too well. But judging from Yovanix's words and Demos's face, I think you're going to have to get used to being called the Queen of Ice and Darkness again.'

'I don't want to think about it. I feel as if my bones are made of glass, and I want to vomit every moment. I'm so tired, but I can't sleep.'

Plexis stirred and a faint grin crossed his face. 'That's all my fault,' he said.

I turned to him, puzzled. 'Oh? How so?'

'It sounds like you're pregnant again,' he said, and then he started to laugh.

Alexander grabbed his arms before he lost control of himself, and the laughter ended in a tired sob. Plexis let his head fall on Alexander's shoulder. 'I'm sorry,' he said. 'I'm just as tired as you are.'

Alexander nodded. 'We're all weary. Let's go home now. I have my soul, I have the people I love and need with me. Here, Nearchus, carry Ashley. I'll pick up your sword for you. Let's go.'

We squared our shoulders and made our way back to the camp. And for a long time my nightmares were assuaged by the glad cry of the child when he spotted his mother and by her exclamations of joy as she ran to meet him.

I didn't speak her language but she made herself very clear. She took off an ornate necklace of amber and gold and carefully placed it over my head. None of my protests could make her take it back. Her eyes were bright and her smile was dazzling. Then she kissed me and held me. She was a mother. Mothers know how to comfort. I cried like a baby in her arms while she crooned in my ear and rocked me back and forth. I was no longer Persephone the Terrible; I was just a woman who had managed to slay a demon and had lost my hand in a terrible accident. I was just someone who needed comforting. She brushed away my tears with her thumbs, holding my face in her hands, and she smiled at me.

Chapter Eighteen

The other people approached me easily after that, patting my shoulders, touching my cheeks, and telling me with sign language how much I meant to them. After a few days of that, I felt almost human again.

Axiom gave me a sleeping potion every night. I slept deeply without any dreams, but when I woke up I felt sluggish and dizzy.

'I'm sorry, I can't give it to you forever,' he said to me one afternoon. 'You'll have to face your demons.'

'I know that, but not tonight, please? I don't want to face them tonight. I …' I cast around for an argument. 'I don't want to wake everyone up, I'll scream; you know how Alexander screams sometimes. He frightens everybody.' My voice dropped.

Axiom's lashes were long and black, sweeping against his cheeks when he lowered his eyes, but he didn't lower them now. 'Ashley, the potion is bad for the baby too. I don't dare give you any more. I'm sorry.' He meant it. His voice was firm. 'We're here with you. No one will blame you for waking them up.'

I stared at him, tears pricking my eyes. 'It was so awful, Axiom, so dreadful. Yovanix saw it, and he will never speak to me again. He starts screaming, even during the day, and you have to give him the potion just to calm him down.'

'Yovanix has lost his mind,' said Axiom. 'He knows not where he is, or who he's with. I give him something to take away the knife-edge of reality, but I am weaning him off it. I only hope it's not too late. If Usse were here, he would know better how to help him. As it is, his eyes give him terrible pain and his throat will not heal, he rips at the stitches. We had to bind his hands to his sides. I'm sorry, Ashley, but I don't know if he will ever recover.'

I blinked and looked down at the ground. 'I didn't see him in time. It was so dark. All I saw were the silhouettes.'

'And just before that, Voltarrix blinded him.'

'I don't understand why,' I whispered.

'In a way it's lucky he did. It gave Paul time to save the child. If the druid had left Yovanix alone, the child would have died.'

'I know that, but can you imagine what Yovanix thinks? All he saw was me coming to cut his throat, and all the other men, immobile, with their heads sliced nearly off their shoulders. What do you think he's going to believe? He thinks I'm a monster. And I am. Who else would have killed those helpless men?' I began to shake again.

Axiom put his hands on my shoulders. 'No, I won't let you say that. Helpless? Perhaps at that moment. It was the only thing to do. Voltarrix was a demon, you said so yourself. But please, try and think of the child you carry. I cannot give you any more of the sleeping potion. I'm sorry.'

I took some deep breaths and was relieved to see I could calm myself. I managed a smile for Axiom. 'All right, you win. No more sleeping potion.'

'I think I'll speak to Alexander and Plexis. I know what would help,' he said. He spoke blandly but his eyes twinkled.

'You do?' I asked. Then I saw his grin. 'Axiom!' I blushed. 'I keep forgetting how well you know me.'

He laughed and shook his head. 'Ten years in a tent with someone is probably a good way to get to know them.'

I nodded thoughtfully. 'And what about you, Axiom? Why have you never married? I don't want to pry, I've never asked you about your affairs, but I have always been curious. You're a free man, and a handsome one at that. Usse married Chirpa. Has there never been a woman to steal your heart?'

'No, Ashley, never. My heart has yet to beat for anyone but my god. Perhaps someday, I will find someone I would love as strongly as I love Him, but that person has not yet crossed my path. However, I am a patient man. I know Yahweh never meant for me to be alone. I have lived with Iskander, Plexis, Usse, Brazza, and you as my family. Your children are my children in my heart. Yahweh gave me a choice, and I followed Iskander.'

'I understand you completely,' I said.

'I knew you would.' Axiom patted my shoulder.

'Sleep, sleep, My Lady. The sun is still bright. Lie down, and if you wake up with a nightmare, the sunlight will give you comfort.'

I slept then, and my dreams oscillated between horror and despair. But each time I opened my eyes the dazzle of light soothed me, and I was able to drop off to sleep once more.

Then the sun set in an orange glow and Plexis and Alexander slid beneath the soft furs with me and held me. Wrapped in their arms, I forgot my fears.

Axiom was right, I thought, a half-smile on my lips. I tingled all over with pleasure.

Plexis moved gently against my back, and Alexander pressed himself against my belly and groaned softly. I stretched, making Plexis moan with pleasure.

'Mmmm, move like that again,' he said teasingly, giving me a nip on the shoulder.

I felt a heat building in my belly, a heaviness that made me arch my back and open my legs. My breath came in quick gasps, echoing the breathing of the two men with me. We moved in unison, our bodies growing slippery with excitement. It flared up quickly; too much time had gone by since we had been together. Need made my movements urgent. I felt a throbbing start in my sex and let myself dissolve into its fulfilment. Plexis gave a strangled cry, his hands grasping my hips. Alexander groaned, driving himself into me. I felt them coming in unison. Another wave of pleasure submerged me and I shuddered in their arms.

Afterwards, we lay in a comfortable tangle, our heads

touching, our arms and legs entwined. I forgot my nightmares, my missing hand, everything. Alexander's mouth roamed lazily over my breast, searching for a nipple. Plexis slept deeply, his face peaceful. There was a calm silence. The dawn had come; a pink light was building on the horizon.

Alexander caught my eye and grinned. He suckled my breast, nuzzling and tugging gently on it. I closed my eyes, my heart starting to thump hard again.

Something else was hard. I opened one eye and peered at Alexander. 'Again?' I mouthed.

He nodded, a faint flush on his cheeks. He lowered his body onto me and moved sinuously. I arched my back, pressing up to meet him, my legs rising of their own accord to wrap around his back. I closed my eyes and saw only darkness. Alexander had chased away my demons. I let my head fall backward and abandoned myself to our pleasure.

We sang the rest of the way back to Orce. The people of that time loved to sing. They sang as they walked, sometimes sad songs about the loved ones they'd lost, and sometimes glad ones celebrating battles and our victory.

Most were made up on the spur of the moment; a man would make up a refrain and the song would be built around it. We had no official bard with us, but most of the men and women had beautiful singing voices. And Alexander came down with laryngitis, which cheered everyone immensely. He'd insisted on singing along. His throat was not up to it however, and he lost his voice. I didn't know if it was due to his wound or to the prayers of everyone around us. Alexander's singing was the worst cacophony imaginable. *He* thought he sounded just fine.

'What do you mean *hush*?' he'd say, a frown on his handsome face. 'I sing just like anyone else. I know *all* the words.' He looked superior. 'I memorize words faster than anyone else,' he said loftily. That was true. He knew *all* the words to *all* the songs he'd ever heard. Too bad about the tunes. He was totally tone-deaf.

He lost his voice, and everyone else sang joyfully on the way to Orce; the children sitting on their father's shoulders, the women wearing crowns of flowers in their hair, and the two Roman soldiers singing in a disciplined fashion with backs straight and heads high. Everyone sang, except Alexander, who had lost his voice, and Yovanix, who had lost his mind.

Yovanix lay on his litter without moving, trying to keep from screaming in fright.

He was still not well. He would wake up from a drug-induced sleep, thrashing his arms and legs and yelling hoarsely. We had to tie him to the stretcher, and we had to tie his arms to his sides so he didn't pluck at the stitches in his neck. Stitches he could not understand. I tried to explain what had happened, but he panicked.

'He'll recover, don't fret. The weird-woman of Orce will heal him,' said Phaleria to me one afternoon. I no longer frightened her. She was more relaxed around me. Some of it was due to the little boy I'd rescued, and some of it was thanks to Demos who had turned his mind from warfare to love and was now wooing Phaleria with songs and stories. She walked with a spring in her step, a lock of red hair twisted around her finger like a ring, and her generous mouth in a wide grin. 'The wise woman will greet us, and we'll ask her to heal him.' She shrugged.

'As easy as that?' I asked, a note of scepticism in my voice.

'Of course! Don't you think he's handsome?' she asked for the thirteenth time that day.

I didn't need to ask to whom she was referring. Demos walked a few paces in front of us, and he turned around and gave a coy wink every four or five steps. 'He's very handsome,' I said seriously. 'And he's strong, kind, a mighty warrior, and never seasick. I think you two will do very well together.'

Phaleria laughed delightedly and linked her arm through mine, startling me. No one had ever done that to me before. I stared at her in wonder, but she just tossed her head and started singing.

Everyone was in a good mood because tomorrow we'd reach Orce. Already, we were travelling down a white dirt road. We'd passed three small settlements, and amazed villagers had greeted long-lost friends and family with joyous cries and tears. It was a fête winding its way down the mountainside towards the sea.

However, I was still depressed. I hadn't faced up to my own problems. Yovanix worried me, and Paul was still acting strangely. He had seen what had happened in the cave, and I think it had further estranged us. On one hand he thought I was wonderful for saving the child, and on the other I was awful to have killed helpless men. I knew how he felt. I held onto Phaleria's arm and tried to join the fun, but my heart wasn't in it.

The sun was setting, turning the fjord into a golden lake in front of the bustling town. Boats bobbed in the harbour, torches were lit in the streets, and a huge feast had been prepared for our arrival.

The townspeople came to greet us. In the front of the crowd was the weird-woman. She raised her arms above her head, making me shudder. However, she was no druid. She was simply waving joyfully, as was everyone else.

The Valerians burst into song as we marched into the village. The weird-woman halted Alexander and touched his face lightly. Her hands brushed against the scars on his throat, and she shook he head from side to side, an expression of awe on her face.

'What magic is this?' she asked.

'It's no magic,' whispered Alexander, his voice shattered. 'It's a way to heal a deep cut without fire.'

She nodded and moved on to Paul. Her hands brushed his face and shoulders. 'The young king,' she said. 'His blood is glowing brighter than the sun. Have no more fear,' she told him. 'A shadow of doubt darkens your mind. You must learn to rely on your instincts, not upon words. Come to see me tomorrow when the sun is overhead. We will talk.'

Then she went to Yovanix. She was blind, so a young

girl held her arm and led her around. I swear to you, most of the time it seemed as if it were the old woman who led the girl. Once next to Yovanix, she stood in silence with her hands hovering above his body, not touching him.

He sensed her though, and he twisted and turned, trying to see with his ruined eyes.

'Hush, don't move. You are in Orce now. Can you smell the sea? The battle is far behind you. Now you will rest and get well.'

'I can never get well,' cried Yovanix. 'My eyes are gone. I am lost in darkness now!'

'There is the darkness of terror and there is the darkness of night; yours is in your soul. You will be able to live once more in the light when your demons have been exorcised. Fear not. I can heal you. Be still.' Her voice grew in power, and Yovanix slumped back onto the stretcher.

His body trembled slightly as she passed her hands over it. I stood nearby, watching. The silence grew and I glanced around. Everyone else had gone into the village. Only Alexander, Paul, Plexis, and I remained behind. The old woman waved her hands over Yovanix, crooning something in a strange tongue.

I turned towards the sea and watched as the sun turned it to a bright orange. The houses were black silhouettes, the torches were spots of yellow. The longhouse echoed with shouts of laughter and song. A huge bonfire was built beside it, and a whole ox turned on a giant spit above a ditch full of glowing red coals.

Sparks shot up in an orange fountain as another log was tossed onto the fire.

The shadow of the mountain grew longer; the molten gold of the sea became navy blue. The festivities continued and Yovanix fell asleep, his mouth open, his face relaxed.

The old woman stepped back and wiped her hands on her dress. 'I can do no more tonight,' she said. 'He will sleep deeply until dawn. I will see to him again tomorrow. He has seen and lived through something no man should endure. But I think he will heal.'

'He will be always blind,' I said to her.

She looked up at me. It was uncanny how she seemed to be able to see past the white clouds in her eyes. 'Ah, the goddess speaks. Poor child, give me your hand.'

I laughed mirthlessly. 'I have but one to give you.'

'One is better than none,' she said simply. She took my hand and held it, her head tipped backwards, her eyes closed. A shudder ran down her spine. It was indescribable. I felt as if a thread were slowly being pulled out of the top of my head. I nearly jerked my hand away but she held it tightly. 'No, let me finish. There are things I can see, things I can heal, things I can change. Yours are not the powers to change, you know that.' Her voice was sly.

I felt very faint. 'Are you an oracle as well?' I asked.

'No, and I speak for no one but myself, but I can hear things that are very distant. A voice said that to you once before. Remember what the voice told you. I can only hear its echo, but it sounds like Balder's voice.' She shook her sightless head and smiled softly. 'A sweeter voice there never was, and when he sings, the birds themselves are struck dumb with admiration. Listen. Close your eyes and listen, Child.'

I closed my eyes and found myself in a green meadow. The impression was so strong that I could smell the grass and feel the warmth of the sun on my bare head. A group of singers was walking over a rise towards me. In front of them was a man dressed in light. His hair was sunlight, his skin glowed, and his eyes were diamond-bright. He saw me and smiled, and then he sang. I have no idea what he said, the language was not mine, but it was the most beautiful music I'd ever heard. I recognized Millis in the chorus behind him. He stood taller than the other men and women around him, as he had in life. He was singing. For the first time I heard his voice, it was warm and vibrant and stirred my heart.

The scene darkened and faded slowly. I waved goodbye and saw my hand was intact. The singers bowed low, sweeping the grass with their arms. They all bowed, even the golden man with the crown of sunshine. His eyes were shining stars. I knew who he was.

'Apollo,' I whispered.

'Goodbye, Child of the Future,' he said, his voice tender and laughing at the same time. 'Goodbye, we shall meet again.'

The scene faded completely and I was standing in darkness. I opened my eyes. The last rays of the setting sun were bathing us in a golden light. I felt warm all over. My body tingled and my eyes were full of tears.

The old woman dropped my hand and smiled.

'That was Balder,' she said.

'I knew him by another name,' I told her.

I looked down at my arm. My hand was gone, but somehow I didn't care. It was only temporary, my mind told me, and so I listened.

Chapter Nineteen

We spent one month in Orce. We needed to recuperate. I was very weak and couldn't eat anything. It was just the nausea of early pregnancy, but that didn't help. I needed rest and food. I lay in a hammock slung between two white birch trees near a blackberry hedge and dozed. When I felt well enough to walk I'd go to the sauna and wash, and then take a quick swim. Even in summer the water was black and deep, and I was unreasonably frightened of monsters lurking beneath the obsidian surface of the lake.

Alexander mocked me gently as he swam in lazy circles. I found it difficult to swim with my missing hand; it was one of the rare times that I really felt its loss. So I only washed off and waded to shore. Then I dressed, lay back in the hammock, and stared at the children filling their baskets with berries, or looked towards the tranquil fjord where boats glided out to the open sea.

I spoke little, but peace was creeping back into my soul. Gradually, I felt the knots loosen and ease, the tension in my muscles dissolve, and my smile came easier each day.

I loved the knoll where my hammock was placed. The

weird-woman chose it. She had insisted on moving me outside the village away from the noise and bustle.

I was not far from the sauna and the lake and I could glimpse the sandy beach through the grove of birch and ash. The children had no fear of me. They offered me berries, chattering like sparrows as they filled their baskets, and they perched on the edge of my hammock to ask me hundreds of questions, questions I couldn't understand or answer unless Paul was with me to translate.

He was often at my side. He seemed to need the peace and quiet as much as I did. He sat on a mossy bank, surrounded by wildflowers, and whittled. Yovanix had taught him how to carve. Paul liked the feel of smooth wood. His pieces were not as detailed as Yovanix's; he liked to make simple, polished things. Right now he was working on a bowl. It was cut from a chunk of maple, and the swirls and gnarls in the wood promised to make the bowl beautiful.

We sat in companionable silence. There was not much to say. He'd come to accept that what he'd done was an accident. He was slower to forgive Plexis. I think he wanted to put the blame of what happened on someone else. Plexis would have taken all the blame if I'd have let him. However, I wouldn't and Paul knew this. He would trust Plexis again. He was young and resilient. Already he confided to me that the whole thing seemed unreal.

'If it weren't for your hand and Yovanix, I would think that I'd just woken up after a bad dream,' he'd said to me.

The sun was a soft dapple on my body, warm where it touched my skin. I shifted in the hammock and closed my eyes. I was no longer afraid of sleep. Now when I shut my eyes I could often catch a glimpse of a green meadow and hear the faint sound of singing in the distance.

I smiled as I slept.

When I woke up the shadows had crept down to the water's edge. Paul was gone, in his place sat Alexander. Of all of us, he was the one who had gained the most from the trip. He'd recovered his soul. His throat had healed admirably. Thanks to Plexis's careful stitching, his scar would soon fade to nothing. Already it was just a faint pattern around the base of his neck.

'Ah, finally!' he said.

'Were you waiting for me to wake?' I asked, sitting up and chasing the last bit of sleep from my eyes.

'Of course.'

'Why didn't you rouse me?'

'And spoil the picture you made? No, I couldn't. You looked so peaceful, as if you were in a marvellous world all by yourself.' His voice held a faint note of jealousy in it. He wanted to share every second of my life. The idea that I could go somewhere wonderful without him obviously rankled. He was funny that way.

I smiled at him. 'I was in an enchanted place, and you were there with me. That's why I was so slow waking.'

'Ah.' He beamed. 'Well, that's good. I've come to get

you. There's someone who wants to speak to you.'

'Who?' I got out of the hammock and unhooked it from the tree. I rolled it into a tight bundle and tucked it under my arm. 'Where is this person? Is it the weird-woman again?'

'No, not her.' He flipped his hand, dismissing the weird-woman to the shadows. 'You'll see.' He tried to look mysterious; he loved surprises. However, he couldn't keep a secret. 'It's someone you've wanted to talk to for a long time.'

'Is it Yovanix?' I stopped. 'Is he, did he, I mean …'

Alexander gave my shoulders a fond squeeze. 'He's better, finally mending. He's been asking for you for a couple days.'

'Why didn't you tell me?' I asked.

'Oh, it was the weird-woman, always by his side, always talking to him. But now she's asked me to get you.'

'So you waited until I woke up. How long ago did she tell you to fetch me?'

He shrugged. 'A few hours ago? I don't know, but you were too peaceful to disturb. I love watching you sleep.' His voice lowered and he grinned. 'You looked so … harmless.'

I hit him on the arm. 'Harmless?'

He chuckled, ducking away. 'That's what I said, my volcano princess. Do you remember I called you that once? You nearly drowned me. I still laugh when I think of it.'

I eyed him sourly. 'You called me a "volcano

230

princess"'?'

'Yes, it was in a river. We were swimming, and you told me that you were called the Ice Queen.'

'That was just something some horrible boy once wrote on the bathroom wall in high school!' I cried.

He put his finger across my lips. 'Hush. Then we made love. Do you remember the first time we made love?' We stopped beneath the sweeping branches of a willow tree. 'We were in my tent. You were drunk, I think, on unwatered wine. You threw yourself on me.'

'I *what*?'

'Well, we sort of threw ourselves on each other.' He sighed and I heard a shiver in his voice. 'And then we made love. You were crying and saying all sorts of silly things, like how much you wanted to stay, and how you hated to leave me. Then we went swimming in the river and you put your face in the hollow of my throat, right here.'

I moved towards him as if in a dream. Our lips touched, so softly, then I pressed my cheek against his throat. I traced his collarbones with my finger, then closed my eyes and breathed in his warm scent. My face did fit perfectly into the hollow of his neck. 'I remember everything except being called a "volcano princess",' I said.

'When you sleep, your face is so soft you look like a young girl. There is something almost painful about the joy I feel when I watch over you, knowing you're carrying a baby inside your belly, knowing that you're mine. I took you from the Time-Senders, and I'll never let you go.' He trembled as he spoke, holding me so tightly my bones cracked.

'What is the matter?' I asked. Something about him was frightening me.

'It's Paul.' He stepped backwards and looked down at me. 'I want to be the one to tell you, I don't want him to have to.'

'What is it?' My heart started to pound. Alexander was looking at me so seriously

'The villagers want Paul to stay here. Here in Orce.'

There was a pause. Then his words sank in. 'No,' I whispered, 'No! He can't, I won't let him. Alex! Why?' I dropped my hammock and clung to him. My heart was breaking. He looked at me and his eyes were bleak.

'Because it's his home,' he said slowly. 'You know that. Search your heart. Isn't this truly the land of your ancestors?'

I felt my knees giving away and I sagged against my husband. He held me easily; his arms were strong. 'Alex, I can't. I can't leave him here. I won't. If he stays, I will stay with him.'

'What about Chiron and Cleopatra? They need you. They have been waiting now for nine months. Will you abandon them?'

'No, of course not! They can come here; we can all stay here. Alex, what are you trying to tell me?'

'It's the wise woman, she made a prophecy. She says he will found a dynasty here. She said his people will be called Vikings. They will travel as far as a new world to leave their mark.'

'And Paul listened to her.' I closed my eyes. 'Why must life be so difficult? All I want is to live in peace with my whole family. I want to grow old and bounce my grandchildren on my knees. Why is this happening to me?' My voice broke.

'I suppose we *could* stay,' Alexander sounded doubtful.

I looked up at him and nearly laughed. 'You have already accepted her words as fact,' I said.

'Well, yes.'

'Paul is a child,' I said, drawing myself up straight and brushing the tears out of my eyes. 'He will come with us now. We'll make sure he gets back here on his twenty-first birthday, when he's old enough to found a dynasty.'

'Well, I started when I was sixteen …' Alexander scratched his head and grinned.

'Don't you dare say another word,' I sputtered. 'I'll handle this.'

'I knew you were going to say that.' He smiled tenderly at me. 'A mother wolf would be less dangerous than you when you feel your children are threatened.'

'I think it's a wonderful thing that Paul will live here and found a dynasty. But until he's a man, he stays with us.' I straightened my shoulders and sighed. 'You're going to have to tell the wise woman that we'll make sure he gets back here in time to accomplish her prediction, all right?'

'All right.' He ran a hand through his hair. 'Shall we hurry? I was supposed to bring you back before sunset.'

I looked at the long shadows lying on the ground and shook my head. 'We might make it back before sunrise if we hurry.'

Chapter Twenty

Yovanix was recuperating. He was sitting by the hearth, drinking from a wooden bowl. I recognized the one Paul had made. He heard us coming and turned to face us. He wore a linen bandage over his eyes. Around his throat was a bandage as well, but the wound was healing at last.

'My Lady?' he asked, tilting his head to the side. He kept trying to see.

I sighed. I kept trying to reach for things. We would get over it, I supposed. 'I'm here. Call me Ashley, will you? It's my name.' I tried to keep the sorrow out of my voice but I couldn't.

He put the bowl down carefully and reached his hands towards me. I took them and held them to my cheek. He didn't know I'd lost a hand, so when he touched the bandage he jerked in surprise. 'What happened?' he asked.

'It was an accident,' I said. 'You look better. How are you feeling?'

'Much better, I assure you.' His voice was not very strong. His throat still hurt. He took a deep breath then pulled me into his arms.

I put my face on his shoulder and started to weep. I

cried and cried, tears wetting his tunic and dripping down his chest while he patted my back awkwardly and murmured in my ear.

'I'm sorry,' he said. 'I didn't mean to blame you. I'm sorry if I hurt you.'

'You didn't hurt me, you saved my life. You did it although you thought I'd come to kill you. Don't you understand? You're the hero of this tale. You were a prisoner of the Eaters of the Dead. They meant to sacrifice you, and I nearly killed you. I was so frightened that I didn't dare look at the people I was slaying,' I sobbed.

'Don't cry. You killed the monsters of the night and set me free.' His voice broke. 'Voltarrix captured me, he wanted to make me one of them. I was fed nothing but raw flesh. I refused to eat, but sometimes my thirst was so great I couldn't help but drink the blood.'

I held my breath. His voice was little more than a whisper in my ear. 'Go on,' I said.

'I had given up hope when they brought the child into the cave. I was dying of thirst and hunger. They were going to kill him and feed him to me, to make me one of them. I knew that if they gave me one morsel of his flesh, I would eat it. I would become like them. I think my mind snapped then, like a dried branch with too much weight upon it. I couldn't bear the pain or the terror any longer. Then you and Paul came, gliding through the frozen darkness, shimmering like wraiths. I saw a knife flash, and I think I prayed you would kill me then. I waited for the end to come. It was just different from what I expected, that's all.' He was silent.

'I'm sorry.' It was all I could say.

'Don't be. I'm not, at least not any more. At first I was out of my mind with terror, and then I started to see a light. Now, sometimes, I find myself in a meadow and it is the most beautiful place I ever saw. When I need it most, it appears to me.'

'Do you see anyone there?' I asked, hesitantly.

'The first time I saw the meadow my brother Anoramix was there,' he said quietly. 'He was walking through knee-deep grass, his head down, like he used to when he was thinking about something. Then he raised his head and saw me. He was surprised at first. He looked closer and smiled, although tears came to his eyes. He spoke to me, but I don't remember what he said. All I can recall is an immense feeling of peace and tranquillity. He walked right up to me and touched my face. I told him he looked well, and he laughed. Since then, I am always alone in the meadow, but I know he is watching me. I feel his presence all the time. It comforts me.'

I nodded. 'I've seen it too. And when I'm there I have both my hands.'

'Perhaps it's the paradise the gods promised us,' said Yovanix.

'If it is, then it's a place we have inside our minds, all of us,' I said.

He was quiet, thinking. 'If that is true, it is the greatest comfort I will ever know.' He rested his head on my shoulder and we stayed like that until the fire burned low and Paul came in to bring us to dinner.

After that, Yovanix and I were often together. His hammock swayed next to mine, and we talked most of the day. His Greek was excellent and he started to teach me some Celtic, although I still thought it sounded more like clay pots breaking than a language. He started to whittle again. He couldn't see, but he could feel, and the animals he made were just as beautiful as before. He even started to play chess with Paul, using the peg-board he'd made on the ship. We talked about what we wanted to do and where we wanted to go.

'Homer was blind,' said Yovanix, 'yet he voyaged extensively. I always wanted to travel.'

'I want you to stay with us,' said Paul. 'You're part of our family now.'

Yovanix grinned, 'Your family is big enough already.'

'And getting bigger,' Paul agreed, reaching over and patting my tummy fondly. He was in my hammock lying next to me, one foot on the ground to make us swing.

'Demos and Phaleria are talking about getting married,' I told them.

'I know,' Yovanix answered. 'They want to live on the dragon boat and trade up and down the coast. Demos wants to make a trip to Alexandria first.'

I smiled, my face in the sun. 'Phaleria is going to take us all back home on her boat.'

'Are we going to sail all the way back?' Paul's voice was high with excitement. 'Will we go to Iberia? And Carthage? Will we? Oh, may we, Mother?'

'I thought you were supposed to stay here and found

a dynasty,' I teased.

'Your idea sounds much better,' said Paul. 'I'll sail home with you and we'll travel, visiting Rome and Pompeii, just like you said. Then when I'm grown, I'll return to Orce.' He scratched his chin. 'I'm not in any hurry to grow up. I think I'd rather travel, like Yovanix. Besides, I promised Yovanix that I'd describe everything I saw to him, so he could see it too. Mother, I promised I'd be his eyes. Can I go? Can Yovanix come with us?'

'I wouldn't leave you two behind for the world,' I said, hugging him tightly. 'Now stop swinging, my stomach is feeling queasy again.'

'You and father are going to have a rough trip,' said Paul.

'I've never been seasick in my life,' I laughed.

I was horribly seasick.

The boat rolled and heeled, and I moaned and clutched my stomach. Pregnancy made me ill. It was dreadful. For the first time I could really sympathize with my husband who was lying next to me. He was seasick, I was ill, and we both moaned in unison when the boat slewed sideways over a huge wave. Above us on deck, I heard Paul's excited shouts, Demos's deeper voice, and Nearchus laughing delightedly at something. The boat rolled again, and I closed my eyes tightly and tried not to feel so dreadfully ill. My bed was soft and comfortable, if only it would stop moving back and forth. I huddled into my covers and tried to take my mind off my nausea.

The voyage had started three days ago. We'd left after

239

the village gave a huge feast in our honour. Paul was presented to all the neighbouring tribes who'd come to see us off. He celebrated his eleventh birthday and was renamed in a ceremony by the old wise woman, who was also the chieftain of the valley. Now they called him Finder of Souls, and they would wait for him to return and take his place in their clan. He would live in the longhouse and marry a Valerian girl and, according the wise woman, his children's children would sail to a new world and bring renown to his tribe.

I was getting used to prophecies and soothsaying, although I can't say I believed in them. Paul was coming with us, and if he wanted to return to Scandinavia when he was grown, fine, he could. It was true he fit in well with the people of Orce. He spoke their language already, learning with the ease of a child. Physically he resembled them, and they obviously adored him. For his birthday they gave him many gifts: two blankets woven in bright colours; bracelets of amber; a helmet – too big for him, but he'd grow into it; a short sword– Alexander winced when he saw it, but Paul promised to be careful; a sacred rock – a whole meteorite, about ten centimetres in diameter and fascinating; a narwhal's horn; a beautiful belt carefully worked in leather and copper; and a puppy.

Paul was speechless with delight. Ever since losing Cerberus he'd taken great pains not to look at the many dogs that populated the village, but I'd seen his sorrowful glances. He missed his hound, so Alexander and I had found him a puppy.

Paul stared at the pointed nose, the round eyes, and

the triangular ears standing straight up on his head. 'He's wonderful,' he breathed. 'What kind is it?'

'I think it's a sort of Spitz,' I said doubtfully. 'Look at his tail, it curls like a corkscrew over his back.' The puppy was only two months old and very small and wiggly. He had soft, dark grey fur on his back, a cream-coloured belly and chest, and four white socks.

'I'll name him Perilous,' said Paul, hugging him tightly. The puppy gave a happy yap and licked his face then snuggled under his chin. 'I'll make sure he's well trained. I'll take good care of him.' His eyes were bright with joy, and he kissed his new dog.

Alexander's expression softened. 'I know you will. You have a way with dogs. You'll love it in Egypt, they have at least twenty different breeds of hound dog, and they come in all shapes, sizes, and colours.'

Paul grinned. 'And in Gaul they have huge mastiffs to hunt the wild boars. Wouldn't you like one of those?'

Alexander had shaken his head. 'I'll leave you the dogs. I have enough trouble with a wife and children to have any pets.'

'Ha, ha, ha. So says the man who had twenty-five elephants,' I'd said, and kissed him soundly.

Chapter Twenty-One

I managed to fall asleep. On the morning of the fourth day I felt better. I was getting my sea legs, or my sea stomach, whatever. I dressed warmly and went up on deck. Paul was sitting next to the mast where he kept his puppy tied so he didn't fall off the boat. The puppy was a fuzzy creature. He looked vaguely like a husky, perhaps bigger and more wolf-like, with a tail that curled over his back in a tight coil. He saw me and yapped. A guard dog then, good.

I sat next to my son and tousled his hair. 'How are you?' I asked.

'I should ask you that,' he said. 'But I don't have to. You look back to normal. Your skin isn't green any more.'

'I feel fine. I'm hungry,' I said, surprising myself. 'I think I'll go see Erati and beg for a piece of bread.'

'Phaleria and Demos are getting married,' Paul said smugly.

'Oh?' I raised my eyebrows. 'And how do you know that?'

'She told me. We're going to stop in the place you called Britain and they're going to get a druid to marry

242

them.'

'A druid?' I made a face. 'I don't think I want to see another druid as long as I live.'

'Don't worry,' said Paul. 'You killed the most dangerous one; the others won't dare touch me when you're around.'

I peered closely at him, trying to see if he was being funny or not.

Phaleria wandered over. When we were at sea she was all business, completely in charge of her ship. Now her face had softened, and I was sure I knew why.

'Up and around? Feeling better, are you?' she asked. Her hair was tightly braided and coiled on top of her head, she wore a short skirt of wool and a linen tunic, over which was a brightly coloured woollen vest. The colourful clothes and houses people lived in had surprised me. When I was living in my own time, I was used to seeing buildings made of steel and concrete, of course. A decree, voted in the Year 85 after the Great Division, stipulated that all houses had to conform with their environment and be ninety-eight per cent non-polluting, which meant solar energy panels and thermal electrical installations. Our houses were all painted subdued colours to blend with the landscape. Not here. People loved colour. Whatever could be painted was painted bright red, yellow, blue, or green, and clothes were no different. The Celts loved patterns and colours, the hems of their sleeves and tunics often had intricately woven borders, and their clothes were rainbow bright. They layered their clothes, wearing vests, leggings, and tunics, and the more colours and stripes the merrier.

Whenever I'd seen a fiction-3D video depicting a tribe in the Iron Age – such as the Celts, or the Vikings – the people had been portrayed as living in plain wooden houses, wearing simple cotton or wool clothes, and looking drab in their monochrome world. The reality was different.

Phaleria was lovely in her butter-yellow tunic with blue and green concentric circles woven into the hem. Her vest was blue with green trim, and her hair had yellow ribbons braided into it. She sat next to me, smoothing the skirt over her knees. She didn't blink when Plexis sat down with us and kissed me. In a time when men often had several wives, I suppose it wasn't unusual for a woman to have two husbands. Human relations were still mutable. Women were freer in Gaul than in Greece. Besides, I was happy. Alexander and Plexis were happy. What else mattered?

'I hear you're going to marry Demos,' I said, snuggling into Plexis's arms.

'We're going to the village where my father was born. I want to marry under the sacred oak.'

'I think that sounds very romantic,' I said.

She shrugged. In those days romance was not an important part of a marriage. That would happen in the Middle Ages, with the advent of chivalry. People were more practical in this century. Traditions were important, pleasing the gods was vital, and the rest was left up to fate. *Que sera, sera. Ut fata trahunt.*

'We'll arrive in six days on the great island where my

family has lived for four generations. They're part of the Iceni tribe.'

'That's great!' I was dying to go to the British Isles and see for myself the Iceni, the best known tribe of Celts in that time. They had organized a revolt against the Romans, and although it failed, it was interesting for several reasons. One was the fact that the leader of the revolt had been a woman, Boadicea. She was the wife of the tribe's king, and she had committed suicide rather than endure Roman domination. That would take place in AD 61, in three centuries. Until then, the Celts were the masters of what would become England. I was also looking forward to buying some belt buckles as gifts for everyone in Alexandria. The Celts were marvellous metalworkers.

I eyed Phaleria with new interest. She was a member of the Iceni. Who could tell, perhaps it would be one of her direct descendants who would lead the rebellion.

By the time we arrived in Britain, Alexander was feeling better. It must be said that the sea was calm and we hardly felt the swells. A brisk wind filled our sails and we made good time, arriving in the evening of the sixth day.

My first glimpse was a disappointment. The beach where we docked was practically uninhabited. There were a few low, thatched huts and a sales counter where a man was doing his best to sell a basket of fish. However, the actual village was an hour's walk inland. We followed a well-worn path through a dense forest, arriving in a valley where fields and pastures surrounded a fortified village. In the pasture grazed sheep – they had black and white spots and, to Alexander's amazement, four curly horns sprouted from their heads. Small black pigs lived in pens under oak trees and shaggy red cattle raised their heads as we approached, setting the bells around their necks ringing. Dogs ran out and barked at us, and the children who tended the flocks of geese cried out in shrill voices.

The village was large, surrounded by a tall wooden fence girded with iron, and the gate was a massive affair that was raised and lowered like a drawbridge. The houses were mostly wooden and shaped like enormous tepees. They were covered with thatch and had no windows in the wintertime. In the summer, several windows were cut out of the thatch and covered with stiff parchment to let in some light. One entered the hut through a door leading directly into a small shed-like hallway where boots, weapons, and cloaks were stored. Inside the huts a fire burned in the centre of the floor, and a caldron hung from a very long metal chain above it. A hole in the roof let out the smoke. Beds were stored on shelves during the day and pulled out at night. A second storey covered half of the hut, with a ladder leading upstairs. Smoked hams and cooking utensils hung from the rafters. Wicker baskets held the family's belongings, and a loom occupied an important place under one of the windows. Near the doorway was a domed clay oven used for cooking the family's bread. The houses were less comfortable, I thought, than the wooden houses in Scandinavia, but they were nice enough, and the people spent more time out of doors here than in the foggy, cold villages on the North Sea.

The hamlet was small but prosperous, and the people were all well fed and healthy. I'd rarely seen such robust children, and I admired the chubby toddler holding onto Phaleria's cousin's skirt.

Her father's family had stayed in the village, while he had left to become a seafaring trader. Phaleria stopped by twice a year to see everyone, to trade, and to deliver mail.

She introduced us, starting with Demos, her future husband. She didn't say anything about Alexander being Alexander the Great, even though the villagers, eager for gossip, asked her if she'd heard anything about what was happening in Greece and Persia. Everyone had heard of Iskander, the great ruler, and Alexander was hard put to stay silent when some of the people started arguing about his accomplishments.

We stayed in a common room, sort of an inn, set aside for travellers. The Celts weren't like the Romans or the Greeks who lived for commerce. The Celts of Britain liked to trade, but they were more interested in their own internal affairs than with the rest of the world. They were insular and independent, not bothering about government or rulers except within their own tribes or villages. And they didn't form a coherent nation, keeping their tribes separate. The leader of each tribe was called a king, but he didn't have as much power as the kings in Egypt or Persia. The tribes didn't pay taxes to anyone, and they minded their own business. To settle disputes concerning land, livestock, or stolen women, they fought between themselves.

One of their favourite pastimes was raiding, don't ask me why. Men just seem incapable of living a tranquil life. They have to stir things up. To keep everyone on their toes, the Celt tribes of Britain would raid each other regularly, stealing sheep, cattle, pigs, or women. Most stolen women ended up marrying their captors, and wars were not usually declared for that reason, more often it was an excuse to have a wedding feast and invite everyone to a fête. If the woman in question was married, that was another problem, a good fight was often the result, and good fights were incredibly bloody.

Cattle were an excellent excuse for a fight, and sheep also, if enough of them disappeared. Pigs were hardly missed, and they were usually smart enough to escape and find their way home anyway. The woods were full of wild and half-wild pigs; they were raided just for practice, often by the children.

Besides raiding, there were the druids who insisted on sacrifices every winter solstice. Then everyone made the journey to Stonehenge, where the druids killed a few virgins, shooting them with arrows made of mistletoe. From what I gathered, this was the winter entertainment. In the summer people went to Stonehenge again. They danced, got drunk, smoked, and generally had a good time in front of huge bonfires. There they killed a few sacrificial victims, usually criminals or people who made trouble for the community. I suppose it was an effective way to encourage good behaviour.

We had learned this from Phaleria as she showed us around. She was a good storyteller, like most people of that time. Our coming to the village was like a new movie coming to the cinema nearest you, after six months of playing the same holo-film. We were expected to provide the entertainment. It was a fair expectation. In a world without instant communication it was important that everyone be proficient in storytelling and entertainment, otherwise boredom set in, winters dragged on and on, and raiding degenerated into a bloody civil war.

We were happy to comply, especially Plexis and Alexander who were both excellent storytellers. Nearchus was shy for a man of his time, and standoffish. However, he was an excellent writer. He wrote about his travels, and as far as I could remember they were still being read three thousand years after he first published them. Not bad for a guy who had trouble playing charades.

My stories were appreciated for their content; I could remember books I'd read nearly verbatim, but I was not an entertaining storyteller. Yovanix had some good tales, he could make people laugh or cry. Demos, I think, was the best. He could tell stories in a way that made you believe you were there with him.

The first evening we ate dinner in the inn, then everyone gathered in the sacred grove and we told stories all night. We sat on a grassy knoll in the form of a natural amphitheatre, with the storyteller at the bottom facing us, his words carrying easily up the slope to our ears. Tall ash trees leaned overhead. I leaned back against Alexander's chest and gazed at the stars just visible through the canopy of leaves.

Paul was sitting next to me holding his puppy in his lap. Plexis sat behind him leaning back on his elbows, his arm fully healed now, his face back to its old puckish expression, his amber eyes dreamy. Yovanix was sitting next to Paul. They had become inseparable. Paul was his guide, leading him everywhere, describing everything with a rare precision. Paul's patience astounded me until I realized that he was truly happy. He had always had an unworldly sweetness about him, and helping others was his vocation in life. With my help, he had decided to train Perilous to be a guide dog for Yovanix. The idea had struck Paul like a revelation, and now he pestered me for hours, begging me to tell him more stories about the dogs that led the blind.

In my time, seeing eye dogs were obsolete; the electronic eye, an implant that enables blind people to 'see', had replaced them. However, I had read about such dogs in my history classes. I had no idea how to go about training such a dog, but I thought if anyone could figure it out, it would be Plexis. He could train any horse, no matter how wild, in a matter of days. When Paul and I had approached him about training Perilous to be a seeing eye dog, he was at first dubious, then enthusiastic. Now half the time his eyes were resting on the puppy, a calculating expression in them.

'The Thief of Souls is dead,' began Demos, and I stiffened in Alexander's arms.

'Shh,' he said. 'Don't worry, it's just a story now. You're safe here with me.' His voice was a soothing whisper in my ear, and I settled back against his broad chest. My heart was thumping though, and I'm sure my expression was as rapt as those of the children sitting cross-legged in the front row.

Demos told how the Queen of Ice and Darkness rose from her home in the underworld and struck down the Thief of Souls as he prepared to sacrifice a child to the blind gods of the Eaters of the Dead. I shuddered in the beginning, but Demos was such a consummate storyteller that I lost myself in his tale. It was a story that happened to someone else, in some other time. The night grew deeper, and still Demos spoke. He told about his journey to the island of ice and fire, where volcanoes spewed white-hot lava into the black sea and at night, the sky was lit by a red glow.

I fell asleep to the sound of his voice, secure in the arms of my husband, with the soft breeze of a late summer night caressing my cheek.

We stayed for one week. Long enough for the resident druid to make the proper sacrifices so Phaleria could marry Demos, and for me to buy plenty of beautiful fibulas and belt buckles for everyone back home.

Fibulas were what people used to keep their cloaks fastened, in case you never saw one. I hadn't seen one before I'd time-travelled; usually I had a magneto-charm on my clothing. Fibulas came in two parts; you sewed one half on one side of the cloak and the other half on the other side. The fibula fit together like the hinge on a door, and you slid a pin down the middle fastening it shut. A chain held the pin, and the fibula could be very simple or extremely ornate. The ones I found in Britain were made of bronze with intricate patterns enamelled in glowing, jewel-like colours.

I saved money to buy pewter from the Iberians and mosaics from Carthage, both of which were on the itinerary on our way back.

We were nearly out of cash. Luckily, Phaleria had offered to sail us back to Alexandria for free; we would have been unable to pay our way on a commercial ship.

Axiom paid the two remaining Roman soldiers generously for their efforts, and he paid the innkeeper at Orce. He paid some of the village men who'd fought, and Alexander insisted on giving money to the widows and orphans Voltarrix had made. Axiom also paid the Phoenician trader who'd taken Plexis aboard his ship. Axiom peered into his money belt and sighed.

'Do you think we should take the green one for Chirpa?' I asked, pointing to a particularly lovely enamelled belt buckle.

'I think it's beautiful,' said Axiom cautiously. 'But it's very expensive. The red one would go better with her hair, and it's half the price of the other.'

I examined the buckle he was pointing at and nodded. 'You're right. We'll take the red one for Chirpa and the green one for Usse. Look at the yellow one; it's just the thing for Brazza!'

Axiom sighed again and paid the merchant. 'I wish you'd bargain more,' he said.

'You know very well I'm hopeless at bargaining. That's why I brought you shopping with me,' I said, watching as the merchant gift-wrapped my packages in soft leather. 'Thank you,' I said, tucking them in my purse. 'Now where? See, over there is a stand with woollen cloaks. Don't they look lovely? Shall we go inspect them? I think I'll get one for Paul, he's growing so fast.'

'Fine, but let me do the talking.' Axiom said, taking me by the elbow and steering me through the market day crowd.

People for miles around had come to the market. Sheep baa'd, cows mooed, pigs squealed, shrieking children ran around everywhere. A newscaster stood on a large stump and called out the news in a loud voice. Merchants hawked their wares, men and women bargained for goods, acquaintances met and exclaimed. Dogs barked and geese honked, and Axiom bargained for a cloak at the top of his lungs, getting a fine, warm one for Paul – at a greatly reduced price!. I bought one for Yovanix. He needed a warm cape, and these were woven with soft wool and sported intricate black and white patterns.

Axiom counted the coins again. I took the cloaks and put them in the basket I held hooked over my arm, my missing hand hidden by a long sleeve. The clothes the Celts wore were voluminous and comfortable. I liked the way they layered their outfits, and everyone wore beautiful belts and lots of jewellery. The Celts loved jewellery. They made it from silver, bronze, and gold, adding amber, precious and semi-precious stones, pearls, and enamel. Men and women wore necklaces, bracelets, rings, and earrings. The Gauls wore torques around their necks, and all the tribes made richly decorated armour. I saw Alexander staring longingly at a helmet made of iron and gold with coral and enamel inlays.

The Celts also made remarkable weapons. Axiom admired a knife and I insisted on buying it for him. He protested, but not for long. Afterwards, he tucked it into his belt and his hand was never far from it. It was a deceptively simple weapon with a perfectly balanced blade and leather-wrapped handle. It was made of iron, smelted in a nearby village. The Celts in Britain, like the Gauls in France, worked with iron and made most of their tools with it.

After we finished shopping, Axiom and I went back to the beach. We were leaving with the tide; Phaleria and Demos were busy readying the ship while the crew took a day off to go to the market.

Back on board, I put away my purchases, using a large woven chest I'd bought in Orce. Into it went all our clothes, the gifts, and the cloaks. Then I went on deck and sat in the sunshine, just relaxing.

Erati arrived later. A farmer drove him in a cart into which he'd loaded all the food for our voyage. Half the food was alive, and I helped put the chickens in their pen. Another small pen made of woven laths was for a nanny goat and her three kids; we would have milk and eggs. Bales of fresh hay were stowed down below, some of which we used as our bedding. Water was stored in huge clay jars; freshly milled flour, dried lentils, and peas were kept in tightly woven sacks. Dried hams hung from the beams. Erati checked to see that the supplies were stored away to his liking. Then he supervised the loading of charcoal used in his clay oven. I was fascinated by the cook's organization. He was a pro, having served Phaleria's father for nearly ten years.

There were even a couple amphorae of wine stored carefully in the hay and a clay jar of rapeseed oil Erati had purchased from the Iceni. When everything was ready, Erati paid the merchant who'd helped unload everything. The man touched his lips with his thumb as a sign of acceptance, climbed back into his cart, and drove away.

Soon the rest of Phaleria's crew came down the path, each carrying a large bundle of goods. Paul and Yovanix came next, and Alexander, Plexis, and Nearchus arrived five minutes later. Alexander held a large bundle, and it was shaped like a helmet. I hid my smile behind a lock of hair. He couldn't resist. I knew he missed his bronze breastplate. It had an enamelled Gorgon's head on the front and was reputed to have been made in the image of Athena's breastplate. Athena, the goddess with the parti-coloured eyes, one blue, one brown, was Alexander's favourite goddess, and he made sacrifices to her every time he set out on a venture. She was also the goddess of wisdom and learning, holding an owl on her arm and an olive branch in her hand. I always thought she was cruel for changing Arachne into a spider, but my own namesake, Persephone, had changed two young boys into lizards for some silly reason I couldn't even remember. Gods and goddesses tended to lose their tempers easily.

That thought whispered through my mind as I watched Alexander climbing on board. He was laughing at something Plexis had said, looking backwards over his shoulder. With his bundle tucked under one arm, he easily climbed the ladder. The sun made his hair shine like burnished bronze and his face seemed open as a child's. It was hard to imagine him losing his temper. However, he had a fearsome temper. It had cost him two friends, and I sometimes wondered if it hadn't also killed his father.

I don't know why I was thinking about that. The day was nearly perfect. Maybe it was the dragon boat itself that stirred my thoughts like dry leaves in the wind. Phaleria had claimed the boat as her own after the druids had destroyed hers. The prow rose six metres above the water in a graceful swan's neck and finished as a dragon's head carved out of wood. It was painted realistically with green scales, white teeth, and a red tongue. The boat was the most splendidly built ship I'd seen in that time. It was wide and solidly made. It had a weighted keel that kept it remarkably stable in heavy seas, and two sails made it easy to manoeuvre. It didn't have as much room down below as Phaleria's old boat – all the passengers shared a common room piled high with fragrant hay. A low cabin with latticed windows had been added to the deck – before there had been nothing. The rowers sat on deck too, another difference. The boat was swift and light, perfect for trading up and down the coast. Phaleria was pleased with it, but something about the fearsome boat roused memories embedded in my genes. My ancestors had voyaged on boats such as these, and Paul had chosen the North as his spiritual home. Already, he spoke wistfully of when he would return.

The wind lifted my hair and I sighed. Perhaps it was just hormones, but my mood was a strange one. I could sense the currents of change running through the world; it was opening like an oyster.

Chapter Twenty-Two

The wind picked up as the tide started to ebb, and Phaleria called out to Titte and Oppi to raise the sails. Vix hauled up the anchor, Nearchus took the rudder, and Kell checked his instruments while Demos and Alexander poled the ship away from the docks. Phaleria stood on the deck and waved to her family and friends who had come to see us off. She would return in six months, hopefully.

We weren't going directly to Alexandria. We were going to stop in Gaul and Iberia, before crossing the Mediterranean to Carthage then back again, putting in at Pompeii and Rome. I was eager to see those great cities, the last time I'd seen them they'd been in ruins. Then we were going back home. The voyage would take about three months, give or take a few weeks depending on the weather and the currents.

Alexander was worried. He was afraid he'd be seasick for the entire trip, but we reassured him he would only be sick for about a week, then he'd feel better. I was feeling well, I was two months pregnant, and while I wasn't exactly over my morning sickness, I had more energy than before. I was slowly getting over the shock of losing a hand, and I was looking forward to travelling. I was a tourist at heart.

I looked over at Alexander and grinned. He'd unwrapped the helmet and was turning it over in his hands, admiring it. He was a warrior; he couldn't look at places without trying to imagine how long it would take to conquer them

He looked at me and winked. 'I think that village would have fallen after three weeks,' he said.

I made a face. How did he do that? 'Are my thoughts so obvious?' I asked him.

'When it comes to me, yes.' He took me in his arms and stroked my hair. 'I bought the helmet for Ptolemy. It's not for me, no matter how much I would appreciate it. It is a gift for him for watching over our children while we were gone.'

'That's right,' I said. 'I'd forgotten they were in Memphis. I hope they're well, and that Ptolemy hasn't already married his son to Cleopatra.'

'Don't worry, he hasn't. He's no longer afraid of me, but he'll always fear you, my Ice Queen.' He chuckled, putting his face close to mine. 'I bought something for you,' he said, and he handed me a small package.

I opened it and gasped. What I saw startled me at first. Then I looked closer. It was a hand, carefully carved from a deer's antler at the place where it spread out in a natural palm. One end was hollow and fit over my wrist. Laces tied it onto my arm, holding it securely in place. The hand was small; the artist had carved a woman's hand like mine, carefully shaping the fingers and the nails. I examined it, turning it over and over, tears blurring my vision. I *was* transparent. Vanity had prompted me to add long sleeves to all my tunics, and I'd taken to holding my arm close to my side. Now, only a careful look would reveal my missing hand. 'Thank you,' I whispered.

'You're welcome.'

'It was your idea, wasn't it?' I asked.

'It was.' He smiled broadly. 'For once, Plexis didn't think of it.'

'He wouldn't have,' I said, sitting on a low bench. 'Come and help me put it on. I want to see how it looks.'

'I'll get one made of ivory in Egypt,' said Alexander. 'But this one is nice because it's so light. In the army, there were hands of all shapes and sizes to replace the ones the soldiers lost. Many had fingers curved just so, to hold shields.' He held his hand out and gripped an invisible shield handle.

'That's interesting,' I said. 'Why; I wonder, didn't anyone find them in the graves?'

'I'm not sure. I don't think people wanted to be buried with them. They knew that they would be whole again in the afterworld. Also, most of my soldiers were cremated. The ivory would have burned.'

'Another thing has been bothering me, but I think I've figured it out,' I said, watching as Alexander adjusted the laces and smoothed them down. 'I wondered why Voltarrix didn't use his powers when we first saw him, the time they ambushed us when we were with the Romans?'

'Yes?' Alexander looked at me, interested now. 'Why didn't he? I didn't think of that.'

'Because we weren't in the Arctic Circle then.'

'And so? I don't understand.'

'It's because of the magnetic pole. He had to be in the Arctic Circle, where the magnetic field is the strongest. It's simple, really. He didn't have the full use of his powers until the earth was tilted towards the sun. The solstice is the when the field is the strongest. The valley was surrounded with high cliffs rich in iron. He needed the summer solstice to steal people's souls. It all works with the magnetic field somehow,' I said thoughtfully, shaking my head. 'And later, in the cave, he was surrounded by iron ore. He didn't need a counter-magnet, he did everything with the force of his thoughts. To voyage in time was beyond him, he didn't have the power to do that, but he could stop time in a limited radius using the earth's natural magnetic properties and his own mind. Amazing. The scientists of my time insisted that the human brain was the most powerful instrument in the world. How they would have loved to study Voltarrix's …' My voice trailed off.

'Will another druid take his place?' asked Alexander.

'I don't know, but it will be too late. Paul was their last chance, and now we're heading towards Rome's territories.'

'It's not Roman yet,' Alexander looked scandalized. 'Carthage is free, Egypt and Greece are independent, Gaul is still Gaul.'

'Not for long,' I said, watching as the land dwindled

into the distance. The water changed colour, becoming deep, ultramarine blue. The first waves started to crest, the boat dipping into a trough then rising over a wave. Alexander smiled weakly and closed his eyes.

'I feel dreadful all of a sudden,' he said.

'Don't worry, I'm here. I'll take care of you, and I'll always love you, even if you turn six shades of green and vomit on me.'

'Sweet.' He clenched his teeth. 'Just one thing, don't mention the words sick, sea, green, or vomit, all right?'

'Deal,' I said, helping him over to the side of the boat where he leaned over and lost his lunch.

'I think I'll be fine now,' he said. 'In fact, I think I feel much better.'

'Do you think the druid's medicine will work?' I was interested. Just before we'd left Britain, the druid that had married Phaleria and Demos had given Alexander a vial of fluid. He was supposed to take three drops whenever he felt seasick. It smelled strongly of mint, and I thought it was probably distilled peppermint leaves. The druids were in charge of the distillery in each village, making alcoholic beverages for the festivals. The Celtic druids used whatever mystical plants were growing nearby. No wonder Roman wine was such a big hit. Mystical plants made bizarre alcoholic beverages.

Alexander and I watched the land disappear. Evening turned the sky deep purple. Erati lit his oven, and soon the smell of baking bread tickled our noses. Phaleria lit the lanterns hanging from the yardarm, and we sat in their orange glow eating our evening meal.

We were mostly silent. Setting out on a long journey does that. I thought of all the journeys I'd taken. The voyage back in time. When we'd gone to India, and when we'd crossed the Himalayas in the winter. Usually we'd been in a hurry, either planning an attack or recuperating from one. Now we were going to take our time, we were going to relax and enjoy our voyage, and nothing was going to spoil it.

I gazed at the stars and frowned. I wondered if the sound I'd just heard was a gust of wind in the sails or the gods laughing at me. I must have looked troubled, because after Alexander finished his bowl of soup, he took three drops of mint potion and draped his arm over my shoulder.

'Don't worry, Ashley. I'm here.' He leaned back against the mast, pulling me to his chest. 'We're together now, I love you, and even if you are the terrible Queen of the Underworld, I'll always stay by your side. Give me a kiss and close your eyes. We'll sleep while the stars look upon us and Nearchus tells a tale of the sea. Listen, just close your eyes and listen.'

I did, but all I heard was the sound of his heart beating. I fell asleep with a smile on my face. If anyone deserved to be King of Heaven and Earth, I thought, just before I dozed off, it was Alexander.

'King of Heaven and Earth,' he said dreamily, reading my thoughts. 'But not of the sea.'

The boat danced upon the waves as the gods looked down upon us. My dreams were diamond-bright with all the stars in the sky leading us towards our future.

Proudly published by Accent Press

www.accentpress.co.uk

Leabharlanna Poiblí Chathair Baile Átha Cliath

Dublin City Public Libraries

9 781786 154835